THE INVESTIGATOR

THE INVESTIGATOR

JOHN SANDFORD

THORNDIKE PRESS
A part of Gale, a Cengage Company

Copyright © 2022 by John Sandford.
Thorndike Press, a part of Gale, a Cengage Company.

Thorndike Press® Large Print Basic.
The text of this Large Print edition is unabridged.
Other aspects of the book may vary from the original edition.
Set in 16 pt. Plantin.

LIBRARY OF CONGRESS CIP DATA ON FILE.
CATALOGUING IN PUBLICATION FOR THIS BOOK
IS AVAILABLE FROM THE LIBRARY OF CONGRESS.

ISBN-13: 978-1-4328-9480-1 (hardcover alk. paper)

Published in 2022 by arrangement with G. P. Putnam's Sons, an imprint of Penguin Publishing Group, a division of Penguin Random House LLC.

LT FIC SANDFORD

Printed in Mexico
Print Number: 01   Print Year: 2022

THE INVESTIGATOR

ONE

Backside of an old brick-and-stucco building on the edge of downtown Tallahassee, Florida, ten o'clock on a muggy evening in early September, a couple weeks before the autumn equinox. The cleaning crew had left, rattling their equipment carts and trash bins across the blacktop to their vans. A few people remained in the building; two cars sat in the parking lot, and there were lighted offices on the second and third floors.

A young woman with crystalline blue eyes and a short brown ponytail sat behind a ragged boxwood hedge, her back against the building's concrete foundation, a rucksack between her knees. Dressed in black jeans, a black long-sleeved blouse, with a reversible red-black jacket, black side out, she was no more than an undifferentiated dark lump behind the hedge. She could turn the jacket to the red side, if needed, so she wouldn't appear so obviously camouflaged for the

7

night. A noisome mosquito buzzed her face, looking for an opening; to her left, a vent pooped vaguely fecal odors out of the building.

Piece by piece, one distraction at a time, the young woman cleared her mind; no more odors, no more bugs. She'd hunted for food as a child and she'd learned that a predator created a vibration that other animals could sense. She'd been in every sense a predator, but if she'd put her back against a tree and cleared her mind, the vibration would fade, she'd become part of the landscape, and the prey animals would go back to whatever they were doing before she arrived. She'd had rabbits hop within six feet of her, unalarmed before they died.

Now, with an empty mind, she'd gone from being a lump to invisible.

The woman was wearing one thin leather glove, and the fingers of that hand were wrapped in hundred-pound test monofilament fishing line. The other end of the transparent line was tied to the loop handle of the building's back door. She waited patiently, unmoving, in the dappled moonlight that filtered through the Chickasaw plum trees on the edge of the parking lot.

At ten minutes after ten, the lights went out in the third-floor office and the young woman brought her mind back to the world, shouldered her pack, and took a switchblade from her hip pocket. Two minutes after that, a middle-aged woman carrying a heavy lawyer's briefcase pushed through the back door, looked both ways, then scurried out to a compact BMW. The building's door, on an automatic door-closer hinge, swung shut behind her. As it was about to lock, the young woman put pressure on the fishing line and held it. The door appeared to be closed, but hadn't latched.

When the departing BMW turned the corner, the young woman eased out from behind the hedge, listening, watching, keeping a steady pressure on the fishing line. She walked to the door, pulled it open, blocked it for a second with a foot, and used the blade to cut the fishing line off the door handle.

She slipped inside, balling the fishing line in her gloved hand, pressed the back of the knife blade against her leg to close it, dropped it into her pocket. Adrenaline beginning to kick in, heart rate picking up.

The target office had been vacant since six o'clock. The young woman turned left, to the fire stairs, and ran rapidly upward on silent, soft-cushioned athletic soles. At the fifth and top floor, she listened for a moment behind the fire door, then opened the door and checked the hallway. The only light came from street-side windows. She hurried down the hall to 504, removed her jacket, and took the battery-powered lock rake from her pack.

She couldn't use the rake on the outer door, because that door had a good security lock, and she would have been standing beneath a light where she couldn't be sure she was unobserved.

This lock was not very good — there was nothing obviously valuable inside except some well-used office equipment. She wrapped the rake in her jacket and pulled the trigger. The pick made a chattering noise, muffled by the jacket. The young woman kept pressure on the rake, felt the lock begin to give, and then turn. She pushed the door open and stepped inside, closed the door, and sat on the floor, listening.

She heard nothing but the creaks and cracks of an aging building, and the low hum of the air-conditioning. Satisfied that she was alone and hadn't raised an alarm, she opened the pack, took out a headlamp, and pulled the elastic bands over her head, centering the light on her forehead. She'd already set it on the lowest power, but she didn't need it yet. She stood and looked around, threw the fishing line in an empty wastebasket.

There was enough light from the office equipment's power LEDs that she could make out a dozen metal desks with standard office chairs, a computer with each desk. Lots of paper on the desks, cardboard boxes stacked in one corner, three corkboards marching down the interior walls, hung with notices, posters, the odd cartoon. She walked down to the left end of the room, to a private office with a closed door. The door was locked, but the rake opened it and she went inside.

Another messy space, more stacks of paper. A big faux-walnut desk, a long library-style table, five metal filing cabinets, a metal side table against the desk, holding a Dell computer and a keyboard. The windows were covered with Venetian blinds, partly open. She closed them, then walked across the room, a thin nylon carpet underfoot, sat in the office chair behind the desk, turned on the headlamp, and pulled out the desk's unused typing tray. There, written on a piece of notepaper taped to the tray, she found the password for the computer, as her informant had promised.

She brought the computer up and began opening files.

The young woman left the building at six-thirty in the morning, now wearing her jacket red side out, the dawn light filtering through the plum trees as she walked beneath them. Her rental car was a half-block away. She put the backpack in the trunk and transferred the lock rake, switchblade, and a short steel crowbar, which she hadn't needed, to a FedEx box already labeled and paid for. The pack still held the file folder of printer paper that she'd taken out of the office. She drove carefully to a FedEx curbside station and dropped in the box of burglary tools. It would arrive back at her Arlington, Virginia, apartment in three days, when she would be there to accept it.

That done, she drove back to the Double-Tree hotel where she was staying, put the DO NOT DISTURB sign on the door, changed into yoga pants and a tank top, put on a sleeping mask, and crawled into bed.

That afternoon, she parked a block from Annette Hart's house, and waited. At five-thirty, Roscoe Anthem pulled up to the curb. He honked once and Hart trotted out of the house, smiling, piled into the car, gave Anthem a peck on the cheek, and they rolled out to I-10, then three and a half hours west to Mobile, Alabama.

Because while you *can* sin in Tallahassee, in many different ways, it was much more fun where the casinos were bigger and your friends were less likely to see you rollin' them bones.

The blue-eyed young woman stayed with them all the way, well back, always behind other cars, shifting lanes from time to time. And she was with them in the casino, at the craps tables, at the blackjack tables, at the slots, always behind a screen of other patrons, talking on her cell phone and pushing the camera button.

Only to be interrupted by a nerdy young card player who eased up behind her to touch her hip and whisper, "You know what? You *really* overclock my processor."

Made her laugh, but she blew him off anyway.

Monday morning, the Washington, D.C., office of Senator Christopher Colles (R-Florida), door closed. Colles and his much-hated executive assistant, Claudia Welp, perched on visitor's chairs, looking across a coffee table at the young woman. Welp pitched her voice down. "Wait: you *broke*

13

into the office?"

"It wasn't exactly a break-in, since it's *Senator Colles's* office and you told me to go there and retrieve some of *his* information," the young woman said.

"I didn't mean for you to break in, for God's sakes," Welp said. "I sent you down there to talk to that secretary."

"But to get to the heart of the matter, did you find anything?" Colles asked.

"Yes. The information you got from Messalina Brown is correct," the young woman said. "Anthem and Hart have stolen about three hundred and forty thousand dollars in campaign funds. I believe they've blown most of it in a casino in Mobile, Alabama. In their defense, they're having a *really* good time."

Colles: "What!"

Welp: "Even so, I'm not sure that justifies breaking into . . ."

"Shut up, Welp," Colles said. "How'd they do it?"

"I wrote a full report yesterday, after I got back to D.C. I've attached the relevant documents and a couple of photographs of the happy couple at Harrah's Gulf Coast casino on Friday night. It's here." She took a file out of her backpack and passed it to Colles.

Welp: "Even if it proves to be true, you've far transgressed . . ."

"Doesn't matter what you believe," Letty Davenport interrupted. "I quit. You guys bore the crap outta me."

TWO

Letty worked in what its denizens called the
bullpen, an open room of low-ranking
senatorial assistants and researchers, each
with his or her own desk and filing cabinet,
surrounded by a hip-high fabric cubicle
wall. Most of the staffers were either recent
Ivy League graduates or smart state school
grads, getting close to power.

As a graduate of a heavyweight West Coast
university, with a master's degree in something useful, combined with her cool reserve
and the way she dressed, Letty was different. She was smart, hard-nosed and hard-
bodied, lean, muscled like a dancer, and occasionally displayed a sharp, dry wit.

The young women in the bullpen noticed
that her clothes carried fashionable labels,
while tending toward the dark and functional, if not quite military. Her jewelry was
sparse but notable, and always gold. One of
the Ivy Leaguers excessively admired a

chain bracelet set with a single, unfaceted green stone, and asked if she could try it on.

Letty was amenable. After the other woman had tried and returned the bracelet, and Letty had gone, a friend asked the Ivy Leaguer, "Well, what did you find out?"

"Harry Winston."

"Really."

"Honest to God," the Ivy Leaguer said. "That stone is a raw fucking uncut emerald, like Belperron used. We could mug her, sell the bracelet, and buy a Benz. Maybe two Benzes."

"*You* could mug her. I've seen her working out, so I'll pass on that."

When Letty finished briefing Colles and Welp on the Tallahassee situation, she left them studying the purloined spreadsheets, dropped her letter of resignation on Welp's desk — two weeks' notice — and walked down to the bullpen. An hour later, Welp called and said, "Get up here. Senator Colles wants to speak with you."

When she walked back into the senator's reception area, Colles, Welp, and a legislative assistant named Leslie Born were huddled in a nook under a portrait of Colles shaking hands with the elder George

Bush. They were arguing about something in low but angry tones; maybe the missing money. Colles saw Letty and snapped, "Get in my office. I'll be there in a minute."

Letty went into Colles's private office and sprawled sideways in one of the comfortable leather club chairs, her legs draped over a well-padded arm. And why not? What was he going to do, fire her?

Colles came in five minutes later, slammed his door. "I apologize for snapping at you out there," he said.

"You should. You were pretty goddamn impolite," Letty said, dropping her feet to the floor.

"You're right, I was. Because you're not the problem. Let me tell you, sweet pea: don't ever get yourself elected to the Senate," Colles said, as he settled behind his desk. He was a tall man, big whitened teeth, ruddy face, carefully groomed gray hair. "There are more numb-nuts around here than in the Florida state legislature, which, believe me, was a whole passel of numb-nuts."

"What do you want?" Letty asked.

Colles smiled at the abruptness. "We bore you. Okay. We bore *me,* most of the time. I used to be this really, really rich real estate developer down in Palm Beach County.

18

Pretty young women would *insist* that I pat them on the ass and I was happy to do it. If I patted anyone on the ass in this place, my face would be on CNN at eight, nine, and ten o'clock, looking like a troll who lives under a bridge and eats children."

"You could probably get away with patting Welp on the ass," Letty suggested.

Colles faked a shudder. "Anyway, I got your letter of resignation. I put it in the shredder."

"I still quit," Letty said, sitting forward. "I don't hold it against you, Senator Colles. You're not a bad guy, for a Republican. I'm in the wrong spot. I realized that a month ago and decided to give it another month before I resigned. The month is up."

"What? Tallahassee scared you?"

"Tallahassee was the best assignment I've had since I've been here," she said. "If it was all Tallahassees, I might have decided to stick around."

"Now we're getting someplace," Colles said. He did a 360-degree twirl in his office chair, and when he came back around, he said, "The Tallahassee thing was . . . impressive. If you'd been caught by the Tallahassee cops, I might have had to fire you. But you weren't. I can use somebody with your talents."

"Doing what? Burglaries?"

"As chairman of the Homeland Security and Governmental Affairs Committee, I've made it my business to oversee DHS operations. There are a couple dozen of what I think of as mission-critical problems that they have to deal with, at any given time. I'm very often unhappy with the results."

"I . . ."

"Shut up for a minute, I'm talking," Colles said. "DHS investigators deal with all kinds of problems, security problems, some of them serious. Like, why can't we protect our nuclear power plants from intruders? We had a guy down in Florida walk into . . . never mind. Anyway, these guys, these investigators, basically do paperwork and interviews. Too often, paperwork and interviews don't get the job done. When there's a problem, the local bureaucrats cover up and lie. They're very good at that. That might even be their primary skill set."

"Okay."

"Now," Colles said. "Have you been here long enough to know what a department's inspector general does?"

"More or less."

"An inspector general basically inquires into a department's failures," Colles said. He steepled his fingers and began to sound like a particularly boring econ lecturer. "They may look into complaints from whistle-blowers or, if it gets in the news, they can look at obvious fuckups. Like why Puerto Rico never got its Hurricane Maria aid from FEMA, outside some rolls of paper towels. They can also examine situations where a necessary investigation simply doesn't produce . . . the needed results. We know there's a problem, but the DHS investigators come up dry. Or they hang the wrong people, the bureaucratically approved scapegoats."

"That's unhelpful," Letty said. She restlessly twisted a gold ring. She was bored, she wanted to move.

"It is. Of course, it's fairly routine in governmental matters. People get hurt all the time, I can't help that," Colles said. "My concern is, the big problems don't get solved. I've personally spoken with several of these DHS investigators, about their investigations. Actually, I didn't just speak to them, I interrogated them in classified subcommittee meetings. They are serious, concerned people for the most part.

"What they aren't, too often, is real good investigators," Colles continued. "Or, let me say, researchers. They go somewhere with a list of questions, and ask the questions, and

21

record the answers, but they don't poke around. They don't sneak. They don't break into offices. What would really help over there is a smart researcher, somebody who knew about money and finance and crowbars and lockpicks and so on. You do. You have a master's degree in economics and a bunch of courses in finance, and graduated with distinction from one of the best universities in the country. Which is why I hired you."

"And because my dad asked you for a favor," Letty said. She was paying attention now: she could smell an offer on the way.

"He didn't press me on it. He really didn't. Lucas said, 'I want to draw your attention to an opportunity.' I looked into it, and here you are," Colles said. "If you were only what your college transcript recorded, I'd probably let you go now. But you're more than that, aren't you?"

Letty shrugged. "Spit it out. The offer, whatever it is."

Colles laughed this time. "I can get you a little tiny office, a closet, really, downstairs. It has a safe, but no window. I think the last guy was put in there because of body-odor issues. I can also get you a government ID from the Homeland Security IG's office. You wouldn't be working for the IG, though.

22

You'd still be working for me, as a liaison with Homeland. You'd go places with an investigator, but we'd call you a 'researcher.' You may sometimes need to do the kind of research you did in Tallahassee."

"That could be dangerous," Letty said. "I could get hurt. Tallahassee was simple. Even then, if I'd run into the wrong cop . . ."

"There could be some . . . dangers, I guess. The IG's investigators, the special agents, can carry sidearms for personal protection. I made some inquiries, the blunt-force definition of 'inquiries,' and the IG's office has agreed that they could issue you a carry permit. Of course, you'd have to demonstrate proficiency before you'd get the permit. I know about your background, from talking to your father, so I'm sure you'd be okay. I know you've thought about the Army, or the CIA, but I can promise you, you'd be as bored in either place as you are in this office. Those are the most ossified bureaucracies in the world. The job I'm talking about, I can almost guarantee won't bore you."

"I . . ." Did he say a *carry permit*?

"I'll stick you out in the wind," Colles added.

"I've already resigned," Letty said. "And I put the letter through the shred-

23

der," Colles said. "You want to quit, you'll have to send me another one. You shouldn't do that. Try this new arrangement. I think it could work out for both of us."

She nibbled on her lower lip, then said, "I'll give it another month, Senator Colles. We can talk again, then."

"Listen, call me Chris," Colles said. "When we're in private, anyway. You're a pretty woman. Makes me feel almost human again, talking to you."

"If I get my gun and you pat me on the ass, I'll shoot you," Letty said.

"Fair enough," Colles said.

With the change in her assignment, neither Colles nor Welp had anything more for her to do that day, except give her the key to the basement closet she'd use as an office. She went down to check it out, and while it *was* bigger than an ordinary closet, it wasn't bigger than, say, a luxury California Closet. The concrete walls were painted a vague pearl-like color, in paint that had begun to flake. The room contained a metal government desk that might have been left over from World War II, a two-drawer locking file cabinet with keys in the top drawer, a broken-down three-wheel chair that squeaked when she pushed it, and a safe buried in a concrete wall. The safe stood open, with nothing in it but a sheet of paper that contained the combination for the old-fashioned mechanical dial. The room did smell faintly of body odor, so Colles may have been correct about the previous occupant.

A busy Sunday would clean it up, she decided. A bucket full of water, a mop, sponges, and some all-surface cleaner. She'd bring in a desk lamp and a cart for her computer, perhaps an imitation oriental carpet for the concrete floor, a powerful LED light for the overhead fixture. She could get a new chair from Office Depot. She would need a coat tree, or a way to sink coat hooks into the concrete wall.

It would do, for now.

When she finished her survey of her new office, she rode the Metro under the Potomac to Arlington. The day had started out gloomy and cool, and by the time she got home, a light mist had moved in, just enough to freshen her face as she walked to her apartment complex.

She changed into a sports bra and briefs, pulled on a tissue-weight rain suit with a hood, and went for a four-mile run on Four Mile Run Trail. Halfway along, she diverted into a wooded park, walked to a silent, isolated depression in the trees. She often visited the place on her daily runs, and sat down on a flagstone.

There was noise, of course; there was always noise around the capital — trucks, cars, trains, planes, endless chatter from people going about their politics. The woods muffled the sounds and blended them, homogenized them, and when she closed her eyes, the odors were natural, rural, earthy, and wet. In five minutes, her workday had slipped away, the personalities, the paperwork, the social tensions. In another five, she was a child again, with only one imperative: stay alive.

Another five, even that was gone. She sat for twenty minutes, unmoving, until a drip of water, falling off a leaf, tagged her nose and brought her back to the world. She sighed and stood up, brushed off the seat of her pants, and made her way back through the trees. She'd never decided *what she was* when she came out of the trees and back to life. Not exactly relaxed, not exactly focused, not exactly clear-minded, or emptied, or any of the other yoga catchwords.

Where she had gone, there was nothing at all.

She was a piece of the rock, a piece of a

tree, a ripple in the creek.

There, but not Letty.

Two days later:

The DHS agent was a sunburned over-muscled hulk who dressed in khaki-colored canvas shirts and cargo pants and boots, even in the warm Virginia summer, topped with a camo baseball hat with a black-and-white American flag on the front panel. He had close-cut dark hair, green eyes, a two-day stubble, a thick neck, and rough sunburned hands. He yanked open the Range Rover's door and climbed in, as Letty got in the passenger side.

He looked over at her, pre-exasperated, as he put the truck in gear. "I don't know what I did to deserve this, but I'll tell you what, sweetheart," he said, in a mild Louisiana accent, "I didn't sign up to train office chicks how to shoot a gun. No offense."

His name was John Kaiser and he was a forty-seven-year-old ex-Army master sergeant and a veteran of the oil wars. He slapped reflective-gold blade-style sunglasses over his eyes, like a shutter coming down.

Letty sat primly in the passenger seat, knees together, an old-fashioned tan leather briefcase by her feet, a practical black purse in her lap. She was wearing black jeans and a dark gray sweatshirt with the sleeves pulled up. She said, mildly enough, "I thought you signed up to do anything Senator Colles asked you to do."

"Colles isn't my boss: Jamie Wiggler is." Wiggler was the Homeland Security inspector general. "I signed up to do security. This isn't security."

They left her apartment complex and drove west out of Arlington, mostly in silence, except that Letty took two calls on her cell phone, listened carefully, and then said, "All right. I can do that," and hung up. After the second call, she took a red Moleskine notebook out of her purse and made a note.

"Do what?" Kaiser asked after a while.

She said, "What Senator Colles asked me to do."

Kaiser shook his head and looked out the window at a convenience store, where a line of locals sat smoking on a concrete curb outside the restrooms. He said again, "This is bullshit. I'm supposed to be doing serious stuff."

"Chris isn't punishing you," Letty said. "You're not doing much right now. Wiggler told me you're back from North Carolina, waiting for another assignment. He thought you could run me through the range. If you didn't like it, you should have told him so. I could have gone with somebody else."

"It's Chris? You're calling Senator Colles *Chris*?" he asked.

"He told me to," she said.

He glanced at her: "Sure. You guys must be really close."

She was blunt: "Close enough to get your ass fired if you're suggesting that Colles and I are sleeping together."

"I wasn't suggesting that," he muttered, rapidly backing off.

"Try harder not to suggest it," she said; her tone did everything but smear blood on the windshield.

Long, long, long silence, except for the off-road wheels buzzing on the blacktop.

The shooting range was out in the Virginia countryside, in a low, unpainted concrete-block building; the back of the building dug into a hillside. They got out, Letty carrying her briefcase, her purse over her shoulder. Kaiser led the way to the building, politely held the steel door for her, and they went inside to a narrow room that stretched across the width of the building. The place was the exact opposite of chic: concrete floor, unpainted walls, shelves of shooting accessories on the outer floor, with two locked racks of rifles and shotguns, mostly black.

The wall behind a glass counter had wide, thick windows that looked out on a ten-station shooting range. Three men were on the firing line, their shots audible but muffled, like distant backfires. Shelves of ammo sat below the windows, and the glass counter case was filled with revolvers and semiauto handguns. The air smelled of gunpowder, Rem Oil, and concrete dust, not at all unpleasant, a candidate for male cologne.

A thin man, maybe sixty, stood behind the counter, ropy muscles, hunched over a newspaper. He was wearing a Rolling Stones tongue T-shirt and an oil-spotted MAGA hat. As they walked in, he folded the paper and said, "Special K. How's they hangin', man?"

Letty: "Special K?"

Kaiser ignored her and said to the gun range man, "Gotta do some training." He gestured between the counter man and Letty. "Letty Davenport — Carl Walls. Carl owns this place."

Walls said, "You're a regular cutie. You got a gun?"

After a second, Letty asked, "You talking

30

to me or Special K?"

Walls snorted and said, "All right. Well, let's get you set up. We have guns for rent, or if you're thinking about buying . . ."

"I'm all set," Letty said. She lifted the briefcase.

Walls: "You got ear and eye protection?"

"I do."

"Then you're good to go," Walls said. "Since you're training, I'll go out there with you, put you on the far end, where you can talk, shuffle some folks down away from you."

Kaiser said to Letty, "I didn't know you had a gun with you."

"You didn't ask," Letty said. "Now you know."

Walls picked up the edge, looked between them: "You guys ain't close friends, huh?"

"We met an hour ago," Kaiser said.

Letty: "It's not looking promising."

Walls shifted his shooters into booths one, three, and five, and put Letty and Kaiser in the ten booth. He clipped a target onto a shooting frame and cranked it fifteen yards downrange. As he did that, Letty was digging in her briefcase and Kaiser said, "Wait, wait, wait. Before you start messin' with a gun, I want to know that you know what

31

you're doing."

"I know what I'm doing," she said. She took out a gray canvas sheath, unzipped it, and extracted a black pistol with a low optical sight.

Kaiser asked, "What the fuck is that?"

Walls said, "I believe it's a Staccato XC. Never seen one in person. It's not stock . . ."

Letty popped the empty magazine out of the pistol, jacked the chamber open, and turned it to show Kaiser that it was empty. "I had it custom-regripped because my hands are small. My dad suggested the checkered cherrywood, because it's pretty. Trigger was already perfect."

"I like a pretty gun," Walls said. "Your dad does guns?"

"He's a U.S. Marshal. He tracked down that cannibal guy out in Vegas. He shot the 1919 killer in Georgia."

Walls said, "Damn."

Kaiser said nothing, but took an ugly tan Sig from his range bag, ejected an empty magazine, took a loaded magazine from the bag, and slapped it home. To Letty, he said, "If you're sure you know what you're doing with your pretty gun . . ."

Letty said, "Hang on a minute."

She put the gun on the range shelf, with a loaded magazine next to it, picked up her purse, extracted a rubber band and a wallet, took all the currency out of the wallet, wrapped the rubber band around it, and then dropped the bundle at the tips of Kaiser's steel-toed boots.

"That's a thousand dollars, fresh out of the ATM," she said, standing too close to him, right in his face. "Five shots, three seconds, cold pistols. Mr. Walls scores it."

Kaiser turned from Letty to Walls and back to Letty, and said, "I spent eight years with Delta. I've pumped out fifty thousand rounds."

"A thousand dollars or shut the fuck up," Letty said.

Kaiser again looked at Walls, who grinned and shrugged. "I wouldn't bet her. If she said that gun was gonna jump up and spit in your ear, I believe you'd wind up with an ear full of spit."

The big man stooped, picked up the money, and handed it back to Letty. "No bet. I can't afford it on my salary, even if you can. Carl can score it. Five rounds, three seconds."

Letty put on her shooting glasses and electronic earmuffs as Walls set up a timer. She kept her hand at her side until Walls asked, "Ready?" and she said, "Ready," and then the timer beeped.

She brought the pistol up and *bapbapbapbapbap,* her elbows and shoulders absorbing the recoil, getting her back on target after each shot.

They pulled the target and Kaiser said, "Huh," and Carl said, "I'd call that as two and a half inches. Could have been two and a quarter, if it hadn't been for that little flier. Right on three seconds. Not bad for a cold pistol. Lot better'n a poke in the eye with a sharp stick."

Kaiser: "I can beat that."

"Then you should have bet the money," Letty said. "Though I wouldn't want to put any extra stress on you. Losing to a *chick*? Could throw some shade on the Delta rep."

"Nice. Two minutes on the range and she's talking trash," Walls said with a happy grin. "I like it, I really do." He ran out a new target and when the timer went *beep!* Kaiser fired his five rounds, *bapbapbapbapbap.* When they pulled the target in, Walls said, "This is gonna be close."

Kaiser: "C'mon, man. I beat her. She had that flier."

"But your group's a tad looser," Walls said. They laid the targets on top of each other and Walls shook his head. "I can't call it. Wait, I *can* call it. It's a tie."

"This is bullshit," Kaiser said. "Like, this rim right here . . ." He pressed a thumbnail into one of his shots that overlapped one of Letty's.

Letty said, "I'll admit it's not bad shooting, even for four seconds."

Walls laughed and clapped her on the back with a heavy hand, like she was a guy, making her half-smile, half-grimace, and said, "I wasn't gonna say nothin', though it wasn't a *whole* four. Three-point-five to be exact."

"Fuck both of you," Kaiser said. He might have suppressed a grin.

Letty slipped a hand into her jeans pocket and pulled out a thin, compact Sig 938. "You got a carry gun on your belt. You want to go again?"

"I got a carry gun, but it's not a toy," Kaiser said. He reached under his shirt, which he'd worn loose. He produced a pistol smaller than either of the bigger guns they'd been shooting, but larger than Letty's carry gun; still an ugly desert tan. "Three shots at seven yards, one and a half seconds."

They spent an hour shooting, burning up ammo, trading pistols, Letty winning some, Kaiser some others, at seven, ten, fifteen, and twenty-five yards. Walls got his own gun, an accurized Kimber .45, but he was older and past it, and wasn't competitive. A couple of the other shooters came over to watch, and one jumped in, but he wasn't competitive, either.

On the way out, Walls said, "You're not a terrible-bad shot, little lady. Come back anytime."

"I will, Mr. Walls."

"You can call me Carl," Walls said.

She nodded. "And you can call me Letty."

In the truck, Kaiser squirmed around in the driver's seat, getting his butt settled in, then said, "I'd kill for that fuckin' Staccato."

"You could sell your Rolex and Range Rover and buy several," Letty said.

"Can't do that," Kaiser said and grunted. "When you're Delta, you spend a lot of time in combat zones. Good pay and no income tax. If you're careful, when you get out, you've got a nice bankroll. The first things you gotta buy are a Range Rover and a Rolex. Couldn't hold my head up with the boys if I didn't."

"What if you're not careful?"

"It's a Prius and an Apple Watch."

"I didn't realize that," Letty said.

"I got a personal question, if you don't

mind," Kaiser said. "I know why I'm good with guns. It was my job. It's still my job, to a certain extent. I don't love guns. They're like hammers. Tools. But why are you a shooter? You a gun freak?"

Letty shrugged. "I grew up with guns and I needed them. Most people don't. All these high-capacity guns flashed by the nutcakes? They're a disaster. If I had my way, there'd be no guns but single-shot hunting rifles and single-shot shotguns. You could do all the target shooting you want with those. You could hunt to your heart's content. Of course, you'd actually have to learn how to hunt or how to hit a target, and most of those dimwits don't want to be bothered. They want to play with guns because they can't get laid, is my opinion."

"So it's women's fault."

"Got me there," Letty said.

Kaiser laughed, then said, "Still, you don't believe in high-capacity weapons, but you . . ."

"I don't believe in them, but that's not where we're at, is it? There are more guns in this country than there are people, so it doesn't matter what I believe. I will *not* be the victim of some lunatic."

"Okay." Kaiser sat staring through the windshield, then said, "Listen. About this morning. I apologize. I was an asshole. You're the best female shooter I've ever seen. But I can tell you something, *Ms. Davenport:* punching paper is a lot different than shooting real live people."

As he put the Range Rover in gear, Letty said. "I know. I've shot three people. Killed two of them. The other one was a cop. I shot him four times, two different occasions. Little .22-short, that was the problem. No punch. He always wore this heavy canvas winter coat. Never did kill him, not for want of trying. Though my dad and another cop did. None of it bothered me much."

Kaiser let the truck coast in a shallow circle across the parking lot. "You're serious?"

"Yes," she said. "If you have your doubts, it's all on the Internet. You could look it up."

She listened, heard her mother's voice and a male rumbling, then the voices went up and her mother began screaming RUN, LETTY! and Letty turned and stepped across the room and picked up her rifle, which was unloaded because her mother made her swear to keep it unloaded in the house, and she fumbled in the pocket of her trapping parka for a box of shells and then heard a crash of breaking glass and a RUN, LETTY! and she broke the gun open and there was a sudden tremendous BOOM and the sounds of fighting stopped . . .

Too late.

She looked wildly around the room, flipped the old turn lock on the door, grabbed the steel-legged kitchen chair at the foot of her bed, and without thinking about it, hurled it through the bedroom window. There were two layers of glass, the regular window and the storm, but the chair was heavy and went through. Running footsteps on the stairs, like some kind of Halloween movie — and Letty threw her parka over the windowsill to protect herself from broken glass, and, still hanging onto the rifle, went out the window.

She hung on to the coat with her left hand and dropped, pulling it after her; the coat snagged on glass and maybe a nail, ripped, held her up for just a second, then everything fell. She landed awkwardly, in a clump of prairie grass, felt her ankle twist, a lancing pain, and hobbled two steps sideways, clutching the parka in the cold, and saw a silhouette at the window and she ran, and there was a noise like a close-in lightning strike and something plucked at her hair and she kept hobbling away and there was another boom and her side was on fire, and then she was around the corner of the house and into the dark.

Hurt, she thought. She touched her side and realized she was bleeding under her arm, and her ankle screamed in pain and something was wrong with her left hand. She touched the hand to her face, and found it bleeding; She'd gashed it on the window glass, she guessed, but she kept going, half-hopping, half-hobbling. *Cold,* she thought. She pinned the rifle between her legs and pulled the parka on. She had no hat or mittens, but she pulled the hood up and began to run as best she could, and her left hand just wasn't working right . . .

She was only a hundred feet from the house when she realized she wasn't alone in the yard. There was a squirt of light and then she heard movement, a crunching on the snow. He was coming after her, whoever he was, and he had a crappy, weak flashlight to help him.

Shells. As she hobbled along, she dug in her coat pocket and found a .22 shell, but her hand wasn't working and she dropped it. Lost in the dark. Dug out another one with the other hand, broke the rifle, got the shell in, snapped it shut. A squirt of light and then the man called, "Letty. You might as well stop. I can see you."

40

That was horseshit, she thought. She could barely tell where he was and he had the partly lit house behind him. She was moving as fast as he was, because he was having trouble following her footprints through the grass that stuck up through the shallow snow — that's what he was using the flashlight for — and there was nothing behind her but darkness. If he kept coming, though . . . She had to do something. She didn't know how badly she was hurt. Had to find someplace to go.

His silhouette lurched in and out of focus in front of the house and she remembered something that Bud, her trapper friend, had told her about bow hunting for deer. If a deer was moving a little too quickly for a good shot, you could whistle, or grunt, and the deer would stop to listen. That's when you let the arrow go.

She turned, got a sense of where the man's silhouette was, leveled the rifle, and called, "Who are you?"

He stopped like a deer and she shot him.

Kaiser dropped Letty at her apartment, with her briefcase and purse. After a microwave risotto, she watched the top of the news on CNN at seven o'clock, then cleared off her kitchen table, got her gun-cleaning equipment from a closet, and cleaned and lubri-

41

cated the Staccato and the Sig 938. When she was sure they were right, she returned to the closet and took out her Colt .45 Gold Cup and Walther PPQ and checked them. Back to the closet for a Daniel Defense AR-10-style semiautomatic rifle.

Her father called her a shooting prodigy. Now she spent an hour pulling pieces off her guns, making sure they were functioning perfectly: a form of meditation, working with your tools. She needed an outdoor range, she thought. She hadn't fired the rifle since she'd been in Washington — too busy, with no time to visit rifle ranges.

The thought occurred to her, then, that with her promised new license, and the military ranges scattered around Washington, perhaps she'd have access?

She'd have to ask.

She'd put the guns away and was on her couch watching the end of the fourteenth season of *Supernatural* when her father called. "Did you quit?" he asked.

"I tried, but Colles talked me out of it. Said he'd find me something more interesting to do," Letty said.

"Any idea what that would be?" Lucas Davenport asked.

"Not exactly. It's with the DHS. He says he'll get me a government ID that will let me carry."

Silence for five seconds. "Ah, jeez, Letty. You sure about this? Is he going to get you into trouble?"

"I hope so, but I don't know. I'll have to see what he's talking about," Letty said.

"You be careful, young lady," Lucas said. "You get in too deep, I'll have to ground you."

"Like that's gonna happen."

"Letty . . ."

"Yeah, yeah, yeah . . . How's Mom?"

When she got off the phone, Letty went back to *Supernatural.* She was thinking about moving on to the fifteenth season when Colles called.

"I got a job for you," he said. "You're gonna need a straw hat."

THREE

Jane Jael Hawkes walked out of her house ten minutes before one o'clock in the afternoon, carrying her backpack, which contained two bottles of water, her wallet, and her nine-millimeter Beretta semiautomatic pistol. The day was hot — 100°F — but not unnaturally so for El Paso, Texas. Rand Low was at the curb in his Ford F-150 crew cab, and she popped the passenger door and climbed in.

Max Sawyer and Terry Duran were sitting in the back and said "Hey," and Low asked, "You up for this?"

"Yes. Drive."

Hawkes was a stocky, hard-faced woman with muscle in her arms and shoulders, originally developed during her teen years in an after-school job lifting batteries in an AutoZone store, and later in U.S. Army gyms. At thirty-four, she had a heavily sun-freckled face and brown hair, cut short; and for all that, she attracted certain kinds of outdoorsy men. She had intelligent eyes, an engaging smile when she used it, and an intensity that fired her face and body and the way she walked.

Low put the truck in gear and they headed out to I-10 on the way to Midland, Texas, four and a half hours away.

Sawyer said, "You didn't really have to come."

Hawkes: "Yes, I did. I made the call, so I go."

She'd made the call to murder a man and a woman she'd never met, or even seen.

The U.S. Army hadn't been what Hawkes thought it would be. When she signed up, she was thinking Iraq, Afghanistan, Syria; armored-up combat patrols on dusty mountain roads or desert tracks where you could see forever. She was thinking adventure, she was thinking movies: *13 Hours, Jarhead, The Hurt Locker, Zero Dark Thirty.*

Instead, she got Fort Polk, Louisiana, bureaucracy, and bugs, working in a job that, in civilian life, would have been called a "gopher." She was supposed to be a 46Q, a public affairs specialist, but she was a gopher. She did take some Army courses that taught her how to use Microsoft programs like Word, PowerPoint, and Excel. She studied hard, because those programs, she thought, would be useful in civilian life. She was wrong about that. You could earn all the Microsoft certifications in the world and still wind up making nine dollars an hour.

Out on I-10, Low put the cruise control at ninety miles an hour and Hawkes told him to back it off to eighty-five. "You get a DPS trooper with an itch and he stops us, we'll be on record as heading out toward Midland."

"You're the worst goddamn backseat driver in the world," Low said, but he backed off to eighty-five.

Hawkes's father had been a white-trash loafer, hard drinker, and sometime over-the-road truck driver out of Houston. Her mother worked occasionally as a house-cleaner and a window-washer for rich people as she tried to take care of her seven children. She took them to church some Sundays and read to them from the Bible some nights, which Hawkes found stultify-ing and often incomprehensible. The Army, Hawkes thought, was one way out of that life, if you couldn't afford community col-lege. She was wrong about that; some things that you were born with you can never escape. She was white trash.

Duran, from the backseat, said, "Let's get some tunes going. What do you got on Sirius?"

They settled on Outlaw Country and got on down the highway, talking off and on about country music. "You know what Sirius needs?" Duran asked. "A Texas music station."

As he spoke, James McMurtry came up on the radio with "We Can't Make It Here." They all shut up to listen, and when McMurtry finished, Hawkes said, "Our theme song. That's our fuckin' theme song, guys."

Hawkes used her quiet time in the Army to read American history, trying to find out why her life was like it was. Some of her reading was reality-based, some of it more peculiar. She was honorably discharged from the Army as a Specialist E-4 and took advantage of the Forever GI Bill to enroll at the University of Texas–El Paso, working part-time in a Fleet & Ranch store, once again lifting batteries. She quit university after two years, when a grad student explained to her that the job market for a woman with a B.A. in history was nonexistent.

Nobody had told her that.

After dropping out, she went full-time at Fleet & Ranch, started by pushing carts of cut lumber around the concrete floor until her back was on fire, but over four years she worked her way up to assistant manager. She should have been the manager, but got sideswiped by a well-spoken bilingual weasel with a necktie, four years younger than she was, and male, with a degree in business.

She'd had no chance.

She continued reading history of the peculiar sort, threading her way through the online world of social media. As somebody stuck to the bottom of the employment ranks, she couldn't help noticing that while climbing through those ranks was difficult enough, holding your spot at the bottom was getting harder all the time, because more "bottom" kept arriving. Plenty of bottom to do the work at nine dollars an hour, if you decided to quit. Didn't take a genius to push a cart of two-by-fours. She was a robot, one that happened to be living and breathing. Sooner, rather than later, a real robot would be doing her job.

Headed southeast out of El Paso, I-10 tracked the agricultural land a mile or so to the south, the ribbon of green fed by the Rio Grande. Fifty miles out of town, the highway jogged to the east, away from the river, and into harder, drier country, running between heavily eroded low red mountains, past isolated small towns until they got to I-20 and turned north, toward the oil patch.

In the backseat, Sawyer was running an off-and-on monologue about guns: "Anyway, I was in this place up in Wichita Falls, Henry's, and I seen this interesting piece, gray synthetic stock, detachable magazine, so I go over to take a closer look, and holy shit! It was one of the original Steyr Scouts designed by Jeff Cooper, you know, the guy who wrote for *Guns & Ammo.* Bolt-action, .308, and it's still mounted with the long eye-relief scope that came with the rifle, and they got the original case with all the case candy . . ."

Duran said, "I don't shoot me no bolt-actions . . ."

Hawkes said, "I read this article said that the more guns a man's got, the shorter his dick is gonna be."

Duran: "So you're saying Max here is a half-incher?"

Sawyer, a short man with thick blond hair, and eyes so pale they were almost white,

smiled: "Okay, boys, let's get 'em out . . .
You, too, Janie."

"Fuck you, Max."

"Anytime, anyplace."

Then there was Rand Low, who was driving, another piece of white trash.

Sawyer said, "Hey, Rand, what do you call four Mexicans in quicksand?"

"I dunno, what?"

"Quatro sinko."

"That sucks," Low said, but he laughed anyway.

Duran said, "I don't get it."

Low had turned his head toward the backseat as he laughed, and Hawkes slapped her hand on the dashboard and barked, "Watch it!"

Low snapped his head back around and hit the brakes, hard. They all rocked forward as he came to a stop at the end of a traffic pileup. They spent fifteen minutes edging up to three DPS cruisers and two wreckers, all with their lightbars flashing blue and red light out into the afternoon. At the front of the line, they found a crowd of cops and relevant civilians standing in the ditch, where a tractor-trailer lay on its side. The left side of a manufactured house, still strapped to the trailer, was crumbled like an aluminum can.

A thin, frightened-looking man in a white T-shirt, jeans, and a bush hat was waving his arms around as he talked to a cop; the driver, Hawkes thought.

Low said, "There's a good 'ol boy gonna need a new job."

As a young man, Rand Low had looked . . . Texan. Large, rawboned, he was permanently angry. He'd been born in Odessa, Texas, where his father worked as a short-order cook and his mother was a waitress. His parents wanted him to learn a trade. They thought the Army might train him in heavy equipment operation, because heavy equipment operators made good money in the oil patch. But the Army recruiter had conned him and he landed in the infantry, carrying a rifle. He saw distant combat — he could hear it, but not see it — and got away uninjured, angered by the restraint imposed on the troops by their officers.

Afghanistan? They could knock it down in a month, he told anyone who'd listen — and enlisted people listened, nodding — if only the Army would turn them loose. The officers said that was crazy talk. You should see the chaplain, they told him. He worried them and they suggested that he find another line of work and finally insisted that he do that. They'd be happy to give him an honorable discharge at the end of his enlistment, but if he stayed on . . . well, then maybe not.

His anger grew in the Army and he carried it out to civilian life in the West Texas oil fields.

If a shopper should back out of a parking space while Rand Low was coming down the supermarket lane, block him for a half-second, you'd hear from him, a bearded, red-faced man in a rage at the audacity of some unlucky woman who occupied the lane ahead of him. Rand Low was coming through and he didn't have that half-second to waste.

"Get the fuck out of the way, bitch, you fuckin' . . ."

Pounding on the steering wheel of his pickup, leaning on the horn. Hitting on the bottle of Lone Star, or Pearl, in the cup-holder.

Low was somewhat tough. Not crazy tough, but maybe eighty-five percent on the male tough-o-meter, what you'd get after two tours in Afghanistan.

One Monday night, at a drive-in burger place in Odessa, Texas, he did his screaming-and-horn act with a woman who rolled down her window to give him the finger. He slammed his Chevy pickup into park and jumped out and went running after her and smacked the trunk of her car with an open hand, hard.

She'd stopped, and as he was about to go around to the driver's-side window to explain the error of her ways, the woman's boyfriend — or possibly her pet gorilla, could have been either — got out of the passenger side of the car, grabbed Low by the neck, dragged him to his pickup, and beat his head against the truck's fender hard enough to dent it and put Low in the hospital for eight days with a concussion and a shattered nose, which was never quite right after that.

Low had learned from that lesson; learned he wasn't jack shit.

He'd gotten out of the hospital with a bill for $47,000, which he had no way to pay, because he had no money and no insurance. His jobs were sporadic enough, and Low was elusive enough, that the hospital eventually wrote off the loss and stopped pursuing him.

But the experience had increased his already volcanic rage with his world. Then he met Jane Jael Hawkes in a military bar in

El Paso, where she worked nights, after her day shift at Fleet & Ranch.

When she was twenty-nine, Hawkes had used her Army computer skills and her reading of American history to start her own website, ResistUS. She chose the name because of the slight pun at the end: *US* for United States, and *US* for . . . us. The view was to the political right and pushed further to the right over the years.

She spun her economic theories out on ResistUS, operating under her middle name, Jael, which she pronounced "Jail," because her mother had fished the name out of the Bible, and she'd pronounced it that way. Jael made no appearances, made no speeches, remained an articulate, mysterious woman known only to people who prowled the hallways of the right-wing darknet. She harvested email addresses of border folks, militia people, sent them anonymous links to her website.

She attracted followers, many ex-military, mostly male, but women as well, all embittered by the lives they were leading. Living in apartments no bigger than cells, or in decaying trailer homes, trying to decide whether to pay the heating bill or the electric bill or to actually buy a steak this month.

Good Americans, hooking up with the woman at ResistUS, and calling themselves Jael-Birds.

"You're a smart guy," she'd told Low, over rum Cokes. "You think you're here by mistake? Hauling pipe for some rich fuckin' oil company? You think BP gives a wide shit about you? We're the modern slaves. Sure, they tell us we're free people, but free to do what? Earn forty grand a year breakin' your fuckin' back? Can you afford a house? Fuck no. Or if you can, it's a shack.

"Why are we pissed on by all those TV people you see on CNN and MSNBC and Fox who make fun of us every chance they get? The people they fly over? The Rust Belt? The Bible Belt? The only time they can see us is when somebody overdoses on OxyContin and they put up a picture of some asshole passed out in the street. For them, that's us. Why should anybody make fun of us because we eat at Olive Garden and not some fruity fish-and-steak place in New York City?"

And Hawkes learned a curious thing about Low, who had little interest in intellectual matters, in history or economics. He could talk. Feed him the words and he could turn them into rage. And he told her something else, one night sitting at the bar:

"You can bullshit all you want, Janie. Bullshit until you drop dead. Nobody'll really give a flying fuck until you do something. Get out there."

"Do what? Get a bunch of guns and go shoot up stop signs, like those fuckin' gun nuts?"

"They're only gun nuts because they don't know what else to be," Low said. "You tell them, but you don't show them. They read all that shit on ResistUS and then what? I'll tell you what. They go watch the football game on ESPN."

She thought about that: how to convert words to action.

She was aware of the militias operating in the El Paso area, because the members hooked up to her ResistUS site. They flew "Don't Tread on Me" flags and Confederate battle flags and wore camo and carried AR-15s and drove Jeeps and bought all that geardo military crap that she'd thought was crap even when she was in the military.

She didn't want that; but she did want something else.

"Here's what we're going to do," she told

Low. "We're going to start a militia, but it'll be a real one. Our own fuckin' army. None of this playing-with-guns shit."

They began to collect members from her ResistUS base and the other local militias. People with military experience and the right kind of enthusiasm. With Low leading, and, tentatively at first, they began to patrol the U.S. border east of El Paso. They found and held illegals for the Border Patrol. Some of the patrolmen began to talk to them about favored crossing points, places where they could use extra eyes.

Hawkes called it "The Land Division," and designed a flag for them, a triangular green mountain on a blue field. The nascent force was asked to standardize vehicles — four-wheelers, either Jeeps or pickups, for those who could afford them. American trucks — F-150s, Rangers, Silverados, Sierras, Colorados. Everybody had guns, of course, twenty different makes of .223 AR-15s or 7.65×39-millimeter AK-47s. They trained, under Hawkes's eyes and Low's direction. They did firing exercises in the barren mountains east of El Paso and north of I-10.

They had cookouts, brats and beer.

Romances sprang up among the troops.

■ ■ ■

Four men sifted out of the collection of veterans and enthusiasts who called themselves Jael-Birds, the hardest of the hardcore. In addition to Low, they were Max Sawyer, their armorer and gun enthusiast; Terrill T. Duran, the oldest of the group, a former Air Force sergeant who had done ten years in a Texas prison for bank robbery and had met Low, who was serving a short stretch for driving a stolen car. And Victor Crain, a recovered meth freak and sometime car thief, who, like Low, had spent time in Afghanistan and who, everyone agreed, was a little nuts. In a good way. He'd been the one to introduce Low to the stolen-car business, but hadn't been arrested when Low was.

The Land Division had been patrolling the border for a year, holding their cookouts and guerrilla training and live-fire exercises out in the desert, when the thing they'd been edging up to actually occurred.

Low and the other three men, in two pickups, were patrolling near Fort Hancock, Texas, when they came across two illegals walking parallel to I-10, headed northwest toward El Paso. The illegals, dirty from their travels, carrying backpacks slung over T-shirts, both wearing ballcaps, one wearing sunglasses, looked over their shoulders as the trucks caught up with them.

"What do you think?" Low asked.

Sawyer, who was riding shotgun, said, "I'm good with it."

Low got on his cell phone, called Crain, who was riding shotgun in the second pickup. "What do you think? What we been talking about?"

"Haven't seen anyone for an hour," Crain said.

Duran, driving the second pickup, said, "I say go for it."

Sawyer said, "I'm with Terry."

The two trucks caught up to the illegals, stopped. The illegals had tried to keep walking, while half-turned to keep an eye on the gringos in the pickups. The four militiamen got out, all with their AKs.

Low took a last look around, then, "Do it."

The illegals were buried in an untracked piece of desert, deep in the soft sand.

The four men didn't talk about it, they all told one another, but somehow, other members of the militia knew, or suspected. A week after the shooting, Hawkes cornered

Low and asked him directly.

Low said, "We had to draw a line and we did."

"You murdered two people?" She was appalled . . . and maybe awestruck.

"We didn't murder them," Low said. "We killed them. There's a difference. They were criminals committing a crime. We were defending the United States of America."

Hawkes was rocked . . . and she nodded, and went along.

The next time she saw Low, she hooked him by his shirt placket, pulled him close, and said, "Here's your mistake: two wetbacks aren't a problem. It's a million wetbacks that are the problem."

Low blinked and said, "That's a line I can use."

A week later, Low stopped over at Hawkes's house with a militia girlfriend, and, sitting at her kitchen table, drinking beer, Hawkes told them, "I read this book about President Lyndon Johnson."

"Yeah?" Low had a hard time keeping up with her reading. He wasn't a reader himself.

"When Johnson started out in Congress, he got a lot of power right away. You know how?"

"You tell me," Low said.

"He took over the committee that raised reelection funds for other congressmen. Before he did that, nobody bothered to raise money for other people, everybody did it for themselves. Johnson raised the big bucks and passed it out to people who'd boost him higher in Congress. It worked. Like he was only a congressman for a couple of terms and he was one of the most powerful people up there. What does that tell you?"

Low had to think about it for a while, then said, "Well . . ."

"Money," Hawkes said. "If you're going to get some real power, you need some real money. We need to figure something out. We need money. Lots of it."

Time passed, months. The patrols continued. Then a man named Roscoe Winks, an oil wildcatter, so he said, wandered into the Ironsides bar where she worked part-time. He was taking a break from the oil patch, he said, a little vacation in the El Paso area. Did she know where a man might find a little . . . uh . . . action? He didn't mean a poker game.

He was a sorry excuse for an oilman, she thought, but they got to talking, and though they at first talked in circles, they eventually got serious. Winks, like Hawkes, was in a perennial financial bind, but Winks had an idea of how he might get out of it, if he had some qualified help, people with some guts. How they might steal themselves some oil and make some real money. Though they'd need twenty thousand dollars to get organized.

She told him to come back: she'd think of something.

She told Low and Sawyer about Winks.

Low asked, "How much are we talking about?"

"Winks says our end could be a million bucks a year. He could give it to us in cash. He's got that all worked out. The money would be clean."

Low: "Terry knows an easy bank up in Lawton, Oklahoma. He knows how we could knock it over, no problem. We been talking about it. Don't know how much we'd get, but it'd be enough to cover Winks."

Hawkes took the next step, looked at Low and nodded.

Duran was right: Low and Duran went into the bank on a payday Friday morning, Sawyer drove the stolen car. They got $39,000. Seed money, for the good of the

USA. They burned the stolen car in a pasture outside Lawton and were back in El Paso by midnight.

"You know who started this way, with a bank robbery?" Hawkes asked, thumbing through the pile of cash on her kitchen table. "Stalin started this way."

Low and Duran looked at each other, then back at Hawkes. Low asked, "Who?"

Winks had a broken-down tank truck. The money from the bank robbery rehabbed the truck's diesel engine and the transmission, gave the tractor unit a fresh coat of fire-engine-red paint, bought some decent recaps for it. A thousand bucks spent on a sandblaster cleaned up the tank. Red paint and careful drawing by one of the militiamen converted the truck into a replica of the vehicles run by the biggest oil-service company in the Permian Basin.

A truck nobody would notice.

And they built themselves a pig. The pig cost eight thousand dollars, created in a machine shop in Waxahachie, Texas, to specifications created by Roscoe Winks.

Somewhat to Hawkes's surprise, Winks's scheme actually worked — small sips of oil from the major oil companies turned into hundreds of thousands of dollars over the two years they were working at it.

Hawkes, with serious money coming in, quit her day job at Fleet & Ranch to spend full-time organizing. She'd been right about the money. The protopopulist groups scattered around the Midwest and Northwest loved the idea of paid-for travel by air, rather than bus or pickup. Money to cover meals and rental cars, even decent motels, instead of the ratholes or back bedrooms they usually had to put up with.

Low became a celebrity among them, a tough guy who showed up at meetings with gun-toting bodyguards in off-road-equipped pickups, some with fuckin' snorkels. And a woman, who stood behind him, her face half covered by a bandanna, who called herself Jael.

Low did the speeches; Hawkes did the thinking and the backroom negotiations.

"We need to galvanize people who think like us," she told her conferees. "We need mythmakers. We need an Alamo. We don't need a bunch of fuckin' crazies running through the Capitol. We need an Alamo that people can be proud of, instead of hiding out like a bunch of chickens."

Nods and questions. Whispered answers. Envelopes full of cash changed hands. They got organized.

More money went to the militia hardcore in El Paso. Those who couldn't afford solid pickups got new ones, and new weapons to go with them, standardized nine-millimeter semiautomatic pistols and ARs and AKs as long guns.

At the end of August, two years after they started stealing oil, they had a target and they had a D-Day. They had their symbol of resistance, their Alamo, though they were the only ones who knew it at the time.

Then, almost at the last minute:

An oil company exec named Boxie Blackburn called Roscoe Winks, to see if he knew anything about some missing oil. Winks panicked and called Hawkes.

"We're right there," Hawkes told Low, later that evening. "We're at the Alamo, but we're gonna have to disappear afterwards. We need that money. We can't get along without it. We spent too much on . . . other stuff, and we still have to pay for the stuff from Bliss."

She never spoke the name of the stuff from Bliss. Bliss was a U.S. Army fort in El Paso. The stuff from Bliss would cost a ton.

"Five more runs," Low said. "We'll tell Winks we want all the money from the last five runs, and we want it now, up front, or he could get hurt — but tell him he can have the truck, the pig, the idea, and he can get his own gang together."

"Kind of like extortion," Hawkes said.

"More than that," Low said. "When Winks gives us the money . . . we're gonna have to get rid of him."

"We'll cross that bridge when we get to it," Hawkes said.

"We're at the bridge," Low insisted. "The caravan is on its way. We know what they're going to do. It's now or never, Janey. We get rid of the Blackburns, we keep the runs going until we move . . . then Winks. The fact is, Winks could give us up. He'd do it, too, if he thought it'd save his own ass."

Hawkes licked her lower lip.

And nodded.

Low watched Boxie Blackburn over a half-dozen weekdays, learning his routine. Although he was a manager, Blackburn was out in the field every day, usually making it home by six o'clock after a late-day stop at his office. He'd be at home for an hour or so, probably cleaning up, and between six-thirty and seven, he'd be out the door with his wife, twice to the Midland Country Club, other times to steak houses.

"He's got a high-end F-150, a Limited," Duran said. "His wife drives a BMW X3. Vic knows a guy who can move them across the border overnight, no questions asked. We'd get ten grand."

"Which is beside the point," Hawkes said.

"I know, but . . . might as well take it," Duran said. "Money is money."

After a gas-and-snacks stop on I-20, they made it into Midland at five-forty on a hot blue-sky afternoon that would have been insufferable if not for the truck's air-conditioning. They pulled into an empty church parking lot on Midland Drive, a block from Cardinal Lane, and waited.

At six o'clock, Hawkes said, "If he doesn't make it home soon, I'm gonna give up. I'm getting kind of screwed up here."

"Well, he will make it home at six," Low said. "Because, *there he is.* Everybody: gloves."

A dark blue F-150 went by on Midland Drive and Low put his truck in gear and followed. In the backseat, Sawyer pulled a Beretta out of a pouch he'd pushed under Low's seat. Duran had his Glock wrapped in a jacket between them, and he took it out and checked it, jacked a shell into the chamber. Sawyer said, "Don't wave that fuckin' thing in my face."

"Getting a little tense there, Maxie?" Duran asked.

"Just not professional," Sawyer said. "Put your gloves on."

Low had turned down Cardinal Lane, a block behind Blackburn's truck. They went past the kind of white board fences that horse people build, the men in the backseat hunched forward to watch as Blackburn slowed, turned into his driveway, waited as a garage door rolled up.

Low said, quietly, "Here we go, boys and girls. Max, stay behind me until I get to him . . ."

"I know, I know . . ."

Low said, "Janie, you just sit. We'll call you if we need you."

Duran: "Rand, where's the tape?"

"Under my feet, I'll bring it," Low said. "Everybody ready?"

Low swung the truck into Blackburn's driveway, and Hawkes said, "Oh my Lord, oh my . . ."

Blackburn was getting out of his truck, shut the door, and then stopped to look at them, the garage door still open. He didn't recognize them, but Low said, "Hey, Boxie!"

Blackburn, Texas-polite, said, "Can I help

you folks?"

Low had been walking toward Blackburn, with Sawyer a step behind, and as they came up to him, Low stepped aside, as though doing a two-step, and Sawyer stepped past him and pressed his heavy black Beretta into Blackburn's belly.

Low, working from a script written in Hawkes's kitchen, said, "Yeah. You can help us. You're a rich guy and we need us some money. We need us some jewelry. Get in the house. You don't fight us, you don't get hurt."

Blackburn was stunned, and scared, staring down at the gun. "I don't have much, I got some, go away, don't hurt anyone . . ."

"Get in the house, motherfucker," Sawyer said. He was also working from the script. He added, "Nobody can see us here."

Blackburn, thinking about his wife inside: "Man, don't . . ."

"Get in the house," Low said, letting some anger out, some crazy. "Get the fuck in the house."

Blackburn led them through the interior garage door into the house, where his wife called: "Boxie? Is that you?"

Hawkes sat in the truck as the men all went inside the house. She cupped her hands over her cheeks and eyes, rocked back and forth in the truck. The men were in there killing them, killing the husband and wife who she'd never met, about whom she knew almost nothing except that the husband had made a phone call to Roscoe Winks, panicking him.

Three minutes passed, five minutes. Nothing moving in the garage. Hawkes mumbled, "Fuck it," and got out of the truck, walked through the garage, opened the door, and saw what looked like two cocoons on the floor, Blackburn and his wife, wrapped in gray duct tape.

She said, "Oh, no . . ." and at the sound of a woman's voice, the wife rolled to her side, her eyes on Hawkes, pleading. The men had plastered a strip of tape across her mouth.

Duran asked, "Max? Bags?"

"Yup." Sawyer took two transparent plastic bags out of his hip pocket, knelt next to Boxie Blackburn and pulled one of the bags over his head, and taped it at his neck. Blackburn began to roll and kick.

Sawyer moved to Blackburn's wife, whose name Hawkes didn't know, and pulled a bag over her head, and Hawkes turned away: "Oh, God. Oh, Jesus."

"You don't have to watch. Go back out to

the truck."

"I made the call. I watch," Hawkes said, and she turned back to the dying couple. Boxie Blackburn went first, trembling violently as his brain died. When the woman died, Hawkes went to the kitchen sink and vomited up everything she'd eaten that day. When she'd finished retching, she washed her face, dried it on her shirtsleeve, and said, "Let's finish it. You all know what to do. Max, get the thermostat . . ."

FOUR

Letty and John Kaiser flew into Oklahoma City on a Tuesday morning after a long Monday getting briefings at Homeland Security headquarters in Washington. The problem involved relatively small amounts of missing crude oil from the Permian Basin in West Texas.

"Now listen," Colles had told Letty. "I want you to talk to an old man named Vermilion Wright in Oklahoma City. He owns an oil company, or most of one. He's been bitching and moaning about oil thefts out in West Texas, where most of his oil wells are located. That's not really what we're worried about. We're worried about what the thieves are buying with the oil money. A couple of Homeland Security agents have been out there and didn't come back with much, which is why the IG's office is now involved. I want you to go out there and see what you can see."

"That's it? That's all you know?"

"Hey, you could at least pretend to be respectful," Colles said. "I'm a fuckin' U.S. senator. And no, that's not all I know. I've set you up to be briefed by a semi-high-level Homeland executive Monday morning. Kaiser will pick you up. I understand you two are buddies now."

"I don't plan to kill him in the immediate future," Letty said.

"Good enough. Monday. Be there and be awake."

Their briefer was a thin, sunburned woman named Billy Greet, who wore khaki slacks and square-shouldered blouses with epaulets, her blond hair pulled back in a tight bun. She might recently have been out in a desert somewhere, because her lips were thin and peeling, her cheekbones sharp and pink.

"Nobody except the oil people really gives a crap about the missing oil — it's the equivalent to about a minute of our daily national supply requirements," she told them. "One fundamental question that nobody can answer is, how is the oil being stolen? Are there thieves loading up trucks and selling the crude on the black market? Is somebody doing something funny with a pipeline? Or is it a purely white-collar deal, with accountants shuffling numbers?"

DHS, Greet said, didn't care about that, because it was a problem best handled by local law enforcement and oil company security officers.

"That was until an Exxon security team picked up rumors that a man named Rand Low is involved in the thefts," she said. "Low is a political extremist who got out of a Texas prison about three years ago."

Greet clicked on a video screen and brought up a mugshot of Low. He was a dark-haired, dark-eyed man with a hatchet face and a prominent, battered nose. "He talked to his parole officer exactly once, then dropped out of sight and hasn't been heard from since. He's from that country out there, West Texas. He spent six years in the Army, got out as a buck sergeant, then he worked oil, as a laborer and a truck driver, before he got involved in politics and started stealing cars, supposedly to raise money for a militia."

While most militias were composed of hapless goofs with guns and confused ideas about America and patriotism, Greet said, Low's militia, according to rumor, had a sharper, more focused edge — anti-immigrant, antigovernment, secretive, and heavily armed.

"We're not sure of this, but we think one of the leaders of the group is a woman, and she might have a sexual relationship with Low. We don't know her real name, if she exists. The militia supposedly has links to other militias around the country, particularly those operating in the Upper Midwest, Wisconsin, Indiana, and Michigan, and the Pacific Northwest, Idaho, Washington, and Oregon. Some of the El Paso people, including Low, were in Portland during the most violent of the riots there. We think his girlfriend might have been with him. If she's real, and we can identify her, we'd *really* like to speak with her."

While the oil thefts weren't important in the overall scheme of things — they didn't threaten national energy security in any way — they had kicked off a lot of cash, by normal standards, and there were indications that the thefts were continuing.

"The oil companies want to stop the thefts. We, DHS, want to know where the money is going, and if the rumor is true, what Low and his friends are buying with it," Greet said. "This is a heck of a lot more than living expenses — they're probably taking in something between a half-million and a million dollars a year, and maybe a lot more. If we can figure out how the oil is being stolen, we can probably identify at least some of the thieves. Then we can turn them over to the Texas Rangers and let the Rangers hold branding irons on their naked feet and get some answers." Pause. "Not really. I didn't actually say that."

"Sounded like you said that," Kaiser said.

"Sitting in an air-conditioned room, fully hydrated, and the poor man is hallucinating," Greet said to Letty.

Letty nodded. "Or it could be simple dementia."

At the end of the day, Letty and Kaiser were ushered into the office of a DHS assistant inspector general, who gave Letty two government identification cards. The first said that she was a congressional employee with an endorsement granting access to the Department of Homeland Security; the second was a DHS sidearm permit.

"We're not too happy about this, frankly, the gun thing, but Senator Colles knows how to twist an arm," the assistant IG said. "You do *not* have arrest powers. You're not a law enforcement officer. The gun permit will allow you to carry a firearm for personal protection only. Do you understand that?"

She did. "Will it allow me to carry it

everywhere?"

"Well, no foreign countries, but anywhere in the U.S. and territories, with the exception of certain high-security facilities where you would have to check it. And you can't fly with it on your person; you'll have to check it to take it on an airplane," the assistant IG said.

Letty didn't say so, but she was pleased. When they left the office, walking down the hall, Kaiser gave her a cell phone–sized package covered with Christmas wrap: "A gift," he said.

Puzzled, she opened it, and found a black alligator leather ID case, sized for her new cards.

She said, "I just . . . I mean . . . John!"

She tipped her head back and laughed: she could carry a gun.

Anywhere.

Oklahoma City was the home of Hughes-Wright Petroleum, run by a billionaire named Vermilion Wright, his business housed in the thirty-seven-story Hughes-Wright Petroleum Center.

During the trip out from Washington, Letty and Kaiser had been talking about the range of employment opportunities she might be interested in, if the DHS well came up dry. On the way into town from the airport, in a rented Ford Explorer, Kaiser said, "The thing you'd hate about the military is the sheer fuckin' boredom and the paperwork. Orders. Every time you go outside . . ."

Letty was driving, Kaiser was picking his teeth with a peppermint-flavored toothpick. "Even if you got picked up by Special Ops, you'd spend ninety percent of your time either sitting around or training. While you're doing that you've got some Ivy League asshole who's never left D.C. yapping in your ear about *combat ethics . . .*"

He was about to go on when Letty asked, "Is that where we're going?" She pointed up through the windshield. "The second building behind the first one? The gold-glass one?"

"They told us the second-tallest building in town and that one is, so it must be it," Kaiser said.

And it was. They found an open space in the underground parking garage and took the elevator to the lobby level, where a security guard checked their appointment status, gave them adhesive paper name tags to stick on their shirts, and sent them to the top floor.

Letty had checked a directory behind the

reception desk and noticed that while Hughes-Wright occupied the top four floors of the building and apparently had naming rights, the rest of the place was occupied by a variety of investment and real estate firms, and smaller oil- and gas-related companies. Nevertheless, the place smelled of oil — not crude, which stank, but like the odor of hot motor oil on a car's dipstick.

That struck her as odd, since so little of the building seemed to have anything to do with oil. Maybe some kind of aerosol spray, an oil-industry version of Febreze?

As they rode up in the elevator, Kaiser said, "While I'm a much better shot than you are, or can ever hope to be, I'll let you do the talking here."

"I let my guns do the talking on the range, but I do think it'd be wise to let me talk here," Letty agreed. "Do you smell oil?"

"Yeah, I do. I was thinking something was wrong with my nose. Maybe they oiled the elevator this morning?"

After the shooting contests at the Virginia range and the DHS briefings, it seemed to Letty that she and Kaiser might fall into a prickly friendship, which was about right, since they were both distinctly prickly. During the briefings, and afterward, and on the trip to OKC, Kaiser had begun playing the part of a surrogate uncle, giving her advice that she didn't need, though he never missed a chance to check her ass.

Which she knew, of course.

He was currently unattached, he'd told her, but the DHS briefing officer, Greet, "kinda liked my whole package," and had mentioned in passing that she, too, was currently unattached. "Gonna call that girl up, when I get back to D.C.," he said.

"If you need any advice about how to talk to women, I'm always here," Letty said. "Believe me, you *do* need that advice."

"*Au contraire,* as we say down in Terrebonne Parish. With the right woman, I speak in poetry."

The elevator doors opened and a woman in a dark green dress was standing there, holding a leather portfolio. "Ms. Davenport? Mr. Kaiser? Mr. Wright is waiting."

Vermilion Wright occupied an expansive wood-and-glass office that overlooked Oklahoma City. He was a tall man, white-haired, angular, deep-set eyes under thick white eyebrows, strong for eighty-five. A recent newspaper story that Letty found on the Net said that he had bad knees from a life of crawling around oil rigs; a bamboo cane lay on one side of his desk.

He stood up when Letty led Kaiser into his office, and stuck out a bony hand to shake with each of them.

"Nice to meet you. Sit down," Wright said. "The last DHS guy in here was about as useful as tits on a bull. I hope you can do something to help us out."

"We're not so much anxious to help you out as we are to find out where the money is going," Letty said, as she took one of the leather visitor chairs and crossed her ankles. "Of course, if we figure that out, we'll probably know who's stealing your oil."

He contemplated her, then asked, "You smart?"

Letty nodded. "Yes."

"Where'd you go to school? What'd you study?"

"Stanford. Economics," she said.

He nodded and smiled. "Went there myself. Back in the fifties. 'Go Cardinal.' Never really gave a shit about college sports, though. You know anything about oil?"

"Only what I read in the Yergin books," she said.

"That's a start," he said. "What'd you think about them?"

"They taught me the difference between investment and fashion," Letty said. "When COVID hit, Exxon's stock went to $30.11.

81

I borrowed a quarter-million dollars from my father and bought eight thousand shares at $31.11, a dollar up from the bottom. I sold out at $67.20."

"So you're up a quarter-million after you pay back your old man," Wright said.

"Not quite. I had to pay capital gains. And the IRS made me pay a year's interest to my dad on the loan."

"So why'd you do that? Bet on Exxon?"

"I checked to see how many electric cars there are. Last year, a little more than five percent of the cars sold in the U.S. were electric or hybrid. The rest run on gasoline or diesel. That's a hair more electric cars than in 2013, but only a hair. The electric cars run on power that mostly comes from natural gas–fired power plants. Guess who supplies the gasoline, diesel, and natural gas? For the time being, electric is fashion, oil is investment. That will change, but not yet."

"You embarrassed about that? Young liberal woman buying oil stock?" Wright asked.

"I had about as much effect as a match in a forest fire."

Wright nodded. "Where'd you put your quarter-million?"

"I'm still thinking about it," Letty said.

Wright gazed at her for another minute, then asked, "Did your boss tell you two why you're here? Why you're here in my office today?"

"Something about a guy you can't find," Kaiser said. "Blackburn?"

Wright turned to Kaiser. "That's right. Boxie Blackburn. Real first name is Bradley, but nobody calls him anything but Boxie," Wright said. "Nobody can find him, four days now. Can't find his wife, either. He works out of our Midland office, does the paperwork for us. I was putting the screws on him to find out where the oil was going, since we should have paper every step along the stream. He was exploring the possibilities and the next thing I hear, he's gone. His cars, too. Nobody at home."

"How much have you lost?" Letty asked.

"Maybe ten or twelve thousand barrels a year, going back a year or two," Wright said.

Letty sat back. "That sounds like a lot."

"Well, we pump a bit more than eighty million barrels a year," Wright said. "The shrinkage is maybe one one-hundredth of one percent — one percent of one percent — and there's always *some* shrinkage, some variation between what we get paid for and what we think we pumped."

"But you're sure you're missing oil?"

"Boxie isn't sure, but I am. The question I got in the back of my head is, Was Boxie involved? Did he think the jig was up? Is he running?"

"I looked at the WTI index this morning and over the past year you've averaged in the mid- to upper fifties per barrel," Letty said. "So you're down roughly a half-million dollars, maybe six hundred thousand, a year."

"That's correct," Wright said. "But we're not the only company that has the problem."

He stood up, turned around, and limped over to his windows. With his back to them, he said, "None of the oil patch companies are anxious to discuss it publicly, but I've had some heart-to-heart talks with a couple other guys. My feeling is, overall, these crooks could be stealing as much as a hundred thousand barrels a year. Maybe more. Chevron, I think, got whacked. They aren't talking, at all, but they've got security guys sniffing around the Permian and I've gotten back some rumors."

"How much are the thieves getting for the oil?" Letty asked.

"I don't know. Because I don't know how much is being stolen. I'm guessing. No matter what they're doing, they'll have some costs, too," Wright said. "Unless . . . and this troubles me . . . it's being stolen on paper. That somebody else is being credited with our oil. Lots of people handle the oil before it winds up in a gas tank. Or the money winds up in our bank account. Stealing actual buckets of oil . . . that'd be complicated. If it's some nerd sitting at a computer and moving numbers around . . . that might be complicated, too, but it's not like you'd have to hire trucking companies to move the oil around."

He turned back to them as Kaiser said, "Whatever it is, even if it's just your oil, it'd be worth doing, for most folks. Now your Boxie guy is missing. Four days, he could be in Panama by now, already moved into the new house. Making bids on a power cat."

Wright jabbed a finger at him: "That's what worries me. He stole it and ran. Or, worse, he poked his nose in somewhere he shouldn't have, and somebody cut it off."

"We'll want to talk to the people in your Midland office," Letty said.

"It's already fixed. They'll answer any questions you have." He turned to Kaiser. "You might want to take a gun. Rough stuff happens out on the patch. There could be a lot of money sticking to the wrong fingers."

They talked for another half an hour, and Letty noted the names of Wright-Hughes employees in Midland. "You going down today?" Wright asked.

"Might as well," Letty said. "Get an early start tomorrow."

"Tomorrow." Wright moaned. "I'm going to Phoenix tomorrow, down to the Mayo to get my knees replaced. Both of them. I'll be out of it for a while, but I will leave strict instructions with Midland: what you want from us, you get."

Letty nodded: "Thank you."

Wright spent another fifteen minutes outlining problems and personnel, speculating on which other companies might have gotten hit — "I talked to the boss over at Lost Land; he thinks they're down between eight and ten thousand" — along with background on Boxie Blackburn.

When they finished talking, Wright picked up his cane and walked with them to the elevators and wished them luck. "Get these guys. I know you have different concerns, but if you can get me names, I have some security people who'd like to talk to them privately."

■ ■ ■ ■

"What do you want to do?" Kaiser asked, as they took the elevator down. The smell of oil was still with them, and outside, the sun poured down like melted butter.

"Get something decent to eat — I couldn't eat that crap on the plane," Letty said. She put on her sunglasses. "Then get outta town."

"Maybe find a rib joint," Kaiser suggested. "Towns like this got good rib joints."

"Fine with me, if I can get a salad."

They wound up at Front Door Barbecue, where Kaiser ingested a year's worth of cholesterol and Letty had an oversized salad with turkey. Satisfied, they walked back to the car, took it out to I-44, and turned south. As they crossed the Canadian River, leaving the city behind, Kaiser said with patent insincerity, "I'll drive if you want."

"I'm good."

"Think I'm gonna kick back then, take a nap," Kaiser said. "Save my energy for the big show."

"You mind some quiet music?"

"That'd be great."

Kaiser had the soldier's knack of going to sleep almost instantly; he did that, and was a silent sleeper, arms crossed, chin on his chest, the bill of his baseball cap resting on his nose.

Letty dialed up a jazz channel, loud enough to mute the road noise, and set the cruise control ten miles an hour over the speed limit. For the trip, she'd dressed in blue jeans and a pale blue, long-sleeved blouse with pearl snap buttons. She wore a Twins ballcap and had the straw cowboy hat, now sitting on the backseat, as recommended by Colles, if she had to go out in the sun.

Interstate 44 was four lanes of pale concrete laid though an agricultural landscape that wasn't exactly rolling — Iowa was rolling — but more like *notched* by creeks and twisting rivers, marked by scrubby trees, Love's truck stops, and weather-beaten small towns.

Letty checked off the towns as they rolled by, but spent much of the trip thinking about the people she'd be talking to. When they got to Midland, she had to get on top of the Hughes-Wright people immediately.

Wright had told them that Dick Grimes, a company vice president who ran the Midland office, was touchy about his territory. Grimes, he'd said, was an oil field veteran who didn't care for anyone's opinions, if that person hadn't spent time as a chain-hand. That automatically eliminated women, and especially young women, and especially young women with college degrees who might be considered snotty.

She decided that she couldn't adopt any particular attitude until she actually met with Grimes: she'd get in his face if she had to, but she'd prefer not to do that. Grimes was a trifle old-fashioned, Wright had said, but he knew everything about oil and where it might be going.

And in the monotony of the drive, she spent a while thinking about a thirtyish legislative aide who, she'd been told, was planning to head back to Ohio and run for Congress, and who should win if he could make it through the primary. He'd been coming around to chat with her, once a day at first, twice a day lately. He had brown eyes and an easy smile; one reason she'd kept going with her birth control pills. On the other hand, she thought, behind those gentle brown eyes, a politician lurked. Not that an appropriate brown-eyed politician couldn't help you through some lonely Washington nights . . .

Letty'd had college romances during her

six years at Stanford, sexual with two guys at long intervals, and a couple of flirtations that hadn't gotten to sex.

She'd enjoyed the two sexual adventures — it had been the men who'd called them off. The second one had told her, during their final dinner together, "My biggest problem is that you're going to do what you're going to do. I'm not really a factor in that, am I?"

She'd argued that he was being unfair, that she was always open to compromises.

"Sure. About whether to have salmon or steak, or pizza or enchiladas. About serious stuff? Not so much. It's your way or the highway, and, well . . . I'm sorry."

She thought it but didn't say it: "Don't let the door hit you in the ass."

For the last year, she hadn't gotten near a bed except to sleep. Something, she thought, would have to be done about that.

They crossed the Red River into Texas, the river about as damp as a kitchen sponge, and twenty minutes later rolled into Wichita Falls, a little short of two hours after they left OKC. She woke Kaiser, who'd been sleeping contentedly, and they got strawberry shakes and a restroom stop at a McDonald's in downtown Wichita Falls.

On the road again, down Highway 277, then several shorter pieces of different highways, dust devils whirling ten stories high across dusty fields. They cut I-20 at Big Springs, rolling fast through country nearly as flat as Kansas, but drier, and browner, with huge pale blue skies hanging overhead.

And it was warm, but not bad, a mildly humid 87 at five o'clock.

After two hours of desultory conversation, Kaiser put himself to sleep again — saving his energy — and she kept her eyes on the highway, let her mind drift: getting on the highway to Midland had been a long and twisting journey . . .

Letty and her mother had been abandoned by her father when she was a toddler, and as a twelve-year-old, she'd been at the center of a series of killings in the rural Red River valley of Minnesota.

The murders had been investigated by Lucas Davenport, at the time an agent for the Minnesota Bureau of Criminal Apprehension. Before the murders had begun, Letty had kept herself and her mother financially afloat, trapping muskrats and racoons and mink out of the local marshes during the winter months. She carried a piece-of-junk single-shot .22, for those times it was necessary to finish a trapped animal. That had taught her to kill without flinching.

Her mother, a sad, depressed alcoholic, had been one of those murdered, and Letty had been wounded herself. She rarely dreamt about it anymore, but sometimes she did, seeing herself in her nightmare, standing out in the dark, and the snow, the temperatures below zero, her hand not working right because of a deep gash caused by broken glass, fumbling to reload her .22 as she was stalked by the killer.

The cop Letty had shot was involved in the murders and deserved every bit of lead he'd gotten; though, as she told Kaiser, she hadn't managed to actually kill him.

When it was all over, Davenport and his wife, Weather, had pulled some political strings and gotten appointed as her guardians, and eventually had adopted her. She never really understood why they did that, other than that she and Lucas Davenport had simply *clicked.* An odd psychic connection that perhaps couldn't be explained; it simply *was,* and, she thought, always would be.

Though she was adopted, the Davenports were every bit her parents, the only ones she'd ever had. The memory of her natural mother had become increasingly one-dimensional. Letty had done more to take care of her mother than her mother had ever done to take care of her, except at the end, when her mother had given up her life to give Letty a chance to live.

Once with the Davenports, everything changed. For the first time there was somebody to take care of her, with all the love and growing-up teenage stresses that implied. In high school, connecting through one of Lucas Davenport's friends, she'd worked as an unpaid intern at a TV station and even made it on-air occasionally. She'd realized then that she didn't need the attention. What she liked about journalism was the research, not the talk; the action, the tension, the stress.

And there was more to it.

Before she'd become Davenport's ward and then adopted daughter, Letty had lost her crappy .22, which had been a personal symbol of her independence. He'd trusted her enough to buy her a new rifle, a pump that she loved even better, but then she'd lost that one, too, taken as evidence after she'd shot the murderous cop a second time.

In addition to all the complicated pieces of their relationship, she and Davenport had bonded over guns. She'd always relied on one, as a trapper out in the Minnesota winter. Davenport was an excellent shot with both handguns and long guns and had trained her in both until she might have been better than he was. Hold that: she *was* better than he was, with handguns, at punching paper, anyway.

What she envied was his ability to make instant life-and-death decisions, never a doubt in his mind and rarely a wrong decision.

One of his investigations ended with a revenge invasion of his own home, while Davenport was away, with two insane drug enforcers kicking the door to kill his wife and children. Letty had shot and killed them both, without flinching and without mercy even when she could have given it, and with no regret whatever.

Lucas Davenport had a couple of other personal peculiarities that had also clicked with Letty. Athletics, for one thing. Davenport was a jock, and Letty enjoyed running with him at night, all over Saint Paul.

And then there was fashion.

Letty couldn't remember actually having new clothes as a child: everything came from secondhand shops. Davenport, though, was a clotheshorse who studied men's fashion magazines and bought tailored suits from Washington and custom shoes from London.

Letty had picked that up, which had amused her adoptive mother, Weather. Weather was a plastic and reconstructive surgeon with a tendency toward the academic. Because the Davenports had money, she also dressed in expensive clothing, but with little sense of style, or even a vague interest in it. She wore hospital scrubs around the house, *borrowed,* as she said, from the hospitals where she was on staff. Going off to work in the morning, she often looked like an advertisement for a wealthy woman's garage sale.

Not Letty, after the meeting of the minds with Lucas. She liked good clothes, she liked good fabrics and perfect fits, Hanro underwear. She knew what worked with her eye color and dark hair because they'd talked about it. She'd once convinced Weather to buy Lucas a Brioni tie for his birthday, because it perfectly chimed with his eyes; he wore it once a week until Letty stole it as a headband, because it perfectly chimed with hers.

On every birthday from age thirteen to

the autumn before, Lucas had given her a ridiculously expensive piece of gold jewelry.

Now, older, as a college graduate, she was sleek, young-womanish, fashionable, with a high-end wardrobe and five-hundred-dollar sunglasses. Maybe even a snowflake . . . unless you happened to catch her uncovered eyes, as Colles had, at her employment interview; the cool assessing crystalline eyes of a wolf, a predator with blood on its teeth.

At six o'clock, she pulled the Explorer into the parking lot of the Homewood Suites in Midland, Texas, and woke Kaiser.

"Good trip," he said, yawning. "I feel *great*. I *could* use a snack."

FIVE

The Hughes-Wright office in Midland opened at seven-thirty and was less than a mile from the hotel. Letty and Kaiser agreed that there was no good reason to get to the office before the employees had a chance to settle in, so they'd meet in the hotel lobby at seven o'clock and find a place to get breakfast before going over.

Letty got up at six o'clock, ran hard for twenty minutes, did a half-hour of yoga stretches and core work, got dressed, thought about it — thought about the hotel and maids — and put the Staccato in her briefcase with a box of nine-millimeter ammo and the Sig 938 in her front jeans pocket inside a Sticky Holster.

She and Kaiser found an IHOP in a strip mall, Letty had pancakes and Kaiser ate sirloin tips with eggs, with coffee for both, and they were out by eight o'clock.

■ ■ ■ ■

The Hughes-Wright office was in a single-story blue-metal building off the I-20 frontage road, five acres of rusty pipe racks and the blue building, with an oil-tank field on three sides and the interstate highway on the fourth. A dozen pickups and SUVs squatted in the parking lot outside the building.

"Gonna be hot," Kaiser said, as they crossed the cracked blacktop to the front door. Letty looked up at the sun-faded blue sky and nodded.

The building's interior was cool, but not cold. Two heavyset women sat behind a reception counter studying computer screens, and they both turned when Letty and Kaiser came through the door. From the way they dressed and did their hair, the two women might have been twins, except that they didn't look alike. One of them said, "Miz Davenport? Mr. Kaiser?"

"Letty and John," Letty said. "Is Mr. Grimes in?"

"Yes, I believe he's waiting to talk to you. Between you and me, he's not in a good mood."

"Maybe we should have brought him a

cheesecake from IHOP," Letty said, smiling at the two women.

"More like a yard-wide lemon sheet cake," the woman said, returning Letty's smile. She pointed at a hallway leading toward the rear of the building. "You go on back, hon. Last office on the left. Dick is skulking in there like an angry armadillo."

Skulking like an angry armadillo, Letty thought, as she started down the hall. Whatever kind of man Grimes might turn out to be, he wasn't the kind of boss who terrorized his employees.

All the offices down the hall had glass doors, three of them occupied by men in T-shirts with pockets or golf shirts; and the place had the same warm oil smell as the building in OKC, but thicker. The last door on the right had a nameplate that said BOXIE BLACKBURN.

To her left, in a larger office, Grimes was sitting behind a wooden desk, talking into a cell phone. She knocked on the glass and he looked up, saw her, and crooked his finger to tell them to come in. They stepped inside and he pointed at two visitor chairs and said into the phone, "I really don't want to hear any shit about it, Ed. You tell Marky I want it up and running by tomorrow morning, or I'll know the reason why it isn't. Yeah. Yeah . . . yeah."

Grimes's office was purely functional: the desk, an expensive office chair behind it, filing cabinets along a wall, a bookcase, and the visitor chairs sitting on a brown carpet dusted with sand. Four pictures hung on the wall behind Grimes, in brown plastic frames: a thin, blond, fiftyish woman with sharp eyes and a sharper nose; and three willowy dark-haired girls, who, though they caught features from both the older woman and Grimes, were all improbably pretty, given their gene pool. A plain Christian cross hung on the wall to the right of them, and Letty noticed a well-worn Bible on the bookcase.

Grimes said "Yeah" one more time, and "Talk to you later."

He punched the phone off and said, "I spoke with Vee — Mr. Wright. He said that as big a pain in the ass as you're likely to be, he wants me to cooperate in every way I can and give you everything you need."

He was a large man, both tall and thick, with close-cropped curly black hair and tangled eyebrows, brown eyes so dark that he didn't seem to have pupils, and a fleshy nose. The two sides of his nose didn't match, and Letty thought he might have had a part of it cut out, like you would with skin cancer. He had a couple other scars on his left cheek, and when he lifted a hand, she saw that he was missing most of his left little finger. He was wearing a pink golf shirt under a gray canvas overshirt, and jeans.

"What'd you think about that?" Letty asked. "About cooperation?"

Grimes scratched the scarred side of his nose and then said, "Well, I didn't like it. Then I thought about it for a while. Since Vee runs the company and has about a billion dollars and, sometimes, a bad temper, I decided I'd cooperate every way I can and give you everything you need. I *do* plan to piss and moan about it from time to time."

"Then we'll get along," Letty said. "I'll tell you what, Dick: you don't have to help us much, other than getting the people around here to listen to us, if we need them to listen. We'll try not to bother you, or worry you, or create any trouble. We don't mind some pissing and moaning. We'll probably do some ourselves."

Grimes nodded. "Then what can I do for you? I mean, right now?"

"I'm sure you know about Mr. Wright's problem with missing oil?"

Grimes shook his head. "He thinks we're short. It's driving me crazy. It's like when my wife sends me to the grocery store to get her some strawberries and the store doesn't have any. When I get home, it turns out that's no excuse. I'm telling you, I looked everywhere and I can't find a leak. Boxie — Boxie Blackburn, our numbers guy, Vee told you about him — couldn't find one, either. Vee says ten or twelve thousand barrels, or more, per year, and he is death on those kinds of numbers. He can smell a leak, so I believe him, but I can't find ten barrels. I'm pulling my hair out."

"You're not losing it at, you know, the pumps? Uh, the rigs?" Letty was unsure of the nomenclature.

"Nawp," he said, a Texas cross between "naw" and "nope."

"You're sure about that?"

"If we are, I can't figure out how. A couple of guys here wonder if there's a phantom pipeline cut somewhere, where somebody takes the oil out before it gets to the tanks. But that's . . . nutso. I can't even think how in the hell you could do that, with nobody seeing it. My personal opinion is, if we're missing oil, it's paperwork somewhere along the way. Somebody's accountant is stealing it."

"Blackburn?"

Grimes stood up. There was only one

window in the office, behind his desk, a high, thin slit whose lower edge was chin high on Grimes. He turned and peered out at a slice of blue sky, then said, "I've known Boxie for twenty goddamn years, since we were both working outside. I can't believe he's stealing it, but . . . where is he? Where's Marcia? We can't find either one of them."

"Talk to the police?"

"Yeah, but they're not too interested at this point. They've gone out to his house, they say both of his cars are gone. Can't find them, but they're gone. They think he and Marcia took off for somewhere. Either for good or evil."

"Would you mind if we poked through Mr. Blackburn's office?"

"Yeah, I'd mind, and so would he, but given what Vee's said, and that you're government people, and the fact that we can't find Boxie or Marcia . . . go ahead," Grimes said. "The door's unlocked, I was in there this morning."

"What about his computer . . . You think it's protected?"

Grimes sat down again, reached across his desk for a scratch pad, and jotted some numbers and letters on it: 71Boxer73. He pushed the note across the desk and Letty picked it up.

"That's his password. He was born in 71, his wife in 73. Clever, huh?"

Kaiser asked, "Do you have any idea why he might have taken off? Okay, maybe he's gone shopping, or maybe he's behind the oil thefts and decided to take off. But maybe . . . he figured something out and said so to the wrong people . . ."

"Like he might be dead?" Grimes's eyebrows scaled up his forehead.

"Gotta ask," Kaiser said.

"I'll tell you guys, there's been some rough shit happened out here in the Permian over the years," Grimes said. "I've known people got killed on the job, even one guy who got shot, murdered — but there's never been any mystery about it. That's what's got me scratching my head: the mystery. Where in the hell are they? If Boxie shows up tomorrow morning and says he and Marcia been out hunting jackrabbits, I'll kick his ass up around his ears. So to answer your question, no, I got no idea where they are, or why they're gone."

A call came in and Grimes checked his phone and said, "I gotta take this," and Letty said, "We'll be across the hall."

They left Grimes's office as he was saying, "Marky? What the hell are you doing out there? Where's my fuckin' shale shaker?"

104

■ ■ ■ ■

Blackburn's office was the same kind of no-frills box that Grimes worked from, family photos on the walls, a woman and two boys and a girl, a full-sized American flag on a side wall, a bookcase stuffed with manuals of some kind, plus miscellaneous nonfiction books and a row of filing cabinets. Letty reached out and tapped one: heavy steel.

The computer was an older Dell. Letty turned it on as Kaiser rattled the filing cabinet drawers, which were locked. The desk drawers weren't, and Letty pulled out the center drawer, hoping to find the filing cabinet keys.

No keys, just the usual amount of middle-drawer crap: pencils, pens, business cards, half-used notepads, an ancient pack of spearmint gum, opened, with two sticks missing, random thumbtacks and paper clips, a four-inch square of what appeared to be lead, a half-inch thick, with nothing on or under it, a mouse pad that looked like a Persian carpet, a Swingline stapler, a yellow book called *Essential Verbs/Spanish,* and, way at the back, a Post-it note, folded in half, with the number *0770* and the words *Security: Bimmer* written in a woman's hand.

And she thought, *Ah.* An alarm code.

She stuck the paper in her hip pocket, stirred through the rest of the junk to make sure she hadn't missed anything, and then went to the desk's file drawers. The files were filled with printouts of spreadsheets having to do with payroll, and individual personnel employment files covering several dozen employees. There was also a drawer full of files on miscellaneous matters, and she riffled through them, and then pulled them out and stacked them on the desktop.

"I think we're wasting our time, but I'm not sure," Letty said to Kaiser. "If he was helping steal the oil, he wouldn't have written anything in a file. What we need is a forensic accountant, and I'm not one. He's got these miscellaneous files . . . Let me thumb through them. Could you stick your head in Grimes's office and ask if he has the filing cabinet keys?"

Kaiser went to do that and Letty started through the files. Several of the folders had personal papers: brochures and sales papers on a Ram pickup, a stack of used checkbook duplicates going back seven years, photos of a man Letty assumed to be Blackburn on a variety of well sites and at business conferences. One folder labeled BASS BOAT had only a single piece of paper in it, and she almost skipped over it. But it had thumb smudge marks on it, as though it were looked at frequently, and when she pulled the paper out, she found a single, ten-character non-word, a jumble of letters, numbers, and symbols. A password.

Kaiser came back. "He doesn't have the keys. I got to run outside, I'll be right back."

"Okay." Letty nodded and turned to the computer, using the password given to them by Grimes. Inside, she found files of correspondence concerning purchase and sales information, a personal file involving travel plans, plane tickets, and reservations, all in the past, and one locked file that asked for a password.

She entered the password from the BASS BOAT folder, and the file opened as Kaiser came back. "What'd you find?" he asked, hanging over her shoulder.

"It's a trouble file — not going to help us, I don't think. Confidential files on people who were fired, caught using drugs, here's one involving a guy who is believed to have stolen a thing called a Ditch Witch, whatever that is . . . ."

"Power ditch digger; we had them in Iraq," Kaiser said. "Good for slit trenches."

"No help here, I don't think."

Kaiser was holding what might have been a man's travel manicure kit, that turned out to be a lockpick set. He took out a pick and a torsion wrench and began opening the file cabinet locks.

"You gotta teach me how to do that," Letty said. "I've used an electric rake . . ."

"You have?" He was only mildly surprised.

"Never mind," she said. "I would like to know how to pick a lock, you know, manually. Quietly."

"Happy to provide you with all kinds of instruction," Kaiser said. "But, uh . . . what are we trying to find?"

"How would I know?" Letty asked. "Something. A note to an accomplice that says, 'Meet me at the oil well where we're stealing the oil this week.' That'd be nice. A note from his wife that says, 'Let's go shoot us some jackrabbits.' Whatever."

She pulled out the drawers. More payroll spreadsheets, copies of tax filings and various business licenses, tanker-truck licensing documents, rental and leasing agreements, maps of oil-rights holdings, and a thick file on a lawsuit involving a drilling-rights dispute between a half-dozen companies that had been settled four years earlier.

"Nothing," she said, pushing the drawers shut. "Like I said, if there's anything, we need an accountant."

"To tell you the truth, I suspect that there's nothing here," Kaiser said. "If you're guilty of something, why would you write it down? If you're not guilty and you figured something out, you'd tell everybody, which he didn't. So . . ."

"You can be pretty annoying," Letty said.

"How's that?"

"By being right. That's annoying," she said.

"I don't mean to annoy you but . . . what do we do next?" he asked.

"Let's go look at Blackburn's house," Letty said.

"Grimes said the cops were already out there," Kaiser said.

"They didn't go inside," Letty said. "If we can find a way, I want to do that."

"Should we tell Grimes?"

"Mmm . . . no."

SIX

Except for the cluster of taller structures downtown, Midland was a flat city, with mid-century single-story houses in sun-faded colors in the residential areas, lots of pickup trucks, burnt lawns, and metal business buildings with miles of chain-link fences around them.

Blackburn's house was in Midland's horse country, rambling houses set back behind fences from Cardinal Lane. There were pastures, bare for the most part, but the Blackburns' house was set in a thin grove of pecan trees with a low split-rail fence running around the edge of the lawn. A sign next to the driveway said PROTECTED BY SATSEC, which Kaiser said was a middling-level security service that rode on satellite TV systems.

The house itself was a white clapboard-and-stone ranch-style; the front door could be seen from Cardinal Lane. The back of

Blackburn's lot adjoined a pasture with another road on the far side of the pasture. The back road had to be the best part of a quarter-mile away, Letty thought, and it'd be unlikely that anyone would notice her messing with the back door, if she were to do that.

A parking pad in front of the garage was hidden from the street by a line of fifteen-foot-tall Italian cypress trees. Letty told Kaiser to back up to the garage doors, where the truck wouldn't be easily seen.

Kaiser stopped the truck's back bumper a foot from the garage door. "That good?"

"That's good. I don't know about locks, the technical aspects. Could you take a look?"

Kaiser showed her a skeptical face, but said, "I guess." He got out of the truck, walked to the front door, pushed the doorbell, stooped to examine the lock, shook his head. He checked the lock on a garage access door, then came back to the truck. "Good locks. I don't know if I could open them, even given some time. And you can see the doors from the street, a guy going by could see what I was doing."

"Then get ready to leave," Letty said. She put on the straw cowboy hat. "If I'm running, let's leave fast."

"What are you doing? Are you going to get us busted? Do the words 'breaking and entering' ring a bell? Does . . ."

"Remember, we're from the government, we're here to help," she said. She touched his shoulder. "Try to center yourself."

Kaiser rubbed his face. "She's planning a felony and she wants me to do some hippie shit. Center myself?"

"Stop with the drama queen," Letty said.

Kaiser had said that the locks were good, so she didn't bother to examine them. Instead, she walked around toward the back of the house. Halfway around, she found a side door going into the garage. The door was thick, solid, with a Medeco lock. She bumped the toe of her shoe against it, and got back a heavy *thunk.* If the back door was the same, they might be out of luck, short of breaking the glass out of a window.

The back door was as solid as the side door. She squatted next to it, peering at the grass around it, and found nothing. There was an inch-wide board over the door. She stood on tiptoe and ran her fingers across it: nothing but dusty grime.

Retracing her steps around the house, she felt along the top of the garage-door trim, found nothing but more dust. Next to the door, though, she saw a smooth gray-green rock half-buried in the grass by the foundation, the only rock she'd seen in the yard. She toed it out of the grass, then picked it up — it was the size of half a baseball and half as heavy. She turned it over, thumbed the hatch she found on the back, and found a mildly corroded brass key.

Polishing the key on her jeans, she fit it in the door lock, jiggled it, turned it, and the door popped open.

"Nice," she said to herself.

The garage was empty, as the police had said; and hot. Four narrow windows pierced the overhead door, so the cops probably looked inside, saw nothing, and called it a day. She crossed the garage to the door leading into the house, tried the key: the lock turned easily. She had in her pocket what she thought was the code for an alarm system, but when she pushed open the door, she was met with silence and a wave of cold air.

An alarm keypad was mounted on the wall near the front door. A note came up on the keypad: garage door open. She went back, closed both the back door to the outside and the connecting door to the house. The keypad blinked out a new message: *5:02 p.m. Sept 15,* then blinked to another message, *Chime Is On.* The alarm was working correctly, she thought, but hadn't been turned on.

When she unlocked and opened the front door, the keypad chimed once, and then went back to the date and time. She walked out to the truck and said, "We're in."

"Ah, boy." Kaiser glanced up and down the street, as if expecting a flock of patrol cars. "You kicked the door? What happened to the security system?"

"The alarm was turned off," Letty said. She held up the key: "And I didn't kick any doors."

"You could have told me," Kaiser said, climbing out of the truck. "I was sitting here sweatin' like a nun in a cucumber patch."

"Well, if I told you, you would have tried to talk me out of breaking in. Then we would have had to go through a lot of tiresome argument. This was easier. Listen, when we go in . . . don't touch anything you don't have to."

"You got a lot of cop shit from your old man," Kaiser said.

"Yes. I did."

They walked quickly through the house — neither one of them mentioned it, but they were checking for bodies or blood and

114

Kaiser had his carry pistol in his hand. An open dining/living room area had eggshell walls and walnut floors and built-in bookcases, mid-century furniture with exposed wooden and chrome legs and patterned fabric. Two long wings came off the central area of the house: a TV theater room and two guest bedrooms, along with laundry and storage areas, were down one wing, with the master bedroom and a home office/library down the other.

After the quick walk-through, finding no bodies, they moved through the house more slowly, still not touching anything. In the kitchen, Letty was walking past the breakfast bar: "Uh-oh."

Kaiser stepped over from the living room: "What?"

She pointed at one of the breakfast-bar stools. The stools were pushed up close to the bar, which made it hard to see, but a woman's purse was sitting on one, partly open. They could see a purse-pack of Kleenex sticking out, and when Letty used a fist to nudge the stool out a few inches, they could see the red-leather corner of a wallet.

"Somebody took her," Letty said. "No way she didn't take her purse. Whoever took her didn't see it and didn't think of it."

"We need to call the cops," Kaiser said. "What are we going to tell them about breaking in?"

"We didn't break in," Letty said. "We used a key from Blackburn's office drawer, apparently left there in case somebody ever needed to enter his house while he was gone. They even left the alarm code with it."

"That's weak," Kaiser said. "Besides, you didn't find the key in his desk drawer."

"Who knows what I found in the desk drawer? The cops would have to prove we did something wrong, and if the Blackburns are . . ."

"Dead?"

". . . missing, then they'd have a hard time proving it. And why would they even want to prove it?" Letty asked.

"Okay. But I'm going to get down on my knees and pray that they're dead," Kaiser said. "Texas jails aren't known for their recreational facilities."

Letty: "Mmm. Listen. Now we have to go through the place more thoroughly — but still fast. Really fast. If they've been taken, it's connected to the oil. What we want is probably on paper, or, more likely, a computer file. We need to go through the office again, and the master bedroom, where

116

somebody might hide stuff. We don't call the cops until we're done."

They found vinyl gloves under the kitchen sink and pulled them on, and moved through the house, fast, opening doors and drawers. The guest bedrooms were still, almost stagnant. They checked the closets, found them empty except for some hangers, and moved on.

The home office was missing a computer — they couldn't tell whether it was a laptop or a desktop, but there was a space for it on a desk pad, a multi-outlet power bar on the floor under the desk, and a Bluetooth printer on top of a low wooden double-wide file cabinet.

Kaiser used his picks to open the file cabinets. There weren't any gaps in the hanging files, and the files all seemed to deal with personal finances and purchases. Letty noted the account numbers at Citibank; the latest statements showed no large withdrawals, and a total of $112,000 in checking and cash savings accounts, and an investment account.

"I'd love to see his investment accounts, the details," Letty said. "If you find anything that might be account passwords . . ."

They found no passwords. "Probably on

his phone," Kaiser said. "I don't think there's anything here."

"You go through the storage cabinets in the hall, I'll take the master bedroom," Letty said, when they finished with the office.

Letty went quickly but carefully through the master bedroom without finding much of interest except a couple of sex toys in the bottom drawer of a dresser full of women's clothing, a four-foot-tall, two-foot-wide safe, and, under a thick set of men's underwear in another dresser, a loaded .357 Magnum with a short barrel and shrouded hammer, and a box of .357 hollow-point cartridges. She left them as they were, though she wouldn't have minded having a .357.

She told Kaiser about the safe. He took a look and shook his head. "We'd need the combination. Or a lot of time and industrial drills."

As they left the bedroom, she asked, "Did you check the garage?"

"No."

"Go check it, but be quick. Men tend to hide things in basements and garages. Since this place doesn't have a basement . . . and remember: it'll be on paper. Or a computer thumb drive. Like that."

"Where do women hide things?" Kaiser asked.

"Bedroom and the kitchen," Letty said. "The refrigerator, among other places. I'll check all that. I think it's more likely that Boxie would do the hiding, not his wife, if it involves stealing oil."

"Your dad teach you that? About the garage and the bedroom?"

"Yes, he did," Letty said.

She followed him down the hall toward the kitchen and the garage door, and he said, "I'm fuckin' freezing."

"Yeah, they like it cold. But it's a dry cold."

"Very funny. Dry . . ." He stopped and peered at a wall thermostat. "Holy cats, they have it set at sixty. I didn't even know they went that low."

"Leave it," she said. "Let's not change anything we don't have to."

They continued on to the kitchen, where Letty began going through the cupboards as Kaiser continued on to the garage.

The Blackburns' kitchen cupboards and refrigerator held no secrets, as far as she could tell, but when she pulled open a drawer to reveal the kitchen wastebaskets, banana peels, coffee grounds, and porkchop bones, she poked around and found two broken cell phones.

119

She picked them carefully out of the garbage, found that both had been smashed with something heavy, like a hammer. She put them back in the garbage with enough food scraps and greasy paper towels on top to look real, yet with enough visible that the cops couldn't miss them.

Always a good idea to give cops something to find; her father had taught her that, too.

Kaiser came out of the garage. "Nothing. I got to thinking, though: both cars are missing. If they were kidnapped, that means there must have been at least three people doing it. One to drive the vehicle they came in, two to drive the Blackburns' cars away. So they scouted and planned it. This wasn't an impulse thing. Of course, if it was the Blackburns running, there'd be no problem, they each took a car."

"Why would they smash their phones to bits before they ran?"

"What?"

She told him about the phones in the wastebasket and he went to look. "They could have done it themselves. They could have bought burners so they couldn't be tracked . . . but nope. There's the purse, too. They're dead."

"Probably." Letty closed her eyes. "Okay.

What did we miss?"

Kaiser shook his head and said, "Listen, Letty, if we're looking for a computer file on a thumb drive, it could be anywhere. If Boxie hid it and he's smart — and he is — we're not going to find it, not unless we come in here with a team and pull everything apart. The baseboards, all the books, the power outlets, empty all the socks and the sport coat sleeves. We could do that, but not if we don't want the cops to know we did it."

"All right," Letty said. She scanned the kitchen. "I don't know what else to do."

"There's a crawl space under the roof," Kaiser said. "Out here, in hot places, they're usually full of insulation, so I didn't check. Think we should? There's a hatch in the garage."

She definitely thought they should look. They took a stepladder off a wall hook and moved it over to the hatch. Kaiser climbed it and yanked open the hatch, and found himself face-to-face with a two-foot layer of pink fiberglass insulation. He took his phone out of his pocket, turned on the flashlight app, and shined it back under the roof. "Nothing but insulation, far as I can see. Nothing disturbed, nothing stinks. There's a little dried sparrow shit."

121

"All right. I'll call Grimes, tell them what we've found, and then call the cops," Letty said. "Let's not talk about digging around in the house. We came, we saw the purse, we called the cops. You better take the gloves and stick them in the truck. Out of sight."

"You'd make a good criminal," Kaiser said, as he came back down the ladder.

"Yeah, well . . ."

"I wouldn't," he said. "I was in jail once, in El Paso. Stationed at Fort Bliss. Went across the river and got stewed, screwed, and tattooed, came back and said something funny to a cop. Wound up in jail overnight. Found out I'm claustrophobic. In jails, anyway."

"One of the things you want to do if you're a criminal is you want to avoid jails," Letty said. "If you get caught, pretend you didn't know what was happening. You know, 'I saw the door was open, I went in to see if anyone was hurt.' Play it stupid."

Letty called Grimes, told him that they'd found a key and a security code in Blackburn's desk and that they'd entered the house. "They're probably dead," she said.

"What? What? Why do you think that?"

She told him about the purse and the broken phones, and that they'd been gone several days but hadn't set the alarm. "We need to get the cops over here."

"Did you . . . see blood or anything?"

"Nothing like that. The place feels like they just left . . . Didn't even bother to empty the garbage." Letty pressed the edge of her phone against her forehead, working through a thought.

"Do you want me to call? I know some people over at Midland police . . ."

"Dick, stay by the phone. Don't call anybody yet. I have to do something . . . only take a minute or two. I'll call you back."

She rang off, turned to Kaiser. "The garbage didn't stink."

"Because it was sixty fuckin' degrees . . . Oh."

"Yes. If somebody had made a check in the first day or two, and the air-conditioning had been set at seventy-two or something reasonable . . ."

"It would have begun to stink. We really didn't spend any time in the guest bedrooms, we didn't check under the beds. If they're here, that's where they'd be," Kaiser said. He led the way through the house to the first guest bedroom with two king-sized beds.

They got down on their knees, next to

separate beds, and Kaiser said, "I got a shoe. Shit, I got a leg. There's a woman under here. It's gotta be Marcia."

Letty could see a dark shape pressed against the wall, and then, like Kaiser, picked out a shoe, saw the leg and the hips and an odd rectangular shape at the head. "Another one here," she said. "It's a man."

Kaiser walked back through the house to one of the storage cupboards where he'd seen a Maglite. They both got on their knees again to look at the bodies, and found the same thing with each. The victims had been bound with duct tape and then smothered with plastic bags tied around their necks.

"Cruel motherfuckers," Kaiser said. "Cruel motherfuckers."

Letty called Grimes first. "We found their bodies under the beds in a guest room." She told him what they'd seen and about the temperature in the house.

"Ah, no. Ah, no . . . I got to get over there."

"The police will probably want you to do the identification. So . . . come on over. I'll call nine-one-one. We'll wait here."

Grimes said, "I am the resurrection and the life. The one who believes in me will live, even though they die; and whoever lives

124

by believing in me will never die. John 11:25."

Letty had seen that Bible in his office. To the Bible verse, he added, "We gotta get the goddamn crazies who did this."

SEVEN

Before she called the police, Letty went out
to the garage door, picked up the key safe
where she'd dropped it, wiped it off, carried
it back into the garage, wiped it again with
a shop towel, and stuck it under a miscellaneous pile of tools and bits and pieces of
unused junk in the bottom drawer of a tool
chest. As she did that, she briefed Kaiser,
talking steadily.

"The cops will separate us. I got the key
and the security code from Blackburn's
desk, where he'd left them in case of emergency. We walked through the house, we
looked in the master bedroom and kitchen,
checked closets, you looked in the garage
and the loft or the attic or whatever it is.
Then I called Grimes and something he said
reminded us of the cold. We didn't find the
telephones in the garbage, the cops will do
that . . . We did see the purse."

She went on for a full minute, Kaiser

listening intently, nodding, as they walked around to the front of the house. Letty had Kaiser lock his sidearm in the truck's glove compartment, and she put her Sig in her briefcase on the floor of the backseat.

"You know, we're allowed to carry these —" Kaiser began.

Letty interrupted. "Cops don't like other people to have guns. What they don't know won't hurt either them or us."

Then she called 911, and told the woman who answered about the bodies under the bed. Five minutes later, the first cop car turned a corner a couple of blocks away.

The Midland cops had gotten there in a hurry, two white SUVs, sirens, flashing lights. One car turned into the driveway, while the other stopped in the street. The first cop out, name tag Frisch, a short man with a brush haircut, hurried up to Kaiser and Letty and asked, "You made the report?"

Kaiser looked at Letty, who said, "Yes. We both work with the Department of Homeland Security. Mr. Blackburn worked for Hughes-Wright Petroleum. When he didn't show up for two days, Hughes-Wright notified you folks. Your officers checked the house but didn't go inside." She nodded at

Kaiser. "John and I are doing research that may involve Hughes-Wright. We arrived in Midland last night, and this morning discussed the situation with the local vice president for Hughes-Wright. He permitted us to check Mr. Blackburn's office, where Mr. Blackburn had left a key to his house along with the alarm code for his security system, in case of emergency. We decided to come out and look at the house. We found two bodies under the beds in the guest room. We believe they are Mr. Blackburn and his wife, Marcia. We don't know them personally, so we're not sure."

A brown sedan was coming fast down the street, showing flashing lights on the grille, and the two cops turned to it and one of them said, "Danny." To Letty and Kaiser he said, "Sergeant Tanner — he'll be running the show. Crime scene'll be next . . ."

The sedan turned into the driveway and stopped next to the patrol car, and a plainclothes cop got out. He nodded at Frisch and asked Letty, "You're the woman who made the report?"

Letty said, "Yes."

And she looked at him and thought, "Hmm."

Tanner was a sun-and-sand-blasted thirty-something, with reddish-blond hair worn long enough to cover the tips of his ears. Not conventionally handsome, he had blue eyes, a narrow nose, and a square chin; he could have been a baseball player, she thought, too bony for football, and at six feet or so, probably not tall enough for Texas basketball.

And he caught her eyes for a second and showed the hint of a smile.

Down the street, two more patrol cars were coming fast. The detective ignored them and asked Kaiser, "You two were together when you found the bodies?"

Kaiser nodded and said, "Yes. We found them together. I'm a security officer with the Department of Homeland Security in Washington, D.C., and Ms. Davenport is a researcher for the U.S. Senate, and assigned to DHS."

Letty dug her new ID case out of her hip pocket and held it open, and Kaiser did the same thing. The detective's eyelids flickered as he realized the situation might be more complicated than he'd at first understood. He said, "I'm Dan Tanner. I'm with the city's Investigative Services. I'll be running the investigation here."

He turned to Frisch and said, "Ari, no need to be abrupt about it, but just for form's sake, we don't want Ms. Davenport or . . ."

Kaiser said, "John Kaiser . . ."

Tanner nodded. ". . . Mr. Kaiser chatting about this until we have time to interview them. So just . . ."

Frisch nodded, smiled at Letty, and said, "I'll keep an eye on them."

Tanner said, "Thank you," and swung an index finger between Kaiser and Letty and asked, "Which one of you is in charge?"

"We're actually associates, neither one of us outranks the other," Letty said. "But I've been asked to coordinate the investigation down here."

Tanner frowned. "Investigation? Into what?"

"Hughes-Wright, and we believe some other oil companies, are missing quite a lot of oil. That's not really our concern, so much as the question of what is happening with the money the stolen oil may be generating. We'd just begun our research when we heard about Mr. Blackburn's disappearance. Your department has a report."

"I'm not aware of that," Tanner said.

"Well, you do. Have a report. This is the fifth day that Mr. Blackburn has been missing. On the second day, Hughes-Wright employees called your department to file a missing-person report, though I understand that it didn't get as far as a formal report. One of your patrol cars checked the house, found both of the Blackburns' cars were missing . . . and your police officers apparently concluded that the Blackburns had left voluntarily."

Tanner: "Huh. You got here last night?" His eyes again snagged on Letty's.

Letty said, "Yes. We got here in the evening, driving down from Oklahoma City after we interviewed Vermilion Wright about the missing oil. This morning we went to Hughes-Wright headquarters, and eventually came here."

"You sound like you're giving dictation," Tanner said.

"I want to be clear," Letty said.

Tanner nodded. "So . . . Ms. Davenport, why don't you show me where the bodies are. Mr. Kaiser, why don't you wait here . . . or you could get in your Explorer and turn on the air-conditioning."

Kaiser said, "Okay. By the way, we called the office manager, Dick Grimes. He's on his way over. He should be here any minute."

Letty followed Tanner to the front stoop; he smelled lightly of clean Texas sweat. When they got to the door, he asked, "You touched the doorknob, right? Going in?"

"I went in the garage door. I thought maybe . . . if something had happened to the Blackburns, maybe the people who did it came and left from the front door. I didn't want to mess with it. I did go *out* through the door, when I didn't see anything that looked like a crime scene when I went in."

"So you touched the inside knob?"

"Yes."

"We'll want to print you, then."

"The FBI has my prints. You can get them through the FBI," Letty said.

Tanner's eyebrows went up. "How'd that happen?"

"We can talk about it later," Letty said. "Right now, why don't I show you the bodies?"

The FBI had her prints. Letty paused, and remembered, in a half-second:

She could hear the gunman pounding up the stairs and she ran toward him, heard him coming down the hallway, lifted the pistol eye-high, stepped sideways, and saw him.

Right there.

Eight feet and coming fast, but his gun pointed sideways toward the bloody wall. He wouldn't have done it that way if he'd believed that her father was upstairs. He would have moved more slowly with the pistol up.

As it was, he had just tensed his diaphragm for what would have been a grunt of surprise, but he never got it out. Tres never had a chance to talk to his saints, to see that their prediction of his early death would be correct. Before he could begin any of that, Letty, shooting for the white spot in his left eye, pulled the shot a bit and sent the .45 slug through the bridge of his nose. As she stepped past his dead, falling body, she shot him a second and third time in the heart.

Letty spent no time worrying about the Mexican boy: he was dead. She heard a burst of shots, one at a time but fast, from the stairs to the housekeeper's apartment above the garage, and she went that way, running lightly, quietly down the stairs, turning the corner, through the living room and the kitchen, to the bottom of the housekeeper's stairs, and then up.

Martinez had gone into the kitchen expecting a close-up shootout with Lucas Davenport, but the kitchen was empty. At the same time, she heard somebody running in the back, and she followed the noise, pushing the pistol out ahead of her, as she'd been trained, found a door going into the garage and, to one side, a carpeted stairway going up.

She heard a door slam at the top of the stairs, but took just a second to pop the garage door and look inside the garage. There were two cars, but no sign of life. She ran up the stairs, heard a heavy thump behind the door, and fired five shots through it, fast as she could, *bam-bam-bam-bam-bam.*

She heard a woman scream something and she kicked at the door, but it didn't budge, and she fired five shots at the doorknob and lock, and then kicked at it, but unlike the usual Hollywood movie sequence, the door remained closed.

Frustrated, she emptied the gun at the door, dropped the empty magazine, took another magazine from her jacket pocket.

A woman's voice, from the stairs below her: "Hey."

Letty was halfway up the stairs when she saw Martinez empty the gun at the door and drop the magazine. She said, "Hey."

Martinez turned, jerking her head around, saw Letty there with the big .45 in her hand. Tres, she barely had time to think, must have failed. She blurted, "I have no gun. I am empty."

She dropped the pistol and the magazine.

Letty said, "Bullshit. You tried to kill my mom and my little sister."

She shot Martinez in the heart. Martinez

didn't go down, but staggered backward, a shocked look on her face. She lifted a hand, and Letty shot her again, in the heart, and Martinez sagged but still brought the hand up, as if to fend off the bullets. There were now only six feet apart, and Letty shot her a third time, in the face, and then Martinez slid down the wall, leaving behind a smear of blood . . .

Tanner was there: "You okay?"

"Just remembering something," Letty said. She sighed, smiled at him.

He nodded and gestured for her to lead, and he followed her through the house to the guest bedroom. He got on his knees, looked under the beds, and said, "Yeah. Okay. Let's get out of here. This is for the crime scene guys now."

Outside, they found Dick Grimes walking up the driveway, accompanied by a uniformed cop. Kaiser got out of the truck to meet him and Tanner nodded at Grimes and said, "Mr. Grimes. We've spoken a time or two — you had those pipe thefts a couple of years ago."

Grimes nodded and said, "How are you, Dan? It's *Dan,* right? Are they both dead?"

"We found two bodies inside. Since you knew them well, we'll ask you to identify them, but that won't be for a while. Our crime scene folks have to work through here."

"Ah, jeez, this is terrible." Grimes produced a paper towel from his pocket and turned away and used it to wipe his face; he was sweating profusely, Letty thought, but then, no: he was wiping away tears. He was crying and trying to hide it.

Tanner patted him on the back and said, "Why don't you go sit in your car . . ." Now he was looking past them down the street. "Here come da chief."

The chief of police walked up the driveway, a heavyset, square-shouldered man with a crew cut and a red face like a canned ham. He eye-checked Letty, Kaiser, and Grimes, took Tanner by the elbow and led him out of earshot, saying, "Excuse us for a minute."

They spoke for two minutes, Tanner gesturing toward the house, then he and the chief walked back over to Letty, Kaiser, and Grimes. The chief said, "I'm Randall Short, I'm the chief here. I'm terribly sorry about this. I can promise you that we'll be all over it. We *will* find the people who did it."

He must have caught a shadow on Letty's face, and he cocked his head and said, "You don't believe me, young lady?"

"I think it's unlikely," Letty said. "They

were killed by professionals, or at least semi-pros. Professional enough that they turned the air-conditioning down to sixty degrees to delay decomposition of the bodies, so nobody would notice an odor, at least, not right away. How many amateurs or impulse killers would think of that? And the way they were killed and the fact that both cars are gone . . . The killings were carefully planned and carried out, and both of the Blackburns' cars were taken so that a routine check would lead the police to think they'd left voluntarily. With both cars gone, that would mean three killers, if they arrived in one car. I wouldn't be surprised if the two stolen cars are now down in Mexico, where you'll never find them."

He stared at her, nonplussed, then said, "Do tell."

"Yes. I do."

"You think *Mexicans* did it?"

Letty shrugged. "I don't know who did it. You could get American professionals to do it, and I'm sure they have competent killers across the border. It's the cars I was thinking about. Getting rid of them permanently, and maybe at a profit, outside normal American police communications systems. If they were in Albuquerque, you'd find them in an hour. In Juárez, not so much.

Besides, Americans, Mexicans, everybody likes money."

The chief raised his eyebrows, creating a half-dozen wrinkles across his forehead, and asked, "Do you read a lot of mystery novels?"

"My father is a U.S. Marshal and was a lead homicide investigator for the city of Minneapolis and for the Minnesota Bureau of Criminal Apprehension. I've talked with him about his cases since I was twelve years old and I was involved in a couple of them. I am now an investigator, a researcher, for the U.S. Senate and the Department of Homeland Security."

Short, the chief, looked at Tanner and then back at Letty. "Involved in your father's cases how?"

Letty said, "He broke up a drug-smuggling ring that had killed some people in the Twin Cities. Two of them got crazy and crashed into our house, trying to kill our family as revenge. I shot and killed both of them. And I once shot a crooked cop. On two different occasions."

The chief leaned away from her and then said, "That's not a story you hear every day."

"It's all true," Kaiser said. "I looked it up. You ought to read about her old man. He's a piece of work."

"Why would you tell us that?" the chief asked Letty.

Letty said, "Because Tanner said he'd need my fingerprints and I told him they were available through the FBI. He wanted to know why, but we put off talking about that — but me shooting those people, that's why. It was going to come out, so I thought I might as well be up front about it."

The chief rubbed his nose and said, "Okay."

Tanner: "We need to talk to Ms. Davenport and Mr. Kaiser separately, and Mr. Grimes here will do the identification . . ."

He explained Grimes's relationship to the Blackburns, and he added, "There may be a problem with some missing oil."

The chief again took Tanner by the elbow, and led him away, and they talked for a while, then the chief waved at Letty, Kaiser, and Grimes and marched back down the driveway to his car. Tanner came over and said, "The chief was explaining how if I didn't solve this, and right quick, I'll be doing the Midland County peyote cactus inventory for the next several years. So we better get after it. Mr. Kaiser, I'd like to talk to you first. Ms. Davenport, if you'd like to wait in your Explorer . . ."

139

■ ■ ■

Tanner took Kaiser to his police cruiser. The crime scene crew arrived while they were talking, and Tanner got out and led them into the house. He came back ten minutes later, talked to Kaiser for another ten minutes. Then Kaiser got out of the cruiser and waved Letty over.

As they passed each other Kaiser muttered, "No problem," and Letty went on and got in the passenger seat of the cop car. Tanner had an iPad in his lap and was reading newspaper stories from the *St. Paul Pioneer Press,* concerning the home invasion that Letty had stopped.

Letty settled in without saying anything, and Tanner read on; at one point he said, "Holy cow," and glanced over at Letty.

"What can I tell you?" Letty said. "That's pretty much the way it was. There were a couple of small errors in that story, but then, my dad says all newspaper stories have a couple of small errors and most of them have more than that. He says that most TV stories are fairy tales; I agree with that, because . . ."

" . . . you worked for a TV station as a school reporter."

"Unpaid intern," Letty said.

"Let me read for another couple of minutes."

He typed and paged, and typed and paged, and said, "My God, your father . . . Kaiser said he was a piece of work, but I had no idea. I mean, I know some of these cases. That shoot-out down in Marfa. That's just couple-three hours south of here . . ."

He read for another minute, whistled once, shook his head, then turned the iPad off and reached into the center console and took out a digital recorder. "I talked to Mr. Kaiser, and now I'm going to ask you a series of questions about how you got to Midland and why, and what you did when you entered the house here. You understand that?"

"Yes."

Tanner turned on the recorder, identified himself with the time, date, and location, asked Letty for her DHS identification card and her Virginia driver's license, read that information into the recorder, and then led her through the decision to drive to Midland, beginning with the possibility of stolen oil.

Letty explained her position with DHS, about Bradley (Boxie) Blackburn's disappearance and the fear that it might have something to do with the missing oil — that he might be involved, or that he might have discovered something that led to his disappearance. She explained her dissatisfaction with the lack of reaction by the Midland Police Department, and her decision that she needed to go to Blackburn's house.

"We had the key and security code, which we took as permission to enter the house in what might be an emergency . . ."

When she finished, Tanner said, "Okay. Good. Clear and succinct. Since this seems to be both a federal and local problem, and your father would have jurisdiction anywhere in the country . . . are you planning to ask him to get involved in this?"

Letty shook her head: "I doubt he'd be interested. He thinks these kinds of cases are best left to people with local knowledge. Besides, I'm working it."

"Okay. Seems like a smart guy," Tanner said.

"He's very smart."

Tanner reached out and turned off the recorder, which he'd placed on the dashboard. "I don't have any more questions, Letty, not right now. I'd like to know more about this disappearing oil. Maybe twelve thousand barrels from Hughes-Wright, maybe more from Lost Land . . . I'll be talking to their manager . . . but you say that Hughes-Wright has lost a half-million dollars, at least. And if it's gone on for a while . . ."

"Exactly. And if there are several victims, the money could get serious," Letty said.

"A half-million isn't serious?"

"Not for these people," Letty said. "We're told Hughes-Wright pumps about a hundred million barrels of petroleum equivalents a year. That's better than six billion dollars at current prices. A half-million isn't exactly a speck, but losing it won't bankrupt anybody."

"But it could be big money for *somebody.*"

"Yes. If you asked around Dallas, you could find somebody to kill your wife for a couple thousand dollars. For a million? You could probably find somebody willing to take a shot at the president."

"I don't have a wife," Tanner said. "Or even a girlfriend, anymore."

"Really. I hope it wasn't a difficult breakup," Letty said.

"I don't know yet," he said. "I haven't mentioned it to her."

Letty had to process the joke, and when she had, she didn't laugh. Instead: "That's a mean thing to say if you really have a girlfriend," Letty said. "That line really sucks. I've heard better lines from guys who were lying on the barroom floor, dead drunk."

"Easy, there," Tanner said. "I'm more sensitive than I seem."

"Yeah, well, right now you're giving me an ice-cream headache, right in the middle of my forehead," Letty said.

"Whatever. I've got to get to my crime scene," Tanner said.

"Good, you should do that," Letty said. A friendship no longer looked likely. "Can we go back into town? John and I? I need to call in to my boss. I need to get on my computer. I need a quiet place to think."

Tanner considered that. "We have to talk some more, all of us. I'm sure you're not lying about your stories, they're too easy to check, though we *will* check. Where are you staying?"

"Homewood Suites," Letty said. "We're there for two nights, but I think it might go longer, now."

"Okay. You can take off," Tanner said. "Don't be running back to Washington without telling me."

Tanner went off to the house to talk with the crime scene crew, and Letty walked over to Kaiser, who was talking with Grimes.

144

Grimes said, "This is the worst thing that ever happened out here."

Letty nodded and said, "They'll be lifting the beds out to get access to the bodies, then you'll do the ID. John and I are headed back to the hotel, to start calling people at DHS."

On the way to the hotel, Kaiser, who was driving, said, "I don't know a damn thing about crime and murder scenes and all that. All I wanted to do when I was a kid was get in the Army and jump out of airplanes — I only went to the community college to make my old man happy. He thought I ought to have a trade. Two weeks after I graduated, I was on my way to basic training. After that . . . I mean, I don't know what you know, from growing up with a high-powered cop. I don't even know what most civilians know, watching cops on TV for twenty-five years. I've been out of it. I don't even know the music that other people my age know. I missed all that."

"You've killed people . . ."

"Not the way you have," Kaiser said. "We were all technical. When we killed people, it was technical. You do this, I'll do that, we'll put a guy up on the roof with an M203, and we smoke them and we move on."

145

"It's gotta be more than that."

"Of course it is, but . . . most of us never got too personally involved with the people on the other side. Shit, sometimes we didn't even know who was *on* the other side. It was a job. It's not like with cops, all up close and personal. If you wanted me to knock down the Blackburns' house and kill everyone in it, I could do that, no sweat, given the personnel and the tools. To sneak in there with enough people to move the cars, to tape them up and kill them with plastic bags, to lower the air temperature, figuring all that out ahead of time . . . man, that's not what we did, to plan that kind of thing. We were killing, but we weren't murdering, if you know what I mean."

"Be careful who you say that to," Letty said.

"Yeah, well . . ."

"You really didn't have to worry too much about consequences, so you didn't have to hide what you were doing," Letty said. "That's what you're telling me."

"That's part of it. You had to be careful about what you did — it is possible to get charged with murder even in a war zone — but as long as you were clean, you were good. The people who judged you were on your side. Here in Texas, you kill somebody, you're on your own."

They drove along in silence, until Letty asked, "What'd you study at the community college?"

"Don't ask."

"C'mon, John."

She waited and he finally sighed and said, "Ceramics."

Letty: "Ceramics? Like . . . making pots?"

" 'Throwing pots' would be the correct terminology, but yeah, that's what I did," Kaiser said. "I threw pots."

"Wow."

"What does that mean?" Kaiser asked.

"It means I'm impressed," Letty said.

"Really?"

"Yeah, really. Were you any good at it?"

"Well, yeah. I spent like nine months in Iraq, with Delta, and started this little school there, taught some Kurdish kids how to clean clay and throw and fire pots," Kaiser said. "By the time I left, they were selling them."

"Wow."

Letty tried to imagine a pottery school in a war zone, until Kaiser asked, "Have you figured anything out?"

"Do you expect me to?"

147

"Yeah, as a matter of fact," he said. "You're already about a week and a half ahead of those cops back there."

Letty looked out her window, at the lines of brick ramblers going by. She said, "Yes, I figured something out. What I figured out is, Blackburn figured something out. He might not have known that he figured it out, because if he knew he had, he would have told somebody. What we need to do is figure out what Blackburn figured out. What could it be?"

"Gimme a clue?"

"Okay. It's not in all that paper back at the office. It has to be something else. Something he thought up but wasn't sure about. He didn't want to embarrass anyone, in case he was wrong. He called somebody, to check on himself, and that got them killed."

"Or maybe there's some connection between him and this militia guy. Maybe they were working together, him and Rand . . ."

"Rand Low," Letty said. "If they were connected, if Blackburn was working with him, why would they kill him?"

"Cover their tracks?"

"What tracks? Nobody has found any tracks," Letty said. "Nobody even seems to know what the tracks might be. If Blackburn hadn't disappeared, we wouldn't have talked to Vermilion Wright, we wouldn't be here, the bodies wouldn't have been found for God-only-knows how long."

"You're getting cantankerous," Kaiser said.

"Cantankerous — pretty big word for a humble potter."

"Fuck you."

"I gotta think, John," Letty said. "Okay? Drop me at the hotel, find a way to amuse yourself. I gotta think."

EIGHT

The Homewood Suites was in a barren hotel zone of the kind common in the Plains states, not much within walking distance except other hotels and a Sam's Club. Letty did her best thinking while running or walking, but Midland wasn't helping, so she wound up buying a couple of Cokes and kicking back in her room, the TV tuned to CNN with the volume turned down.

With her back against a pile of pillows, she watched the silent talking head while doodling on a Rhodia legal pad.

She thought briefly about the Blackburns. The discovery of their bodies hadn't particularly upset her — she didn't know them and they'd been hardly visible under the beds. She'd seen dead bodies, bodies still leaking blood, of people she'd actually known. She'd dismissed the Blackburn killings, as such: there was nothing for her in their murders. If there was anything at all, the crime scene people would find it. Or not.

The operative fact about the Blackburns was quite simple: they had been murdered.

The operative question was: Why? What had Boxie Blackburn done to get him killed? Then she mentally corrected herself: there were two dead, not one. Had Marcia been the cause of their deaths? That seemed unlikely, but the possibility had to be considered.

She considered it for one minute, then dismissed the idea. Marcia was collateral damage.

Collateral damage: nothing more.

Letty had never doubted the love of her adoptive parents, but her relationship with them was not the same. She and her father, Lucas Davenport, had bonded almost instantly, within hours of their meeting, he in his forties, she at age twelve. Her relationship with her mother, Weather, had taken time. When they'd eventually become intimate, Weather had told Letty that she'd worried about Letty's early years and how that dark time might have shaped her.

"You can be very harsh," Weather said. "You're almost exactly like your father that way. You even look like him. When people see you together, they assume you're his natural daughter. Your eyes are exactly the same, ice crystals. You shot those two people, you saved my life, I went into shock . . . but you didn't even seem to be affected. Had to be done, so you did it. When Lucas got back and saw what had happened . . . he was happy. *You* were happy. I was absolutely freaked out. I felt like I was going crazy for a while, I was afraid to be in the house alone. I still have nightmares, sometimes. But you . . ."

"You think I'm a psychopath?" Letty asked.

"No, of course not. You're exactly like Lucas, and I *know* he's not a psychopath," Weather said. "And I know you're not. You're just . . ."

Letty grinned at her: "A high-functioning sociopath, maybe?"

"I'm trying to be serious, here," Weather said. "I'm saying that you make very cold judgments about people, about their worth. You don't cut them any slack for being . . . human."

Letty had shrugged. "People are what they are. Most people, honestly, don't interest me. Some do, of course. You're interesting. Dad's interesting — a lot of cops are interesting. Virgil Flowers is interesting. Social

152

workers are interesting. Really bad people are interesting, and so are really good people. A guy who gets up, goes to the store, works, comes home and sits on the couch and drinks beer and watches football or reruns . . . not interesting. Some studies are interesting. Logic is interesting. Facts are interesting. Bullshit isn't, and people who peddle bullshit usually aren't. Unless they're criminals."

"Some people would say bullshit is the grease that gets people through life," Weather said.

"Other people," Letty said. "Not me."

Weather talked to Lucas about the conversation and Lucas snuck back around to Letty and told her, on a nighttime five-mile jog/walk, "I've been through all that self-questioning, the shit you're going through. I used to chase a lot of women . . ."

"I heard about that," Letty said, wryly. "Including from some of the women."

"I wondered, to myself, am I some sort of predator? I got to the point where I said, no, I'm not — I like women. That's all. I like them a lot," Lucas said. "I've killed a number of people and I don't worry about it. Am I a psycho? A sociopath? I've thought about it, but nope. I'll tell you what I am and what you are — we're pragmatists. Really harsh pragmatists, to pick up on what Weather told me about your conversation. We see things as they are, we project out consequences of our actions, very pragmatically. We don't stir in a lot of hope, we don't turn blind eyes."

Letty mulled that over as they jogged and said, finally, "I'll have to work through that, but I think you're right. I killed two people; Mom said she freaked out, but she thought I had no reaction to it. She was wrong, I did react. I thought about it a lot. There's no pleasure in it, I didn't get off on it, even afterwards."

"But no regrets."

"That's right. No regrets," Letty said. "More than that, though. I stopped thinking about it because what's the point? Those people are dead. Maybe I stuffed it all in a box at the back of my brain, and put the box in my brain's attic. Maybe someday I'll take it back out and look at it and freak out, but . . . not yet."

"There you go . . . give me fifty yards to the driveway," Lucas said.

"Dream on. Twenty yards. You're lucky to get that."

Sitting on the bed in the Homewood Suites, Letty whittled down what she knew about the Blackburns, about Dick Grimes, about the theft of the oil. Had Blackburn solved the problem? Grimes, Vermilion Wright had said, knew more about oil than almost anyone; and Grimes himself had said that Wright knew so much about oil that he could virtually *feel* when something was wrong in the oil fields. But the two men couldn't figure out how the oil was being stolen.

Blackburn might have. And then somebody had figured out that he knew, and had come to his house and killed him and his wife. What had Blackburn discovered? She'd covered two full pages of the Rhodia tablet with a variety of symbols, squares, cartoon faces, when an idea popped into her head. She called Dick Grimes.

"Are you still at the Blackburns' house?"

"Yes. They're almost done inside, Tanner said they'll be coming to get me."

Letty: "Vermilion Wright said a lot more oil than your ten or twelve thousand barrels was being stolen. That some company called Lost Land had been hurt and he thought that Chevron had been hit pretty hard. So let's pretend that *you* guys stole it . . ."

"What?"

"Stay with me for a minute," Letty said. "Wright said you guys pump a hundred million barrels a year, more or less. What if some guy came to you and offered to sell you a hundred thousand barrels of crude at a good price. Say . . . twenty-five bucks a barrel, and you knew it had to be stolen. I mean, would you commit a crime, an actual crime, that you could go to jail for, and maybe ruin the company, to boost your oil production by one-tenth of one percent?"

"No, of course not," Grimes said. "That'd be chicken feed. Too much risk, not enough reward, even if they gave it to us for free. Which they wouldn't. If they wanted half, so we'd get, mmm, say two and a half million dollars, and then we got taxes and everything else . . . No."

"I assume Chevron and Exxon and BP wouldn't be interested . . . what about a company like Lost Land? I don't know anything about them."

"They're smaller than we are, but they still pump eighty million. So no, I don't think they'd be interested."

"You see where I'm going with this?" Letty asked.

"Not right off the top of my head," Grimes admitted.

"Well, I think you guys have been going at it backwards, trying to figure out how the oil is being stolen. I'm thinking, okay, it's *being* stolen. Let's *assume* that. That it's not something buried in paperwork or accounting, but physically stolen. Buckets of crude oil. And Boxie Blackburn figured it out."

"I'm listening. What'd he figure out and why are we going at it backwards?"

"Because I believe what he did was, he started asking, who would be *buying* it? Not who was stealing it, or selling it. Whoever buys it from the thieves would have to be somebody who is small enough to take the risk. They'd also need an excuse for having a hundred thousand barrels of oil for sale. The buyer would need a way to get it to a refinery . . ."

"Okay. Yeah. I see where you're going," Grimes said. He was suddenly interested, his voice pitching up. "Letty, listen to me: this is a very solid idea. We can work with it, but it could be dangerous, talking about this. I know some people . . . Vee knows some people . . . we could call up some people . . ."

"What people are you talking about?"

"Pipeline people. Refinery people. Trucking companies. You can't get a bucket of crude oil and put it in your truck's fuel tank. They're not selling it retail. It has to be run through a refinery and that oil is accounted for. I talked to Vee's secretary an hour ago and she said he's out of the operating room with his new knees, but he should be able to talk to us tomorrow morning, and he'll want to. This is something we can figure out. We need to ask, what small-time wild-catter who was maybe putting out a hundred thousand barrels a year, or less — maybe a lot less — suddenly bumped up another hundred thousand barrels or so? Not a one percent increase, but a hundred percent increase."

"Like somebody said, it's not much money for you top guys, but it's a lot of money for somebody," Letty said.

"Exactly . . . Listen, Tanner just came out of the house. I think they're gonna want me to go look."

"Go. Call me back and tell me if we're correct, that it's the Blackburns under the beds."

"I will. Soon as I know. Damn. I think you could be on the right track about the sales."

Letty got up, brushed her teeth, called Kaiser. "You find a way to amuse yourself?"

"I drove all over town," Kaiser said. "I'm still doing it. It's a complicated place, not all that easy to get around. One area is a big circle thing, but most of it is little squares.

North of here . . . man, you wouldn't believe it. It's pumpjacks as far as the eye can see. Hundreds of them. Thousands of power poles."

"I'd like to see that. Maybe you could roll me around town a little?"

"Ten minutes, out front," Kaiser said. "You figure anything out?"

"Maybe," Letty said. "Tell you about it when you get here."

Letty was waiting out in front of the hotel when Grimes called back. "Okay. My God, that's not something I ever want to see again, but it's them. Boxie and Marcia, smothered with those bags, their eyes . . ."

"Easy," Letty said. "They're not suffering anymore, they're gone."

"Okay, okay, I gotta get home. I gotta, I don't know . . ." Grimes stuttered off into silence.

"We'll see you tomorrow morning," Letty said. "You take care."

He rang off as Kaiser pulled in. Letty got in the Explorer and said, "Let's see the sights."

"Did Grimes call?"

"Yes. He identified them. It was the Blackburns," she said.

"Are we over our heads yet?"

"Not yet," Letty said.

As they drove through the city, Letty told Kaiser about the possibility of finding a buyer for the oil, rather than searching for the thieves.

"There must be dozens of small companies out here," Kaiser said. "Guys who have, like, one well. Okay. Maybe not *one* well, but you know . . . small-timers."

"I don't know anything about that," Letty said. "But there aren't hundreds of pipelines or hundreds of trucking companies or hundreds of railroads. Those people must have data on their customers. You'd just print out a list of oil shipments and run your finger down it, see who got a bump in the last year."

"Could work," Kaiser said. "Of course, with the post-COVID boom, there could be a lot of companies showing an increase."

"Didn't think of that, but you're right. On the other hand, Grimes and Wright would probably know which ones are legit and which ones aren't. We'll see."

Kaiser took Letty on a tour of the city and then the countryside around it, down white-dust service roads through the oil fields that not only surrounded the town but penetrated it, and then down through Midland's near-twin city of Odessa. The Permian oil fields amounted to the biggest machine she'd ever seen, Letty decided, a level plain marked by endless acres of weeds and machinery. She said, "Those pumpjacks, the pointy top part — the way they go up and down, they remind me of herons sniping frogs off a pond."

"The oil's not just here — it goes all the way across the border into New Mexico," Kaiser said. "I went past a billboard that said the Permian Basin covers eighty-six thousand square miles, and if it was a state, it'd be the twelfth largest. Ahead of Utah."

"A little bleak out here," Letty said, as they took a rural highway past endless rows of pumpjacks.

"It changes if you go west — cotton fields and so on. There are some nice neighborhoods in town, and some shitholes, too."

"If you were Rand Low, where would you hide?"

"Not here. Too many people around. I looked on my iPad and there are small towns all over the place, oil workers coming and going, renting rooms . . . A lot of temporary housing for the fracking boom. He could be anywhere. About the only way

161

you could dig him out would be to put his face on all the TV stations, or put up billboards and keep that going until somebody spotted him. Don't think that's going to happen," Kaiser said.

"Depends on what he's up to," Letty said. "If it's something serious and we can't find him, maybe the TV stations would listen."

They had dinner together at a diner, then went back to the hotel. Letty spent the evening reading oil industry websites — *Oil and Gas Journal, Rigzone, Oil and Gas People,* a couple of big oil associations, trying to pick up on the industry vibe.

In the morning, she ran six easy miles on the West Texas plain, did her yoga, got dressed, thought about it, and slipped the Sig 938 and the Sticky Holster in her front jeans pocket. She got a cup of coffee and she and Kaiser were at the Hughes-Wright office at eight o'clock. The two front office women were both on their feet, talking in hushed voices. When Letty came through the door they turned to her, and one of them said, "This is so awful. Are you okay, girl?"

"I'm okay," Letty said. "Is Dick back in his office?"

162

"Got here one minute ago. He was talking on his phone to Mr. Wright. Go on back."

Grimes was still on his phone, and when he saw Letty and Kaiser in the hallway, he waved them in and said into the phone, "They just got here. I'm putting you on speaker."

Wright said, "Letty, John. This is a terrible thing. Boxie had kids, and now they've lost both their parents; this is . . . this is a fucking catastrophe. Now, Dick and I are talking about your idea. Looking at the sales end of things. I don't know why I didn't think of it myself. Getting old, I guess."

"How are your knees?" Kaiser asked.

"I'm told they'll work fine, but I'll have the scars from hell. Anyway, the best way to figure out this oil sales idea of yours is for me to start calling people I know," Wright said. He stopped to cough, cleared his throat. "Every time I go to a hospital, I get sick. Anyway, I'll get Jessie — you met her, my secretary — to put together a list of phone numbers. I'll be calling them all morning, if I don't cough up a lung, first."

"If we're right, and it's a wildcatter, how does the oil get to him?" Letty asked.

"Truck. That's the only way I can see it happening. Once it's at a known company, they're probably shipping it out by a commercial trucking company or pipeline. I can't see them trucking it out of there themselves, a tanker truck only carries about a hundred and ninety barrels. They'd need a lot of trucks, too many for a small operator. They're probably using several of the commercial trucking companies, so none of them notice the sudden production increase. I'll hit them all. We use them ourselves, so they'll talk to me."

"How about refiners?" Letty asked. "They'd have to have computerized accounts . . ."

"Yeah, I'll do them, next," Wright said. "The doctors here are gonna have me walking around later today, so . . . I don't know how far I'll get. Give me your phone numbers — I'll call you direct when I have something."

"We have to talk to the cops," Letty said. "We made statements yesterday, after we found the bodies. We'll have to go in and read them and sign them. We won't talk to the cops about this sales thing until we hear back from you. If we told the cops, they'd start calling everybody and people would start freezing up."

"Guess you're right about that," Wright said. "We can hold that between us for now."

■ ■ ■ ■

Outside, Kaiser glanced up at the clear blue sky and said, "Too nice a day to talk to the cops."

"We've got other possibilities," Letty said. "Rand Low had some buddies out here before he went to prison. His FBI file has a list — a couple of them testified against him at his trial."

"Right here in Midland?"

"No, let me look." She took her laptop from her briefcase, called up the file that Greet, the DHS briefer, had given them. "One is a guy named Brody Rivers, also known as Stony Rivers, last known address was in Lubbock, which I don't think is too far from here. Another is named Victor Crain, don't know much about him, except he may have been in a militia with Low."

"One thing I learned when I was down here in the Army — nothing in Texas is close to anything else," Kaiser said. "Lubbock is a couple of hours from here. El Paso is quite a bit farther, bet it's four or five hours."

"It's early," Letty said. "Why don't we hit up Tanner at the police station, if he's there, sign our statements and take off? We'll be back before Wright will have anything on the sales."

That's what they did. The Midland police station was a tan cube with a high set of stairs out front and a couple of long-haired kids sitting on them, like they were waiting for either a ride or their dealer. Inside, they were told that Tanner was at the Blackburn house and would have to be present when they signed. Letty told the uniformed sergeant they spoke to that they were going to Lubbock, and asked her to tell Tanner that they'd be back in the afternoon.

On the road out of town, Kaiser behind the wheel again, he fished around on the satellite radio until he found the Red Hot Chili Peppers doing "Scar Tissue" and he said, "Ah . . ."

"One of my favorite old-timey bands," Letty said.

"Old-timey? Watch your mouth. I grew up with them," Kaiser said. " 'Californication.' 'Scar Tissue.' 'Snow.' 'Give It Away.' Any band that can do 'Give It Away' and cover 'Brandy' . . . that's a knockout band."

"They covered 'Brandy'? The Looking Glass's 'Brandy'?"

"That exact song," Kaiser said. "In concert. You can see it on YouTube. Flea is awesome."

And a while later, Letty said, "I love driving through these mountains, the curvy road, the views."

Kaiser glanced at her as though she were having a stroke. Then: "Oh. You were being funny. I'm cracking up over here."

Letty looked out across the hot flat plain, at the distant, circular horizon that wrapped around them like the edge of an old LP record, at the billiard-table highway that dwindled to a pinpoint ahead of them.

"At least you don't have to worry about not seeing the oncoming eighteen-wheeler," Kaiser said. "You can see it fifteen miles out."

Two hours into Lubbock, talking occasionally, listening to music, Letty reading snatches out of the FBI's file on Brody (Stony) Rivers. Rivers had testified against Rand Low at Low's car theft trial. Rivers had been charged with conspiracy in the thefts, but was cut loose in return for his testimony. There were a few interesting details — Low's public defender protested at his sentence of two years for a first-time offense, but the file also noted that Low had been caught driving a stolen Mercedes that happened to belong to a district court judge.

That note made Letty smile, which Kaiser caught, and he asked, "What?"

When she told him, he said, "Not exactly a criminal mastermind, huh?"

Letty plugged Rivers's FBI-file address into her cell phone, which took them to Bois d'Arc Village on the west side of Lubbock, a downscale mobile home park. The homes were numbered, but in no particularly rational way, as if home number 1 had simply been the first to show up and park, with 2 and 3 in other parts of the place.

As they rolled through the park, Letty said, "You notice anything . . . weird?"

"All trailer parks are weird," Kaiser said. "I should know — I lived in one for a year."

"Count the pickup trucks," Letty said.

A minute later, Kaiser said, "Okay, that's weird. There aren't any. Or maybe I saw one back by the gate."

"One or two or three, but . . . everywhere else out here, they're the default vehicle."

"Maybe people who live here can't afford them. Average car here is what? Ten years old? Fifteen?" He pointed through the windshield at a car parked in front of a mobile home. "When was the last time you saw a landau roof?"

"I didn't know what a landau roof was, until you pointed it out," Letty said.

All of the homes were set behind a continuous, waist-high chain-link fence, and the place was absolutely still, no walkers, no loungers, not even a dog behind the fences. The Brody Rivers home was ill-kept, even for the trailer park, and, unlike the others, seemed to be partially constructed of wooden planks, now peeling and warped. A variety of plastic children's toys were scattered around a cramped lot of compacted gray dirt.

"Tough place," Kaiser said, as they pulled off the street and parked. "The question now is, should *you* knock, because you look like a small, harmless orphan girl who is no threat to anyone? Or should I knock, because I'm a large threatening presence who might rip your heart out if you don't talk?"

"I was thinking that if you knocked, and they shot you, you're so thick that they wouldn't get complete penetration," Letty said. "I could use your body as a shield while I returned fire. If I knock and they shoot me, they *would* get complete penetration, and probably smack you down, too. We'd both be dead, instead of just one of us."

"We're well matched in catastrophic think-

169

ing," Kaiser said. "I just flipped a mental coin. You get to knock."

"Fair is fair," Letty said. "Let's go."

Letty led the way through the chain-link gate, across a yard that smelled of weeds, dust, and a hint of garbage, up to the trailer's front door, and knocked; the door had a vinyl outer shell that flexed, muffling every knock, and Kaiser said, "Gotta bang on it harder." She did. A curtain moved in a window next to the door and then the slit window scraped left and a woman's voice asked, "What do you want?"

"We need to talk to Brody," Letty said.

"He ain't here. And he don't call himself Brody."

"Then we need to talk to you. We're . . . from the government," Letty said.

"Cops?"

"No. I'm a researcher for the Department of Homeland Security."

From the ensuing silence, it seemed likely that the voice's owner was thinking it over. Then she said, "Okay."

The woman who opened the door was thin, narrow-shouldered, dressed in tights and a plain blue T-shirt. Her blond hair hung loose down her back and showed a dark-brown part. She had suspicious brown

170

eyes and a scattering of acne around a long, sallow face.

"Stony took off in June, ain't seen him since. Hasn't called," the woman said.

"Do you guys share a checking account?" Letty asked.

The woman snorted. "If I ever saw him around my checkbook, I'd shoot him," she said.

The woman's name was Kaylee Turner. She had two children with Stony Rivers, both in school, and worked nights in a Stripes convenience store. "Stony takes off every once in a while. He's been gone for a long time, this time. When I heard the gate open, I thought it might be him. I don't get many visitors and he always comes back."

"We actually need to talk to a man named Rand Low, who used to hang out with Stony . . ." Kaiser said. He wiped sweat off his forehead with the back of a hand.

Turner snorted again. "Hang out is not exactly what they did. Rand was driving stolen cars for some gang that was selling them in Mexico. Stony knew about it, might even have driven a couple himself. When the cops grabbed them, Stony agreed to talk about it in court. If Rand knew where Stony lived . . ." The thought hung her up, then

171

she blurted, "Shit! You think Rand found him?"

"You think Rand would hurt him?" Kaiser asked.

"Hell yes. Rand is a killer," Turner said. "The people around him, they'll kill you, too. That crazy posse of his."

"Did you and Stony share a credit card or anything?" Letty asked.

"No, we kept our money separate. I want the kids to eat. He'd spend every damn dime, if I let him. Which I don't." She turned back to the house, then said, "Come on in for a minute. It's hot out here. I want to look for something."

Letty and Kaiser followed her inside. The trailer was cool and neat enough, but smelled like SpaghettiOs flavored with cat urine. A gray-and-white cat was sitting on the back of a couch, staring at them; didn't move. At the far end of the trailer, Letty could see an old exercise treadmill, and beyond that, through a door, the corner of an unmade bed.

"Give me one minute," Turner said. She was back in less than a minute, carrying a plastic cube filled with envelopes. "I throw Stony's stuff in here. He gets letters and bills and shit . . ."

She dug around in the bin, pulled an

envelope, then another, both unopened. She handed them to Letty and said, "Credit card statements. He had a bank account with Wells Fargo, but he got those statements on his cell phone."

Visa card. Letty said, "Uh, he's your husband. I suspect it'd be technically better, legally, if you opened them."

"Give them over here, then," Turner said. Letty handed the envelopes back to her, and she ripped them open, glanced at the bills, and handed them to Letty. "The last two months, he hasn't charged a single fuckin' thing. That ain't right. That fuckin' Rand probably took him."

Letty waited.

"Somebody killed him," Turner said. She put her hands to her face, squeezed. Then, "Maybe . . . Maybe he's still out there? Maybe he's hiding someplace where he can't use his charge card?"

"Maybe," Letty said. "Kaylee, we're doing this research, maybe we'll find him. Do you know any names, people in Rand Low's posse? Anything would help."

"Well, I know two for sure. Max Sawyer, not a bad guy. He loves his guns. He might have shot some people, that's the rumor, but . . . he never gave me no trouble at all. If he was gonna try to fuck something, I believe it'd be a .30-30. Then there's Victor Crain, he is a *bad* man. He once caught me back by the washing machine when Stony was out in the yard with the grill, pushed me into a corner and put his hands on everything I got. Handsome man, though. Max was not a bad guy, but he and Vic was best friends, which I could never figure out. They were both in Rand's posse, Vic was in the car-stealing gang. This was back before Rand went to prison."

"What do you know about this posse? Was it just guys playing with guns? Was it political?" Letty asked.

"Yeah, they played with guns. They all had guns. They talked about being tactical, they wanted everybody to buy four-wheel-drive pickups with big tires so they could go cross-country. They talked about being white people, which seemed a little crazy to me. You're white, so what? You know? That's like saying you eat pork chops. I always thought they were like pretend Nazis. They have this little sticker they put on their car bumpers. Blue sticker with a green triangle on it, pointing up. I guess it was supposed to be a mountain. They were like an outlaw motorcycle gang, but with trucks."

"Was there a woman with them?"

"Everybody had a woman. Or at least said

they did. If you didn't, it was like you were queer . . . They had this thing they did, joking with each other. They'd be talking about women they knew and they'd snap their fingers and point down to the ground, like they were telling some chick to drop down to her knees and blow them. I told Stony if he ever really did that to me, he best be wearing his armored jock strap 'cause if he weren't, I'd kick his junk off."

Turner kept asking for reassurance that Rivers might still be out there somewhere, not charging anything on his Visa card. Letty wasn't interested in lying to her, so Kaiser did it, telling Turner that Rivers probably didn't come back because he didn't want to endanger her or the children.

"That's probably it," she said, showing some relief. "The kids, he loved the kids. Loves the kids."

Letty asked if she could keep one of the Visa bills — "Maybe we could use some government computer to trace him," she said. "We'll let you know."

Turner glanced toward the back of the mobile home, to the bedroom. "He left his laptop, which sorta worries me, because he usually took it when he was going somewhere. Didn't use it for much of anything but email and porn . . . ."

"Mind if I take a look?" Letty asked. "Could give me an idea where he went."

Turner had to think about that, then said, "I guess. If he's dead, it can't hurt him. If he's alive, and you find him, then at least I'd know."

She went back to the bedroom and fished a laptop out from under a bed and brought it back to the living room, dragging the power cord. An aging Gateway running Windows 7, the machine produced a long list of porn sites, a shorter list of right-wing political sites, and dozens of emails going back six years. Almost all the emails were routine spam, never deleted, but one, from a sender who called himself RamJam, said, "Don't put this shit in email. Delete it."

Rivers apparently had deleted the offending email, but not the comment about it. The delete file was empty, so he apparently knew enough to take the last step to get rid of it.

Letty noted RamJam's email address, and continued scrolling through the mail. Kaiser chatted with Turner as Letty worked, to keep Turner thinking about something other than the laptop.

When Letty first moved in with the Davenports, in Saint Paul, Davenport had a desktop police radio tuned to the police channels. He never listened to it, and Letty asked if she could keep it in her bedroom. When she tired of listening to the cops, she fished around on the dozens of other channels available on the radio and stumbled on the cell phone frequencies.

Many of the cell phone calls involved apparent drug deals and followed a simple format: "Uh, hey man, this is me." "Where you at?" "Down to the corner." "How's the corner?" "It's all right. You working?" "I'm working." "See you then, ten minutes?" "See you."

Some of Rivers's emails had the same clipped feel: "Let's get coffee." "What time?" "Ten." "See you then."

Letty couldn't tell exactly what was going on, but *something* was going on.

When she was done with the email, she checked the other files on the machine, but found nothing useful. The photo file, for which she had hopes, was filled with porn. She shut down the computer and twisted the bar stool she was on, to talk with Turner.

"These people that Stony was hanging with, back in the Rand Low days — did you know them? Other than Crain and Sawyer?"

"I couldn't tell you much about them, those I met," Turner said. "Oil workers, most of them, the ones that had jobs. Some had been to prison. Most of them were in the Army, some of them a long time ago. Talk about it all the time. Stony never was in the Army, he felt kind of out of it when these other guys would be talking about Willy Pete or MREs or Charlie Foxtrot and that shit."

"Names?"

She shook her head. "That was all a while ago."

"How tight was Stony with Rand Low?"

"Rand was the one everybody listened to. He was . . . intense. Stony liked him for that. I knew Rand would get him in trouble, but Stony did what Rand told him . . . right up to the trial."

"If I were to go hunting for him . . . Rand Low?"

"Not a good idea, girl. But if you *was* to look for him, he wouldn't be up here, he'd be down in the oil patch or even further down south. That whole bunch would cross over to Mexico, to Juárez, what they called the tolerance zone, and get laid. Like a fraternity initiation. Then it got too danger-ous to go to Juárez, they were having the dope wars over there, so they started hitting a place they called Pussy Park in El Paso. Stony said he never went for that, but I expect he was lying. Rand and his boys would be someplace between Midland and El Paso, if I had to guess."

Back in the truck, Kaiser said, "We don't know for sure that he's a dead mother-fucker."

"No, but he's a dead motherfucker," Letty said.

Their DHS briefer, Billy Greet, had told them to call if they needed information support during their research. On the way back to Midland, Letty called Greet, gave her Rivers's credit card number, told her about the bank account at Wells Fargo.

"Are you in your car?" Greet asked.

"Yeah, we're in Lubbock, Texas, we're heading south to Midland, should be there in two hours," Letty said.

"I'll be back to you before then — this won't take long," Greet said.

"While you're at it, we have a couple more names to check — it'd be great if we could get some addresses," Letty said. She gave Greet the two names they'd gotten from Turner, Max Sawyer and Victor Crain. She added RamJam's email address to see what might come of that.

When Letty was off the phone, Kaiser

said, "We're crossing over into some dangerous territory here. These guys, this posse, they might have killed the Blackburns and maybe Rivers. We really need to tell the cops about it."

Letty: "Mmm."

Greet called back when they were halfway to Midland. "It's not looking that good for Rivers. His Wells Fargo statement for March shows that he had a little over four hundred dollars in his account — four hundred and thirteen dollars. He earned a few cents of interest since then, but hasn't made any withdrawals. Visa's put a hold on his account, it's on hold since the first of May — he hasn't paid the minimum the last two months and he hasn't charged anything. I think he may be in trouble."

"You're wrong about that," Letty said. "I don't think he's troubled. Not anymore."

"Okay. There's that. Max Sawyer is on probation for a gun law violation, possession of a fully automatic rifle, which he said had been left with him by the wife of a friend. The friend had died, and the woman didn't want guns around her children. She testified to that, but the federal prosecutor thought she was lying. The U.S. attorney out there isn't real big on gun violations, so he let Sawyer plead to a lesser charge, a misdemeanor. He got a fine and no jail time. He wasn't convicted of a felony, so he can legally own guns. At the time he was arrested, he had a house in the town of Monahans. Utility bills in his name are still being sent there."

As Letty took down the address, Kaiser said, "He had a machine gun. That's not good. What about Crain?"

"Not much on Crain, couple of minor drug busts in El Paso," Greet said. "Got fingerprints and a mugshot from those. Never did any time or anything. He shows an address in Monahans that's right around the block from Sawyer. I'll text you mugshots for both of them. RamJam, that email, is a dead end. Hasn't been active in years."

Letty took down Crain's address and said, "We'll check on them. If it looks iffy, we'll get a Texas cop to go with us."

"That would be smart," Greet said. A few minutes after they ended the call, Letty's phone dinged, and she found the mugshots of Sawyer and Crain. She showed them to Kaiser, who nodded and said, "Got 'em."

They took one more call before they got to Midland.

Vermilion Wright said, "My goddamn

knees now hurt so bad I can barely talk, but — I got something for you."

NINE

Wright had a name and he thought it was a good one.

"He's a wildcatter named Roscoe Winks, a piece of white trash if there ever was one," Wright said. "He's got a half-dozen played-out wells up west of Seminole. He's been pumping five or six thousand barrels a year for ten years, limping along, not hardly paying his bills. Two or three years ago he put down an exploratory well up in North Dakota and came up with nothing but dust, and that damn near broke him. Maybe it did. Last year, he jumped up to better than ninety thousand barrels, put on a pipeline out of Midland."

"Six thousand barrels, though. That's what, three hundred thousand bucks? Not bad for one guy," Kaiser said.

"Not one guy — he's got expenses, got people he's got to pay, shipping costs, power for the pumpjacks, and all that. Be lucky if he was clearing fifty thousand before this big bump-up."

Letty asked, "Is it possible that the extra oil came out of the ground? That he started fracking or something?"

"Nawp. I got an old hunting buddy out that way, name of Lowell Harp, who knows Roscoe," Wright said. "He says Roscoe ain't got a pot to piss in or a window to throw it out of. Said he's dead in the water. Lowell was completely surprised to hear Roscoe was suddenly doing so well. You got to talk to Lowell."

They got name spellings and addresses for Roscoe Winks and Lowell Harp, and a phone number for Harp. "Lowell runs a half-dozen gas stations in towns around the Seminole area, does all right for himself. You can trust him." Harp, Wright said, was a cousin to his wife.

Letty thanked him and said they'd try to interview Harp the next day. "We've got to go talk to the Midland police some more. Probably won't be finished until it's too late to get out there today."

"I'll tell Lowell to expect you."

When they got off the phone, Kaiser said, "We did all right talking to Miz Turner, and we did even better sittin' in the truck taking phone calls. It's almost like we're professionals."

"These guys . . . Sawyer, Crain, and Winks . . . sound pretty hardcore," Letty said. "We need to decide how we'll handle them. Maybe talk to Dan Tanner, see what he recommends."

"Don't want to get in any dusty-road shoot-outs," Kaiser said. "Though I expect we'd do okay, if it came to that."

"A machine gun was mentioned," Letty said.

"Ahh . . . right. Let me reconsider."

They were back in Midland before two o'clock and drove straight to the police headquarters. Tanner was there. He gave them lightly edited printouts of their statements, which they read and signed. Letty told him about Max Sawyer and Victor Crain, and their relationship to Rand Low. She showed him the two mugshots.

"You think they might be related to the Blackburn homicides?"

"They could be, but we don't know," Letty said. "DHS was told that a Chevron security team heard a rumor that Low was involved in the oil thefts. Now Blackburn was probably murdered because of the oil thefts. So the connection is a rumor."

Tanner pinched his already narrow nose, thinking about it, then said, "Okay. Monahans is only about an hour from here. Why don't we run down and ask them about it? We can bust Low if we find him, for violating his parole."

Letty shrugged: "I'd like to stop at a Stripes and get an ice cream and a Coke, but I'm good to go."

Kaiser: "What she said."

"I know an investigator for the Monahans PD," Tanner said. "I'll call her, see if she can go along."

They went down in two cars, in heavy truck traffic, Tanner leading, made a quick stop at a Stripes, where all three of them got ice-cream bars, and Letty added a Coke and Kaiser got a Diet Pepsi, and they continued south through Odessa and another thirty-five miles or so into Monahans.

As they followed Tanner, Letty looked out at the highway and asked, "You know how you can tell Texas has low taxes? Because they don't pick up any of the crap that gets thrown on the highway. Road gators everywhere, those white plastic bags hung up in the weeds everywhere. *Everywhere.* Like some kind of bizarre flowers."

Kaiser: "Says the fuckin' California snowflake . . . Of course, you're right. Texas magnolias."

"Texas magnolias," Letty repeated. "I like it."

Monahans looked mostly like a dusty intersection with dusty intersection businesses; and later like a flat dusty town with buildings and housing scattered around somewhat haphazardly, with ninety percent of the structures either yellow or beige.

The Monahans investigator, a woman named Casey Pugh, was waiting at the edge of town, waved at Tanner when he slowed at the end of the off-ramp, then followed their little convoy to a tiny beige house on South Allen Avenue. The house might have been built during World War II and was worn by time and neglect. The only decoration was a narrow wooden two-step stoop that led up to the front door.

They parked and got out of their cars. The house was surrounded by a chain-link fence, with a worn spot in the dead grass around a single tired evergreen tree. A sign on the gate said BAD DOG, and a chain was looped around the tree, but nothing was on the end of it.

Tanner introduced Letty and Kaiser to Pugh. Tanner and Pugh had spoken by phone on the way down, and Pugh had been filled in on the Blackburn murders, the oil thefts, and the possibility that Max Sawyer might know something about it.

Pugh was a parched-looking woman, tight through the jaw, with blunt cheekbones under deep-set eyes, and had a solid Texas accent. She said, "Might not be anybody here, but if there is, watch out for the dog. Hate messing with dogs. They're my best friends, truth be told. I got four, but you put them with a bad guy . . ."

"We had Belgian Malinois in Iraq," Kaiser agreed, putting a hand on the top rail of the fence. "You don't want one of those bad boys hanging from your throat."

They all looked at the house for another minute, then Tanner said, "Fuck it. I don't see a dog," and unlatched the gate and stepped through. The other three lined up behind him, but as Tanner started up the dirt path leading to the front door, a white-and-pink pit bull came out from under the stoop like a rocket and, without a single bark or whine, hit Tanner in the upper leg, knocking him down.

Tanner screamed and thrashed, the dog's jaws sunk deep in his thigh, its head whipping back and forth, ripping Tanner's leg. Kaiser shoved Letty and Pugh aside and grabbed the dog by its hind legs and lifted it straight up.

The pit let go of Tanner and twisted to bite Kaiser, but Kaiser threw it over the fence and shouted at Letty and Pugh, "Inside, inside," and when they were through the gate, slammed it. The pit hit the fence, but it was too high for the dog to get over. Tanner, pushing himself to his feet, pulled his gun and, stumbling to the gate, as Kaiser and Pugh shouted "No!," shot the dog in the head.

The dog dropped and Tanner went down at the same time, groaning, and Letty shouted into a sudden silence, "He's hurt, he's hurt."

A double-hand-sized bloodstain was already spreading across Tanner's pant leg, and Kaiser pushed Tanner flat and said, "Let me look, let me look."

He pushed his fingers through dog-bite holes in Tanner's pant leg and ripped the fabric, wiped Tanner's leg with his hand, turned to Pugh and said, "He's pumping blood. The dog hit his femoral artery. Didn't rip it open, probably poked a hole in it. You got a hospital here?"

"Yes — Ward Memorial."

"Got to get him there, *right now,*" Kaiser said. "Let's put him in your car, you drive . . . I'll keep pressure."

A short, square-shouldered blond man exploded out of the house, a pistol in his hand. He was wearing an Army-green T-shirt with a Walther logo. "Who fired . . . Did you shoot my dog?"

Pugh pointed a finger at him. "You're under arrest. You're under arrest. Drop the gun."

"Fuck that," the man shouted. "Who the fuck are you?"

"Police," Pugh shouted. "Your dog attacked us —"

"You shot my dog —"

Tanner cried out, "Oh, God," as Pugh put her hand under her jacket, on what might have been a gun.

"Pull that fuckin' gun and I'll kill you," the man shouted. "This is my property."

"We gotta move him," Kaiser shouted. "We gotta get him going."

Letty had stepped sideways from the shouting group of cops and Kaiser, and now she slipped the 938 out of her pocket and pointed it at the man's head, two feet from his ear. "If the cop tells me to shoot you, I'll blow your brains out."

The man cocked his head toward her, took in her tone of voice and the nine-millimeter hole at the end of the pistol, and said, "This is my property . . ."

Letty, chill as ice: "Drop the gun or I'll kill you. I'll kill you right now."

Again, a brief assessment, then he half-stooped, carefully dropped the gun on a shoe-sized patch of grass. "Don't shoot."

Kaiser was bent over Tanner: "Hey! Hey! We gotta get him going."

"Take him to my car, it's open, put him on the backseat," Pugh said. She had her weapon out now. "Go to the fence," she told the blond man. "Go to the fence."

The man stepped over to the fence and Pugh cuffed him to the solid top rail as Kaiser carried Tanner to Pugh's car, Tanner groaning, "Hurts, hurts," and slid him into the backseat, then climbed in on top of him.

Pugh said to Letty, "Stay with him, I'll get a patrol car here right away," and she jogged to her car and a moment later, it turned a corner and was out of sight.

The man said to Letty, "Killed Rooter. Killed my dog."

"I'm sorry," she said. And she was.

"Did you kill it?" he asked.

"No."

"Would you have killed me?" he asked.

"Without thinking twice," Letty said. "Are you Max Sawyer?"

"Yeah. Who the fuck are you?"

"Another gun nut," she said. "You want a drink of water?"

He didn't want a drink of water, but his back hurt, he said, and he could use a chair. "There's a kitchen chair right straight back from the door and there's a beer on the table, only half drunk."

Letty looked at the handcuff holding him to the fence, then nodded and went inside the house, got the wooden kitchen chair and the bottle of Dos Equis and carried them outside. Sawyer sat in the chair and said, "You're too young to be a cop."

"I'm a researcher with the Department of Homeland Security," she said. "We're trying to locate Rand Low, has to do with people stealing oil."

"What's your name?"

"Letty. What about Low?"

Sawyer had yellow haystack hair and looked a bit like the prime minister of Great Britain. He chugged the rest of the beer and lobbed the bottle across the yard. "I wouldn't know about that," he said. "Haven't seen Rand since the day he went to prison. I expect he's over in San Antonio. I doubt he has anything to do with stealin' oil."

"Well, he does. Maybe he cut you out of

the money — we're thinking it's around five million a year. He doesn't keep it all, of course, but he keeps plenty," Letty said.

Sawyer smirked at her and said, "You don't know shit. You must be cruising on looks alone, honey, because you got no idea what you're talking about."

Letty smiled: she was right, and Sawyer wasn't bright enough to know that he'd confirmed it. "I know one thing. You're going to prison, on account of threatening a cop with a gun. That's ag assault. You get out, you'll never be allowed to carry another gun for the rest of your life. Not buy one, not have one, not shoot one. If you were to help us find Rand Low, the charge could go away."

Sawyer turned away: "Fuck you."

"The only thing you're gonna be fuckin' is some hairy-butted old biker in the state pen," Letty said.

That made Sawyer laugh. "I like your style," he said. "And your gun, though it's not exactly a target shooter."

"I got a Staccato XC for that," Letty said.

Sawyer's eyebrows went up. "No shit? I'd like to see that. You got an optical on it?"

"Leupold Delta Point Pro."

"Oh, man. Listen, when I bail out — you guys got nothing on me — why don't you come down and let me try that out? If you're in the neighborhood?"

They talked guns, Sawyer testing her on the details, then Letty nodded up the street, where a white Monahans cop car had turned the corner. "Here comes your ride. I understand the Texas state government is trying to make its prisons more comfortable. You can relax in the sunshine, get free eats and free medical, it's almost like a vacation. When you're not spending time with that biker."

"You can be a mean little bitch," Sawyer said. "Even if you've got good guns."

"Maybe I'll see you again sometime," Letty said.

"Bring your guns," Sawyer said. A threat.

She pushed it back at him. "I will."

Sawyer smiled and nodded. "Looking forward to it."

The Monahans patrol car pulled over and a sunburned cop got out. He stepped over the body of the dead dog at the gate. "I understand there was a gun involved," he said to Letty, while ignoring Sawyer.

Letty pointed her finger at the pistol still sitting on the burnt grass. The cop looked at it, then asked, "Will you be around?"

"I'm waiting for a ride," Letty said.

"Could you wait until Casey gets back? I'd want her to take charge of the gun. I'll take the subject here to the lockup."

"Might check him for weapons — nobody's done that yet, they didn't have time," Letty said.

"Bad bite?"

"Yeah, Tanner was bleeding hard," Letty said. "Haven't heard anything yet. He's an investigator for Midland."

"Oh, sure, I know him, Dan Tanner. Too bad." He turned to Sawyer. "You gonna give me a hard time?"

"No, but I want to lock up my house and I want a receipt for the Gold Cup," Sawyer said.

"You'll get it. Where are your keys?" the cop asked.

"In the house, on the stove."

Letty said, "I'll get them."

She picked up the chair Sawyer had been sitting on, carried it inside, saw the keys on the stove, picked them up, closed the front door as she left the house, made a show of locking it while not actually locking it. Sawyer was on his way to the backseat of the patrol car, his hands cuffed behind him, and she caught up and said, "I'll slide the keys in your pocket."

He turned his hip toward her and she

slipped the keys into his pocket. "That 938 doesn't print on your jeans at all," Sawyer said.

"Got a Sticky Holster," she said.

"I seen those at gun shows, never had one," Sawyer said. "Maybe I'll check them out. Don't even print on skinny jeans."

The cop said, "Watch your head," and put him in the backseat of the patrol car. To Letty, he said, "I'll call Casey and tell her you're waiting, watching the gun."

When he was out of sight, Letty called Kaiser. "Are you still at the hospital?"

"Yeah, it's going to be a while. They're prepping Tanner for surgery, but the surgeon isn't here yet. They've slowed down the bleeding."

"Well, I'll be sitting on the stoop at Sawyer's house."

She got off the phone, walked up to the stoop, pushed through the unlocked door, and started picking through the place. Although the house was small, it did have two bedrooms, no more than ten by twelve feet each. Sawyer had been sleeping in one and using the other for storage. The storage room had a locked closet with a good heavy lock that appeared to be new; she couldn't budge the door.

Sawyer had a laptop, an old Vaio. She turned it on, and it came up without a password. She went to the email: nothing in the inbox, outbox, or trash. Since that's impossible, she understood that he'd wiped his mailboxes after each use. She checked Internet Explorer and found a list of gun blogs. Nothing useful.

She turned the computer off, wiped her prints with a paper towel, and began searching through drawers and boxes and jars; in a kitchen cupboard, she found a lidless Rubbermaid cooking container with miscellaneous detritus — pens, pencils, rubber bands, a garage door opener with no battery, and the house didn't have a garage, anyway, and a half-dozen keys. There were two identical keys that fit the front door. She put one back in the box and kept the other.

A shiny brass key was mixed with the other junk, and when she tried it in the bedroom closet door, the lock gave way. Inside the closet she found four rifles and a combat shotgun in a gun rack. A half-dozen handguns sat on top of their cases, arranged on a plastic bookcase. Two range bags sat on the floor and held ammo, earmuffs, and cleaning equipment.

A cell phone was placed carefully on one

of the bookcase shelves. She turned it on and it came up without a password. No texts, either incoming or outgoing, but she found four saved phone numbers under "contacts." The contacts themselves were Alpha, Bravo, Charlie, and Delta, which she suspected were not real names. She displayed them all, took a shot of them with her own iPhone camera, turned off the cell phone, and put it back on the bookcase shelf.

When she looked out the back door, she saw a tan Jeep parked in the backyard. She'd seen a jean jacket hanging on a hook by the front door, and when she checked the pockets, found a key fob for the Jeep. In the backyard, she climbed into the hot vehicle, started it up, cranked the air conditioner, called up the navigation system, and checked saved addresses and recent trips and photographed them with her phone. A search of the car turned up nothing but another pistol, a large-frame Smith & Wesson .44 Magnum, tucked under the front seat.

"Texas," she said aloud. She'd been told that when a car with Texas plates approached the Canadian border, the Canadian border cops would disassemble it, searching for the handgun they knew must be in there somewhere.

Letty had been in the house or the Jeep for twenty minutes: fourteen minutes too long, by normal burglary standards. Back in the house, she looked out the window toward the street, saw nothing of interest except the Colt still lying on the grass where Sawyer had dropped it.

She risked another five minutes, hurrying, hunting for anything that might be useful, not finding it. Then she went outside, locked the door, dropped the key in the weeds by the corner of the house where she could find it again if she needed to, sat in the Explorer, and called Kaiser.

"What's going on over there?"

"Waiting to see what's happening with Tanner," Kaiser said.

"Would you ask Casey to either come back for a minute and pick up Sawyer's gun or call another cop to come over and get it? I'm sitting here doing nothing, but I can't leave until the gun does."

Pugh showed up ten minutes later, Kaiser with her. Kaiser said, "Gonna be a while before Tanner can get around, he got ripped up good. He's going to need physical therapy and probably more work on that artery by a vascular specialist."

Pugh took a photo of Sawyer's gun with her cell phone, then picked it up and put it in a plastic bag. She asked Letty, "Is the house locked up?"

"Yeah. Sawyer asked me to lock it before your cop took him to jail. Sawyer's got the keys in his pocket."

"Too bad," Pugh said. "If it was unlocked we'd have to secure it. Give us a chance to poke around. See what we can see."

Kaiser looked at Letty, then looked away.

On the way to the cars, stepping around the dead pink-and-white pit bull, Pugh said, "I'll get the dog taken care of."

When she and Kaiser had said good-bye to Pugh and were in the Explorer, Letty asked, "Any point in going to the hospital?"

"Not today — Tanner's out of it, and he will be for a while. We could run down tomorrow morning."

"We'll do that," she said, as she took the Explorer through a U-turn.

"I assume you ransacked the house," Kaiser said. "You being a natural-born criminal."

"And his Jeep," Letty said. "He's got a closet full of guns and in that very same closet, a cell phone with four numbers saved. I took a picture of them. His Jeep's nav system had a long list of the last destinations. Think DHS can track them?"

"If you give them five minutes," Kaiser said. "They've got access to some weird technological shit."

"Speaking of weird shit . . . I think I'm losing mine," Letty said. "You know how I grew up; basically, a shitkicker, saved by the Davenports. Anyway, I get out here, talking to these people, I'm falling back into shitkicker talk. I said, 'free eats' and 'right comfortable.' I thought Stanford had drained all that out of me."

"Got to consider the bright side," Kaiser said. "This DHS gig falls apart, you could write country songs." He looked out at the street and asked, "We going?"

"We've got another guy to find, remember? Victor Crain lives on the other side of this block."

"Ah, man. In all the ruckus, I forgot about him. Think we should get Pugh back?"

"Not right now. Let's see what we can see."

Letty took them around the block, then down a dusty dirt alley that separated the houses on Allen Avenue from the houses on Bruce Avenue. "There's the house and there's Victor Crain," Letty said, two-thirds of the way down the track. Crain was a muscular man with full-sleeve tattoos and was wearing a white T-shirt; he had well-oiled brown hair striped with white.

They were moving slowly, and as they passed Crain and his black Ford pickup, Kaiser looked out the side window and lifted a hand to Crain, who was loading a cardboard box into the pickup. Crain flipped a hand back at them and then they were past.

"I had to wave at him or he would have figured out something was up. He's going somewhere," Kaiser said.

"Probably heard the shot when Tanner killed that dog," Letty said. "Poor goddamn mutt."

Kaiser said, "Pits can be great dogs, treated right."

Letty nodded and said, "I'm taking a left up ahead. Let's get back where he won't see us but we can see him if he moves."

They wound up two blocks away, partly concealed by a school bus that had been converted into an RV, looking across three yards to Crain's pickup. They could see Crain moving back and forth from the house. After one last trip, carrying a rifle case, he was in the truck, driving away.

Letty waited until he'd gotten to the end

of the block, then went to the end of the block that she and Kaiser were on, in time to see the pickup turn toward the main drag. They followed, with a half-dozen cars between Crain's truck and the Explorer, saw him turn south, and Kaiser said, "Headed for I-20."

"Probably."

He was. They saw him take the on-ramp to I-20 south, followed, let more cars get between them, and then got up on the highway. A mile later, Kaiser said, "He's doing about fifty. He's checking for slow cars behind him. There's an off-ramp coming up. Get off there."

Letty got off, followed a couple of signs to the on-ramp, and got back on I-20. Crain was now two or three miles ahead of them, but on the flat highway, they could still see his truck.

"Hang back, don't close up," Kaiser said. "He won't be able to see us this far back."

They followed him southwest, through Pecos, to the small town of Toyah, where they lost him. They were still more than a mile back when they saw him take the exit. When they got off the highway, there were no moving black Ford pickups in sight.

"Now what?" Letty asked.

"Drive around," Kaiser said. They did, for fifteen minutes, but Crain had disappeared.

"He could be in a garage," Letty said.

"Or he could be cutting cross-country," Kaiser said. He had a map up on his iPad screen. "There are a lot of back highways coming out of here. No way we could track him anyway — we'd be the only two vehicles on some of these roads."

"Give up, then?"

"When at first you don't succeed, say 'Fuck it' and go home," Kaiser said. "We've got those addresses on Sawyer's cell and nav system, maybe one of them will point us out here somewhere."

On the way back to Midland, they stopped at Monahans to check on Tanner, and were told that he'd been moved by ambulance to the hospital at Odessa, where they had a vascular surgeon.

They found the hospital in Odessa as it was getting dark and were told that Tanner had been stabilized. He'd been sedated and was asleep, preparing for a seven-o'clock surgery the next morning.

"We *tried* to be nice," Kaiser said, as they rolled out of the parking lot.

TEN

At the hotel, Letty pulled Sawyer's cell phone data off her iPhone photos, retyped it, and sent it to Billy Greet in Washington, asking for help in determining locations. The information from the Jeep's navigation system was a different kind of problem — there were eighty addresses, and by entering them into Google Maps, she found that most were commercial buildings like hardware stores, restaurants, and coffee shops.

While it was possible that those sites were used for meetings with friends, it was also possible that Sawyer was simply going out for dinner or to buy hammers. One address in San Antonio went to a western-wear store, one in Midland to a Home Depot.

An address in El Paso went to a residence on Pear Tree Lane and might be a possibility. Another went to an address that Google didn't know about, off State Highway 132. She called up a map, and found that Highway 132 ran east of Toyah, where they'd lost Crain. She sent both addresses to Greet and went to bed.

Greet called the next morning as Letty was getting back from her run — Washington was an hour ahead of Midland — and said that the El Paso address went to a woman named Alice Serrano who had been convicted of assault in New Mexico eight years earlier but had served no jail time and had no known connection to Low or to any radical group. Greet hadn't been able to find the address on Highway 132. "It's so sparsely populated out there that it's possible they have some kind of informal numbering system."

"Why would it be in the Jeep's nav system if the address isn't real?" Letty asked.

"Just because it's in the nav system doesn't mean that it was found. You know what I'd do? I'd go into this Toyah place, to the post office, and ask about it. Mail carriers know all that stuff."

"Maybe we'll do that. We've got another guy to look at before we go running out there, though. Vermilion Wright thinks he knows who's buying the oil."

"You're moving, Letty," Greet said. "But take care. I grew up in Oklahoma oil country, and it can be rough out there."

"We've already figured that out," Letty said. She told Greet about the dog attack.

"I gotta say, the cop was an idiot for busting through a gate with a BAD DOG sign on it."

Kaiser called, and they went back to IHOP for pancakes and to plot out the day. They decided to go out to Seminole to talk to Vermilion Wright's friend, Lowell Harp, and to check out Roscoe Winks's oil operation. Letty called Harp during a second cup of coffee, and they arranged to meet at one of Harp's convenience stores.

Seminole was as easy to get to from Odessa as it was from Midland, so they swung by the Odessa hospital to check on Tanner. There, they were told that Tanner was still in the operating room. When they asked about his condition, a nurse asked if they were relatives. Letty showed the nurse her DHS identification and he grudgingly conceded that Tanner was listed in fair condition, which was the second-highest level, below "good" and above "serious," "critical," and "unresponsive."

"Does 'unresponsive' mean the same as dead?" Kaiser asked.

"Yeah, pretty much, except we could still get in there and harvest some organs," the nurse said.

"I didn't need to hear that," Kaiser said. Out in the car, he muttered, "Harvest some organs," a couple of times, until Letty told him to shut up, and then he said, "I got your organ right here."

Seminole was an hour out of Odessa, through a forest of pumpjacks and the small city of Andrews. They met Harp at a wind-scoured Elko gas station and convenience store. He was a tall man with a deeply lined face and a gray mustache, wearing a straw cowboy hat and boots as though he'd done that all his life, which he probably had; Letty pegged him at somewhere between seventy and eighty, but, given the obvious wear and tear, couldn't make a closer estimate.

The store had a combination storage room and office, with two chairs wedged inside. Harp took one, offered the other to Letty, and said to Kaiser, "I'm old and she's female. You're gonna have to stand, John."

"Roscoe Winks," Letty said, as they sat down, knees-to-knees.

Harp smiled, showing a row of thick teeth under the mustache. "Roscoe Winks. He's a crook, he surely is. Always has been. Vee tells me that Roscoe might be stealing oil, and I gotta say, the only reason that he hasn't been doing that before is that he hadn't figured out how to do it. He's been bankrupt about six times, screws over people he's hired to do work for him, lies about everything, cheats at everything, been married four times, and drinks. He does tell some good stories when he's in his cups."

Letty: "Is he violent?"

"Oh, no. Not because he wouldn't like to be, but Roscoe's yellow. A coward. I wouldn't put it past him to hire somebody to beat you up, but he wouldn't do it himself."

"You're painting an attractive picture," Kaiser said.

"Did I mention that he's ugly?"

Made Letty laugh.

"I made you laugh," Harp said, reaching out to pat Letty on the knee and maybe a piece of her thigh. "But listen here: when I say he could hire somebody to beat you up, he knows people like that. I believe he would do that if you were a threat. Maybe worse. There are places not far from here that no white man has ever walked over, make good burying grounds. You don't want to disappear."

"We're very up-front and careful," Letty said. "Where would we find Mr. Winks?"

Harp got a sheet of paper out of an office printer, took a yellow pencil stub from his shirt pocket, licked the tip once, and drew a map. "You go on out north of town, and about the time you might think you're past the last of the pumpjacks, you'll go another mile and there'll be this little patch of them. There's a sign that says WINKS OIL CORP. You can't miss it."

They thanked Harp, and in the car, Kaiser said, "Nasty old man had your shirt and pants off about four times in there."

"I liked him," Letty said. "Old, but still got it going on. And confident about it."

"Whatever," Kaiser grumped.

They drove north out of town, past fields of pumpjacks and later cotton, with tumbleweeds blowing across the highway on a hot breeze, and spotted Winks Oil Corp. just as Harp said they would. Letty had grown up in the billiard-table-flat countryside of Minnesota's Red River valley and the sprawling rectangular fields that surrounded her hometown. That had given her an eye for acreage.

The Winks property, she thought, with her country eye, covered a half-section, or about three hundred and twenty acres. Pumpjacks were scattered across the nearly perfectly flat land. A small metal building and two green oil storage tanks squatted at the edge of the land closest to the highway. A red Chevy pickup was parked outside the building, but nothing moved.

"Now what?" Kaiser asked.

"They're right on the highway," Letty said. "I can't believe that they'd roll a renegade oil truck down there and start pumping oil into those tanks, during the daytime."

"Uh-oh."

"Lot of weeds," Letty said, looking at the fields surrounding the pumpjacks. "You could sit in those weeds and not only wouldn't anybody see you, they couldn't find you, even if they knew you were out there."

"Uh-oh."

"Let's head back to Midland. Didn't I see a Dick's store there?"

She had.

Kaiser bitched and moaned all the way through the sporting goods store, but Letty paid him little attention, picking out a Bushnell two-person tent that was mostly mesh.

"DHS ain't gonna pay for it, no way they gonna expense that," Kaiser told her.

"I'll claim I spent the money on gasoline."

"No way I'll support —"

"Shut up."

"What are the chances that the truck would even show up tonight?" Kaiser asked. "Fool's errand if you ask me."

"Do the numbers," Letty said. She paused by a shelf of sleeping-bag liners, decided against, and pushed the shopping cart on down the aisle. "Wright thinks they could be stealing a hundred thousand barrels a year. If a full tanker holds only a hundred and ninety barrels, they're stealing every night, and some nights, twice. We know they're working now — so, the chances are good."

"That fuckin' tent you bought has an orange trim *designed* to make it more visible at night," Kaiser said.

"Camo tape will cover it. I saw some by the checkout."

They returned to the hotel, where she practiced setting up the tent — it used flexible tent poles to form a low dome — and she covered the orange trim with the camo tape. Kaiser showed her how to use the Canon image-stabilized binoculars that he kept in his bug-out bag. That didn't take long, as the glasses had only one button.

The sun didn't go down until almost nine

o'clock, and a half-hour after sunset, they were driving back to the Winks site. Kaiser would drop her off a quarter-mile away. A fence ran along the roadside ditch that she'd have to cross, and Kaiser said, "Pick up your feet. That way, you'll step on the rattler instead of kicking it."

"Shut up."

"I'll be on the phone, sweating . . ."

". . . like a nun in a Delta barracks."

"I wasn't going to say that, but that would be the case," Kaiser said. He was worried, and showed it. "Talk to me, goddamn it, Letty. You got both guns? I know a guy who lost his sidearm crawling across a field. Try not to do that. I can be back here in two minutes. So talk to me. Talk to me. When you're out there, call me every fifteen minutes."

"I'll call when it's necessary. I've got you on my favorites list."

"Okay, we're coming up on it. I don't want to hit the brakes and show the brake lights, so I'll roll to a stop. Goddamn it, what am I doing? Here we go . . ."

They rolled to a stop, and Letty slipped out of the Explorer, carrying her pack and the tent, and squatted next to the ditch on the right side of the road as Kaiser accelerated away.

There was no moon and only a hint of light on the western horizon; the ditch smelled of gravel dust and mold. When Kaiser was well down the road, Letty scuttled across it into the left ditch, then duck-walked across the ditch to the fence.

She watched, listened, stood up, crossed the fence, stooped, and walked a slow, careful four hundred yards across the open field, past a slowly cranking pumpjack smelling of oil, into an acre-sized patch of bone-colored, thigh-high weeds that smelled of herb-flavored dust. Again she waited, then took the tent out of its carry bag and set it up, crawled inside, snake-free. Fifty yards away, through the tent's mesh, she could see the oil tanks next to the Winks building. The building was dark, with a single pole light by the road.

Time passed, nothing happened. Two hours after she settled into the tent, a narrow crescent new moon poked over the eastern horizon; two hours after that, the Milky Way was rising overhead. Letty was wearing a dark sweatshirt, and she pulled the neck opening over her head, slipped an arm out of the sleeve so her arm and hand were inside the shirt, opened her phone, the light contained by the shirt, and called Kaiser.

"I was sitting here sweatin' . . ."

"Like a nun?"

"No. Bullets. Why didn't you call?"

"Because nothing happened. Nothing. I've seen two pickups and they didn't stop. Anyway, I'm set here," she told him. "You good?"

"I'm good as long as nobody is checking pumpjacks. I was afraid to call you because I wasn't sure you had the phone's ringer turned off." Kaiser was parked behind a pumpjack on a parallel road a mile away. "You got that 938 in your pocket?"

"I do. And the phone's on vibrate."

"Okay. Now, don't move. That's what people see: movement."

Letty clicked off, sprawled across the tent, plugged an earbud into one ear, and called up a playlist of quiet music, an old "Jazz for a Rainy Day" that a college friend had suggested.

She waited. At some point, a light-footed animal walked by, she thought possibly a coyote, because it was sniffing at her; she didn't try to see it, because it might also have been a skunk, if they had skunks in Midland. As a trapper, she'd learned that skunks were not to be messed with, as they tended to shoot first and ask questions later. For the buck-sixty she'd get for a skunk

215

carcass, the stress wasn't worth it.

Her phone vibrated and Kaiser asked, "Nothing?"

"Haven't even seen another car. There's nothing out here."

"All the better to steal the oil," Kaiser said. "I've been sitting here thinking . . ."

"I hope they don't hear the grinding noise out at the road."

"I'm laughing myself sick. Listen: if somebody is stealing oil from wherever they steal it, they're probably doing it in the deepdark. Then, they've got to drive to Winks and unload. I believe they might wait until it's real late, after midnight, before they load, and then they'd unload at Winks even later. You might have a long wait."

"I'll nap some. I'm close enough to hear anything as noisy as a truck."

She did that. She'd known that the nights still got cool, so she'd folded a jacket and put it inside the pack. She hadn't needed it. Now, left inside the pack, it worked well as a pillow. With the quiet jazz and the dark of the night — the sliver of moon was straight overhead, providing about as much light as a firefly — and the long day, she dozed, waking every hour or so when Kaiser called, or when a pickup rolled past. None of the trucks stopped at Winks, and it was nearly three o'clock when she heard the tanker truck coming in.

It slowed, turned at Winks, rolled behind the tanks where she couldn't see it. She called Kaiser and told him about it. "Get ready. It came in from the south, so it'll probably be going back out that way. Hey: don't call me. I'll call you."

"What are you doing?" Kaiser asked.

"What you told me not to," Letty said. "I can't see the truck from where I am. But don't worry, I won't get closer, I'll just crawl around in a circle until I can see it."

"Goddamn it, Letty . . ."

"I'm going."

She clicked off, unzipped the tent, and began circling through the patches of weeds. She'd been a hunter when she was young and hungry, had needed to get close to poach sitting pheasants and ducks with her little .22-short, and she knew how it was done; and in her black jeans and sweatshirt, she was close to invisible.

She'd made a mistake on the original surveillance site, the tent, she thought, as she moved slowly through the night. She should have gone farther across the field, which would give her a view down the length of the driveway loop, instead of the side of it. She would have been able to see what the driver was doing, but now he was hidden by the tanks.

No way to fix that. She ghosted through the night, no sound except the grinding of a pump, coming from the area of the tanks. She moved a hundred yards in a circle, toward the head of the driveway loop, but still fifty yards out. From a clump of weeds, she looked down toward the tanks. She could see the nose of the truck and a single man standing outside the cab, talking into a cell phone, a splash of light on his face.

She moved closer, took the binoculars out of her backpack, and studied the man. The cell phone light was bright enough to illuminate the side of his face, but the front of his face was turned away from her. She sat, not moving, five minutes, seven minutes, then another man walked around the end of the truck and said something to the man with the phone. She couldn't see his face. The man with the phone nodded, turned it off.

They walked out of sight, to the back of the truck, did something she couldn't see, then walked separately to the driver and passenger doors and climbed inside. She saw the second man's face in the cab light, but not clearly. They started the truck and

drove through the driveway loop, the headlights playing off the weeds above Letty's
head.

When the truck was broadside to her, she
risked getting to her knees. She could make
out a logo on the side of the tank, a faux-
antique script that said *Yorktown*.

When it had gone through the bend, she
turned her back to the truck, did the inside-
the-shirt trick, and called Kaiser: "They're
leaving. They're going south."

"I'm on it."

Kaiser wouldn't be able to pick her up
before tracking the tanker. She was tempted
to walk down to check out the Winks building, but resisted the impulse. Instead, she
walked carefully and silently back to the
tent, pulled the sweatshirt over her head,
and called Kaiser again.

"I'm not behind him," Kaiser said. "I'm
running parallel off to the east. We're still
headed south. I'll call when anything
changes."

Still under the sweatshirt, she used her
phone to look up Yorktown trucking and
found Yorktown Oil Services Ltd. out of
Midland. She opened up the website and
read, "The largest independent oil trucking
company in the Permian Basin, with more

than a hundred clean, modern trucks . . ."

She closed the phone and pulled the shirt back down, lay back on the pack, and dozed. Sometime later, she heard what she thought was a voice. Her phone clock said 5:14. She pushed herself up, peering through the mesh toward the road. She could see a flashlight coming toward her down the side of the road, and when it was closer, saw two men half-walking, half-jogging along the shoulder.

They went on by, and eventually out of sight. She never learned why they might be out there, running in the night.

Kaiser called: "I think I spotted that address on Highway 132. There's some kind of pit out there. Maybe a gravel pit, I don't know. I'm not on the same road . . . I'm north of it. The truck drove down in the pit where I can't see it anymore. I marked it on the nav's GPS. You want me to sit here and watch, or head back to you?"

"What can you do if you watch?"

"Not much. I can't get close without tipping them off that I'm here."

"Then head on back," Letty said. "We'll check it tomorrow."

"Okay. I won't make it there before sunrise. Stay hidden."

"Call when you get close. I'll get some sleep."

Kaiser called when he estimated that he was fifteen minutes out. Pickups had been passing on the road, but none had turned at Winks. Letty folded up the tent and put it in its carry bag, did her duckwalk away from the Winks building past the pumpjack to the fence, waited until there were no trucks coming from either direction, then crossed the fence and the road, and sprawled in weeds. The sun was fully above the horizon, promising another hot day, when Kaiser called again.

"I'm a minute out. You should be able to see me."

She got to her knees, saw him, and a minute later was in the truck.

"You okay?" he asked.

"I'm fine. Got some sleep. Been a while since I've slept outside, it was kinda nice. No rattlers as far as I could tell. Want me to drive?"

Kaiser was happy to stay behind the wheel, so Letty got on her phone and called Greet in Washington. "We saw an oil tank truck delivering oil to a company that is probably selling it for the thieves," Letty told her. "I don't think the truck is legit — they hide it, and we know where they're hiding it."

"We might want to bring in the FBI," Greet said.

"We still don't know where they're getting the oil," Letty said. "If you want to wait for a couple of days, we'll probably get that."

"I'll talk to my boss. Things get complicated when we go to the FBI, so it's not like they're going to show up at your hotel tomorrow morning."

"My concern is that they'll go for the oil thieves, which I'm not sure will deal with the whole threat," Letty said. "If these guys are using the money to do something dangerous . . . they might already be under way with it. We should probably try to figure that out before we jump them. Try to figure out everybody involved, not just the truck drivers."

"I'll tell the boss. If you do need some FBI backup right away, call me, twenty-four/seven."

"I will," Letty said. She hung up and pulled the visor down to shade her eyes from the harsh, low-angle sunlight. "Another day, another two hundred and seventy-four dollars and forty-three cents."

"Really? I think I make more than that. Three-thirty something. I should be the boss of you," Kaiser said. He asked, "So . . . boss. Are we going back out tonight?"

Letty said, "I believe we should. I'd like to know where that truck is getting the oil and something about the people driving it. If the FBI drops a net on them, it'll be 'Gimme a lawyer.' By the time that gets sorted out, the militia will be gone."

"If there is a militia," Kaiser said. "If they're not buying houses in Panama for their retirements."

"What's your thing about Panama? You thought the Blackburns might be there."

Kaiser shrugged. "It's nice down there. I might retire there."

"Okay. Listen, I'm not sleepy, let's go see Tanner. Then we can go back to the hotel, take naps, think things over."

Tanner was pallid, melancholy, but tried to smile when Letty and Kaiser showed up. He pointed a finger at Kaiser and said, "You probably saved my life, bro. Gracias."

"No problemo," Kaiser said. "How are you doing?"

"I'll be on my back for a while. They don't want any stress on the muscles around the artery. The doc had to cut out a piece of it where the dog bite wrecked it, and pull together the ends."

Kaiser shook his head and said, "In that case, I wouldn't be in any rush to get out of here. You're gonna need some physical therapy when you do. You're lucky that mutt didn't hit about six inches further toward the middle."

"I thought about that, about the time he was chewing on my leg," Tanner said. He looked at Letty. "You guys getting anyplace with the investigation?"

"We're generating names — Max Sawyer may or may not be kept in jail for a while, depending on what the Monahans cops want to do," Letty said. "None of us were wearing uniforms and his dog got shot, so . . . an assault charge might be tough. He didn't actually point his gun at anyone. Dog is dead . . ."

"Fuckin' dog," Tanner said. "Goddamn leg, hurts. Not only the surgery, I got the bruise from hell."

"Get some drugs, man. We'll try to keep you up on what we're doing," Kaiser said.

"Yeah, do that."

After a little more talk, Letty and Kaiser left the hospital and Kaiser said, "We're not that far from Monahans. Want to run down there and see what Sawyer has to say for himself?"

"No. We made a mistake there," Letty

said, as she settled into the Explorer. "Tanner wanted to talk to him about the Blackburn murders, but the only way we get to him for *that* is if he's involved in the oil thefts. He'll figure that out. Probably has, by now. Victor Crain did — he's already running. So we've probably told the whole goddamn group that we're sniffing after them. Maybe if we let sleeping dogs lie . . ."

"If I were them, I'd call everything off and dig a hole and pull it in after myself," Kaiser said.

"So would I," Letty said. "But they did the oil thing anyway, last night. After Crain would have talked to them. They didn't stop . . ."

"You think they can't? That they need the money?"

"Or they're trying to squeeze the last bit of blood out of the rock, before they go crazy."

As they were driving back toward Midland, Letty got Pugh at the station in Monahans. Pugh said that they had charged Sawyer with assault on a police officer, though the charge wouldn't hold.

"He can legally own a gun, and a dog, and Tanner walked through a warning sign, and none of us were in uniform, we didn't have a warrant," Pugh said. "Sawyer's never been convicted of a felony. We were hoping that he'd talk to us, but he didn't and he's got a lawyer now. We're SOL. We're gonna have to cut him loose."

"All right," Letty said. "Listen, we'd really appreciate it if you wouldn't ask him about any oil thefts. I'm sure they're already spooked, but if we could take it easy . . ."

"I'll let that slide. I'll push him on his gun, push his lawyer on the gun, make it seem like a gun thing, that Tanner had a rumor on the murder investigation."

"Great. Make it seem like it wasn't even a big deal, us going to his house. It was a routine check, until the dog attacked Tanner."

"I can do that, although I'm gonna feel a little stupid," Pugh said.

"Only for a while," Letty said.

"Fair warning: he'll be out by this evening," Pugh said. "He goes out to a range up in Pecos, and some of our guys know him from there. They say he's got a *lot* of guns."

"Okay. We're warned. Hey, Casey — Thanks."

When she was off the phone, Kaiser asked, "What are we doing tonight?"

226

"I want to look at satellite photos," Letty said. "We want to get as far away from the tanker truck parking pit as we can and still see it, if it pulls out."

"I got the spot," Kaiser said.

"So we can do some more recon late this afternoon, before dark. Until then . . . Let's get breakfast, not pancakes, head back to the hotel, get cleaned up, and take a nap."

"You know what we need to do?" Kaiser asked. "It's so flat out here, people are visible from so far away, I'd feel better if we had a rifle with us. If these guys really are some kind of nutcake militia . . ."

"You had me at 'rifle,' " Letty said.

"Well, we can legally buy one, even though we don't live here, if our supervisor gives us a letter of authorization on an official government letterhead," Kaiser said. "If we called Greet right now, she could scan a letter and send us a PDF that we could print at the hotel."

"Wonder if there's a decent gun shop in Midland?" Letty asked.

Kaiser glanced at her.

"Just kiddin'," Letty said. She picked up her phone and punched in Greet's number. "If this works, we'll go shopping before we go back out there."

ELEVEN

Victor Crain had rented a house behind Max Sawyer's for the simple reason that it'd been empty and that Sawyer knew the landlord. He'd heard a gunshot, and when he looked out his back window, he'd seen the commotion in Sawyer's yard and decided it was time to book.

He hadn't been in the place for long and most of his possessions were still in boxes. When no cops showed up at his door, he repacked the few things that he'd unpacked when he rented the place, hauled them out to his pickup, and left town.

On the way, he watched for cop cars, or anyone who might be tracking him, and saw nothing suspicious. He called Jane Hawkes and said, "Sawyer's been busted. He might have tried something, I heard a shot."

Hawkes: "Shit! Shit! Why . . ." There was a breakdown in reception, and Crain next heard ". . . now? We're so close!"

"I bagged out of my house," Crain said. "I'm gonna bunk down at the shack."

". . . R.J. can . . . ask around."

"You're breaking up," Crain said. "Where are you?"

"Rand and me and . . . big hole . . . almost done."

"Gonna work?"

"Yes. We're gonna drive the pickup . . . today. Make sure."

"Hope it don't rain . . ."

"It'll be fine. I'll probably see you up to the shack . . . nights . . . late. I gotta get . . . Midland and . . . some of the boys up there."

"See you then," Crain said. "Find out about Max."

Hawkes was standing on the side of a mountain where the only trail was cut out of the dirt by off-road four-wheelers. She could get a pickup from I-10 southeast to what they called "the hole," and she could get the same pickup from the town of Pershing northwest to the hole, but the hole was a problem.

The hole was actually an arroyo slicing down the mountain right into the Rio Grande, created by storm runoff. The solution to the problem was to knock the edges off the hole with a Bobcat, using the loose

229

dirt to fill in the rocky bottom, covering stones the size of footballs. Getting a trailer up to the hole with the Bobcat was a trial, and the Bobcat itself was the smallest one made, which didn't help. They'd spent ten days working on the road, trailering the machine as far as they could, then using it to smooth entry and exit lines and knock down center mounds on the two-tracks until they got to the hole.

Not everybody would have a four-wheeler, they thought, so after knocking the edges off the hole and partially filling it, they widened the bottom, building a parking platform. If some couldn't make it up the slope, they'd pull the truck off until everybody else was through, then they'd use a winch to pull the truck up the far side.

Once across the hole, they'd be fine, even in the dark.

"What do you think?" Hawkes asked Rand Low, looking down the hole.

"We gotta pack it better if we're gonna put sixty or seventy or eighty pickups across it. But I could take the truck down there now and get it out. Those rocks down there actually make a decent foundation."

"If you can't get out, we'd have a long walk," Hawkes said, hands on her hips.

"Ah, we're good," Low said. "Let's give it a shot. If it doesn't work, we'll pull it out with the Bobcat."

They were all soaked with sweat and brown with dust. Terrill Duran was wearing a bandanna around his face as he worked the Bobcat. He killed the engine and walked over and asked, "You wanna try?"

"We're talking about it," Hawkes said doubtfully. "If you guys think so . . . Take it easy."

Low got in the pickup, eased it up to the hole, then let it roll down over the edge, slowly, to the bottom, fifteen feet below, across the built-up pad, then up the other side.

At the top, on the far side, Low got out and called, "It's soft, we need to pack it some more, but it'll work fine. I think we're done with it."

"C'mon over," Duran called back to him. "I'll push some more dirt down and we can pack it, and then we can run the truck up and down it for a while."

They gave it another hour, rolling the pickup and the tiny Bobcat up and down the arroyo wall, until the dirt was solid. When they were finished packing, they took a heavy-bristled push broom out of the truck and pushed white surface dirt back over the raw earth of the refashioned arroyo. When they were done, Low stuck a couple of rod-mounted red reflectors into the dirt on both sides of the track into the hole.

"How about we go into Pershing and check in to the motel, like we talked about?"

"Waste of money, if we leave tonight," Crain said. "And it's a risk."

"We got the money," Low said. "Not much risk. And I stink. We all stink. Instead of stinking all the way back to El Paso, I'd like to get cleaned up and maybe spend an hour in the pool. We all brought our swimsuits."

"Sounds good to me, I'm dehydrated as hell," Hawkes said. "If it rains, we're screwed."

"No rain for at least a couple weeks, last time I looked," Duran said.

Hawkes told them about the call from Crain.

"R.J. goes on duty at eleven o'clock, he'll still be asleep. I'll wait until ten to call him," Hawkes said. "We need to know what happened to Max."

"Max won't give us up," Low said. "Though I sorta don't think that he ought to come on the raid with us. If they think

232

he was with us, something to do with us, they'd be right back in his face. He ought to be somewhere that gives him an alibi. I don't want to lose that boy."

"I'll think about it," Hawkes said. "You might be right."

"What about the oil?" Duran asked. "Think we ought to quit?"

"I'll talk to Terry about it, but I don't want to quit yet," Hawkes said. "The raid is costing us a chunk. We got forty-four people coming in from out of town and I'm sending them two thousand bucks apiece for travel money, gas, food, and motels. It's a solid three days from Seattle down to El Paso. Less for other people, but those ones from Seattle and Michigan got a long haul."

"I worry if that's enough guys. Forty from out of town, sixty-some of ours. Some of the out-of-towners might chicken out when they hear the whole plan."

"Not many," Hawkes said. "I know them all personally and they are the hardcore."

"Better be," Duran said. "It's not like the assholes here in Pershing don't have guns. And the FBI and maybe the National Guard is gonna be on us like flies on shit."

"We worked it all out," Hawkes said. "It'll all be fine."

Pershing, Texas, had two things going for it: a bridge across the Rio Grande, to Mexico; and it was home to the second-largest battery in America, which wasn't as much of a tourist attraction as the locals thought it should be, being a group of electrical lumps inside a concrete-block building.

Located halfway between its border-crossing competitors at El Paso and Presidio, and southwest of the town of Van Horn, Texas, its only link to the rest of the U.S. was a single narrow highway that connected to I-10 at Van Horn. The road was used largely by semi-trailer truck traffic hoping to avoid the traffic jams at El Paso, and also as a shortcut to I-20 and highway routes going northeast into the U.S., and from the U.S. southwest into Mexico.

The Pershing residents didn't know it, but Hawkes, Low, and Crain had just finished forging a second road out. An existing dirt road led out of the town, a mile northwest along the Rio Grande, to the Pershing Sportsmen's Club, which amounted to a clearing in the brush where the sportsmen had set up a shooting range, with a mountain bluff as the backstop. A two-lane track led farther northwest out of the sportsmen's club, used only occasionally by four-wheelers and dirt bikes.

Those tracks dead-ended at the Arroyo Grande, the ditch that Hawkes and the others had just crossed. Once across the arroyo, more four-wheeler tracks connected north to agricultural access roads for fields along the river. While Hawkes and her crew had spent most of their time working on the arroyo, they'd also smoothed tougher patches along the four-wheeler tracks, back as far as the farm roads.

A hot, disheveled town of eighteen hundred souls, Pershing was one of the most isolated towns in the lower forty-eight states. Electric power flowed along a single line of power poles from Van Horn, which was the reason for the second-biggest battery. When the power went out, as it occasionally did during thunderstorms, the town would have been out of luck without the battery backup.

Pershing lived on the bridge and what went across it in both directions. There was a substantial U.S. government Customs and Border Protection post, which provided the best jobs in town, along with three bars and a motel, an auto-parts store, a couple of different brands of dollar stores, two convenience stores, one small supermarket, two churches, a café, a Subway and a Regio's Pizza, and a green-painted concrete-block jail surrounded by Spanish bayonet plants.

The town had no city hall, police station, or municipal court — all city meetings were held in the elementary school. The tallest structure in town was a cell phone tower in a vacant lot at the top of a ridge on the north edge of town, next to a cylindrical water tower.

Ochoa, the Mexican town on the south side of the river, was even smaller — a Customs station, a scattering of manufactured houses, a cantina and a convenience store with gas and diesel, and a two-acre hard-surfaced parking lot for trucks waiting to make the crossing.

Pershing had had its fifteen minutes of fame a year and a half earlier, when a "caravan" of Central Americans had arrived at the bridge without food, water, or a place to sleep except the concrete parking lot on the Mexican side. They had been expected to go to El Paso, but at the last minute the motley collection of old cars, buses, and bicycles had swerved north, with the idea that they might be shown more mercy at the smaller city.

And they had. Pershing's mayor, Harry

Lopez, with the consent of the other four members of the city council, had invited the refugees into the United States, and had pressured a harried supervisor at the Customs post to allow them through for humanitarian reasons. Lopez and the council members had their stories in the *New York Times,* the *Washington Post,* the *L.A. Times,* and most of the networks. Even when the moment passed, Lopez and the councilmen were left as secular saints, to be occasionally consulted on immigrant matters by the media.

Since that day, called the Great Crossing in Pershing, Hawkes and Low had been up and down every street in town; had detailed maps, now with extensive annotations, and satellite photos. They knew where the mayor and the council members and all four cops lived, and where the Customs officers and border patrolmen lived, and who carried guns. They knew how big the I-beams were that supported the Chihuahua Bridge.

They'd done their reconnaissance in several different pickups and Jeeps, much of it during the COVID-19 crisis, which allowed them to wear masks without comment.

After a final crossing of the Arroyo Grande, they drove southeast along the four-wheeler tracks, past the gun range, and into Pershing. Nobody paid any attention; they weren't the only Bobcat in town. They checked into the Lariat Motel, took turns in the shower, and then plunged into the cool water of the pool.

"This is fuckin' . . . exquisite," Hawkes said, pulling up her vocabulary after surfacing in the pool. "My God, why doesn't everyone have a pool?"

They laughed, but they all knew why, and they didn't have to say it: you don't have a pool if you make nine dollars an hour.

With the sun dropping low in the afternoon sky, they dressed and headed back to El Paso, three hours away. They arrived at dark, dropped the Bobcat and trailer at the rental agency, and drove over to Hawkes's house. She had turned the family room into a war room, maps on the walls, three long folding tables surrounded by folding chairs, three laptops on the tables along with an office printer. A thirty-six-inch television hung from the wall, above a rack of identical black rifles.

Hawkes led the way in, hit the lights, turned on one of the laptops, and brought up the National Weather Service.

"Still no rain in sight," she said. "That's the last big worry. The hole bothers me."

Duran laughed. "My last big worry is getting out of there without any holes in my chest."

"If we do it right, we'll be good," Hawkes said. "We need to make sure Rodriguez gets down there with his camera."

"A thousand bucks . . . He'll be there. He'd be there for free if he knew."

"Can't tell him," Hawkes said. "I'll give you an extra thousand to take along. If he won't go for one, he'll go for two."

Rodriguez ran a freelance video-news truck in the El Paso region. The truck had satellite-link capability.

They talked some more about the logistics and scheduling, then Hawkes said, "What we need to do now is find out what the hell happened with Max. Why the cops were on him."

"What I'm thinking is . . . What I'm afraid is . . . Blackburns," Duran said.

Low said, "How would they make that connection? We didn't touch a goddamn thing in there. There weren't any prints, there's no DNA. We got in and out clean.

They didn't even find them for four or five days."

Hawkes checked her watch. "I'll talk to R.J. tonight. You guys ought to get some sleep: it's gonna be busy tomorrow. I need to clean out the house, box up what I'm taking with me."

When the men had gone, Hawkes went to her computer and out to her darknet site. Another man had dropped out, but they still had a hundred and ten people committed.

After working through the incoming mail, she checked her watch again, and called R.J.

"Have you heard about Max?" she asked.

"No. What happened?"

"He was busted, this afternoon. There was some shooting. At his house."

"If somebody got shot, I'll hear about it," R.J. said. He was a cop in Odessa. "Probably get back to you in an hour or so, if you're still up."

"I'll be up."

She went out to Netflix, skipped through two episodes of *The Queen's Gambit,* one of her favorite streaming programs of all time. She paused it halfway through the finale, where the American girl beat the Russians, when R.J. called back.

"Here's the deal," he said. "A Midland investigator named Dan Tanner — good guy, I know him — who is checking out a double murder went to Max's place, but nobody knows exactly why. Supposedly working the murder. Max's pit bull attacked him, bit him real bad, put him in the hospital. Dog was shot. Max got arrested for pulling a gun on the cops, but I'm told it's probably a bad bust. Nobody was in uniform, he came out with a gun after somebody shot the dog in his front yard."

"Goddamn it . . ."

"Yeah, but like I said, it doesn't sound like much. One thing, there were three other people there. There was a Monahans investigator named Pugh, I know her, too, she's okay, and then two federal people. There's a big guy from the Department of Homeland Security and a woman who's working with him, like an assistant, or something. Really young, doesn't seem like much. But the guy is definitely a threat."

"Homeland Security . . . ah, man," Hawkes said.

"Yeah. That was my thought. Homeland Security isn't here to see who's stealing oil."

"You gotta stay on top of this, R.J. This is critical."

"I will. I'll start checking things out. I'll

try to find where the Homeland Security people are staying. Maybe you could put some guys on them, track them, see what they're doing."

"Call me back if you find anything out," Hawkes said.

She had people coming from all over the country. She had her own people armoring up.

And Homeland Security was poking its nose in.

Not ideal.

The day had been a long one, and she had a minor, familiar headache: she'd insisted on working on the road building, and the hot weather sucked the water out of her. Low had explained that she had a much higher skin-to-meat ratio than the males did, which meant that she evaporated water faster — something he'd learned as a laborer up in the oil patch.

She drank a final bottle of water with an Aleve and went to bed, lay awake, and thought of what was up ahead of her. She'd be a fugitive, for sure. She had people to pass her along, like the Underground Railroad, but she'd probably be caught in the end.

Some nights, dreaming of that end, she

thought about fighting it out. She'd be armed, she knew how to use her guns, but she had no illusions about the cops who'd be hunting her. They'd know how to use theirs, too. She'd die, but she'd be a legend.

On other nights, she thought of accepting her capture — if they'd let her do that — and then standing mute during her trial and imprisonment. Once inside the Bureau of Prisons, wherever they sent her, she'd continue her writings. They couldn't entirely stop that; her work could be smuggled out, if nothing else.

Would that make her a legend? She was unsure of that. She wrote reasonably well, she thought, but wasn't exactly a poet. Low spoke better than she did, where the rage and hurt was right out there for everybody to see and hear. Still, as a writer, she was good enough.

Sometimes she imagined herself in movie-like visions, hiking through the mountains with a rifle on her shoulder or, alternatively, riding through the mountains on a sorrel stallion, and then she'd laugh at herself, for the vanity. She'd have a Subaru for the beginning of her run, there wouldn't be any sorrel stallions in her future . . .

All she really wanted was for people to recognize that she'd never had a chance and that seventy percent of them were the same way — people without a chance. To understand that the bottom people were all in it together.

You might sympathize with the immigrants from the south on an individual basis, but their effect was to create an even lower bottom than already existed, she believed. There was no way to raise yourself up, if the bottom kept falling out beneath you. The Democrats bragged about the idea of a fifteen-dollar-an-hour minimum wage: How many of those Democrats could live on thirty-one thousand dollars a year? And the Republicans were worse: they pretended to believe that paying fifteen dollars an hour would cause McDonald's to go broke. Poor fuckin' McDonald's.

She rolled over in the night, the anger causing her to thrash about like a beached salmon, tangle herself up in the sheets.

Not for much longer. In a week, she'd be up in the Rocky Mountains.

Or dead.

TWELVE

Hyman Drago's Hunting and Tactical Equipment was a gun nut's dream store, Letty thought, as she cruised slowly down two long aisles of rifles and shotguns. She'd been in a lot of gun stores, but she had to admit that Drago's was a good one. Kaiser was walking on the opposite side of the gun aisles, totally focused. He would stop, touch a gun, move on. A clerk had asked each of them if they needed help, and they'd both politely declined, saying they would call for it when they needed it.

The guns were locked in the racks, most with metal or synthetic stocks, a surprising number with wood. Letty favored wood, found wood warm in the winter. With an inadequate pair of gloves, a metal stock would freeze your fingers . . .

Letty's natural mother had survived on child support checks and drank away a good part of the money. Letty had eaten school

245

lunches eagerly, unsweetened instant oat-meal at breakfast with powdered milk that came in huge blue-and-white boxes that seemed to last forever, and, too often, peanut butter sandwiches for dinner, especially in the last week before a new support check came in.

After the Davenports adopted her, she never again drank powdered milk or ate peanut butter, in any form; real whole milk she barely tolerated.

Letty started trapping when she was six, initially coached by a farmer named Bartles, who also loaned her rusty Victor jump traps until she could buy some of her own. When a muskrat or racoon survived the initial trapping, she killed it with a corn knife she'd found in a shed behind her house. Later, when the trapping started to bring in some discretionary funds, the same farmer sold her an ancient break-open .22 rifle, accurate out to about ten feet, for eight dollars, plus a partially used brick of .22-short ammunition, good for killing racoons.

At first, she hated killing animals. The distaste faded as she killed more of them. She never liked it, but something in her heart changed. If it was necessary, she'd do it, and it was necessary to eat.

The thing that drew her to guns was their

precision, lethality, and simplicity. Aside from the gun, her entire life was chaotic — she often missed school when her mother was too drunk in the morning to take her, was often late with schoolwork because of the missed days, sometimes had an exceptional load of muskrats and no time to both get them to the buyer and go to school on the same day.

Guns represented order and life. They were simple, clean, understandable, useful. She knew that her .22 was a piece of junk, perhaps seventy years older than she was, with a stock that had split and had been poorly repaired, but she cared for it as though it were her first piece of jewelry. That feeling had never gone away.

"Here we go," Kaiser called to Letty from across the rack of long guns. "It's not a rifle, but it's probably what we need."

The floor clerk was keeping an eye on them and Kaiser waved him over. Kaiser touched the barrel as Letty joined them and said, "Used Remington 870 shotgun, it'll take rifled slugs. Magazine-loaded. Decent sling, not great, but we're not going to be marching across Texas."

The clerk said, "Rifled slugs are fine. So is buckshot, if you'd prefer that. And any other shot loads, as far as that goes."

"I've never been much into shotguns," Letty said.

"Not much to know," Kaiser said. "The thing is, with this version you can change loads in a hurry and those slugs will knock the crap out of anything they hit. Up close, the buckshot . . . number-three buckshot has about twenty pellets at about .25 caliber each . . . Doesn't have the range of a rifle, but for our purposes, last chance self-defense . . ."

"Perfect for that," the clerk said.

Kaiser looked at Letty. "You think a twelve-gauge might rock you back a little too much? Gonna kick like a horse if we're shooting slugs."

"I've shot skeet some, so . . . no. On the other hand, I was shooting light loads."

"If you got in a position where you had to shoot it, I doubt you'd much notice the recoil," Kaiser said. "Besides, I sorta think it might be my gun for the time being."

Letty said, "If that's your pick, you're the combat guy."

Then Kaiser and the clerk got involved in a protracted discussion of condition, with the clerk arguing that the gun was used only by a little old lady on weekends during deer season, while Kaiser suggested it appeared to be a worn-out competition shooter that could blow up at any minute. Kaiser got the gun, an included hard case with a TSA-approved lock, four boxes of shells and three extra magazines, for $660, which Letty put on her American Express card.

"I'm going to keep it," she told Kaiser, as she carried it out to the car. "I always knew I should have a shotgun, but I never got around to it."

Kaiser was exceptionally pleased with himself. "I stole this sucker. It's damn near new. I bet it hasn't had a hundred shells run through it."

"So you took advantage of that poor sales clerk?"

"The thing had a layer of dust on the trigger guard. I bet it was in that rack for two years, nobody even picked it up. For law enforcement kind of stuff, it's better than a rifle."

"You think there's a range where we could shoot it, around Midland?" Letty asked.

Kaiser glanced at her.

"Just kiddin'."

They found a sporting clays place out in the countryside where Letty could spend time working with the gun. Like Kaiser said, the shotgun rocked her back on her heels;

249

half a box of slugs and half a box of buck-shot left her with a sore shoulder. And it was heavy: she wouldn't have wanted to carry it around the fields in the Red River valley, but if she had to shoot it in self-defense, it'd work fine out to perhaps sixty or seventy yards with slugs, forty or fifty with buckshot.

They were done with the range at two o'clock and went back to the hotel. "Try to sleep," she told Kaiser. "I'll call you around five . . . We'll hit the McDonald's for dinner and get out there where we can see the tanker come out of its hole."

"Five o'clock," he said.

In her room, Letty got on her laptop and called up a manual for the shotgun, disas-sembled it, reassembled it, and did it all over again. When she was satisfied she knew the gun, she spent five minutes dropping and reseating the mags. When she could do it with her eyes closed, by feel, she put the gun back in its case and crawled into bed, which felt cool and soft after the night on the ground.

At five-thirty, they hit the McDonald's halfway between Midland and Odessa, and by six-fifteen, were running along County Road 132, which was little better than a dirt track, where Kaiser had seen the oil tanker disappear. The whole countryside was a flat wasteland of low brush punctuated by dozens of pumpjacks and hundreds of power poles, one of the ugliest landscapes Letty had ever encountered.

Kaiser thought the truck may have been driven into a borrow pit or natural swale, but as they got closer, it appeared instead to have been driven into a dry creek bed that ran generally parallel to the track. "Had to be right around in here," he said. "I checked the GPS, I was almost straight north of them, and . . . there we go."

He pointed at a dusty track that went over the edge of the creek bank and onto the creek bed itself. The arroyo was deep enough to hide the truck, and as they went farther along the road, they could see no sign of it. "Wonder why they're hiding it? It's a big company, right?"

"I don't think it's real. Maybe we'll find out," Letty said. She pointed through the windshield. "Did you see that building last night?"

On the creek side of the road, but fifty or sixty yards from the creek bed, a small corrugated steel building squatted ten yards off the road. The building showed streaks of rust down its sides, and corrosion where it met the earth. Kaiser shook his head. "No. I wouldn't have seen it without lights inside. All I could see of the truck were its lights."

"Don't slow down. I'm going to make a movie with my cell phone," Letty said. They went on by. The building was no more than twenty feet square, with power coming in from one of the poles that fed the pump-jacks. A TV antenna was mounted on a pole behind the building, and an old-fashioned outhouse stood by itself behind the building and to one side.

"What the hell is this place doing out in the middle of nowhere?" Kaiser asked.

"It's like a line shack," Letty said. "Maybe . . . for people working the oil? Maybe maintenance on the pumpjacks? Or ag workers? We did see that one field with the center-pivot irrigator. Actually? I have no idea."

"I wouldn't know a center-pivot irrigator if one was stuck up my ass," Kaiser said. "But over there . . . See the footpath coming out of the creek? The truck is down there and those guys are walking up here. They could be in the shack right now."

"Don't think so," Letty said. "There'd be at least one pickup. They're not going out to the grocery store in that tanker."

They went on by and continued until the road was about to disappear into raw dirt; but before that happened, they crossed another track going north, and took it, and a mile later, another road going west toward the interstate. "This is where we want to be tonight," Kaiser said. Letty unbuckled and turned in her seat, looked past Kaiser's head with his binoculars. "I can see the building . . ."

She pointed ahead where a waist-high clump of weeds reached almost to the road. "See if you can get behind the weeds without getting stuck."

Kaiser drove in behind the weeds and stopped. "This will work," Letty said. "If that truck is in there, no way they'd see us way up here. If they go out after dark with their lights on, we'll have a front-row seat."

"More than an hour to sunset," Kaiser said. "We can't sit here. Somebody might come by and wonder what we're doing. But we gotta be back here when we can still see well enough to drive without headlights."

"We can turn off the headlights if we have to. But the taillights . . ."

"Duct tape and blackout cloth," Kaiser said.

"Let's go up to Odessa and visit Tanner," Letty suggested. "He'll think it's nice of us, and we'll have a comfortable place to sit while we wait. Get a couple Cokes. There's a Walmart up there, we could get the tape and the blackout cloth."

" 'Cause we really don't give a shit about Tanner."

"I didn't say that."

Tanner was grumpy but relaxed: he'd been given a dose of OxyContin, which he found pleasant, as had Vermilion Wright, with his knee surgery. "Not going to piss on people for using OxyContin anymore," he said. "Doesn't affect your thinking, but it does make the pain go away."

"Take a dozen pills a day for a month and see how you feel," Kaiser said. "You'll be selling the tires off your squad car to pay for a fix."

The conversation more or less slipped downhill from that, and after a while, Tanner said, "I gotta get some sleep. I want to thank you guys for coming by," and so they left.

"That was refreshing," Kaiser said, as they crossed the parking lot.

"Did what we needed and I got to pee," Letty said. "Let's run over to Walmart and get the tape and cloth for the taillights. It'll be close to dark before we get back to our bush."

By ten after nine, they were parked in the weeds at the side of the track. They hadn't bothered to cover the taillights on the way out, because they could get stopped by cops and because they'd be a mile away from the tanker and the building that went with it. Parked in their bush, Letty spent some time hunting for a decent music station on the satellite radio. There was no traffic: not a single car or truck. In the distance, they could see the lights from I-20, but no moon, as yet.

After a while, Kaiser said, "I'm gonna z-out."

"Okay." Letty cleared out her mind and sat.

At midnight, to the south, a set of headlights bounced and ricocheted along the road that led to the small building and within a minute or so was followed by a second set of lights. Letty nudged Kaiser, who yawned and asked, "We on?"

"We're on," Letty said.

The two trucks stopped at the corrugated

metal building and a light came on inside it. Twenty minutes later, the light went out, and while they couldn't see the men, they could see two brilliant flashlight beams as the men behind them crossed the distant road and then disappeared into the creek bed. Five minutes after that, the tanker truck rolled out of the creek bed, onto the road, and started out toward the interstate highway.

When all they could see were the tiny dots of the red running lights on the back of the tanker, Kaiser cranked up the Explorer and they went after it, running parallel to it and a mile north. Seven or eight minutes later, as the truck was approaching the interstate, Kaiser leaned on the gas and they closed in.

The tanker turned northeast toward Odessa. They followed it into the city, where it got off, turning right into the industrial section of town. Kaiser stayed well back, Letty tracking the three red lights on the back of the truck with the binoculars. A quarter-mile off the highway, the truck took a right onto a narrow street into a jumble of metal buildings. Kaiser turned off the Explorer's headlights and followed, but pulled off the road when they saw taillights flare on the truck.

"What do you want to do?"

"How far are they from us, do you think?" Letty asked.

"Maybe . . . half a mile. Maybe not quite that," Kaiser said.

"Let's ditch the Explorer and hike down there. See what's going on."

"We could lose them coming out . . ." Kaiser said.

"If they're stealing oil, we sorta know where they're going," Letty said.

They found a semicircular drive where they could park behind a pile of unidentifiable rusting machinery that appeared abandoned, probably oil field equipment. Kaiser got a flashlight from his gear bag, and they hurried out to the street, to find that the tanker had disappeared.

"I'm sure he stopped — they were doing something down there," Kaiser said.

"Probably pulled off," Letty said. "If they didn't, we've lost them, so we might as well run down there and find out."

The moon had come up, slightly fuller than the night before, and the track was so light-colored that they could jog along it. When they were close to the place they'd last seen the tanker, they heard some quiet rattling coming from a long, high shedlike metal building behind an eight-foot chain-link fence. They edged closer, up to the gate, and found a chain loosely wrapped around the gatepost and the leading edge of the gate, and an unlocked combination padlock holding the chain in place.

Kaiser carefully pulled the lock off the chain and whispered, "Need to use my cell phone flashlight." He turned his back to the gate and holding the padlock against his chest, turned on his cell phone light, allowing a needle point of light to shine through his fingers and onto the padlock. The lock was of the type that required four letters to be aligned: they were currently reading POOH.

"Like Winnie," Letty whispered.

Kaiser whispered back, "When people go into a place with a lock like this, they don't scramble the letters until they go back out."

"Good to know."

They heard more mechanical noises from the shed, but muffled, as if people were moving carefully, on tiptoe. Kaiser unwrapped the chain and they slipped through the gate, rewrapped the chain, and walked in the dark to the end of the shed.

Both ends of the shed were open and the tanker was parked inside. They were looking at the back of the truck, and saw two men walking along the side of the truck, carrying something that resembled a scuba tank.

"What the hell is that?" Kaiser whispered.

"No idea."

The men carried the object to the passenger-side door on the truck, and one of them stood on the external step, opened the door, and took out a plastic sack. They pulled the sack over the thing, whatever it was, then one of the men stood on the step and pulled the passenger seat back. The object was at least somewhat heavy, because it took both of them to get it into the truck and behind the seat.

"The thing had some kind of coupling coming out of the end," Letty whispered. "See that?"

"Yup."

When the object was in the truck, one man pulled the seat back and climbed inside, while the other man walked around the truck to the driver's-side door. The truck started, pulled carefully out of the shed. The passenger got out at the gate, pulled it open, and the truck drove through. The passenger wrapped the chain around the gate, locked it, and got back in the tanker, which rolled away down the street.

"Let's go see what we can see," Kaiser said.

Using the flashlight, they walked into the shed. There they found an installation of heavy pipes, some of them a foot in diameter, coming out of the ground, running along for fifty feet or so, then disappearing back into the ground. There were several even larger pipes on top, and a number of smaller ones running into short vertical installations.

"A pipeline," Kaiser said. "How in the heck would they get the oil out of it?"

"There are a lot of thingees here . . ." Letty said, walking along the installation.

"Good. We just have to find somebody who knows what a thingee is."

"Vee Wright would know," Letty said. "Valves. That's what I was thinking of. Not thingees. Stand back and put some light on this thing, I'll try to take a picture with my phone."

They did that. With Kaiser playing his flashlight across the pipes, Letty took a dozen shots from different angles. The photos weren't great, but you could see the pipes clearly enough.

"Let's go," Letty said. "Gotta hope you were right about the POOH."

Kaiser was correct: POOH opened the lock. They relocked the chains after they were out, and jogged back to the Explorer.

As they pulled out of the hiding spot, Kaiser said, "They gotta be an hour and a half from Winks's. We can probably get there in time to see them unloading . . ."

"We know where they're going," Letty said. "I want to go back to that house, that shack, where they parked their trucks. I want photos of their license tags."

Kaiser didn't argue. They headed back to the I-20, took a wrong turn on the way, got lost, found their way back, and turned southwest down I-20. Earlier that night at the Walmart, Kaiser had bought two on-sale black T-shirts and a roll of duct tape. Once they were onto the back roads, he pulled off and taped the shirts over the Explorer's taillights. A half-hour later, they were approaching the metal shed, which was dark.

When they got there, Letty said, "I'll get the photos. And I want to try the door . . ."

She hopped out, ran to the door, tried it: locked.

Next, she went to the trucks, took photos of the license tags. Both trucks were locked. Kaiser had gotten out of the Explorer, the engine still running, and said, "I got my picks, I could probably open the trucks . . ."

"Could have alarms," Letty said. "How

about the building? Could you open that lock?"

He checked and said, "I can do this one, it'll take three or four minutes."

"There's a door on the back . . ."

They hurried around to the back; Kaiser looked at the lock and said, "This one is easier. This is a piece of junk."

"See what you can do. I'll go out to the road to keep watch."

Five minutes later, Kaiser came around the shed and said, "It's open. It's a latch lock. When you come back out, if you pull it closed behind yourself, it'll lock automatically."

"Okay," Letty said. "Give me the flash. You keep watch."

Kaiser had left the door open an inch or so. Letty pushed inside and found a stuffy room with a single Army-style bunk; a counter with a microwave, two glasses, and a cup; a bowl and some spoons; a table and chair; an old fat television; a ten-gallon Igloo water tank; an office refrigerator; and a trash can. In one corner, nine cardboard moving boxes were piled atop one another, three boxes high, three wide.

The inside air held residual heat from the day, so the air-conditioning hadn't been running. A pile of gun magazines and newspapers sat on the floor by one of the beds; the papers, Letty noticed, were from El Paso.

Aside from the printed matter, there was little paper, but one piece, from the trash can, came from an auto dealership and was a receipt for routine maintenance on a pickup truck. The owner's name was printed across the top: (Mr.) Terrill T. Duran, with a home address in Monahans and a phone number below it. Letty stuffed it into her hip pocket.

She was uncertain about what to do with the boxes. They resembled the moving boxes that Crain had been putting in his truck when they passed him in the alley in Monahans.

She scraped her lower lip with her teeth, decided that she had to look.

She pulled a box off the top row, found it unsealed. Boots and clothing. She set it aside. Pulled another box off the top row: more clothing. A third box contained gun equipment — a green metal forestock rest from Remington, exactly like one she had — and earmuffs and ammo for a .223 and a nine-millimeter.

She was down to the second level of boxes, and moved the first boxes back a bit on the floor so she could keep them in order. The first box on the second level was heavy. When she opened it, she found propaganda pamphlets for the Land Division, which promoted a citizen patrol of the Mexican border.

She stuffed a couple leaflets into her pocket. The next box was also heavy and contained what appeared to be privately printed books called *ResistUS!* She thumbed quickly through one, found a photo of a masked woman in a khaki-colored blouse and jeans, captioned "Jael." There was a Jeep in the background of the photo and it looked contemporary.

She took a book, dropped it on the floor near the door.

The next box held more ammo and three bowling trophies.

The bottom three boxes contained clothes, boots, silverware, dishes.

As she was kneeling next to the bottom row of boxes, she thought about the bodies under the beds at the Blackburns' and she shined her flashlight under the bunk. Nothing there but air, but, turning the other way, she caught the reflection of something under the cookware shelf. She crawled over and found a .223 rifle slung on bungee cords.

She was about to unsling it when her phone buzzed. Kaiser: "Somebody's coming in. Get out here."

"I gotta, I gotta . . ." The boxes were still on the floor. "Kaiser: Go. Go now. I'll run out the back and get in the creek bed. I'll call you and tell you where to meet. I got a thing I gotta do, or they'll know we were here. Go. Go."

"Going."

Letty heard him pull away, scrabbled across to the boxes, and began repiling them. One tried to fall off the top of the pile, but she pushed it back, stepped toward the back door. Saw the *ResistUS!* book on the floor, picked it up. Nothing else seemed to be out of place. She turned the flashlight off, went out the back door and pulled it shut, heard the lock click. As she did that, headlights swung across the front of the building.

She walked straight away from the shed, toward the creek bed. There wasn't much cover, so she broke into a careful jog, unable to use the flashlight. A light came on in the building and she could see her shadow on the ground in front of her. Had to hurry . . .

She nearly fell into the creek bed. There was little warning, nothing but a sharp dirt edge and then the arroyo below. She couldn't see how deep it was. She sat down, her feet over the edge, and turned back to the building, saw a tan Jeep sitting on the shoulder of the road, bathed in the light from a window. Then the back door popped open and a woman stood there in the light, the rifle in her hands. The woman shouted, "Vic? Vic? That you?"

Letty slipped over the edge of the cutbank, flicked the flash on and off. The bank was steep, but walkable, crumbling dirt, heavily cut up by foot tracks going up and down. The woman at the house shouted again, "Vic! Terry! That you?"

At the bottom of the creek bed, she turned right and began walking east as quickly as she could; dropped the book, stooped, snatched it off the ground, and hurried on. The creek bottom was eroded and uneven and the going was difficult. She was a hundred yards or so up the creek bed when a light cut across the creek. She pressed herself into an eroded crevice, squatted, and froze. The woman was standing above the truck's parking spot, shining a brilliant white light along the arroyo.

She'd stopped shouting: if there was anyone in the arroyo, she'd apparently realized it wasn't Vic or Terry.

After scanning the creek bed, she shined the light down the arroyo wall directly in front of her, examining something. Tracks, Letty thought. She was looking at the place Letty had gone over the side. Then the woman turned, and the flashlight went out, and the woman fired a shot down the arroyo, past Letty, and then a dozen more shots, quickly, spraying them down the creek bed, first one way, then the other.

One came close enough that Letty could differentiate between the crack of a slug breaking the sound barrier ten feet away and the boom of the shot itself. She didn't move.

The shooting stopped, the light came back on, scanning the creek bed. Then it began to fade in a stuttering way, as if the woman were running away from the creek bed but shining the light back toward it as she ran. Letty waited, heard what sounded like the building door closing, then a car started. She got up and began to walk again. On the way, she called Kaiser.

"Are you okay?" he asked. "I was afraid to call, afraid I'd give you away. I saw the muzzle flashes, there were so many that I figured he didn't know where you were . . ."

"It was a she . . . and I'm good. I'm in the creek bed, heading east," Letty said. "When

I cross that road, the road going north, I'll come up and run along it."

"I'll come down there. I'll pick you up."

"Don't let her see you. She's got a .223." Letty clicked off, worried that the lighted face of the phone would pinpoint her.

In the pale moonlight, Letty could see the rim of the arroyo wall above her. Another hundred yards and it curved slightly to the north. When she could no longer see the glow of lights from the shack, she turned the flashlight on and began to run. The bottom of the arroyo was studded with water-worn stones the size of her fist; she'd been lucky not to twist an ankle.

She'd gone only a short distance when her phone vibrated again: Kaiser. "Where are you?"

"Still in the creek."

"You gotta run. She's turned her truck down the creek bed, she's behind you and I think she's coming in your direction."

"I'm running."

Another hundred yards and a culvert pipe appeared ahead of her. She looked back but couldn't see headlights; the truck's lights would still be behind the curve in the creek bed.

At the culvert, she climbed the bank onto the north road, turned off the flashlight, and began running hard. Down to the south-west, she could see the light from the back window of the building, and along the line of the creek bed, the glow of headlights coming her way. No way that the Jeep could get out of the creek bed without going back, but the headlights were closing on her.

She ran faster. Another minute, a few more hundred yards, and Kaiser was there, waiting in the Explorer, lights out. Through the open passenger-side window, he said, "I've taped over the interior lights. Get in."

She climbed in the passenger side, breathing hard, and pulled the door shut and he asked, "You okay?"

"I'm fine."

"Scared?" He stepped on the gas and they accelerated down the moonlit track.

"Give me five minutes," Letty said. "I didn't have time before."

"Been there and done that," Kaiser said. He was looking in the rearview mirror. "Was it worth the trouble?"

"Yeah. I got some stuff. I got two new names. A guy named Terry Duran, for sure — I've got his address and phone number. And I got a book by a woman named Jael, wearing a mask. Vic's in the shed. Our friend Victor Crain. Not much else in the place except a .223 hidden under a shelf.

The person shooting at me was a woman driving a tan Jeep. Jael? Maybe. I couldn't see her. It'll take a while for her to get out of that creek bed. There's not much space to turn around — she might have to back out," she said.

"You actually got quite a bit."

"I'll send Greet an email tonight," Letty said. "We'll have something by tomorrow morning."

"Good," Kaiser said. "I'm feeling kind of spooked out here in the dark. In Iraq, we were the guys in the night. It was the targets who were out driving around."

They continued north without lights, until they could no longer see the glow from the shack. Kaiser stopped, stripped the T-shirts off the taillights, and they turned toward the interstate.

Letty was silent, thinking, then said, "I hardly touched anything in there. I dug through a bunch of boxes, but I restacked them before I left. I got out and locked the door on the way, maybe . . . she saw my flashlight in the window? I was careful to keep it pointed at the floor."

Kaiser thought about that, then said, "Maybe she smelled you?"

"I smell?"

"You use a little perfume," Kaiser said.

"Not very much . . . a dab in the morning."

"But I bet you smell like nothing that's ever been in that fuckin' hut. She might have walked in, and instead of smelling microwave burrito farts, she smelled a flower . . ."

"She thought I was Vic or Terry. That's the names she was calling . . ."

"She might not have known why she thought somebody was there. She sensed it. Sometimes that happens when you go into a place. You don't know *why* you know, but you know there's somebody inside. Or was just inside."

Letty said, "Huh."

"If we go after her, you might switch perfume, 'cause she seems like the aggressive sort," Kaiser said.

THIRTEEN

Letty sent an email to Greet at DHS, got towels from the bathroom, spread them on the carpet, lay down, and cleared her mind. When she'd thoroughly relaxed, she brought a couple of considerations to the surface.

First: she had to pay more attention to Kaiser. He knew things that were valuable to her, but he was not an instinctive teacher. That valuable information remained dormant until something occurred to bring it up.

She hadn't spent any time thinking about how vehicles were seen in the night, but he obviously had, or at least he'd had training that impressed itself on him. Without any heavy thinking, he'd blacked out the Explorer so they could invisibly travel midnight roads without being seen, and he'd anticipated the need in advance.

He knew what might give her away — perfume — when surreptitiously entering a building. Or perhaps it had been sweat, she thought. She'd been restacking those boxes in a hurry.

Kaiser hadn't panicked or argued when she'd told him to drive away from the metal building without her. He hadn't called her when she was being shot at. He could pick locks with silent manual picks. He knew a lot about a lot of guns, she knew a lot about a few.

Second: she'd considered the trip to Oklahoma City and then to Midland as an interesting and even entertaining research opportunity. It was that, and more: tonight, she'd been shot at, and if the woman had been better at stalking, she might have killed Letty, instead of firing wildly up and down the creek bed. *I am not on a lark,* Letty thought. *I'd better start paying attention to that.*

Though she *had* done some things correctly, she thought. They'd solved part of the puzzle: who was stealing (in the bigger picture) a relatively insignificant amount of oil. She hadn't yet learned what was being done with the money that came from the thefts. Whatever it was, it was important enough for at least three killers to have cooperated in executing the Blackburns.

That suggested that the oil thefts would

273

continue. If the killers had simply wanted to seal themselves away from detection, and were willing to give up the thefts, they could have killed Roscoe Winks. As it was, Winks was still out there and could give them up. She would not, she thought, rest easy if she were Winks.

A new thought:

If the Blackburns had been killed because Boxie Blackburn had uncovered exactly what Letty and Kaiser had, then the killers might be coming for them.

She rolled up off the floor, picked up the towels, then got the *ResistUS!* book she'd stolen from the shed. She sprawled across the bed, turned on the bedside reading light, and started paging through it. The book had been written by Jael herself and there was no publication date or publisher listed. The inside pages were inexpensive pulp, the covers flimsy and printed in black-and-white.

She spent an hour with it. Jael, whatever her real name, offered economic theories of the homegrown kind: resentful, zero-sum arguments in which one group can win only if another group loses. In her examples, lower-income working Americans were losing to illegal immigrants.

Jael argued that big corporations — she

274

mentioned chain stores and fast-food outlets specifically — promoted the inflow of immigrants to keep wages low. She argued that when any city or town sheltered enough Spanish-speaking immigrants, the immigrants naturally had to learn English to survive — and at a certain point, all the surviving retail establishments would hire only bilingual employees, and push native English speakers out of those jobs.

Jael wasn't *all* wrong, but she was mostly wrong. She wrote from a ground-level perspective that included only what she could see. She wasn't a bad writer, for a propagandist. For every example, she cited a real-world situation that seemed to support it.

Her solution was simple: seal the border, round up the illegals who were already here, and drive them back across it.

We didn't create the conditions that made them refugees. They should go home and fix whatever their problems are, instead of coming here and making problems for good Americans.

Before she went to bed that night, Letty called Kaiser in his room and said, "I have some instructions for you."

"Do tell."

"Yes. I got shot at. The Blackburns were murdered and Brody Rivers is missing. I expect that they now know about you and me, poking around. So make sure that ugly SIG of yours is loaded and put it on the floor next to your nightstand, on the side away from the door. If somebody comes through the door, you want to roll off the bed and land on top of the gun."

Silence. Then, "Yes. I see. You're doing the same?"

"I already have, with both guns."

Nothing happened that night.

The next morning, Letty was getting dressed and not putting on a dab of her Tom Ford Fucking Fabulous perfume when Greet called from Washington.

"Getting interesting," Greet said, cheerfully. "I've been digging up everything I can find, hitting every source I know of. Terrill T. Duran and Victor Crain were and maybe still are members of a militia that might be called the Land Division or Command, and might have been running around the Big Bend area in Jeeps and pickups with guns. Jael might be its leader. That's gotta be the militia that Rand Low is involved with."

"Lot of 'mights' and 'maybes' there," Letty

said. "But I found a book called *ResistUS!* by this Jael and I've got a pamphlet on the Land Division, so there must be something to it."

"Good! I'll want to see that stuff. They were supposedly chasing down illegal immigrants and holding them for the Border Patrol, although there were rumors that they also killed some of them. That last part may be myth. Not a single person ever came forward with any serious information about killings. Something you should be aware of — they supposedly had the tacit support of some local law enforcement agencies out there. Local sheriffs. Maybe some members of the Border Patrol."

"That sounds bad," Letty said.

"Be circumspect. Just because a guy has a badge doesn't mean he isn't a looney tunes," Greet said. "We got nothing on this Jael, except the name, which has gotta be a nom de guerre. There's a whole story about the original Jael on Wiki if you're curious."

"I've got a photograph, though she's wearing a mask," Letty said. "I'll take a picture with my cell phone and text it to you."

"Terrific. Where'd you get it?"

"At that shack where I got shot at," Letty said.

Pregnant silence. "You know, without a

search warrant . . ."

"The door was open when I got to it," Letty not quite lied. She didn't mention that it had been opened by Kaiser. "We knew a crime was in progress, perpetrated by the residents of the place. Besides, I don't need a warrant. I'm not a law enforcement officer. What about Duran?"

"I'm not sure I agree on your status there," Greet said. "But . . . Duran. We know he was there at the same time as Low. The prison rumor is that Duran was basically an armed robber up and down the mountain west, specializing in suburban banks. Nothing on his politics, if he has any. After Duran got out of Preston Smith — Low was already out — two unknown men robbed a bank in Lawton, Oklahoma, and got away with $39,000. In terms of body build and height, could have been Low and Duran. Ski masks over sunglasses, rubber gloves. They used a stolen car that was later found burning in a field outside Lawton. Very nicely done. Efficient. No DNA or prints. Nobody hurt, clean getaway."

"So if that was them, they might not be total dumbasses," Letty said.

"Not dumb, but probably crazy. I personally prefer dumb."

"How about arrest warrants?"

"There's a warrant out for Low, for the parole violation. You knew that. Nothing current for Duran or Crain. You've got those mugshots of Sawyer and Crain. I'll send one of Duran."

"Thanks. They're the ones stealing the oil. Duran and Crain. Kaiser and I more or less witnessed it, though we couldn't swear that they actually took any oil. We could probably set it up so the FBI could bag them."

"You don't think you scared them off last night?"

"I doubt it," Letty said. "I doubt they can even be sure that there was somebody out there. They didn't actually see me. They never saw us any other place, where they were stealing the oil or unloading it."

"Okay. I'll talk to the boss, and if he approves, I'll go to our FBI liaison," Greet said. "Tell them that we don't want to talk to local law yet. See what they say."

"Call me," Letty said. "We're going to check Terry Duran's address. Maybe we'll spot Crain there."

"Careful."

When she was ready to go, Letty called Kaiser and suggested that they hit the McDonald's for breakfast. "Bacon, egg, and cheese biscuit, mmm-mmm."

"My heart's already clogging up, hearing that," Kaiser said. "But I guess this job comes with sacrifices."

"I'm going to call Vee Wright and Senator Colles and I want you to hear the calls," Letty said. "We can do that from the car."

"Am I being informed, or implicated?" Kaiser asked.

"Take your pick, John."

In the car, Letty called Vee Wright, who was awake in his Phoenix hospital room. He was, he said, in moderate pain. "They got me out of bed and walking around. Couple of pills and I should be good to go."

"That's great. Listen, we might have found your oil thieves . . . I'm going to text you a photograph of some pipes, right . . . now." She pushed a button on her cell phone.

She told Wright about tracking the tanker truck and about the scene at what she thought was a pipeline, about the men loading what looked like a scuba-diving tank into the truck.

Wright said, "I got your picture . . . All right, all right. That might explain some things . . . like a scuba tank? Did you see any fixtures on it?"

"We couldn't see it very well — it was

280

dark, and they were pulling a bag over it, but there was something sticking out of one end."

"I think what they did was built themselves a pig."

Pipelines, he said, had a variety of internal monitoring and maintenance jobs done by "pigs," which were metal or plastic tanks that were dropped into pipelines and pushed along by the oil inside the pipes. They were also used to separate batches of oil from different companies.

"You put a pig in a pipeline through a launcher. The launcher inserts the pig into a stream of oil that pushes it along. I suspect they made themselves a pig that somehow gets into the stream and then maybe . . . expands? Or extrudes some feetlike things that cause the pig to jam in the line? The oil would back up through the launcher and you could pump it out to your truck. Interesting. That would explain why they steal it from a bunch of different companies. They wouldn't know which batch of oil they're getting."

"You were right about Winks. That's where they're unloading it," Letty said.

"All right. Good. Let's get the FBI on it, right quick . . ."

"Not too quick, or we'll miss some of

these guys," Letty said. "The other thing is, we don't know if they killed the Blackburns. We've got work to do before we can establish that, even as a probability." And she lied a bit: "Our DHS people are coordinating with the FBI right now. We could have something before you're back in your office. We want to make sure we get them all, and we get them for the murders."

"Excellent work. Excellent," Wright said. "I'm willing to let them steal the oil for a little while, anyway, if we can hang them on the murders. You go ahead and do that."

Colles was not in his office, but a secretary who knew Letty said he would call back that afternoon. "There's an interagency cluster-fuck going on about museum construction on the Mall. He's in the middle of it."

At the McDonald's, Letty summarized what they'd figured out. "We've got three guys we're pretty sure of: Duran, Crain, and Max Sawyer. They all live too close together in Monahans not to be linked up. Greet says Duran is in this Land Division and I found that militia stuff in Crain's moving boxes. Any of them could point us at Low and Jael, if we had a way to convince them to do that."

"That's not really us, that kind of action, squeezing people," Kaiser said. He lifted up the top of his biscuit, looked at the bacon below it, frowned, put the biscuit back together, and took a bite. He winced, swallowed, and asked, "Why would they even believe us?"

"That's a problem," Letty conceded. "Something wrong with that sandwich?"

"Yeah, I'm probably gonna eat about four of them," Kaiser said. "Say what you like about McDonald's, they can make a sandwich . . . and, not to change the subject, it might be time to call in the local cops."

"We can't be sure of them. Probably okay, but possibly not: that's what Greet told me," Letty said. "I've got a feeling that what we need to do will be boring: we need to pick one of these guys and watch him. See who he's talking to."

"Greet could help with that — DHS has all kinds of cybersecurity and intelligence units; one of them should be able to get Duran's cell phones and see who he's talking to."

"Good. I gotta learn about DHS resources."

Kaiser poked a finger at Letty. "If Duran's got any brains, he'll have a burner phone, but the intelligence guys can get at that if

283

they know where he lives, and if he makes calls from that location."

"I've got his address. He's on the other side of Monahans from Sawyer's place."

They called Greet from the car, and she said she'd make inquiries about identifying cell phones calling from a particular location, but without the phone number. "I've never done that, but I think we can. There might be a price on it — I don't know. If we have to rent an airplane or send out special equipment. If they're at all security-aware, they're probably calling from one unidentified burner to another."

She said she would get back when she'd learned something.

The outdoor temperature had turned up several notches by the time they got to Monahans. Letty was driving as they cruised Max Sawyer's and Victor Crain's houses, and both seemed unoccupied, inert. Sawyer's Jeep was gone.

They drove across town, passing through a much richer area of sprawling brick ramblers, and then back into a more run-down neighborhood. At Duran's address, they found the two pickups they'd seen the night before, along with a tan Jeep that was newer and a higher trim level than Sawyer's.

There was no way to know for sure, but the Jeep might have been the one driven by the woman who'd shot at Letty. The Jeep was pulled into Duran's yard, and was sitting sideways to the street.

"We need the Jeep's plates, and we're not going to get them with a cell phone," Letty said. "Why don't we have a decent camera with a telephoto lens?"

"We don't need an Axel Adams photo, all we need is the tag number," Kaiser said. They were sitting at a stop sign, looking down the block at Crain's house. "I'm rolling down my window. Drive on past, don't slow down at all. I'll keep my head below the window, put my phone on video, nothing sticking up but the phone."

"Ansel," Letty said.

"What?"

"Ansel Adams."

"No, I'm talking about the other guy. Axel Adams, from over in Lafourche Parish."

Letty said, "Oh."

Kaiser laughed and said, "Gotcha."

Letty drove by the house and, at the end of the block, turned a corner and pulled over into the shade of a tree. "You get it?" she asked.

Kaiser was peering at his phone: "No.

Can't see it, the way the Jeep's parked. We really need to know who she is . . . if it's Jael. She was quick to jump you with that gun last night. If that's actually her."

"It's her, she had that Jeep," Letty said, letting a little irritation show.

"You don't know that one hundred per-cent."

"I *feel* it," Letty said. "Not only is it her, that gang killed the Blackburns and would be perfectly happy to kill us. This is about more than stolen oil."

"Remember what about six people have said — it's only a little oil to the oil compa-nies, but it's a hell of a lot of money for anyone else," Kaiser said. "Worth killing for."

"All right, all right," Letty said. "Let's find a place where we can watch them."

They found a spot on the opposite side of the block where they could see the cluster of vehicles by looking between houses. They'd been there for twenty minutes when a police cruiser pulled up behind them, lights flashing, and a cop got out.

Kaiser said, "Ah, shit. Busted."

Letty rolled down the driver's-side win-dow, took her ID case from a hip pocket, and held it open outside the window, where

286

the cop could see what would appear to be a badge case. The cop came cautiously up, took the case, looked at it, and handed it back.

"We had a call from a neighbor," the cop said.

"If you want somebody to verify our investigation, you could call Casey Pugh," Letty said. "We were here a couple days ago, when the dog bit the Midland investigator."

"I heard about the dog," the cop said. "You got something going on right this minute?"

Letty said, "Yes, unless our targets see a cop car with flashing lights. Which would make it harder to run our surveillance."

"Sorry. I'll move on. I'll call that neighbor . . ."

"Is the neighbor on this block? I'd hate to have it turn out to be the people we're watching," Kaiser said.

"Yes, it's . . ." The cop gestured to a house across the street. Letty and Kaiser looked and saw a curtain move.

"Okay. Talk to Casey," Letty said.

The cop went on his way and Kaiser said, "Hope they didn't see that."

"No help for it," Letty said. "Can't blame the cop."

They sat for another hour, watching the

needle slowly drop on the gas gauge, and then got movement. A man that Letty recognized as Duran came out of the house, followed by Crain, and they both got in Crain's truck. An athletic woman and an unknown man — not Low — got into the Jeep. They did U-turns on the street and headed toward the interstate.

"That woman . . ." Letty said.

"Yeah."

"Right body shape, judging from the photo in the *ResistUS!* book."

"That's something . . . and, hey, stay back," Kaiser said. "The interstate is a pipe, once they're in it. We don't have to be on their bumpers."

Letty said nothing, and a moment later, Kaiser said, "I may have mentioned that before."

"Yes. You have," Letty said.

"Getting snippy."

"John . . ."

They stayed close enough to see the two vehicles, moving as a loose convoy, turn south on I-20. Maybe going to the shack, or the arroyo with the hidden truck? With Letty and Kaiser a mile and a half back, they watched as the convoy went through Pecos and Toyah and a couple other small towns, and then another fifty miles onto I-10, the Jeep leading.

"Goddamn it, we could pass them and get the Jeep's plate, but we'd have to pass Crain first, and he saw this truck in his alley," Letty said.

"Gonna have to do something. If they head west, like they're going to El Paso, we're gonna need a gas stop," Kaiser said. He leaned over toward Letty, looking at the gas gauge. "We got maybe another eighty or hundred miles."

The landscape got rougher and drier as they went farther south, mountains ahead, plains fading behind them; all of it was desert. Shortly after merging onto I-10, and with Kaiser and Letty still undecided about what to do, the convoy got off at a local highway, turned left under the interstate, and continued south.

"Way back, now," Kaiser said. "Way back. Nobody else out here . . ."

Letty stayed way back, barely in touch, but close enough to see the two vehicles slow and turn off the highway on a dirt track that went east toward a range of low mountains.

"Now what?" Letty asked.

Kaiser was peering at a satellite image on his iPad. "That road goes nowhere. It's a dead end, up in the mountains. There's a whole snarl of tracks up there. No sign of a house or water or anything, it's like something for off-roaders, a recreational trail."

"Follow?"

"Well, they're going over a big hump, and then straight until they get into that snarl. Once they go over the hump, they won't be able to see us coming. Of course, if they're *luring* us up there . . . it's a great place for an ambush."

They were coming to the turnoff. "Talk to me," Letty said.

Kaiser had his binoculars out. "They're over the hump. I can still see some dust . . . If we follow them, take it slow. We don't want to kick up a cloud behind us."

"Fuck it," Letty said. She took the turn.

Kaiser looked through the binoculars for another minute, then said, "I don't see anything moving. But . . ." He unbuckled his seat belt, knelt on the seat, and fished the shotgun case off the floor in the backseat. Turned around again, extracted the shotgun from its case, slapped in a load of five slug rounds, and put the rest of the magazines on the floor between his feet.

Letty said, "Now I wish I had my AR-10 with me."

Kaiser: "Yeah, that'd be the one to have.

Scoped?"

"Leupold variable. My dad took me to a junkyard in the countryside north of Saint Paul and we spent some time shooting at junked cars, to see what would happen," Letty said. "The .308s went through everything, like the car doors were tissue paper."

"Hunting rounds?"

"No, Dad had some steel core stuff he got somewhere," Letty said. "Might even have been AP."

"Which is illegal in a lot of places," Kaiser said.

"I was with a cop."

Three-quarters of a mile off the highway, the track pitched up onto what Kaiser said was the hump. "Don't go over it . . . When it starts to flatten, let me out," Kaiser said.

They went on for another twenty seconds, then Kaiser got out and jogged ahead with the shotgun. As Letty watched, he got to the top of the slope, knelt, glassed the road ahead, then jogged back. "They're around a turn up ahead, but I don't know how much farther they went. It's a half-mile or more to the snarl and the dead end. If we want to watch, we need to hide the truck and walk in."

"Can you see her plates?"

"Nope. She's sideways again," Kaiser said.
"Miserable bitch."
"You said it, not me."

Letty turned the Explorer around and they coasted back the way they came, until Kaiser said, "Probably could get in there . . ."

He pointed at a crack in the rugged rock, filled with dried weeds. Tire tracks from what must have been an off-road vehicle were barely visible in the brush.

"Avis is gonna kick our asses," Letty said, as she made the turn and drove through the scratchy brush. The new trail curved into the mountain, and she stopped as soon as they were out of sight of the main track. They got out, Letty put on her straw hat and got two warm bottles of water from the floor and put them in her pack, next to the Staccato case.

Kaiser was walking out toward the main track, kicking the occasional clump of weeds back to an upright position. At the trail they stopped to listen, then started up the hill. They were approaching the crest when . . .

Boom!

Or not quite a boom. More like a hollow *crump!*

Kaiser froze, then said, "Holy shit. Our

boys got themselves some C-4, or something like it. Maybe . . . dynamite. Do they still make dynamite?"

"I dunno. Let's go see," Letty said. "They're around that rock up ahead, if we run . . ."

"If it was just a test, they could be coming out . . ."

"So we run faster."

They ran as fast as they could, trying to stay off the loose dirt, into the harder tire tracks where their footprints couldn't be seen. As they approached a spot where the road turned, they slowed and eased up to a house-sized boulder that defined the turn, and peeked around it.

The two vehicles were parked near a wide eroded crevice that cut toward the top of the mountains. The three men and the woman were standing behind the Jeep, talking. The unknown male, Letty thought, might be explaining something.

Letty got out her phone and took a half-dozen photos at the greatest possible enlargement, and Kaiser whispered, "Still gonna be about the size of ants."

"Next time we do this, we bring a decent camera with a telephoto lens," Letty whispered back.

After another minute of talk, the four

people trudged into the crevice and disappeared. The unknown man was carrying an olive drab tool bag. When they reemerged, the woman and one of the men were looking at their watches. Then they all turned to the crevice, and *crump!*

Louder this time. "They're burying the charge," Kaiser whispered. "You notice there are no wires, no cell phones in their hands . . . the charge was on a timer."

The four walked back into the crevice, were out of sight for four or five minutes. When they walked back out, Crain and Duran were carrying what might have been short lengths of railroad ties, but a reddish color, rather than brown. They dropped whatever they were in the back of Crain's truck with a metallic *clang*. They talked for a moment, then went to their vehicles.

"Let's hide," Kaiser said. "Like, right now."

A jumble of broken rock and boulders rose behind them, and they found a spot where they could sit down and not be seen. They heard the vehicles go by, and when the truck noises had faded, climbed out from behind the rock.

"We need to see what they were blowing up," Kaiser said. They walked to the crevice, then up inside it, and found a narrow crack in a bluff that showed burn signs. "It's C-4," Kaiser said. "Smell it? And here . . ." He picked up a piece of green plastic wrapper from the ground. "It's military stuff — at least, this is the way the military stuff is wrapped."

He showed Letty a piece of green cellophane wrapper with yellow lettering.

Letty was kneeling next to the crevice, saw something deep inside that didn't look like rock. She reached in and pulled it out, a sharp-edged scrap of heavy metal, c-shaped, the size of her hand from the heel to her fingertips.

Kaiser took it and turned it in his hand and said, "Oh . . . Good Lord. You see any more of this in there?"

Letty used her phone as a flashlight, saw one more piece of metal, pulled it out and handed it to him.

"You know what this is?" Kaiser asked.

"No, but I believe you do. And I don't like the look on your face."

"It's a piece of I-beam," Kaiser said. "You know, like the beams that hold up buildings? Those two pieces they loaded into Crain's truck — that used to be three feet of I-beam and they used the C-4 to cut it in half."

"A test and a demonstration," Letty said.

"We need to back out of here. A crime scene crew might find identifiable fragments of . . . whatever."

"If we hurry, we might be able to see where they're going . . ."

They jogged back to the Explorer, but by the time they got there, the convoy had made the turn at the highway and was nearly to the interstate.

"Gonna lose them," Letty said.

"Now we know what kind of trouble we're talking about," Kaiser said, his voice as sober as she'd ever heard it. "This is bad shit, Letty. This isn't for us anymore. Not running on our own. We need to bring in the FBI and the ATF. A whole team. Maybe a SWAT squad."

"You're right. You drive," Letty said. "I need to talk to Colles and Greet on the way back. Get this rodeo started."

FOURTEEN

Hawkes and a man named Coffey drove west toward El Paso, while Duran and Crain went back north toward Monahans. On I-10, driving into the sun, Hawkes asked Coffey how long it would take to get the C-4.

Coffey said, "I need to set up an alibi and I didn't want to do that until I knew you had the money."

"There's two envelopes in the center console," Hawkes said. "Take the top one, count it, then put it back. Count the second one, put it in your pocket."

Coffey did that, smiled, put the second envelope in his leg pocket and said, "Pleasure doing business with you. How late do you stay up at night?"

"As late as I have to."

"I'll knock on your door at ten o'clock, sharp. Have the first envelope there. If I can't get it tonight, I'll call on your burner phone. If I don't show up and don't call, I'll be in the stockade."

"I don't want to hear that," Hawkes said.

"Yeah, well, you get caught stealing C-4 in the Army, you're shit outta luck," Coffey said. "Not only prison, I'd get a dishonorable, lose sixteen years of good time and my pension. So: I won't get caught. Won't even take a chance of it."

"I understand that," she said. "Where'd you get that stuff we set off today? Why didn't you take it all then?"

"Because it would be missed," Coffey said. "The stuff we set off today, the Army thinks was set off during training last year. I picked it up then. Never hurts to have a little C-4 around."

"Okay."

"All said and done, I'll be at your garage door at ten o'clock. You should erase my demo from your cell phone," Coffey said. "If you get caught, they might find a way to link it to me."

"All it shows is your hands," Hawkes said.

"That might be enough. Who knows? So erase it after you've run through it enough. A goddamn three-year-old could do it."

"I'll look at it a couple more times, then get rid of it," she agreed.

Hawkes dropped Sergeant First Class

George Coffey at a strip mall where he'd left his car, across Highway 54 from the Cassidy Gate at Fort Bliss, then drove home. She and Coffey had worked over the plan to steal the C-4 a half-dozen times and she could see no fault in it. The Army checked the explosive dump only about once a month, so they should be long gone before the Army even knew the stuff was missing — a hundred pounds of plastic explosive, plus detonators and digital timers.

In the very cold come-to-Jesus talk they'd had before the deal was made, Coffey had asked, "Why the extra detonators and timers? You want thirty, that's way more than you'll need."

"Because after you deliver, we're going to pick out detonators at random, and timers at random, and a chunk of C-4, take it out in the desert, and we're going to set them off ourselves. If they don't work, we're gonna call off the attack and then three of our people will come looking for you. They'll kill you. They've killed before — one was an Army sniper — and they'll put you down. You screw us on anything, C-4, detonators, timers, we'll kill you. You turn us in, we'll kill you."

"Go easy, there," Coffey said. "There's no

way the Army can trace me on this if they don't catch me right in the dump. They won't do that. I got that all figured out and I'm not exactly a virgin. After your attack, I'm sure as shit not gonna talk to anyone about it."

"Just sayin' how it is," Hawkes had said.

Now the plan was rolling, and Coffey had the first hundred thousand dollars in his pocket. Whether or not he got the additional hundred and fifty thousand remained to be seen. The handover could be delicate, but from the research they'd done on Coffey, he appeared to be an experienced black-marketeer of government supplies and equipment.

At home, Hawkes made a chicken sandwich and spent a half-hour sitting in the bathtub, staring up at the bubbled paint on the ceiling. Everything in the rented house had been painted or repaired with the cheapest possible materials, but that wasn't a huge problem because she'd never lived in anything much better and because she'd soon be gone.

She toweled off and was putting on shorts and a T-shirt when R.J., the cop from Odessa, called. "I spent some time watching that DHS guy today, after my shift. They went to a McDonald's and then drove down to Monahans and parked down there. I couldn't tell what they were doing, and I couldn't hang too close or they would have spotted me. After a while they headed south down I-20 and I had to break off. I lost them."

"No! What time was this? Where were they parked in Monahans?"

R.J. didn't know the exact street, but said it was on the south side of town. The time, Hawkes realized, fit the time she was there with Duran, Crain, and Coffey. Had they been tracked down I-20? Were they being watched? Was Crain's house bugged? They'd seen no sign of a tail, and Duran said he'd watched for one.

"Listen, is there any way you can get up to their hotel right now? See if they're there?"

"I guess. My shift starts in two hours, I haven't eaten . . ."

"R.J.! This is critical. I was in Monahans . . ."

She told him the story, and when she finished, he said, "I'm walking out to my car right now. I'll be up there in twenty minutes. I'll call you."

As she waited for the cop to call back,

Hawkes went over the day — the meeting at Crain's place, the C-4 demo, the return to El Paso. There'd been no sign of being tracked. At Crain's, halfway through the meeting, she'd seen a cop car a block away, lights flashing, probably a traffic stop, nothing to do with them.

There'd been no sign of being tracked when they were up the mountain checking out the C-4 sample, and that should have been pretty obvious. She hadn't been home for more than an hour when R.J. called, so if the DHS people were back at their hotel, there'd be no way they could have tracked her to El Paso.

"We're too close, we're too close," she said aloud.

Then R.J. called back. "They're at the hotel. Their car is there."

"Man! That's like you lifted a boulder off my back."

"Yes. Still, I don't know where they went down I-20 . . ."

"Maybe . . . I dunno. At least they're not on top of me."

"If you're really under heavy surveillance, there'd be more than one set of watchers. But that's not the feeling I've gotten from talking to the guys up at Midland. After Dan Tanner got hurt, the murder investigation was taken over by another guy and I talked to him about the case. He said the DHS guys signed their statements and never came back."

"I hope you were careful about talking to the cop."

"Oh, sure. His old lady runs a bar up there, and I knew he usually goes there at night. I went up there and played it like I was just bumping into him and was interested because of Dan Tanner getting bit by that dog."

"Okay. Okay, that's good. If anything comes up . . ."

"I can't watch them full-time. You really ought to have somebody who can."

"Let me think about that," Hawkes said.

She didn't have to think about it, because if Coffey came through that night with the C-4, she'd freeze everybody in place, and then . . . bang!

Max Sawyer arrived at nine o'clock, got out of his Jeep, looked up and down the street, moved his AR-15, wrapped in a blanket to obscure its outline, into the garage. "You hear from Coffey?"

"Not yet. He's supposed to show up at ten o'clock if he gets the stuff without a problem, or call if there is a problem."

"You gonna pay him the rest?"

"If he's got the stuff. But we might have another problem." Hawkes told him about the DHS people showing up in Monahans at the same time she was there.

"You know what? R.J. says he doesn't know exactly what they were watching. I bet they were watching my place. But I didn't go anywhere."

"Then why did they go south on I-20? Unless . . ."

"What?"

Hawkes said, "I was out at the shed a couple nights ago and thought maybe somebody had been in there and was sneaking out the back when I got there. I really . . . felt somebody. I even fired off some shots down the creek bed, with Terry's AR, but I never saw anybody. I thought maybe I was imagining things. I sorta thought it might be a woman and I guess this DHS guy has got a woman assistant . . ."

"I don't think she's his assistant. I think she might be running the show," Sawyer said. "She's mean as a snake. Knows a lot about guns. Pulled this little Sig nine on me after that cop got bit by Rooter. When things cooled down, I asked her if she'd have shot me. She said 'yes.' Something about her . . . I believed her."

"If it was her, then they know about the tanker," Hawkes said. "They might have followed it, they might know about Winks."

"Ah, boy."

"So I need to warn Terry and Vic off," Hawkes said.

"You want me to take care of Winks?" Sawyer asked.

"Think you can?"

"Sure. Happy to do it, and we'll have to do it sometime, anyway," Sawyer said. "I'll tell him we need to meet this morning, before the next delivery. Nothing much out there at three o'clock in the morning. Good spot for me to take him out."

"Consider the possibility," Hawkes said. "We're so close . . . You better move your Jeep around the corner, where Coffee won't see it . . . And hey, I'm really sorry about Rooter, him getting shot. I liked that dog."

"Me, too. I'll fix Tanner's clock someday, when enough time has passed."

Coffey pulled up in front of Hawkes's house at ten minutes after ten o'clock. Hawkes had resisted calling him, but had started to sweat. When she saw him through the door window, backing into the driveway, she muttered, "About time," and called to Sawyer, in the garage, "He's here."

She went out the front door, to the drive-way, as Coffey got out of the truck.

"How'd it go?" she asked. Nice night, cool now, bright stars.

"Smooth as a baby's butt," he said. "I want the other envelope."

"And I want to see the stuff. Let's get it into the garage. You're late."

"Lift the garage door up," Coffey said. He yanked open the tailgate on his truck, and Hawkes could see cardboard boxes inside.

She nodded, pulled the garage door up. Sawyer was standing there with his rifle.

"What's *he* all about?" Coffey asked.

"We've got a hundred and fifty thousand dollars in cash, and we didn't want you robbing us," Hawkes said. "Maybe you noticed, we don't entirely trust you."

"Yeah, I noticed."

"So let's see the stuff."

"Okay, but we've got to hurry," Coffey said. He grabbed a box and carried it into the garage, where he said to Hawkes, "Grab those small boxes, they're not so heavy."

There were five heavy boxes. Sawyer didn't help unload, but stood by with his rifle. Even so, the truck was empty in three or four minutes, and they pulled down the garage door with the three of them inside.

"Gotta hurry now, gotta hurry," Coffey

said. He used a pocketknife to cut the tape on the top of the four heavy boxes, and began lifting out bricks of C-4. "The smaller boxes are the timers and the detonators. You use them like I showed you, like you made those videos with your phone. It's all here and that's all I got to say."

He looked at his watch. "Time's about up. Gimme the money."

"What are you talking about?" Hawkes said. "Why the rush?"

"Because you got the guy with the gun here. I thought you might decide there wouldn't be any more money . . ."

"And . . ."

"I snuck into your yard fifteen minutes ago and buried a brick of C-4 next to your house and it's going to go off in . . . eight minutes. There'll be a hundred cops here five minutes later. If you shoot me, or don't give me the money, that brick is gonna blow the ass off this house, and probably the neighbor's," Coffey said. "If the shock wave is strong enough, it could detonate this stuff inside here and then the whole block will go up. So . . . I gotta run . . . When I get in my car, I'll call you and tell you exactly how to find the C-4 and you can pull the detonator and the timer. Not hard to find."

"You motherfucker," Sawyer said, pointing the rifle at Coffey's chest.

"Gimme the money," Coffey said to Hawkes.

"How do we know you'll call?"

"Because if I didn't, the brick will blow and the cops will come and you'll probably tell them who sold you the stuff . . . I sure as shit don't want that to happen, but it won't make any difference to me if gunboy shoots me."

Hawkes shook her head, then said to Sawyer, "Lift up the door."

She ran inside, got the manila envelope off the kitchen counter, ran back out, and thrust it at Coffey. "Maybe you'd like to count it later?"

Coffey thumbed the money in the envelope, then hurried out to his truck. He got in, leaned his head out the window toward Hawkes and said, "Fuck a phone call. The brick is right at the back corner of the garage. There's a white plastic poker chip sitting on top of it so you can see it. Pull the detonator, yank the timer off like I showed you. You got . . ." He looked at his watch. "About five minutes."

They found the poker chip in one minute and pulled the detonator and then the timer. Coffey hadn't been bluffing; the time showed 3:45 when they killed it. Hawkes began to laugh: "Didn't see that coming. He's a smart guy, to set us up like that."

"I'm not laughing," Sawyer said. "Scared the shit out of me."

"Yeah, well . . . Let's go talk about Roscoe Winks."

Sawyer said, "I gotta move if I'm going to get there tonight. One good thing — I was at Ironsides until an hour ago, so I got a built-in alibi. Bartender can put me here in El Paso."

"You might like this killing thing too much," Hawkes said.

"Does give me a little woody," Sawyer said. And, "Hey, that was a joke."

"But neither one of us is laughing," Hawkes said. "You better get going."

Inside, it occurred to her that Sawyer had been asking her permission; and once again, she'd nodded.

FIFTEEN

Letty and Kaiser talked to Billy Greet at DHS, as they were driving back toward Midland. Greet was appalled to hear about the explosives.

"My God, they could be planning something like Oklahoma City. Or worse, if they were learning how to cut I-beams. They could be planning to bring down a whole building."

"That's why we need the FBI on this, and ATF," Letty said. "We probably need an FBI SWAT team and an ATF explosives team, in case, you know . . ."

"Worst-case scenario," Greet said. "Listen, you know what time it is here?"

"Six?"

"Yes. People are gone. I'll start raising hell, but it's hard to get anything done at dinnertime. It's hard to get people to answer their phones."

"I don't know what to say. That's your territory," Letty said.

Greet: "The other thing is, they're still apparently stealing and selling the oil to support their militia and whatever they're planning to do, right?"

Kaiser said, "Right. That's what we think."

"They can't have gotten paid yet for the oil you saw them stealing," Greet said. "It might not even have been delivered to wherever this Winks guy takes it. And they gotta know we'll be all over them if they pull off this attack . . ."

"So if they're still stealing, they're probably not ready to pull the trigger yet," Letty said. "That's good, Billy. That hadn't occurred to me."

"It's when they stop the oil that we've got to be worried," Greet said. "I'll get things going here tonight, but I can tell you from past experience, we're not going to get much done until day after tomorrow at the earliest. Tomorrow there'll be a bunch of meetings, the FBI guy there in Midland will probably want to talk to you . . ."

"We'll talk to him," Letty said. "They've got the C-4 now, John is familiar with the stuff from the Army, and he says that's what it is. I agree about the oil deliveries, but I think they're not far away from whatever they're planning. Probably ought to get a surveillance team down here."

"I'll get it going," Greet said.

When Greet was off the phone, Kaiser asked, "You want to know what I think?"

"Probably the same thing I think," Letty said. "Let's get dinner, get some bottles of water and the tent, and head out to Winks's. See if they're still delivering. Maybe smuggle some pillows out of the motel, get some sleep while we're out there."

"That's exactly what I think," Kaiser said. "Though, you know, in Delta we didn't use pillows. We used rocks."

"Of course you did," Letty said. "I'll take a pillow, we'll see if we can pick up a rock for you at Costco. Or you could make do with a concrete block."

They got a recommendation for an Italian restaurant from the desk clerk at the hotel, smuggled a couple of pillows out to the car, ate dinner, and, as it was getting dark, headed toward Winks's property.

"There's a spot a half-mile or so out where I can hide the car," Kaiser said. "Not where I hid the first night out. The first night, I couldn't come out behind them. That won't be a problem tonight."

They got to Winks's in full dark, cruised it once — the building was dark — then drove a long rectangle and came out, as Kaiser said, a couple hundred yards off the road and perhaps a half mile from Winks's, with the car parked behind a pumpjack. Kaiser gathered up the tent and pillows, and asked, "Shotgun?"

"Yes."

"You carry it, then," Kaiser said. "I got these fuckin' pillows."

They loaded the shotgun with buckshot, then walked slowly in the starlight along the road, talking quietly until they got close to Winks's. There, they crossed the fence and Letty led the way farther into the field than she'd been the first night, so they were looking down the length of the driveway and could see both the area where the oil truck unloaded into the oil tanks and the front of the building.

They set the tent up on a flat spot in another patch of weeds, as Letty did the first night, put down the pillows, and crawled inside, tight, shoulder to shoulder. "Not bad," Kaiser said. "Unless we have to get out of here in a hurry."

"If we do, I'll slide out first, being skinnier," Letty said. "If you've got to, don't worry about the tent. This net won't slow down your buckshot."

They settled in, watched the building in

the bare illumination of the pole light, then Kaiser yawned and asked, "You want to watch first? I could sleep awhile."

"Sleep," Letty said. "I'm wide awake."

"Don't let me go more than three hours," Kaiser said. "You need downtime, too."

Letty spent the three hours listening to music with her iPhone AirPods, and reading her phone inside her sweatshirt. At one o'clock, she woke Kaiser: "Nothing."

"I got it, you sleep," he said. He yawned again. "I actually feel pretty good."

Letty took a while to doze off, finally locked into a memory of a fishing trip with her parents to the north woods of Wisconsin, and slept. She had no idea how long she'd been down when Kaiser nudged her hard, and then, in the next instant, breathed, "Shhh."

She'd been sleeping on her back, head on the motel pillow. She opened her eyes, carefully rolled over in place, feeling the tension in Kaiser's shoulder as he looked out through the mesh and the weeds. A pickup had turned down into the parking lot. The driver parked at the front door to the building. An older man got out of the cab, thin, gray hair to his shoulders.

"Winks," Letty whispered. She'd seen photos of him, but not the man.

"Think so."

Winks stretched, dug in the pocket of his jeans for keys, unlocked the door, went inside. Lights came on and Winks pulled the door shut.

"What time is it?" Letty asked.

"Ten after three," Kaiser said. "You've been sleeping like a log for two hours."

They watched for twenty minutes, occasionally saw a flash of Winks's red shirt through the front window. He appeared to be working at a desk, standing up, sitting down, out of sight. Twice, he stood and looked out through the window, toward the road, then disappeared again.

"He's waiting for someone," Letty suggested.

"Could be. Odd time to be doing paperwork. Maybe he wants to be here for a delivery?"

Then they saw headlights approaching from the south, slowing, and a tan Jeep turned in under the pole light.

"That's Sawyer," Letty said.

Winks stood up and looked out the window as Sawyer got out of the Jeep and walked toward the door. Winks opened it from the inside.

Kaiser: "Did Sawyer pull a gun?"

"I think he did," Letty said. "Yo, man, you

think . . ."

Sawyer walked through the open door and they heard a voice, uncertain which man, and then . . .

Crack!

"He fuckin' shot him," Kaiser said. He sounded astonished.

Letty already had her pack open. She pulled out the Staccato case, unzipped it, took out the gun, and jacked a round into the chamber.

Kaiser: "Wait!"

"No. I'm going."

She slid out the back of the tent, and Kaiser pushed his way after her, keeping the shotgun pointed at the building's front door. Letty moved to her right, until the nearest oil tank was between her and the front door, and then ran lightly toward it, Kaiser a step behind her. Letty looked around the oil tank, then ran on to the next one, watching the door.

As she got to the tank, the lights in the building went out and Sawyer stepped outside, pulling the door shut behind him, moving toward his truck.

Letty shouted, "Stop there! Get on the ground! Get on the ground or I'll kill you."

Sawyer froze, then said, "That you, girlie? Letty?"

"Get on the ground. I'm looking at your forehead with my red dot."

"Don't shoot, I'm going down . . ." Sawyer slowly knelt, then flattened out in the dirt.

"Take your gun out, don't point it, push it away from you. Push it over there . . . If you fuckin' try anything, I'll kill you."

"Like I said, you're a mean little bitch. The gun's on my back . . ."

"I know. Roll up and take it with your off hand and push it . . ."

Kaiser came up beside her with the shotgun as Sawyer rolled up on his side, reached to his back with his left hand, caught his pistol with his fingertips, and tossed it off to his left. "That's the second time you made me throw a good gun down in the dirt."

Letty asked, "You kill Winks?"

Without thinking, she stepped to her left, bumping Kaiser, and Kaiser said, "No," and swung the shotgun to his left, and at that instant, Sawyer pulled a second pistol with his good hand and Kaiser said "Shit!" or something like that, and pushed Letty and followed her down behind the oil tank as Sawyer fired twice at them, the slugs whanging off the oil tank.

Letty did a quick peek and he fired again, and she switched the Staccato to her left hand, did another quick peek at Sawyer, who'd scrambled to his feet, and she shot him, low, she thought, and he screamed and went down and she shot him again as he was rolling under his Jeep and he turned and fired half a magazine off the side of the oil tank.

Kaiser grabbed Letty by the arm, jerked her away from the edge of the tank, stepped sideways and fired three rounds under the Jeep.

"That had to . . ."

"I don't think . . ."

Sawyer, from behind the Jeep, shouted, "You a pussy? C'mon out and we'll settle it . . . We'll both come out and we'll settle it head-to-head, gunslinger." He laughed, and the laugh sounded like a scream.

Letty looked up at Kaiser, who shrugged and whispered, "What the fuck?"

"All right, I'm stepping out now," Letty cried. "Let's see what you got, cowboy."

One second later, Sawyer popped up at the back of his Jeep, his gun hand aimed where Letty should have been. Nothing of Letty protruded from behind the oil tank except her left eye and left hand and she shot Sawyer in the forehead.

"Moron," she said, as he went down. "Watched way too much TV."

"That it?" Kaiser asked.

Seconds passed, shuffling their feet, peeking around the tank. With no movement, Kaiser whispered, "I've got buckshot loaded, I'm going to step around the next tank where I can see behind the Jeep, you stay here and keep focused on the hood . . ."

"I hit him above his right eye," Letty said. "He's gone."

Kaiser said, "Okay, but you stay here."

He went to his right, around the back of the Jeep, peeked to the side. "He's . . . down."

"I'll go around the front," Letty said. She followed the muzzle of the Staccato around the front of the Jeep. Sawyer was crumbled on the ground, faceup, eyes open, a massive wound above his right eye, what might have been a smile on his face.

"He's gone," Letty said.

"Don't ever go walking into me again," Kaiser said. "And don't ever say somebody's 'gone' until you stick your finger in the bullet hole. A lot of fuckin' guys were killed by men they knew were dead."

"Sorry."

Kaiser looked up at the pole light, then back at Sawyer. "Gotta check Winks. I mean really — this is . . ."

They found the old man in his office chair, slumped to one side, a single bullet wound in the heart.

"Sawyer shot him quick to minimize the time he was inside," Letty said. "Cuts down on the biologics you might be leaving behind."

She took her cell phone from her pocket, punched in Billy Greet's personal number in Washington. Greet answered on the third ring and groaned. "You know what time it is here?"

"Yes. It's about five minutes after we shot a guy to death at the Winks Oil Company," Letty said. "Oh, we shot him after he killed Winks himself, so the oil thefts are probably over and the Land Division may be rolling. You awake yet?"

Greet was awake. "There really is no point in doing anything right now, but I'll be up at six and at the office by seven and I'll be screaming my head off. Right now, you should find out what county you're in down there. Call the sheriff's office, get some cops on the scene."

"They'll probably want our guns and we really don't want to give them up," Letty said. "We'll need some Washington heat to keep them. I mean, people could be looking to kill us after this. We need them."

"That I can help with," Greet said. "We

320

shovel a lot of money out the door to sheriff's departments everywhere. Grants. I'll have the guy in that office call your local sheriff and whisper sweetly in his ear. I can probably get that done before I go back to bed."

"Thank you."

After Greet hung up, Letty called Senator Colles and got the same initial reaction: "It's almost five o'clock here, what in God's name . . ."

"I shot and killed a guy here in Texas, one of the guys who was stealing the oil, about a minute after he killed the guy who was buying it. Purely self-defense, but I thought you should know. I've talked to Billy Greet."

Long silence, then, "Is this gonna come back to bite me in the butt?"

"Don't see how," Letty said. "If you want to turn on the propaganda machine — keep it in idle for now — there's a possibility you'll be a national hero."

She filled him in on the investigation and how his crew of two investigators may have stopped a terrorist attack using U.S. Army plastic explosive.

"I can work with that," Colles said. "Now I'm going back to bed."

■ ■ ■ ■

"Guess we should figure out who the sheriff is here, and call," Letty said to Kaiser. Kaiser was looking at her oddly, and she asked, "What?"

"You okay?"

"Well, yeah — no bullet holes or anything," Letty said.

"But . . . you just killed Max Sawyer? I'm not seeing a reaction there."

"He was trying to kill us," Letty said. She shrugged. "I'm supposed to be embarrassed?"

"Never mind," he said. He added, "I *would* like to keep the shotgun. I would also like to stay out of jail."

"When the cops get here," Letty said. "Make yourself as important as you possibly can."

Texas has roughly a billion counties, and after pulling up a map on Kaiser's iPad, they couldn't decide which one they were in. They finally called the Odessa Police Department, described their location, and were told that they most likely were in Santa Anna County. The cop who answered the phone gave them an emergency number for the county sheriff's office.

Letty called, explained the situation, and was told that an officer would be on the way. Ten minutes later, a patrol car rolled in the driveway, stopped with its headlights on them and on Sawyer's body beside the Jeep.

A deputy got out, a pistol in his hand, and called, "Are you . . . ?"

"Yes. We're agents with the Department of Homeland Security in Washington, D.C.," Kaiser called back. "We have one man shot and dead here in the driveway, you can see him. There's another victim in the building, also dead, shot by the man out here. The dead man."

"How did he get dead?" the deputy called.

"We shot him after he shot the man inside. We believe the man inside is Roscoe Winks, the owner of this company. We don't know that for sure. Both men were involved in a high-level oil theft ring operating out of Monahans."

"You keep standing there where I can see you — I'm going to call for more help," the deputy said.

Fifteen minutes later, another patrol car rolled in, and five minutes after that, the sheriff himself, in his personal SUV. The two deputies conferred with the sheriff, still back at the beginning of the driveway, then they heard the sheriff ask, "You haven't even looked?"

"We think these two are still armed . . ."

"They called us so they could shoot some deputies they don't know?" The sheriff sounded exasperated and he marched down the driveway toward Kaiser and Letty, followed by the deputies, and asked, "You got ID? You say Roscoe's in there?"

"Yes, this guy" — Letty pointed at Sawyer's body — "walked right in and shot him first thing, didn't even bother to shut the door," Letty said. "Anyway . . . what's your name, Sheriff?"

"Clayton Rhodes, I got a card in my truck, I'll give it to you later." Rhodes was a stocky older man with a sun- and wind-lined face, white hair. He was wearing chinos and a white shirt under a blue sport jacket. "About those IDs?"

Kaiser and Letty showed him their IDs and Rhodes asked one of the deputies for a flashlight so he could read them. He did that, looked up at Letty, and said, "U.S. Senate, huh?" then put his flashlight on Sawyer's body and said, "Bless my soul. This boy's been shot and then shot again. Who did that?"

Letty said, "Me. He was shooting at us

and I had to put a couple of hasty shots out there, hit him in the legs, I think. You might find some buckshot in him, too, from three shots fired by Agent Kaiser with his shotgun. I put the cherry on the cake with that shot above his eye."

Her speech had fallen into a country rhythm and the sheriff was bobbing his head, bottom lip pushed out, as he listened, then said, "Well, ain't you a regular Annie fuckin' Oakley." He didn't sound especially surprised, and asked, "You say Roscoe's inside?"

"Yes."

"Let's go see," the sheriff said. They all went to the building door and the sheriff looked in, then backed away, let the deputies look, then said, "Something for the crime scene people to do. Don't think Roscoe's going to walk away from that, though. Bad end to a bad man. A piss-poor one, anyway."

"They were stealing oil . . ." Letty began.

The sheriff held up a hand. "Let's go sit in my car where we can get comfortable. I want to hear the whole story."

He told the deputies to get a medical examiner going and to get the crime scene people out there. To Letty and Kaiser, he said, "We got two trained crime scene deputies, got cameras and swabs and everything. They do a bang-up job, in my opinion. You'll need to talk to them."

On the walk up the driveway to his car, he took a phone call, listened for a minute, then said, "Yes, this is him. I'm with them now. Uh-huh. Uh-huh. I haven't even asked for their guns. Should I? Uh-huh. Uh-huh. All right, I'm about to get their story, but we're already good friends. Say, is it warm out there in Washington? Uh-huh. Okay today, but it's supposed to be hotter 'n hell tomorrow."

When he got off the phone he said, "That was Washington, D.C., twisting my arm."

"Sorry about that," Kaiser said.

"Didn't sound like much of a twist," Letty added.

"No problem at all," Rhodes said. "I now got the personal cell phone number for the man who runs the grants assistance office. I woulda given you a thousand American dollars for that, this afternoon, and now I got it for free. Not counting what happened to Roscoe, of course, and all the bother we're gonna have to put up with."

They sat in the sheriff's Suburban, Letty in the front with the sheriff, Kaiser in the back, and Letty outlined the entire situation.

When she finished, the sheriff covered his face with both hands and rubbed up and down, then said, "I don't need this kind of monkey business."

"I don't really think you'll get much of it," Letty said. "Winks Oil is the only part of it that's in Santa Anna County, as far as we know. The oil is actually stolen on the other side of Odessa and it's delivered here. We would like to spend some time in Winks's office and go through his records, bank stuff and so on."

"We can fix you up to do that, but we'd want to get our crime scene people done in there first. You could probably get in tomorrow afternoon," Rhodes said. "About your guns — that was what the guy from Washington wanted to talk about — I don't think we'll need them. From what I saw, all your shots were through-and-through, so we won't be recovering any slugs to compare to yours. If we do, by some chance, we'd want you to come in and borrow us your guns for a minute or two, so the crime scene boys can shoot them into some Jell-O stuff."

"Gelatin," Kaiser said from the backseat.

"Yeah, gelatin. Y'all pretty sure they're not going to blow up anything in Santa Anna County?"

"No reason to think so," Letty said.

Kaiser, from the backseat: "Is there anything here to blow up?"

"Watch it," said Rhodes, with a tight smile. "Though we *are* what you'd call 'rural,' at least for big-city folks like you."

"I grew up in a place that makes Santa Anna County look like Los Angeles," Letty said.

"Thought you might have some country girl in you," Rhodes said. "Stick around tonight as long as you want, we'll need full statements from you no later than tomorrow. Tomorrow morning, my office, would be good. Are you the pair that was with Dan Tanner when that bulldog bit him in the balls?"

"Pit bull, not bulldog, and it got him in the thigh, not the balls," Kaiser said. "Then he shot the dog and we took him to the hospital. Tanner, not the dog."

"Poor damn dog," Rhodes said. "Though the story was more interesting when it was Dan Tanner's balls that got bit."

Letty agreed, bobbing her head like the sheriff: "Yes. It was."

They both laughed.

Kaiser, in the backseat, said, "C'mon, guys, that's not funny . . ."

SIXTEEN

R.J., the Odessa cop, called Hawkes at five o'clock in the morning, yanking her out of bed. "Listen: I just heard that there was a shooting at Winks's. Two guys were killed. One was Winks and I believe the other one was your man. I'm hearing he got in a shootout with that DHS guy."

"Oh my God! Max is dead?"

"I don't have names or too many details, but somebody's dead. The guy who killed Winks is apparently dead. I'll try to get more, but I thought you should hear about this right now."

"Thanks, R.J. We owe you," she said. "What do you know about the DHS guy?"

"Only that he's a big guy, and that's about it."

Hawkes didn't have to think about the problem. She called Victor Crain in Monahans. Crain, groggy with sleep, said, "Yeah,

Duran's here, he's bagged out in the back. He was drinking late, but he oughta be sober enough now."

"You gotta get out to the shack and the truck," Hawkes said. "You gotta burn them. Take some gas out there and set them on fire. There'll be DNA and fingerprints all over the place, and the only thing that'll wipe them out is fire. If you can't get it done, the cops will be holding Winks and everything else over our heads forever."

"If they were at Winks's, they probably know about the truck," Crain said.

Hawkes thought about the night she'd been out at the shack, and thought she'd seen a figure going out the back. She hadn't been certain there'd really been anybody there, but now it seemed more likely. "Is Terry's stuff still out there?"

"Most of it. We moved a box of clothes up here."

"Listen: you get some gas and cruise the place. If there was a shooting, the cops'll all be doing bureaucratic stuff for a while, making reports and all that. We got a chance. You cruise the place and if you can get in, burn it. Burn the truck, too. We've got no more use for it now. Can you get gas without buying it?"

"Yeah, I got an aftermarket tank in my

truck bed, I can pull some out of that," Crain said. "We'll go check it out. I got a gas can. Where's Rand?"

"He's here at his apartment, but that's too far away to get to the shack. You gotta do it."

"We're on the way," Crain said.

He shook Duran out of bed, and the two men drove out of Monahans in the dark. They scouted the shack and the truck from the road to the north, saw nothing moving, then made a pass on the road in front of the shack.

"Still nothing moving," Duran said.

"Could be somebody inside," Crain said. He drove on by and continued to the first intersection, a half-mile away.

"You spooked?" Duran asked.

"Man, they killed Max."

"Yeah. But if we don't burn that place, we're cooked. You and me. We gotta get back there," Duran said.

Crain turned around, drove back to the shack, and they found it empty. They carried Duran's boxes out to the truck, along with the AR-15, dumped all the paper garbage in the middle of the floor, piled some cotton blankets on top of it, ready to be burned.

That done, they ran down to the truck,

331

hosed the interior with a pail of gasoline, and touched off the fire. They'd always handled the truck's hoses with gloved hands, so that shouldn't be a problem. At the shack, they broke the wooden kitchen bar off the wall, and stacked it on top of the blanket, along with the wooden chair.

The sun wasn't quite up, but the sky in the east was getting bright when they moved the pickup, trailed a pail of gas out to the road, and set it off.

The interior of the shack exploded with flame, burning hot and nearly smokeless.

"Let's get the fuck out of here," said Duran, and they jogged to the truck and were gone.

Two miles down the road, Duran looked back. There was a wisp of smoke hanging over the shack, but he couldn't actually see any flame.

"I think we're good," he said.

"Call Jane. Let her know."

The day after the shootings was paperwork hell for Letty and Kaiser. A couple of reporters heard about the shoot-out, apparently from Santa Anna sheriff's deputies, and called around, asking questions. Rhodes, the sheriff, held a brief press conference in which he said that federal agents had arrived at the scene just as Roscoe Winks was being murdered, and in an ensuing shoot-out, the gunman, whose identity had not yet been confirmed, was shot and killed.

In essence, a nothing-burger for the bigger city news outlets, and the small towns no longer had newspapers or reporters.

Letty and Kaiser made statements at the FBI offices in Midland, and to the Santa Anna Sheriff's Department and led two Midland FBI agents and an ATF explosives agent to the tanker truck and the building next to it, only to find them gutted by fire. Nobody had reported the fires, probably because they were far out in the countryside.

The ATF agent, whose name was Burrell, sniffed at the building and truck and said, "Doused them down with gasoline and touched it off. Won't be anything to work with, I'm afraid."

The metal building was still warm from the fire, which Burrell thought must have happened before dawn. "But, hell, I'm no expert on residual temperatures. Seems likely that it wasn't much of a fire and not long ago. If they burned it before daylight, the fire wouldn't have been too visible, and you wouldn't see the smoke at all."

"There's an outhouse in the back," Letty

said. "Couldn't you get some biologics out of that?"

"Somebody could," Burrell said, wrinkling his nose. "Not me. I don't do poop. Ask the FBI."

The FBI agents agreed that somewhere in the FBI's ecology there probably was a guy who did poop and they'd look for him, if that became necessary. They took the VIN off the tanker truck, and before they left the site, it had been traced to Roscoe Winks.

"No help there," Kaiser said.

Kaiser and Letty kicked through some of the rubble in the shed. The remnants of the mattress on the steel bunk smelled like burned chicken feathers. The cardboard boxes that Letty had searched had been removed, along with the rifle.

"What do you think?" Kaiser asked.

"Somebody tipped them off to the shooting at Winks's, and they hustled up here and burned everything they couldn't move. Didn't need the truck anymore with Winks dead. We got them worried."

"Where would they have gotten the tip?"

"A cop," Letty said. "Cops would have been the people who would have known about this in the middle of the night, early enough that these guys could feel confident about coming out here and setting the fires . . ."

"Yeah. That doesn't make me feel any better," Kaiser said.

"Now we call Rhodes and see if he'll let us in Winks's office," Letty said. She looked around the site. "There's nothing more for us here."

Letty and Kaiser, trailed by an FBI agent in a separate car, drove out to Winks's early in the afternoon and found two sheriff's deputies sitting in the shade of an oil tank, reading their phones. Both bodies had been removed, the deputies said, and the crime scene crew had finished their work.

Winks had used a Windows laptop, which was sitting on his desk, lid closed. His cell phone was sitting beside it. The FBI agent opened the computer, brought it up. The computer asked for a password.

"What do you do here?" Letty asked.

The agent was digging in his briefcase, and took out a thumb drive. "I've got an offline NT password and registry editor here . . . I can edit the registry and reset the password."

Kaiser: "It's that easy?"

"Yeah, it is," the agent said. "Of course, if he's encrypted his files, we're out of luck . . ."

They stood around, watching as he worked: five minutes later, he said, "We're in, and the files are *not* encrypted. Dummy. What are we looking for?"

"Let me in there," Letty said. "Emails first."

They found dozens of receipts for oil pick-ups by a half-dozen different oil service companies, but nothing that suggested a connection to the suppliers of the oil, the thieves. Winks had saved a number of websites, but all but one were commercial and routine. The FBI agent pointed to a link in the browser and said, "Click on this."

They did, and found it led to an empty website.

"I'm thinking what they did was, they talked here," he said. "Whoever is on the other end wiped it out after every conversation. Or Winks did."

"Why do you think that?" Kaiser asked.

Letty: "Because of the website ID."

"Exactly," the agent said. "Fifteen random numbers and letters dot com. Not something anyone would find by accident. The only way you could find it would be if you came to this machine, or the other one, and found it like we did. But with nothing there . . . we're shut out."

"What about his cell phone?"

"That will take a while, unless you find something written down somewhere. We'll have to go fight Apple about it."

"Damn it," Letty said. "You know what we're talking about here. These people may be getting ready to blow something up. Why don't you tell Apple *that*?"

"We will. Today. Is there anything else I can help you with?"

"How about recovering deleted files? Deleted emails."

"I can try to go to his ISP for that . . . He's not in any cloud that I can see, so it's not up there. The ISP, you know, we're dealing with sticky bureaucracies here. Sometimes they don't even answer the phone."

"Not even for the FBI?"

"We can get to them eventually, but it can take time. I'll push it as hard as I can."

Winks's office gave up nothing useful. Letty called the sheriff and asked him to contact the state patrol to see if anyone whose name they had — Sawyer, Duran, Crain, Low — had any traffic tickets of any kind, from anywhere.

Rhodes called back and said that Sawyer had gotten a speeding ticket in the past twelve months in El Paso. "You going down there?"

"Actually, I think we've seen something about El Paso," Letty said. "I've got to read through my notes."

"If you go, take it easy down there, girl. Things can get rough on the border."

"But not in Santa Anna County?"

"We're peace-loving folks here, by and large," Rhodes said. "With a few outliers."

"Are we going to El Paso?" Kaiser asked.

"Those guys spent a lot of time down there," Letty said. "It's probably the head-quarters of this Jeep militia. I mean, the militia patrols the border and the border isn't here. This was the moneymaker."

"So we go down there and talk to who?" Kaiser asked. Then, "Should have a big FBI office, maybe they've got something on the El Paso area militias? Wouldn't be surprised if there's a half-dozen of them."

"Maybe the Border Patrol would have something. Can't be many militias that have a woman as a leader."

"You know who'd have something?" Kaiser asked.

"Who?"

"Google. Or Bing."

■ ■ ■ ■

Google and Bing did have a lot of information on border militias, but none mentioned a woman as a leader, though there seemed to be a lot of women in the militias in general. "We're gonna have to go down there," Letty said.

They were sitting in the hotel lounge with Kaiser's iPad on the bar. Letty got carded every time she ordered alcohol in Washington or Virginia, but the Texas bartender hadn't even looked like he was going to ask. He slid a margarita across the bar with Kaiser's beer, and Kaiser asked, "You're only gonna have one, right?"

"Right. I don't like alcohol, but this day made me thirsty. For more than water."

"Good. Have one and quit," Kaiser said. "I'd hate to see what you'd do if you were liquored up. Probably start fights in the parking lot."

"My mother — my natural mother — was an alcoholic. She didn't wait to get into the parking lot. She'd fight you right in the bar," Letty said. "I've done some reading and some authorities think alcoholism might run in families. Not because of culture, but because of DNA. Something in the genes.

So I'm careful."

"I was an alcoholic for a while, but it was cultural," Kaiser mused. "Right after I re-upped for the first time, with the Army. I was twenty-four, just made sergeant, thought about quitting, but the thing was, I was good at it and I liked it. I re-upped for six years and I started drinking. Like every-body else. This was up in North Carolina. Then some guys and I went to this crappy resort on the Outer Banks when we were on leave, I was with this chick who didn't drink . . . We had this little cabin to ourselves and there was a garbage can out back. We weren't cooking, we were eating every meal in a diner or restaurant, so I wasn't putting anything in the garbage can. This girl would clean up my beer cans and throw them away every morning. Toward the end of the week, I picked them up myself one morning and took them out back and the damn trash can was half-full of beer cans. Just beer cans. I thought, *Holy shit, I'm an alcoholic.*"

"And you quit?"

"Not right away, but yeah. Then I got made a staff sergeant and I was already Ranger-qualified, and decided to try out for Delta. And I made it. Culture changed. Figured I could drink two beers a day and I've stuck to that."

"No women in Delta," Letty said.

"No, but there are in the CIA's Special Operations Group. Some Delta guys wind up there, if they're smart enough. Tough bunch."

"You never were?"

"No. SOG is usually small missions, a team taking out one particular target, or maybe exfiltrating somebody from hostile territory," Kaiser said. "If you think about them as assassins, you wouldn't be far wrong. Or, sometimes, Boy Scouts, doing a good deed. I was more interested in bigger actions. Taking and holding something until the Rangers get there. Cleaning out a town. That kind of thing."

"You ever get shot?"

"No, not shot. Wounded, twice, shrapnel. Walked back with the team once. The other time, they medevacked me, gave me a painkiller lollipop while they flew me in to a hospital. Assholes got me in the back of the left leg and across my butt and up my back, almost to my shoulder. Bleeding like crazy; medic stuffed bandages into the cuts. It was an IED, an improvised explosive device, made out of an artillery shell and a cell phone. I walked right past it and probably thirty or forty yards down the road before it was set off. Killed two of the team outright, wounded four of us."

"My God. That sounds . . ."

"What?"

"Interesting."

Kaiser laughed. "You better stay away from SOG. They'd get you killed for sure. When Sawyer was shooting at you, you stood there shooting back like bullets was flies, like you were going to live forever."

"Hey. I had one eye exposed, and my hand. He never saw me," Letty said. "And I'm sorry about bumping you off-line. That won't happen again."

"Yeah, well." He laughed again. "You sorta scare me, man."

"Don't mean to," Letty said.

"I know, but you do," Kaiser said. "I don't want to be there if you get killed."

"Huh. So — El Paso?"

"You're running this boat. If you say so, it's El Paso."

They met at the front desk the next morning, agreed they'd slept well, stopped a last time at the IHOP for pancakes and at a convenience store for a cheap Styrofoam cooler, ice, and bottles of water, and aimed the Explorer south down I-20.

El Paso was almost due west of Midland, but they had to drive four hours first southwest and then northwest to get there, interstate all the way, I-20 and I-10. The landscape changed, the plains dwindling in the rearview mirror, sere, dirty brown mountains poking up along the highway, cut by the Rio Grande, which defined the greater El Paso area. El Paso sat on one side of the river, Juárez, Mexico, twice as big, on the other; together, two million people, with a dome of haze visible for a hundred miles.

"The mountains here . . . They look like big piles of dirt," Letty said.

"And hardly a ski resort among them," Kaiser said.

Letty opened her laptop on the way, combing through her notes. After a while, she said, "I knew we'd run into an El Paso address somewhere along the way. The addresses I got out of Max Sawyer's Jeep. Alice Serrano, on Pear Tree Lane. We could swing by her place on the way into town, see what we can see."

"What do we know about her?"

"Almost nothing. Convicted of assault in New Mexico years ago, didn't serve any jail time," Letty said. "Nothing since then. She's either innocent or guilty as hell but keeping her head down. What do you want to do?"

"I'm good to go, and it's still early, so why not?" Kaiser said. "Dig one of those waters out of the cooler, will you? I'm getting dry."

"It is dry," Letty said, peering out at the landscape through her sunglasses. "And hot. I'd hate like hell to walk across this country."

Pear Tree Lane was buried in a housing development of single-story brick and stucco houses with flat roofs built on gently curving blacktop streets. The houses, mostly earth-colored, had minimal lawns and little foliage around them, cypress trees here and there, some pines, an occasional palm. The backyards were tight boxes pressed against similar tiny backyards from the next street over.

They cruised by Alice Serrano's house. An old Pontiac slumped in the left half of the short driveway, like it might have been there, unmoving, forever. The back window was covered with dust, and one tire was visibly low.

"Doesn't look like the house belonging to a leader of the revolution," Kaiser said. They continued down the block, around the corner. "You want to make another pass?"

"One more," Letty said.

They made another pass, still saw nothing moving in Serrano's house.

"Maybe she's at work — I mean, it's likely

she's at work," Kaiser said.

"All right. Let's go find the hotel." A minute later, she frowned and added, "I saw something back there that wasn't right. Saw it on the first pass, didn't see it on the second. Don't know what it was . . ."

"Don't focus on it. Let it marinate. It'll come floating up," Kaiser said.

They checked into another Homewood Suites, which was located just off I-10, not far from Serrano's house. They took a half-hour to get cleaned up and stash their luggage, then got back in the car and drove to the El Paso FBI offices, which were inside a boring white stone-and-glass building with the homogenized appearance of a newer post office.

After clearing through security, they met with Special Agent Klaus Anders, who told them that El Paso had at least a half-dozen known militias, and maybe a dozen more that were either inactive, fictional, or secret.

"They patrol the border, where they're allowed to. Mostly getting in the Border Patrol's hair. Texas doesn't pay too much attention to them, but New Mexico has cracked down," Anders said. He was a tall man, in his late twenties or early thirties, Letty thought. He wore glasses with gun-metal rims and had the pallor of a person who spent a lot of time indoors.

He took a paper map out of a desk drawer, and unfolded it, and the three of them bent over it. "El Paso ought to be in New Mexico . . . We're way out on the tip of this triangle that sticks into New Mexico," he said, tapping the map. "I can give you the names and addresses of several of the leaders of the local militias . . . and fill you in on their backgrounds. Most of them have criminal records of one kind or another."

Letty: "We'd be particularly interested in one run by a woman, or involving men named . . ."

"Duran, Low, Crain, or Sawyer, though I understand you took Sawyer off the books," Anders interrupted, nodding at Kaiser. "The Midland office filled me in. I don't know of a militia run by a woman, although there was one, years ago, before my time here. No criminal record, her bunch did some patrolling, but weren't involved in any kind of threats or violence. There is one odd thing, though . . ."

"We like odd things," Letty said.

"We're hearing rumors that some other militias, not from the El Paso area, but up in the northwest, have been talking to a hard-right anti-immigration activist somewhere down in this area and it's a woman. She apparently runs a darknet site that we haven't been able to find, not that anybody's been looking that hard."

"Anything about money?" Letty asked.

"Funny you should ask — yes. Our guys up in Portland say that one of their local militias has apparently gotten some funding through her. We've got informants in most of those militias, but not in leadership roles. So what we get is rumor," Anders said.

"That might be the woman we want — you should have been briefed about the oil thefts up in the Midland-Odessa area."

"Yeah. You think that money went north?"

"Some of it, maybe," Letty said. "Though the guys we've seen aren't exactly philanthropists. And we think some of it was used to buy C-4, and they might be planning to blow up a building. We saw them apparently learning how to cut an I-beam with timed explosions."

"I heard that . . . I was told the ATF is on it."

"Any sign that anything here is about to blow up?" Kaiser asked. "No pun intended . . ."

"Yes. There is," Anders said. "You heard about the Caravana Viacrucis del Migrante de Libertad?"

Letty said, "The Caravan of the Migrants' Way of the Cross of Freedom?"

"Something like that. It's a caravan coming up from Central America, and the Mexicans aren't doing much to slow it down," Anders said. "Word is, it's headed here and there are more than thirteen hundred people in it. Buses, cars, people walking. It's not far south of Juárez. Border Patrol is in an uproar, they're bringing in reinforcements."

"I don't mean to be offensive and I don't want to seem like an entitled East Coast witch. With what John and I have found, apparently a militia with heavy financial means from oil thefts — could be well over a million dollars — and a willingness to kill people, three murdered so far, that we know of, and another probable, and who apparently have access to high explosives and are training to use it . . . why are we talking to a relatively junior FBI agent? Why isn't there some crisis-management team working here?" Letty asked.

Kaiser jumped in. "I was in the military for a long time and got wounded when some asshole set off an IED on my squad. What are you going to say if this caravan crunches into the border and gets wiped by a bunch of IEDs? C-4 is wonderful for that . . ."

"I'm not all *that* junior," Anders said. "I was designated to talk with you, when we were told you were coming. We have other preparations under way, we've got a task force that's . . . tasked with working out the probabilities and coordinating with local law enforcement . . . I'd point out that neither one of you is a trained investigator, from what we've been told . . ."

Outside, in the heat, walking to the car, Letty said to Kaiser, "Tasked with working out the probabilities, my incredibly well-toned ass. How long do you think it'll take them to put a report together?"

"Jeez, who knows? Anders didn't even look like he went outside," Kaiser said. "What's he really going to know about a militia? And he was their militia guy."

"And, unfortunately, we're not trained investigators," Letty said, looking back at the building. "Maybe I should call Colles and get him to light a fire under their butts."

"We could try that," Kaiser said. "But you know what? Nothing moves slower than a bureaucracy. The only way you get speed from an organization like DHS or the FBI is if one person engineers it. Orders out the SWAT squad on his own authority. And he

349

better be right, because if he pulls the fire alarm and there's no fire, he'll be in major career trouble. Safety is in numbers and numbers move slow."

"When you're right, you're right," Letty said. They started back to the hotel, and a time and temperature sign off I-10 said that it was ninety-six degrees at three o'clock. "Listen, we're not going to learn anything by driving around El Paso. Let's get on our computers. Read everything we can find on the local militias. Then there's something we haven't spent a lot of time talking about . . ."

"Which is . . ."

"Why Winks was murdered," Letty said. "I can think of one good reason: they didn't need him anymore. Or they couldn't use him anymore, which is the same thing. He was a loose end, and they needed to seal that off."

"We did talk about this — that they killed the Blackburns because Boxie Blackburn had figured something out. They didn't want to kill Winks, which would have sealed them off even better, but he was their money man. That made sense to me. Then they went and killed Winks anyway, which means something changed."

"Yes. Us," Letty said. "We went after

Sawyer, and I asked Sawyer about Low, and about stealing oil, which was a mistake. Sawyer told them about that, and they decided to clean up their operation. Kill Winks, burn the truck and that shack. But would they have done all that if they weren't about to pull the trigger on something bigger?"

"I don't know. We do have to be careful about one thing — becoming overly paranoid," Kaiser said. "Maybe nothing much is happening?"

"Three murders," Letty said. "That's something. That's the death penalty in Texas, and they're not shy about using it down here."

As they were approaching the hotel, Kaiser, who'd made the trip mostly in silence, said, "A local cop might know more than the Feds. Somebody who grew up here. I wonder if the El Paso cops have somebody who specializes in the militias?"

"I'll find somebody to ask. And I'll call Colles," Letty said.

"Don't forget that you think you saw something down by Alice Serrano's house. You were going to remember what that was."

"I'll call you when I remember," Letty

said. "Meet for dinner at seven, and we can figure out what we're going to do tomorrow."

SEVENTEEN

Letty spoke to Billy Greet at DHS about the FBI response to the warnings of imminent trouble, and Greet asked, "Letty, are you sure that trouble is really *imminent*?"

"No. No more than people who warned about Osama Bin Laden were sure that Nine-Eleven was imminent. I'm fairly sure that something is under way — when it takes place, I don't know."

"I can tell you that the FBI is moving, but . . . not so fast as you want them to," Greet said. "Frankly, you're part of the question — you're a new twenty-four-year-old employee, and . . ."

"I got the same attitude from the agent we talked to. So, all right, I'll continue poking around with John. But if the federal building blows up, don't call me to complain."

"Letty!"

"Two words, Billy: C-4, I-beams. They're

not making firecrackers."

"It's the end of day, here. I'll press this tomorrow morning. Promise."

When she finished with Greet, Letty went to her computer and began digging through years of news stories coughed up by Google and Bing without making much progress. There were women in the local militias, and some had happily spoken to the media about their political beliefs, which stretched from hard right to the seriously dysfunctional, Democrats-drink-the-blood-of-white-babies fringe.

None of them seemed likely as the organizers of a major conspiracy. Some of the women might be willing to kill, given the opportunity, Letty thought, but — to steal a phrase from Kaiser — they couldn't lead a Marine into a whorehouse, much less manage a huge conspiracy.

The evening was still too hot for a run, and the local area didn't seem particularly congenial to running, so she brought up a heavy-duty YouTube yoga session, took a shower, and went down to the lobby to meet Kaiser.

"Where to?"

He shook his head. "If you're not thinking gourmet, I'm told we could walk a block or so to a pizza joint."

"That's fine," she said.

The pizza place was nice enough, and they went halves on a mushroom (Letty) and pepperoni (Kaiser). "Did you talk to the cops?" Kaiser asked.

She shook her head. "I'll try them in the morning if we can't think of anything better. You find anything online?"

"Nothing that feels right. I wonder if we should have stayed up at Midland? We had something to chew on there."

"Hard to tell," Letty said. She told him about her conversation with Greet. "I think we're on our own."

They walked back to the hotel and Kaiser said he'd probably be tasting pepperoni in the back of his throat all night, but the pizza had been good enough. As they passed a Chevron gas station, Letty stopped and put a hand to her forehead.

"What?"

"That thing I thought I saw back on Pear Tree Lane. There's that Chevron sign . . ."

"What?"

"The Chevron logo . . ." She pointed at the sign on the outside of the station.

"The V's?"

"Yes. Remember when we were talking to

Kaylee Turner up in Lubbock? She said the members of the militia, the gang, whatever it was, had blue stickers on their bumpers with green triangles. That's what I saw. A sticker. Those chevrons reminded me."

Kaiser looked up at the Chevron sign again, said, "Okay."

"That's why I saw the thing only once, going down the street — it was on the back bumper of a truck. When we came back, we were going in the other direction, so I wouldn't see it."

"We need to take another ride past what's-her-name's house, Serrano."

"I don't think . . . It wasn't by Serrano's house. It was on the other side of the street, it was on my side, not yours."

They thought about that as they walked into the hotel, then Letty said, "I wonder if they were smart enough to put a nearby address into visitors' navigation systems, instead of the real address they were going to. Then, you know, the nav system gets you on the block, but you have to do that last hundred feet on your own."

"Sure, they say, 'Go to the pink house on the other side of the street.' Good security. I don't know if they'd be smart enough to do that."

"I don't know, either," Letty said. "I'm

going back to the computer. Most places are online with tax assessment and collection information. I'll see if I can spot a likely house . . ."

"What name are you looking for?"

"Don't know that, either. I'll just be browsing for something interesting."

They said "good night," and Letty went up to her room, got online, and found that El Paso County didn't show a Pear Tree Lane in their records, although she was pretty sure she had the name right — and it did show up on Google and Bing. She messed around with various options, but came up empty.

They'd have to go back the next day.

Kaiser called just before she got in bed. "You know how you gave me those instructions, up in Midland, about putting my gun on the floor beside the bed?"

"Yes. We should do that here, too," Letty said.

"Yeah, but now I have some instructions for you."

"Okay."

"You know the little peephole in your door? It works both ways. Make a spit wad out of toilet paper and push it in the hole so nobody can look in from the outside. As a woman, you ought to be doing that anyway. Keep the chain on the door. If somebody knocks, stand behind the wall to the side of the door, not behind the door, when you ask who it is. And just because they say, 'Housekeeping,' don't automatically believe them. If you open the door on the chain, they can kick it without any trouble at all. Yank the chain right off the wall. If they do that, they'll come down on that front foot, inside the door, and when they turn to you, they should be looking straight down a nine-millimeter hole."

"Got it."

As she was making the spit wad out of toilet paper, she thought, *Not to be paranoid at all, but that's why I have to pay more attention to him.*

After she'd blocked the peephole, she went to her laptop and did a Google search on peephole intrusions — and learned that women were not only watched, but had actually been filmed through the peephole as they undressed inside their locked rooms.

Yet another reason, Letty thought, that all women should be issued guns at birth.

The next day they went back to Pear Tree Lane first thing, but found no pickups parked on the street. "Damn it, I think it was about here," Letty said, as they rolled down Pear Tree. "That's what I've got in my mind's eye, anyway. Let's go over to the assessor's office, see if they can help us out."

The tax office was located in a scuffed-up brown-brick building with a scuffed-up yard; they were waited on by a scuffed-up counter clerk with a waxed black Hercule Poirot mustache and a friendly demeanor. There was nothing particularly interesting on the list of owners on Pear Tree Lane, except that a half-dozen houses were owned by the same company. The company's mailing address was in Denver, Colorado.

"Rentals," said the clerk. "You can buy them in there for a hundred thousand, get twelve hundred a month in rent. That's a fourteen percent return. Try getting that from a bank."

"Rats," Kaiser said, when they were back outside. "Why can't anything be simple?"

"We may have to go to the simplest thing — knock on doors," Letty said.

"Gonna be a million degrees out there," Kaiser said glumly.

Letty insisted, so they did it, walking along the three hundred yards of Pear Tree Lane like a couple of hopeless coupon-book salesmen, met with empty houses, people who spoke no English, and when they actually found somebody to talk to, no comprehension. "Jael? No, ain't nobody by that name. What kind of name is that, anyway?"

But: a woman who owned a Jeep? Yes, she worked at the Fleet & Ranch store and a downtown bar at nights, or had, anyway. Friendly sort. "Why would you want her?"

There was no Jeep in sight at the house where the woman lived — one of the rentals — but there was a garage, so the Jeep might be inside. The garage had no windows, and the house appeared to be closed up, tight, maybe even grim.

"Want to knock?" Kaiser asked.

"Got your carry?"

Kaiser patted his waist, under the loose cotton shirt.

"Keep it handy. Let's go knock," Letty said.

They did, but got no answer. "Probably at work," Kaiser said.

"The neighbors are probably going to tell her that we were asking, too," Letty said. She looked back at the house, then up and down the street. "Damn it. I think this was about where I saw that truck parked. The one with the sticker. This might be her house."

"Don't start thinking about coming back

at night," Kaiser said. "I don't think this would be a street where you'd want to do that."

Kaiser drove, taking them back to the hotel, while Letty called Greet at DHS. "We need to have you call the Yandel Investment Corp. in Denver, Colorado, and see if they can give you the name of the woman who rents one of their houses in El Paso . . ." She gave Greet the house number. "If you get her name, we need you to turn that through NCIS to see what kind of record she has . . . and maybe see if you could get her tax returns, figure out exactly what she's been doing here in El Paso."

"Tax returns will take a court order, but, it's usually fairly quick," Greet said. "I talked to Senator Colles, he's been goosing the FBI, but I haven't heard back. Things are moving, but I can't guarantee how fast they'll be going."

"I already had that lecture from John," Letty said. "Call us soon as you can get this stuff. There's a chance this woman could be Jael."

Hawkes had been watching them through a window as they worked the street. That anyone should be working the street was unusual enough, but that it should be a big, tough man with a slender young woman rang alarm bells.

Soon enough, they were knocking at her door. She was sitting in a bedroom, on the floor, arms wrapped around her legs. Trying not to breathe. They knocked some more, then walked away. Without moving a curtain, she stood up and watched them go.

She called Low. "Those investigators are here. They don't know exactly where I am, they're knocking on doors up and down the street. But it's them."

"Damn. If they call the cops . . ."

They talked about what Hawkes should do if the investigators came back before she could get out — cross the backyard, climb the fence, Low would pick her up on the next street. She'd been ready to abandon the house anyway, she'd sold everything of value, including her Jeep, packed the clothes she'd need for her escape. Now she carried her bag out to the Subaru in the garage, along with three grocery sacks full of books, a box of dishes and silverware, bedding, including her pillows, and a six-pack cooler, and loaded up the car.

She did the landlord's rep, who was nice enough, a thin, pale man with a tentative smile, who'd always been polite with her, the favor of emptying out the refrigerator, taking anything that might spoil to the garbage can, pouring two quarts of milk down the sink. When she was done, she stood in her bedroom, moving back and forth between windows on opposite walls, looking up and down the street.

No sign of a cop, or any unknown car, or the Explorer.

When she was satisfied, she took a last turn around the house, looking for anything she might have missed. She didn't bother to try to wipe out fingerprints, or any of that. The Feds would figure out soon enough who she was, and the Army not only had her fingerprints, they had samples of her DNA.

Turned one last time at the garage door: she'd lived in the house for three years, felt no affection for it at all. Shook her head, ran the garage door up, backed out, and a minute later, was gone for good.

"Her name is Jane Jael Hawkes and she has no criminal record at all," Greet told Letty. "But she's your girl. How many women you know with a middle name like Jael?"

Letty was sprawled on her bed, her phone set to "speaker." Kaiser sat on a corner chair, immersed in a beat-up copy of Alan Furst's novel *Red Gold,* which Letty had loaned him. "She was in the Army until twelve years ago, clean record there. She's really invisible, no presence on social media, at least, none we can find, no mentions in the local newspapers. Military records show she used the G.I. Bill to go to college at UTEP. Don't have her tax records yet."

"Army — stationed at Fort Bliss?" Letty asked.

"No, Fort Polk, Louisiana."

"Is Fort Bliss a place where you might get some military C-4?"

"Oh . . . heck, I don't know," Greet said. "I wouldn't be surprised, I guess."

Letty said, "Hang on for one minute . . . I need to check my computer." She did that, then came back to Greet: "Billy, the commanding general at Fort Bliss is named Thomas D. Creighton, he's a major general. Could you give him a ring and ask him if we could come over to chat with him?"

"Two-stars are pretty important," Greet said. "I mean, I'm pretty important, and I'm only the equivalent of a colonel."

In the corner, Kaiser looked up from the book and raised an eyebrow.

"Could you call him?" Letty asked. "Tell him you're a three-star and if he doesn't talk to us, he'll be a one-star by dinnertime."

"I'll get back to you on that," Greet said.

"Billy — this is important."

"I know."

From the corner, Kaiser said, "I hope nobody stole it from Bliss."

"It'd help to know that," Letty said.

"Yeah, but if that stuff is gone, some poor bastard is going to get cornholed — excuse the expression — and it'll most likely be the wrong guy."

Greet called back a half-hour later: "General Creighton will see you at two o'clock. Please be on time."

Kaiser stood up and said, "I'm going back to my room to read this book for a while. We're not that far away, but if we're talking to a two-star, we should be early — I'll see you downstairs at one o'clock."

The Fort Bliss headquarters building was impressive enough, done in a faux southwestern style. They were early, but Kaiser had a long amiable chat with a sergeant major about employment opportunities after the military, and the sergeant major did them the favor of taking them into Creighton's office early.

Creighton, a tall, watery-eyed man with a permanent sunburn, pointed them at visitor

365

chairs and said, "DHS. Are you guys bad news?"

"I hope not, sir," Kaiser said. "We're tracking some people, we think right-wing militia, who we think are up to serious no-good. We followed them out into the mountains back east of here, almost to I-20, and they found themselves a crack in the terrain and they used some C-4 to cut an I-beam in half. We weren't in a position to challenge them, so we don't know where they went. We think a bunch of them operate out of the El Paso area."

Letty had taken her cell phone out, called up a photo with the C-4 wrapper they'd found at the site of the C-4 test, and passed it across the desk to Creighton. He looked at it and said, "Damn."

Kaiser nodded. "Yes, sir."

Creighton called, "Sergeant major!"

The sergeant major stuck his head in the office. "Yes, sir?"

"I want to talk to Captain Colin sometime in the next two minutes. Can you make that happen?"

The sergeant major said, "I believe so, sir."

"And could you tell Roxanne that we'd like three cups of coffee in here . . ." He looked at Letty and Kaiser. "Or soft drinks?"

Letty said, "Coffee's fine, thank you."

The sergeant major disappeared, and the general turned to Kaiser. "So you were out there, snoopin' and poopin', with nothing but your dick in your hand . . ."

"Yes, sir, and while it's a beautiful thing in itself, it ain't worth a damn in a fight."

The two men laughed and then the general apologized to Letty, saying, "Sorry about that, young lady. Old, old joke. I spotted Mr. Kaiser as a former NCO . . . what rank, Sergeant?"

"Master sergeant," Kaiser said. "Task Force Green."

"Really? Hell of an outfit. And now you're DHS . . ."

The two ignored Letty as they talked Army, the general probing Kaiser's background and assignments, until they heard hurried footfalls in the outside hallway and then the outer office. The sergeant major stepped in and said, "Captain Colin, sir."

Captain Colin was a gawky young man, bespectacled, a heavy ring on one hand, who carried what might have been a permanent worried look. "Yes, sir?"

"Are we missing any C-4?"

The worried look intensified. Colin glanced at Letty and Kaiser and said, "We better not be. I can get an instant audit done in fifteen minutes or so."

"Do that," Creighton said. "I've got about twenty minutes to spend with these folks from the Department of Homeland Security, and I need the answer before they have to go."

"Sir!" Colin disappeared.

"West Pointer," Creighton said. "He'll have a few stars someday, if he doesn't foul up." He turned his watery eyes on Letty. "So they tell me you shot that poor man three times all by yourself, and the last shot in the head. Is that true?"

Letty nodded. "It seemed like a reasonable thing to do, at the time."

They spent fifteen minutes talking about the investigation and the theft of oil, and the general said, "Now you've got me worried. What are they going to blow up?"

"Something with I-beams," Letty said. "A building."

"Lord help us," Creighton said.

Colin walked back into the office without ceremony, nodded at Creighton, and blurted, "Sir, I need to talk to you privately."

Creighton turned to Letty and Kaiser, then back to Colin and said, "Okay." To Letty and Kaiser, "Could you excuse us?"

They went to sit in the outer office. Letty said, "They're missing some C-4."

Kaiser nodded: "Yup."

Fifteen minutes later, the sergeant major took a phone call, then came over and said, "I'm afraid General Creighton was called away. He, uh, went out to his car, out the back entrance."

Letty spread her hands: "You're telling me he isn't going to talk to us anymore?"

"That's . . . what it boils down to," the sergeant major said.

"Tell him to go fuck himself," Letty said.

She turned away as the sergeant major muttered, "I don't think so."

Letty turned back: "We're the people on top of this. If he doesn't cooperate, he could have a heck of a lot bigger problem than he has now. What's he gonna do, investigate? Find these people? Stop them from blowing up a building somewhere? Or is he gonna try to hide the fact that his C-4 got stolen?"

"I can't help you," the sergeant major said.

Letty and Kaiser walked out the front door, into the heat. Kaiser said, "We've got to . . ."

Letty held up a hand, pointed down to the end of the building. "Isn't that the Colin guy? The captain?"

Colin was standing just off the street, talking urgently on a cell phone, facing sideways away from them, as if waiting for a ride.

Kaiser, "Yeah, I think . . ."

Letty was already jogging toward Colin. He didn't see or hear Letty coming until she was almost on top of him. When he realized that somebody was running up to him, he turned, saw her, and frantically waved her away.

"I can't talk to you," he said, holding the cell phone against his chest to muffle the microphone.

"You better," Letty said. "Creighton has screwed himself. Kaiser and I are the only people who can stop this."

"The FBI . . ."

"The FBI is in meetings and will probably be there for a week. We have reason to believe something is already under way. Tell me what you found out. I'll put in a good word for you at your court-martial . . ."

"My court . . . Go the fuck away."

"If a building blows up, you and Creighton could be in deep trouble for not helping us out. If we stop it and it's nothing more than a theft that went nowhere, who's even to know? But we need to know what you know," Letty said. "Creighton said if you stay in the Army, you'll eventually be a general. You want to stay in? Or do you want to be the guy who blocked an inquiry into what happens with a bunch of stolen explosives?"

Colin looked down at his phone, then punched the end button.

"We don't know anything, not for sure," he said. "We sent the guy in charge over to the dump. After a quick look, he came back and said we might be missing some C-4. Where it went and who took it, he doesn't know. We're going to get our own investigators involved. If we can find the thief, that should help stop . . . stop whatever might happen."

Letty asked, "How much was stolen?"

"I got a car coming, I got to get out there," Colin said. He looked down the street, and then said, "Go away, I don't want anybody to see me talking to you."

"How much?"

Colin took off his hat, rubbed a hand across his head, then said, "A hundred pounds. With detonators and individual digital timers."

"How precise are the timers? Could they be set so everything blows at once?"

"Yes. Now go away."

Letty jogged back to Kaiser, said, "Hundred pounds."

Kaiser said, "That ain't optimal."

Letty asked what he meant, then called Greet at home, who asked, "Is it bad news? I assume it's bad."

371

"They're missing a hundred pounds of C-4, with detonators and digital timers," Letty said. "The good news is, Kaiser says it'd probably be a smaller building. They'd need more to bring down a skyscraper, depending on how smart they are."

"Well, that brightens my day," Greet said, appalled. "A smaller building. You mean, like the federal building in Oklahoma City?"

"I bring the news, I don't editorialize on it," Letty said.

EIGHTEEN

Letty and Kaiser sat in the Explorer, in silence, until Letty asked, "How much do you really like your job?"

"A lot. I depend on it," Kaiser said. "If I stick with it, I can retire at sixty-five with two full pensions and Medicare."

"I mean, other than that," Letty said.

"Does get boring sometimes. Not so much lately. Sweetie."

"We need to go back to that Hawkes woman's house," Letty said. "We need to get inside."

"Ah . . ." Kaiser shook his head. "Tell you what. Let's go to this Fleet & Ranch store and ask about her. If she's there, we can tell her, you know, we need help finding some people involved in right-wing activities, maybe on her street."

"Then you're willing to break into her house if we go to Fleet & Ranch first?"

"Maybe. I'm willing to be the lookout, anyway," Kaiser said.

The store manager's name was Benjamin Rojas, and they spoke to him on the store's sales floor.

"Jane worked for us for . . . I don't know . . . several years," Rojas said. "She quit about a year and a half ago, but I know she's still in town. I've seen her around, I think she works at a bar."

"You know which bar?"

"Mmm . . . wait a minute." He got on his cell phone, found a number, called it, and said, "Angela, could you come up to the contractor's door for a minute? Right away?"

Angela hurried around a corner, a husky Hispanic woman in a red carpenter's apron. Rojas introduced Letty and Kaiser to her, then asked, "Do you know what bar Jane Hawkes works at now?"

"She used to work at Ironsides, but I don't think she works there anymore. I go there most nights with my man and I don't see her."

"You ever see her around town?" Letty asked.

"I do, sometimes . . . well, once or twice since she quit here." She frowned. "I don't know, I think she might have inherited money or something. Last time I saw her, she was driving by in a Jeep Rubicon. Those cost some money."

"They do," Kaiser said. "Like forty thousand."

They pushed Rojas and Angela on Hawkes's political opinions. Rojas had no idea, but Angela said, "Sometimes bad things came out. She didn't like Mexicans and Hondurans coming across the border. She wanted Trump's wall to be built, but she thought Trump was an asshole. Excuse the language."

"Sort of a right-winger, then," Kaiser said. "Anti-immigrant."

"Yes, she was," Angela said. "She had all these theories, about how the illegals keep the working people down. But she was friendly to us who work here in the store. Not so much anti-Mexican, or anti-Hispanic, just anti-immigrant. Lots of Mexican people even agree with her."

"She had a problem with me," Rojas said. "I jumped over her to the manager's job. And, you know, I'm Hispanic, though my family's been in Texas for two hundred years. So there's that."

Out in the parking lot, Letty said, "We have

to do it, John. She's Jael. We have to either talk to her or go into her house. We walk up to the door and if nobody answers, you use your picks. I'll body-block for you."

"That's a watchful neighborhood," Kaiser said. "I think it's fifty percent that somebody calls the El Paso cops."

Letty said, "C'mon, man. She came into that supposed inheritance and bought that Jeep about the time the oil thefts started."

"I got that," Kaiser said. They were leaving the parking lot and stopped to let a tumbleweed blow by. "Okay. All right, you got me. Let's go."

Nobody answered their knock. Letty used her body to block sight lines from one side, and Kaiser used his to block from the other direction as he worked his picks into a lock that he said was a piece of junk. Still, he took three minutes to get it open and they were both sweating by the time he did. Literally sweating, the backs of their shirts soaking wet with perspiration. When the lock popped, Letty pushed on the door with her knuckles, and when it was open called, "Hello? Hey, anybody here? Hello?"

"Quick, now," Kaiser said, as they went inside and he pushed the door closed. "The cops could still be coming."

One minute in the house, and Letty said, "She's gone. She was here, there's stuff in the garbage can that probably was dumped yesterday. There's a milk carton that doesn't smell spoiled yet. No clothes, no bedding, no towels, no bathroom stuff . . . nothing but junky furniture and an old TV."

Kaiser agreed. "She's moved on."

"They're close to whatever they're planning to do, she's already running," Letty said. "We need to talk to Greet. We need to see her bank accounts and credit cards . . ."

They called Greet as they were driving out of Pear Tree Lane, and told her that they'd looked through the windows of Hawkes's house and it appeared that she'd vacated the place. "Not like a standard move-out," Letty said. "She took clothes and personal stuff, dishes and bedding, cleaned out the refrigerator, but she left behind her bed and chest of drawers and other furniture, a microwave and TV."

"You saw all that through the windows? The inside of a fridge?"

"Try to focus, here, Billy," Letty said.

"You think she's on the run?" Greet asked.

"That's what we think."

"Okay, I admit that's scary. Unless they just wanted the C-4 because, you know, they *wanted* it. Like those goofs running around with ARs."

"Blowing up an I-beam seems like a very specific *want,*" Letty said.

"We can put out a request for her Jeep — if she owned it, I can get the tag number and put the Texas highway patrol on it and the El Paso police. I can probably get her credit card purchases; the bank accounts might take longer."

"You gotta do it fast as you can; if she cleaned out her bank account . . ."

"Okay. I'll get all of that today. You guys be careful."

"I don't know what we do next," Letty admitted. "Guess we wait for Greet to call."

They hadn't gotten to the hotel before Greet called.

"First thing I tried was tracking Hawkes's Jeep. Guess what? She sold it yesterday morning. Went down with the buyer and registered the transfer with the Texas DMV. She got almost thirty thousand dollars for it — twenty-nine, nine."

"Billy . . ."

"I know, I know, that's bad. Real bad," Greet said.

"I just thought of something," Letty said. "Damn it, I should have thought of it when

I was talking to the general. You need to call him back, or talk to the sergeant major who sits outside his office. They've got a captain there, I don't know his full name, but his last name is Colin. I need to talk to him. Immediately."

"I'll call," Greet promised. "And he *will* call you back, because I will be screaming at them."

Colin did call back, as they drove into the hotel parking lot. "I'm in enough trouble, with the general asking why you're calling me."

"I don't care about how much trouble you're in," Letty said. "Listen to me. When this unknown guy was showing our suspects . . . the people we know about . . . how to use the C-4, I took some photographs with my iPhone. We were too far away from them, for the photos to be much good, but I took them on the telephoto setting. Maybe you can do something with them. If he was the guy supplying the C-4, and he probably was . . ."

Colin: "Send it to me! Now!"

Letty sent the best of the photos, and Colin said, "I got a guy who can work with this."

"If you get anything, call us back," Letty said.

"Maybe," Colin said, and he clicked off.

"Fuck that guy," Letty said.

"Fuck the whole Army. It's CYA, every day."

"Covering your ass won't cut it, if they blow up El Paso," Letty said, as they walked across the parking lot to the hotel. "What if they're planning to blow up the Army headquarters?"

"From what I've read, the militias are usually full of ex-military," Kaiser said. "I don't think they'd do that."

"Can't see them blowing up a government building, they're all pretty well guarded."

"No, they're not . . . not if it's done like Oklahoma City, where a truck pulls up in the street and *boom,*" Kaiser said. "But the Oklahoma bomb was huge. A lot bigger than a hundred pounds of C-4."

"If they were learning how to cut an I-beam, they must be inside some place . . . must be able to get inside with explosives and detonators and all that."

"Whatever it is, I believe they're going to do it soon, since Hawkes just evacuated the war zone," Kaiser said. He held the door for her, and said, "Let's find a place to sit

380

and talk. I wonder where Low is? We haven't heard from Low. Or even seen him."

"Now, that's a thought," Letty said. She cupped her hands over her nose and mouth, thinking, then said, "Probably doesn't have a driver's license, at least, not a current one, or his parole officer could find him. Same goes for truck registration."

"Greet says his cell phone has to be a burner," Kaiser said. "We need regular bills that aren't on a government computer that everybody is wired into, that the parole officer would be accessing."

"Utility bills. Greet already looked at some for Sawyer and Crain," Letty suggested. "They usually go to the address where the service is."

Kaiser ticked a finger at her: "That might be the thing. We could get Greet to call."

"She might be tired of us asking for her help," Letty said. "And it's after hours in Washington."

"Fuck her. That's her job. Call," Kaiser said.

Letty called Greet, who was still in her office and said that she would do what she could. "Problem is, places are closing down for the day. It's getting late. And to tell you the truth, I don't think it'll do any good."

"Tell me why," Letty said.

"Because he's gone underground. His parole officer can't find him, you haven't seen him. He's got a fake ID and it's a good one. I think Hawkes is gone, too. Do you think she sold her Jeep and now is walking around with thirty thousand dollars in her pocket? I don't think so, either. She bought another vehicle, but she hasn't registered one. Bought it under a fake name, with a fake ID, or a private sale, or all of that. But I'll bet dollars to donuts that she's got wheels."

"How do we find them?"

"I don't know," Greet said. "I've been researching Hawkes, she was in the Army and did okay there, she's bright, that shows up on her Army intelligence tests. We have good pictures of her now, from the Army and her college ID. If we distribute them all over, some cop will eventually spot her, but that's not going to happen tomorrow or even next week."

"Send them to my phone — the pictures," Letty said.

"Yes."

After talking with Greet, Letty called Pugh, the Monahans cop, and asked if she could go by Crain's and Duran's houses in Monahans to see if lights were on, if there were parked vehicles out in front of them.

"We could go back up there, if they're around," Letty told Kaiser.

"Four and a half hours gone," Kaiser said.

"What would we do for four and a half hours, if we stayed here?" Letty asked. "We're stuck."

Pugh called back fifteen minutes later and said both houses were dark, with no vehicles around.

"They're all moving," Kaiser said. "It's under way, whatever it is."

"It's like a fuckin' nightmare," Letty said. "One of those where you're trying to find your school locker and you keep running from one to the next, and it's never yours."

Letty and Kaiser went up to their rooms to wash their faces and hands, then walked back to the pizza place again to get dinner.

Greet called as they were finishing the pizza and said, "I'm not getting anywhere. I can't find anyone to talk to at the electric company; the gas company says they don't have a Rand Low in their billing system. He has a driver's license, he renewed it when he got out of prison, but he doesn't live at the address on his license, not anymore, and that's the same address that's on his truck tag.

"His truck tag wasn't renewed, but a guy at the state patrol office said he's probably peeling the renewal sticker off somebody else's truck and putting it on his own. Nothing on any of the big three cell services, he's probably got a burner. I don't see a Visa card under his name, but I did find an active Visa and an active MasterCard under Hawkes's name, so he could be using one of those . . . The state patrol hasn't issued recent traffic tickets to Crain, Duran, Low, or Hawkes. So far, I've struck out with the banks."

"Billy, I know you gotta be annoyed with us . . ."

"No, no, we need you to keep pushing, I'm here all night if you need me to be," Greet said.

"We know they're anti-immigrant. Would the Border Patrol have anything under their names?"

"Shit. If you didn't hear it, I just slapped my forehead. Let me see who I can wake up and ask."

Letty and Kaiser walked back to the hotel, frustrated, agreed that if Greet called back with anything significant, Letty could wake up Kaiser anytime. "I'm going to finish that Furst book and then go to bed," Kaiser said. "Maybe things will get clearer overnight."

"Or blow up," Letty said.

"Wash your mouth out with soap."

Greet called back at ten o'clock, which would be midnight, Washington time — Letty had been confused about time zones for a bit, until she found out that El Paso was in the Mountain Time Zone, unlike the rest of Texas. "I was looking for the right Border Patrol intelligence guy, and it turns out he's in a motel in El Paso. He's there because there's a big caravan of Central Americans headed your way, fifteen hundred people or so . . ."

"I saw something in the El Paso paper," Letty said. "They're supposed to get here when? Day after tomorrow?"

"That's what this guy thinks. Maybe as soon as tomorrow night. Anyway, he says that there has been a militia patrolling along the river southeast of El Paso for several years. They've been especially active the last year or two . . ."

"Because they got operational money," Letty said.

"Maybe. They've actually spotted and stopped a number of illegals and called in the Border Patrol. He said that they are armed. They claim that they only carry weapons in case they should run into armed drug mules coming across."

"That doesn't sound so terrible, if you gotta have a militia in the first place," Letty said.

"Maybe not. But here's the relevant part. He thinks that the militia may be run by a woman. His border patrolmen have encountered her a few times and she does the talking, not the guys. And she drives a Jeep."

"That's her," Letty said. "Jane Jael Hawkes."

"I sent her Army ID photos and her driver's license photos to the intelligence guy, he'll put them in front of people who've met her. That won't happen until tomorrow, though."

"All right. Well, I don't know what we're doing tomorrow, but something is going on. If you can think of anything, let me know."

"Try not to break into any more houses," Greet said.

"I can't promise anything," Letty said. "You know what? I'm scared. I finally got there."

NINETEEN

Back up in the mountains well east of El Paso, ten miles off I-10, Hawkes could see almost forever to the southeast, with the orange ball of the sun dropping toward the horizon at her right hand. Curls of pale dust rose from the wheels of the pickups winding up the desert road toward the meet. It was hot, but no longer oppressive, and would cool quickly in the night. The skies were perfectly clear, and the stars and the moon would be a spectacle.

"We already got sixty and we're still an hour away," Rand Low said. He was exultant, pacing back and forth on a rocky ridge above the meeting area. Down below, sixty pickups were parked in a semicircle around what would be a bonfire later in the evening, after it got dark.

Militia folks wandered among the trucks, introducing themselves, drinking a little beer, eating cheese sandwiches, men and women in jeans and boots and cotton shirts, a sprinkling of camo. The license plates were from all over, Washington State, Oregon, Idaho, Michigan, Wisconsin, New Mexico, Arizona, four dozen from Texas. "We'll have seventy, eighty trucks before the night's done, more than a hundred guns."

"Wonder how many of them are FBI?" Crain asked, with a tight grin.

"Might be one or two, but I sorta doubt it," Hawkes said. "These are the cream of the crop. I've looked at every one of them six ways to Sunday. Still, we can't take a chance."

"Some of those boys and girls are gonna be right surprised tomorrow morning, when we tell them the truth," Low said.

"If they want to bail, they can bail. We'll tell them the truth then," Hawkes said. "If there's FBI among them, it'll be too late for them to do anything."

"Down there!" Low said. "Two more trucks. Goddamn, they're coming in now."

"Read your talk some more," Hawkes said. Low had a speech written by Hawkes, meant to be delivered as the high point of the evening, something to get people churned. "You're not gonna be able to read it when you get down there."

"I know, I know, I know. I'm gonna shout

it out there, gonna preach," Low crowed. He looked down at the papers in his hand, curled into a tube. He'd already read it twenty times. Then, suddenly subdued, he asked, "How many you think will buy it?"

"All of them, until tomorrow morning," Hawkes said, looking at the people walking among the trucks. "Some might drop out then and they'll live to regret it. This will be the day when people will ask, 'Were you there?' This is where we draw the line."

"Ah, God." Low scrubbed at his hairline with open hands. "I ain't felt like this since high school football."

Duran was climbing the slope toward them, and when he came up, out of breath, he said, "I talked to Borrego. It's definitely happening."

"Of course it is," Hawkes said. "I've known for two months."

"Look at this," Low said. More trucks climbing the mountain, five, six more, long rolling cigars of dust trailing behind them. Down below, a dozen men and women had clustered around a guy who was demonstrating a long, dark, heavy rifle. "That's a Barrett fifty."

"And that's probably a guy we don't need, a show-off," Hawkes said.

"C'mon, give the guy a break," Low said.

"I wouldn't mind trying it myself."

"Bet ol' Max would have loved to try it," Low said.

"But ol' Max is deader'n a doornail," Hawkes said. She started thumbing her cell phone. "I heard some more about that from R.J. He wasn't killed by that big DHS guy, he was shot by the girl. R.J. says she put three rounds in him, two in his legs and one in his forehead. The story is, her name is Letty Davenport and she's a killer. R.J. says she's killed before and she took Max down like he was the village ding-a-ling."

She pushed a button on her phone and held it so Low could see the screen. "This is her, Letty Davenport. Picture's six or seven years old. I'm going to pull it and send it around to our main guys."

"If I see her, she's dead," Low said. He reached behind his back and pulled his Beretta, popped the mag, slapped it back in place, just because he liked to do it.

"Says you," Hawkes said. "How many people you killed in an actual stand-up gunfight?"

Low glanced sideways at her: "What's got on your tits?"

"I'm . . . anxious," Hawkes said. She put the phone away. "Also tired. I spent five hours buying potato chips and weenies and ketchup and charcoal and lighter and KFC and bread and salami. I had to go to three KFCs to get all that chicken. And marshmallows and buns and pickles and Pepsi and water and beer and milk and cereal . . ."

"We get the picture," Duran said. "Hey: there's more coming up."

Down below, more long trails of dust, more pickups rolling in.

Hawkes reached back to her days in American history: "It's like . . . It's like fuckin' Shiloh. Good ol' boys and girls going to war."

Full dark came quickly, not much twilight on the desert, and pinewood fires popped up around the meeting place. A woman named July Null had set up a cafeteria off the back of three El Paso pickups, and people were lining up with paper plates for the food. A truck or two came in after dark, but Low had been right: there were eighty-two trucks altogether and maybe a hundred and ten people — seventy percent men, but a larger number of women than they'd expected.

A Honda gas generator ran smoothly off to one side and provided power for a dozen lights and a speaker and microphone, which had been set up on top of Low's pickup bed. Several people were wearing cowboy-style bandanna masks and pulled-down hats, not wanting to show their faces. Hawkes hadn't bothered: the Feds would know who she was if she pulled this off. She wandered among the crowd, shaking hands and taking hugs from old acquaintances, compliments from people who knew her by name but had never met her.

The place smelled like a small-town carnival, she thought; it was the odor of mustard and ketchup and chopped onions on roasting wieners that did it. And maybe a little whiff of poop — *ladies in that ravine, gentlemen in the other, and watch your step, there's a deep hole back there, and be sure to use the garden trowel to drop some dirt on top of your business.*

Hawkes took the microphone for one minute and said, "We're going to have a pep talk by one of our own El Paso boys, but right now I want to encourage you to eat — we still got plenty of KFC — and to introduce yourself around. If you're a little shy, don't worry about it, go meet people. We want to be a unified force when we get to town tomorrow. Now: we've got members of our El Paso group who will be directing traffic tomorrow. They don't outrank you —

nobody outranks anyone here — but we've been talking to them about directing traffic. We want everyone to sign up with these groups, so you know where you'll be tomorrow. Something else — we'll be getting up early in the morning, so try to get some sleep, even if it's hard. I hope everybody has a sleeping bag, like we asked you to bring, but if you don't, we've got some extras on this truck over here . . ."

She pointed to the next truck over, and Crain held up two sleeping bags.

Hawkes went on. "Try to stay up until we tamp down the fires and kill the lights. For those of you who come from places that are wetter than us, you'll be amazed by the stars you'll see tonight. So. Fifteen more minutes for dinner, you can put your trash, paper plates and all that, in the bags below this truck. Then we'll have the pep talk. Tomorrow morning, we'll talk about specific assignments."

One of her El Paso women shouted, "The Hawk is out," and Hawkes smiled and climbed down from the truck.

As she came down, Low climbed up and took the microphone. A big man with shoulder-length black hair, he was dressed in a black T-shirt under a black sport coat, black jeans, and black combat boots. He was carrying a black AR-15 with a thirty-round mag banged onto the bottom of it. As the crowd tightened around the truck, he peeled off the jacket to reveal a tan leather shoulder holster with his Beretta. Hawkes had calculated the effect, and she'd been correct: a ripple of *ooo* rolled through the crowd. Low flashed his smile and picked up the microphone.

"I've been asked to coordinate our action tomorrow. In your invitation to the party, we noted that Texas has open carry of long guns, but you need a license to carry a handgun, either open or concealed. That's not really here nor there tomorrow — carry whatever you have — but we don't want anybody recklessly shooting them off . . ."

He went on about guns for a while, answered a couple of shouted questions, spoke about the media — "They're gonna be all over us, calling us Nazis and all that bullcrap . . ." — and then began to preach.

"This country should be a paradise. There should be a job for every working man, and how long the liberals been talking about that, and what have we got? Sold out to the Chinese and the Mexicans and everybody else we could be sold out to. The Vietnamese, who killed fifty thousand American

394

boys back in the sixties and seventies . . .
We got any veterans here?"

Hawkes marveled. When she was sitting in
a McDonald's with him, Low came off as a
Texas hick, white trash, gobbling fries with
oil-stained fingers, chewing with his mouth
open, spitting pieces of Quarter Pounder
around the table, dribbling ketchup on his
shirt . . .

On a rifle range, he was a dangerous man,
to himself and everyone around him. He
never seemed to know quite where his gun
was pointed, whether it was a rifle or a
pistol, and if you sat next to him long
enough, the muzzle would inevitably track
across your nose, with his finger on the trigger . . .

But.

Get him to talk at a meeting, and he came
alive. He couldn't write his speeches, but he
could deliver them, working into a kind of
controlled frenzy that animated crowds and
made even the skeptical pay close attention.

". . . goddamned wetbacks taking over
our country? I don't think so, that ain't
gonna happen, as we say up in Crocket
County . . ."

When he climbed down from the truck to
continuing applause, Crain cut the genera-

tors, and the lights snapped out. Overhead, the stars were tiny suns, pouring their light over the gathering, bringing out another long sustained *ooooo* . . .

Hawkes wrapped an arm around Low's waist and said, "You did it. You got them. Now, tomorrow morning, we got to keep them."

"I'm worried about the first part of that, where you tell them we've been lying to them . . ."

"It'll grab their attention . . ."

"It might be better if you started off sayin' we're worried that there are spies among us. Even one would be too many. So I lied to you a little last night."

Hawkes considered, and said, "You could be right. I think either way is okay. I'll sleep on it. You worry about what you're gonna say. I'll take care of mine."

Low nodded and, looking out over the encampment, where people were crawling into their truck beds, or standing around talking, or smoking, random laughs and giggles, and said, "I'll remember this night for the rest of my life."

"We all will."

Hawkes lay awake for a long time, lying on a yoga mat next to Crain, in the back of

396

Crain's truck, both of them wrapped in lightweight sleeping bags. Crain, from long practice in prison, was asleep almost immediately, and snoring. Hawkes ran through the whole scheme for the next day.

She remembered a quotation she'd seen in one of her history books, from a German general: "No battle plan survives contact with the enemy."

She was thinking about that when she dozed off; hours later, she heard her phone beep at her, opened her eyes, and saw the night sky, and down to the horizon, Orion's Belt, pointing down at the town of Pershing, Texas. Her mouth was dry and tasted bad; she sat up, kicked out of her sleeping bag, looked again at Orion's Belt. An omen, she thought, and it gave her confidence.

Pershing was named after Black Jack Pershing, an American general who chased Pancho Villa all over northern Mexico, and never did catch him.

By dawn, the encampment was awake, eating breakfast. There wasn't enough cereal to go around, though she'd bought fifty boxes of Honey Nut Cheerios and twenty gallons of milk that had been kept cool in a stock watering tank full of ice. There was a little early-morning grouching and bitching, the group winding up for the action in El Paso, though it wouldn't exactly be in El Paso.

The militias rekindled a couple of fires, burning the last of the pinewood, people spitting toothpaste into the sand and scuffing more sand over it, and there was a line at the latrines for a while.

Hawkes let that go on for forty-five minutes, then climbed up on top of the truck with the microphone and amp. "If we could crowd in around here, we've got some important stuff to talk about this morning. I'm going to start things off and I'm going to tell you three shocking things. First thing. I would not be totally surprised if there was an FBI informant among us. Or, maybe, an out-and-out FBI agent, a spy. That is just the way it is. That's life. Because of that possibility, that we have a flea in our ear, here's the second shocking thing. We lied to you last night, getting you whipped up for an action in El Paso. We're not going to El Paso. We're going to a town called Pershing, Texas.

"You remember Pershing. A year and a half ago, a caravan from Central America, more than a thousand people, came up here, like it was headed for El Paso, planning to rush the border. At the last minute, the whole caravan swerved down a side highway, used mostly by trucks headed for the eastern part of the States. That highway runs through the town of Ochoa, Mexico, on the Rio Grande, and across the bridge to Pershing, here in the States.

"The whole thing was stopped on the Mexican side, all those illegals packed into a parking lot. The mayor of Pershing declared a human disaster and invited them across the bridge, and the gutless men at the Customs and Border Protection station allowed them through. We have word that the same thing will happen again today, this evening — a caravan has already turned off the main Mexican highway and is headed for Pershing. We're gonna go down there and we're gonna stop them. I can promise you, this will be a great day for our kind of people. I'll tell you something else: we're not gonna get arrested, we're not going to jail. Some of our El Paso people are walking around right now, putting duct tape on your license plates, covering up the numbers.

"We're not far from the highway that runs from I-10 to Pershing, which is why we chose this place, which I know some of you thought was too far from El Paso . . . We picked it because we're not going to El Paso."

She spoke for ten more minutes, outlining the detailed plan for invading Pershing, holding it, and then . . .

"We'll talk more about the details this afternoon. Each of you will get a small file folder with an informational packet, which you should look at when you have a break. We think we have things fixed so nobody gets busted. Again, because there might be an FBI agent here — hello there, wherever you are, you fuckin' rat, if you're really out there — we don't want to talk about it right now," she said. "Okay, next thing. How many of you guys have used chain saws? Raise your hands . . ."

A lot of them had. Hawkes got them working on sign-up lists, organized by her El Paso faithful, depending on what they could do, and what they were willing to do.

When she was done, Low talked for ten more minutes, winding up the crowd. There were doubters, but not many.

When he had them shouting, the El Paso people passed out clip-on American flags that could be attached to truck windows.

Hawkes took the microphone back.

"I know most of you hadn't counted on what we're doing. You've got families you're worried about, you're worried about getting arrested, and all of that. Even if we were arrested, I don't think there's a jury in Texas that would convict us. Nevertheless, it would be tough," she said. "If you don't feel right about this, here's what you do. Get in our convoy, go on down to I-10 with us. We'll be going under the bridge and turning left. You turn right on this side of the bridge, and it'll take you straight into El Paso. We'd suggest you keep going, scatter back to wherever you're from. We won't hold it against you: but I'll tell you what, you'll be missing the greatest day that ever came to people like us. You'll miss the beginning of the revolution. You'll miss being genuine American heroes."

There was some stirring around, after she got off the truck, and Low shouted, "Load 'em up! Load 'em up! We're going down the hill as a convoy, no matter which way you turn at I-10."

They spent twenty minutes loading up and lining up, the pickups spaced so they wouldn't be bumping into one another in the dust they'd be kicking up. Two El Paso women ran down the line of trucks, telling the drivers to close up once they were on the highway. "Lights on! If a highway patrol should try to pull us over, we ain't pulling over. We think we know where they're at, and they're not where we're going. But we're a convoy. We keep rolling on no matter what!"

Hawkes rode with Low. When they were set, Low hit his horn a half-dozen times, and led the way down the mountain.

"Think we'll lose many?" he asked Hawkes. "Guys turning right?"

"Bet it's not ten," Hawkes said. "Most of these guys are hot to trot."

She looked up at the sky: Orion's Belt had faded away with the dawn.

TWENTY

Stepping back:

After talking to Greet, Letty got ready for bed but couldn't sleep. If Hawkes was the leader of an El Paso area militia and she'd gone on the run before being pressured by any authority, then she must be considering some action that would require her to run.

An action that would happen soon. But what?

Though she was tired from the day, Letty began looking at online satellite maps of El Paso and the surrounding areas, picking out possible targets. The militia was believed to have been patrolling east of the city, in the rough country on the American side of the Rio Grande; there wasn't much out there. Once you got past the agricultural strip fed by the Rio Grande, there was nothing but dry mountains and desert.

El Paso had the usual federal buildings of any big city, but an attack on a building didn't feel right. The amount of money collected from the oil thefts suggested a large operation involving a number of people. A bomb designed to blow up a building took one man, one truck, one timer, and one detonator . . . and C-4 would be the wrong way to go about it.

She thought about the C-4. The stuff was a powerful explosive, all right, and Hawkes and her friends had been testing it on an I-beam. Not enough to bring down a skyscraper, she'd been told, but she wasn't sure she believed that. Say you had a huge heavy building and blew out all the supports on one side . . . wouldn't that bring the whole thing down?

She didn't know. She dug around on Google and found an Arcelor-Mittal site that made her feel foolish, with its models of building structures. *Of course* buildings weren't supported only around their perimeter. They were supported by beams that rose up all through the building, and some of those beams were far heavier and thicker than the I-beam that Hawkes and her friends had cut in the test explosion.

And she found an image of the federal building in Oklahoma City after the terrorist bombing. The truck bomb had taken off the building's façade and a chunk of the interior, but the rest of the structure remained standing. That bomb was far more powerful than a hundred pounds of C-4.

So: not a building?

She shut down the computer and turned to the nightstand clock: almost midnight. She turned off the lights and tried to sleep, and failed. Bored in the dark, bereft of ideas, she got the remote, turned on the television, piled pillows under her head, and began clicking around through the cable channels.

Got caught by an old movie called *High Fidelity,* a rom-com about a guy who ran a Chicago record store. She missed the first part of it, but watched it right to the happy ending, yawned, clicked through the available channels.

She caught a repeat tape of a local news channel. A weary-looking brunette with unsubtle makeup was saying, ". . . may not be coming to El Paso after all. Reports from Mexico say that at least part of the caravan broke off the main highway and are headed toward the border crossing at Pershing. How much of the caravan is continuing to El Paso and how much is going to Pershing is uncertain, but the caravans should arrive in either place late tomorrow, if their progress continues as it has the last few weeks.

Pershing, if you will remember, was the site of a controversial crossing nineteen months ago . . ."

Letty remembered.

A Central American caravan of men, women, and children, apparently headed north to El Paso, had turned east at a small Mexican town instead of continuing north, and had arrived at a crossing at Ochoa, Mexico, linked across the Rio Grande with the town of Pershing.

There was almost nothing at Ochoa except a Mexican border station, a couple dozen houses mostly inhabited by the border guards, a gas station/convenience store, and a huge parking lot for Mexican eighteen-wheelers headed for the U.S.

Pershing was larger, although Letty wasn't certain how much larger. If she remembered correctly — she climbed out of bed and fired up her computer and found that she did remember correctly — it was also a small town.

Pershing's main claim to fame occurred when the Central American caravan, including large numbers of children, showed up at the Mexican side of the bridge with almost nothing in the way of food, water, or shelter. The mayor of Pershing, Harold Lopez, with support from all the city commissioners, had become a hero to a segment of the American political community when he invited the refugees to cross the bridge, and shouted down the Border Patrol when patrolmen tried to stop them.

"Food and water for babies," Lopez had shouted at the El Paso news crew that had shown up to record the confrontation. The Border Patrol cracked when the news crew reported that a baby had died, possibly of dehydration, and the caravan crossed the bridge. Once inside the U.S., members of the caravan had to be processed through the American legal system. That could take months, and might well result in many of the refugees remaining in the country.

Letty reviewed the whole story in the Google links, then checked the mileage to Pershing. Kaiser had already told her that nothing in Texas was close to anything else, and he was right. Pershing was the only crossing between El Paso and Presidio, Texas, and was about sixty miles southwest of the I-10 town of Van Horn. The last stretch, between Van Horn and Pershing, was on a two-lane highway through the mountains, apparently designed expressly for truck traffic. Altogether, Pershing was about three road hours southeast of El Paso.

And she thought, *Hawkes* — Jael — *is already running.*

At two o'clock in the morning, she called Kaiser, who answered with a groan and, "Aw, what happened?"

"Did you get any sleep at all?" Letty asked.

"Yeah, I finished the book at ten, I was sleeping like a baby until eight seconds ago," he said.

"Get up, pack up, we need to hit the road."

Kaiser's voice sharpened up: "What happened?"

"Nothing, yet, as far as I know. I'll meet you in the lobby in half an hour, we're checking out. You're driving. I haven't slept at all, and I need some. Half-hour."

She clicked off and went to get dressed and pack her clothes.

In the lobby, Kaiser asked, "Can you tell me now?"

"After we get checked out and we're in the car," Letty said. "This might not make you happy."

"I'm already not happy," Kaiser said.

Outside, the air was cool and felt a bit damp, compared to the afternoon's blow-dryer heat. Stars were bright overhead, and while waiting for Kaiser to catch up, Letty twisted in circles, face turned to the sky. More stars than she'd seen even in deep rural Minnesota; but on the other hand, in deep rural Minnesota, in the winter, you had the rippling yellow, purple, and blue-gray curtains of the northern lights.

"So tell me," Kaiser said, throwing his duffel and shotgun case in the back of the Explorer.

"Let's get on I-10," Letty said. She walked around to the passenger side, dropped the seat back so she might possibly get some sleep. "We're going east."

When they were moving, she laid it out for him: an anti-immigrant militia with the leader on the run for no good reason they could yet see, a town celebrated for allowing an entire immigrant caravan to cross the border, and now another caravan on the way to the same place.

"The only thing I could think of is that the caravan is triggering them. I don't know what they're going to do, but there's a good chance they'll do it in Pershing. That's what I think."

"How would they know that this caravan is going to turn toward Pershing?" Kaiser asked.

"If you weren't a dumbass, and you were steering a caravan, where would you go?"

"But what if they *are* dumbasses, and they really *are* going to El Paso?"

"Late-night news channel says the caravan split last night. I think Hawkes, or Low, or whoever is running this thing, knew this was going to happen. I think they're going down there to block the caravan. If they're not, well, El Paso doesn't need the two of us. They've got city cops, FBI, ATF, Texas Rangers, sheriff's deputies . . . The Pershing website says they have four part-time cops."

Kaiser, blinking into the night, was silent for a minute, or perhaps two minutes, then said, "All right. I know pretty young women don't actually have rectums, but if you *did* have one, I understand that's where you pulled this idea from. The weird thing about it is, I believe you. Should we call the Feds?"

"At three o'clock in the morning? You think anyone would even answer?"

"Okay. We should call Greet as soon as she might possibly be awake," Kaiser said. "More people than us need to know about this . . ."

"They know about the caravan. Whether they've linked it to this militia activity, I don't know."

"They haven't," Kaiser said. "I've got no way to know that, but they haven't."

"Unfortunately, you're correct," Letty

said. "You're three hours from Pershing, something less than two hours from Van Horn, where you turn. I'm going to try to take a nap. If I'm not awake when you make the turn, wake me up then. I want to see the highway into Pershing."

Kaiser woke her at four-thirty. "We're coming up to Van Horn. There's a Love's Travel Stop on the other side of town, not far. We could gas up and buy some stuff to eat and drink. I don't know what they'll have in Pershing. I think we should stop."

Letty yawned. "Good. I have to pee anyway. I ran out of the hotel without hitting the bathroom. Too cranked up."

At the Love's, they got gas and they both hit the restroom and then Kaiser piled up crackers and cookies and potato chips and jerky and energy bars and Diet Coke, and Letty got two six-packs of water and some black licorice and string cheese and bananas, and they both got large cups of coffee, and got back on the highway, a mile to the Pershing exit.

The Pershing highway was well maintained but crooked. It began on rolling desert, then quickly cut through the mountains, running along the top of a ridge, outcrops of reddish rock and dirt on one

411

side, a deep fall-off on the other. Yellow and red reflectors marked danger spots, so many of them that they might have been an art installation. At some of the wider spots, they saw what appeared in their headlights to be the edges of agricultural fields, but they weren't sure of that. In the sixty miles between I-10 and the outer edge of Pershing, they saw no more than a dozen houses, marked by pole lights.

"You still all right to drive?" Letty asked, after a series of quick left-right jogs in the highway.

"Good right now, but I'm tired," Kaiser said. "I-10 was great. Ninety miles per hour, light traffic, no cops. I was reading my phone and as far as I could tell, there's one motel in Pershing, a Lariat Inn. A couple reviews said it's okay. 'Clean' was the operative word. I doubt the militia will be there at six o'clock in the morning. If they're not, we oughta bunk out."

"I could do that," Letty said. "I'd like at least to drive around town soon as we get there, see what there is to see. Shouldn't take more than a few minutes."

"First light's around six-thirty, so there won't be much."

Halfway down the highway, they got stuck

behind a tractor-trailer headed toward the border crossing, and followed it for twenty miles before Kaiser could get around it in the face of sporadic truck traffic going the other way. He said, "I could be wrong, but if somebody wanted to use that C-4 to blow up one of these rock outcrops, you could probably block the highway for a week . . . speaking as a guy who spent too much time in dirka-dirka-stan."

"The rocks aren't held up by I-beams," Letty said.

"True. But a brick of C-4 here, another one there . . . It doesn't have just one use. You could make some effective IEDs out of that stuff. C-4, detonator, burner phone, *boom.*"

"Thank you for that. You should teach confidence-building classes when you get back to Washington."

They saw a scattering of lights ahead, followed by a band of darkness. The lights surrounded an oversized parking lot for semi-trailer trucks. "Waiting to cross, or already across coming this way," Kaiser said. "Guys sleeping before they take on that highway."

Then there was a long, dark strip of highway, nothing but the oncoming white lines in the headlights and the occasionally squashed jackrabbit, then a thick grove of palm trees, and after another five miles, the lights of the town.

Kaiser drove a couple of blocks into it, then began circling through the side streets. While the highway had been smooth, well-maintained blacktop, the residential streets in town were heavily patched blacktop, oiled dirt, or plain dirt. Most of the newer houses were the manufactured type, as far as Letty could tell, double-wides brought in by truck and set up on concrete slabs. Others were concrete block, with deteriorating frame houses sprinkled among them, along with bare-brick adobes from the nineteenth century. Most of the light came from scattered porch lights; only the highway, which led downhill to the well-lit Customs station, had streetlights. An oversized truck parking lot sat to one side of the station, with a single waiting truck.

"Seen enough?" Kaiser asked, as he turned away from the border.

"Yes, but I didn't see your Lariat Inn."

"We skipped most of the main drag circling around town. It'll be along there, somewhere . . ."

A small town: they found the Lariat Inn in two minutes, a single-story row of twenty-four narrow rooms with eight or ten cars pulled nose-in to the doors. An aging white wooden sign said FREE WI-FI, and hanging under that, another sign, that appeared to be permanent, that said, VACANCY. They went inside the office, rang a bell on the desk, and a sleepy elderly man came out of a back room, yawned and asked, "What can I do you for?"

"Got a couple rooms?" Letty asked. A clock on the wall clicked to six-fifteen.

"I do, but I'll have to charge you for a full day if you check in now," he said.

"That's fine," she said.

"Connecting or not connecting?" His eyes clicked between the two of them.

Letty looked at Kaiser and asked, "What do you think, Uncle John?"

"As widely separated as possible," Kaiser said to the old man.

They checked in, and outside, Kaiser said, "I got that 'Uncle John' shit. Very funny. But in a deal like this, separate the rooms so one can be at least a temporary bolt-hole, if they spot the other one."

"See, you know some criminal stuff," Letty said.

Kaiser held the room keys separately in his two balled fists and said, "Choose. Then I can't be accused of taking the good one."

Letty chose. Her door came up first, and

as Kaiser walked to his, he called back, "Not a fuckin' thing going on here. Wake me up when you're ready to go back to El Paso."

Letty's room was, as advertised, clean; the pillowcase smelled freshly laundered. Letty fell onto the bed and slept as though dead for two and a half hours, when her phone rang: Kaiser.

"What?" she croaked.

"Look out your window," he said.

She rolled off the bed. A line of pickup trucks was rolling by the motel: a long line, spaced out. In many of them, an armed man or woman sat in the truck bed, rifles pointing to the sky.

Letty: "Oh, shit."

"I left the shotgun in the truck," Kaiser said.

"I'd get it while you can," Letty said. "I'll call Greet."

Greet answered on the first ring. "I was about to call. Do you know about a refugee caravan . . ."

Letty interrupted: "We're in a motel in Pershing, Texas, up the hill from the border crossing. A whole lot of pickup trucks are going by. I've counted thirty so far, and some went by before I started counting. There are guys with guns. I don't know . . .

a TV truck just went by, the kind with a satellite link, so whatever this is, it'll be on TV. Billy, this could be bad. They keep coming. Here come some more now. There are a lot of them."

"I'm calling everybody. You stay in touch. You say they've got guns?"

"Lots of guns. Long guns, ARs. I think they're taking over the town . . ." she said. Then, "Kaiser's calling me, he's in another room. I'll call you back."

Still looking out the window, she switched to Kaiser.

He said, "Got my shotgun. What do you think?"

"We need to get out there," Letty said. "I want to take a shower, but I'll be done and dressed in ten minutes. Let's ask the old guy if there's a diner we can walk to. We'll probably hear some stuff there, if there is one."

"Saw a pizza place, but not a diner."

"Gotta be somewhere you can get breakfast," Letty said.

"Ten minutes," Kaiser said.

Letty took a two-minute shower and brushed her teeth, dressed in jeans and a white blouse, tightly tucked in, slipped the 938 into its Sticky Holster, and checked to make sure it wasn't printing on her pocket.

She was reaching for the doorknob when Kaiser knocked. "You got your baby gun?"

"I do."

"I don't want to carry until I know what's going on," he said. "If anyone checked me, they'd find it. I'll be counting on you for protection."

"I'm a better shot anyway," Letty said. "Think you could slide a couple extra mags in your sock?"

"Of course. What else are socks for?"

The old guy was standing outside the office, looking down the hill toward the Customs and Border Protection station. He turned when he heard them coming and said, "Something going on."

"No kidding," Kaiser said. "I haven't seen that many black pickups since I got caught in a goatfuck at an Air Force base in Grand Forks, North Dakota."

"Those guys got guns." The old guy cocked his head. "You guys with them?"

Letty shook her head. "No. We're just . . . You don't think . . ."

The old man said, "I don't know what to think. I gotta talk to my wife, see what she thinks."

As he turned back to the motel door, Letty asked, "Is there a diner here where we could get breakfast?"

The old guy said, "Up the hill, on this side. Jeff's. Food is decent, but I'd stay away from the open-faced beef sandwich, that sucker will repeat on you. If you tell them that Roger sent you, he'll put a dollar in a jar for me."

Kaiser asked, "Diner? Given the situation . . ."

"Best place to hear stuff in a small town," Letty said. "Diners and beauty shops. Beauty shops won't be open yet. But first . . . there's people walking down the hill. Let's get in with them."

A couple of dozen townspeople were walking, in small groups, in fits and starts, down toward the Customs and Border Protection station.

"We should split up, in case somebody saw us in Midland or Monahans," Kaiser said. "We're more conspicuous together. Watch your phone."

Letty joined a group of women walking down the hill, Kaiser went off on his own. They stopped at a concrete wall that marked the edge of the parking lot around the border station. Letty did a quick count of the pickups that clustered around the station and came up with fifty-two, almost all of them black. One or two men with rifles were standing behind each of the trucks. Another truck came down the hill, and one left.

A man dressed head-to-foot in camo, and wearing a heavy military-style bulletproof vest, was standing near the front entrance of the Customs station and was shouting through the door. Letty couldn't make out the words but could hear somebody inside shouting back.

After several minutes of that, the man in the vest turned and walked away from the entrance, between two trucks, where he joined three men and a woman; Letty thought the woman was Hawkes. The woman was masked with a cowboy-style bandanna but had Hawkes's build.

The group talked for a moment, then two of the men walked away, stopping at each pickup in the cluster, to speak to the militiamen standing behind the trucks.

"Oh, no. They're going to shoot," said a woman in Letty's group.

As Letty watched, the woman — Hawkes? — raised a pistol above her head, pointed it at the sky, and then fired a single shot: *Bam*.

Immediately, the men standing behind the trucks began firing their weapons, all pointed above the station and downriver.

The din was terrific and a number of the townspeople began running back up the hill, away from the station. Letty noticed some of the men firing their guns were laughing.

A demonstration, she thought.

After ten or fifteen seconds, the shooting stopped, and the man who'd been shouting through the door walked back up to it and began shouting again. A minute later, he waved toward two other men who were standing behind trucks, and the men put down their rifles and walked up to the station and followed the first man inside.

Kaiser had eased into Letty's group of women, and said to her, quietly, "The border guys quit."

"Yeah."

"I'll be at the diner."

Letty followed him five minutes later. Nothing more had happened at the station — the men who'd gone inside hadn't come back out — and as she walked past the motel on the shoulder of the road, four pickups went by, moving fast, one of them flying a pale blue flag with a bright green triangle on it, another flying a Confederate battle flag. Two of the trucks had men sitting in the back, holding rifles. One of the men waved at her.

The diner was a low red building with wide windows facing the street. It was half-full, or half-empty, depending on your philosophical view of things, but almost all the customers and two of the waitresses were crowded into the brown leatherette booths with windows facing the highway, watching the pickups going by. Everyone turned to look at Letty as she walked in, then looked back outside as somebody called, "Here come some more."

Three more pickups streamed by, another one flying the Land Division flag.

Kaiser was sitting in a booth on a side wall. They could still see enough of the street that they could count pickup trucks, they could watch the front door, and were far enough from the crowd that they could speak quietly.

Kaiser leaned across the table to Letty and said, "You're the Fed who shot Max Sawyer. I have to think that they got a description of you from somebody, if not your whole name and address. From the cop you think they're talking to. There were a couple pictures of you on the Internet. I mention this because . . . if you look around . . . you don't

422

look like a single other woman in this town. Nobody that I've seen."

A dozen women were standing at the windows; they tended toward bulk, with elaborately coiffed hair, mostly wearing yoga-style pants and loose tops meant to disguise the extra weight. Kaiser was right. She looked like none of them, and if the militiamen had seen her Internet photos, they'd pick her out in a minute.

A waitress drifted over, wearing a pink uniform with a white apron. "We're having some excitement here, hons. Jeff says we're still serving, though, so . . ."

"Tell Jeff to put a dollar in Roger's jar," Letty said.

"You're not with . . ." The waitress tilted her head toward the windows.

"We're not," Kaiser said. "We'd like to get out of here if we could. We heard some shooting." He didn't say they'd been there.

"Down to the border," the waitress said. "I don't think you can leave town. One of the guys here has a wife on her way to Van Horn and she called and said the road is blocked about five miles out of town . . . There's a big stand of palm trees there, we call it Palm Grove Corner, because you go around a corner there . . ."

"Saw it when we came in last night,"

Kaiser said.

The waitress: "Lucy, this guy's wife, said they cut down all the palm trees and piled them across the road and they're behind the palms with guns and not letting anyone through."

Letty said, "That's not good."

"It's a crying shame, is what it is. Those trees were there for a hundred years, I bet," the waitress said. "You still want to eat, honey?"

Kaiser said, "Yes. We better. Don't know what's going on, or how long it's gonna last, we better stock up now . . . What's good?"

"Most everything, but I'd personally stay away from the open-faced beef sandwich . . ."

When the waitress came back with pancakes and hash browns, Letty asked, "Is there a thrift store here in town?"

"Yes, there is. You go on up the hill to the next street, turn right, and it's two blocks. Mavis Thrift, it's called. Run by Mavis Sparks."

Kaiser was tasting the hash browns: "Gonna need ketchup."

The waitress brought a bottle of ketchup, and Letty called Greet: "There was shooting down by the border station, a demonstration of firepower, and I think the Customs and Border Protection quit. Probably disarmed. We've also been told we can't leave town because the militia cut down a grove of palm trees and dropped them across the highway and they've got armed men backing up the roadblock."

"Jesus! It's an invasion."

"That's exactly what it is," Letty said. "There's supposed to be a town meeting at noon, called by the militia. I'm not in a good place to talk. I'll be calling you."

"I'll pass along what you have to say. People are freaking out, they're talking about sending the Army down there."

One of the men by the front windows turned and said, "Shouldn't we be doing something?"

Another: "Like what? These people are like the Army."

Another: "You think they'd really shoot us?"

Another: "You heard that gunfire."

The first man said, "I'll tell you all what: I'm going back up to my house. If they try to dig me outta there, they'll have a problem on their hands. I got a shotgun and I'll kill any asshole tries to come in there."

A couple of other men agreed. One said,

"That's the best thing. Hole up in your house. They can't dig us all out. I'll kill a couple of them fuckers myself."

Another: "Easy, easy, let's see what they do . . ."

The argument was continuing when three men armed with AR-15s pushed through the door and one said, "Hiya, folks, hope you're okay in here . . ."

One of the men near the windows asked, "What are you guys doing?"

"We're borrowing your town for a couple of days," the lead militiaman said. "There's a caravan headed here and we're not going to let it cross. But the main thing is, we don't mean any of you harm. We really don't want to hurt anyone. You heard that shooting, it all went up in the air, to convince the Customs people that they shouldn't try to take us on. They agreed. They won't do that. You shouldn't do that, either: the fact is, you should be with us. We'll be talking about that at a noon meeting down by the border station . . ."

One of the men was scanning the diner as the leader went on and his eyes stopped when they got to Letty. He looked at her for a moment, then turned to a man by the window, who said, "You know, there are a hell of a lot more guns in this town than you got . . ."

"We don't want a war, no way," the leader said. "But if you want one, we got it."

When the militiamen left a minute later, Kaiser said quietly, "That guy was checking you out."

"Yes. Let's get out of here."

They left the diner during a lull in the pickup traffic and hotfooted it up the hill to the first street, turned right, and hurried along to Mavis Thrift, which appeared to be closed. "There's somebody in there," Kaiser said, peering through the door window. He knocked until a woman came to the door and shouted, "We're closed."

"We need help," Letty shouted back through the glass.

The woman fussed for a minute, but finally let them in. "I need some of everything and I'll pay cash," Letty told her.

"Are you . . ."

"No, we're not with them."

The woman, like those in the diner, was on the heavy side. She had a face that might have had a permanent worried frown graven into it, overlaid by a whole new set of worries from that morning.

"They been shooting people up, whoever

they are," the woman said. "I got a gun, but I'm no damn good with it."

"Hiding out is the way to go," Kaiser said. "I don't think they've shot anyone yet."

The woman nodded, then asked, "What can I do for you, young lady?"

"I need some clothes and a mirror," Letty said.

Twenty minutes later, Kaiser said, "Hell, I wouldn't recognize you if you walked right past me. I've never seen pants that exact color."

"They look nice," Mavis said to Letty. "Don't show off your figure so good as the skinny jeans, though. I think your dad would agree with that."

The woman smiled at Kaiser, who said, "I guess."

"That's okay," Letty said. She batted her eyes at Kaiser, then checked herself in a cracked, full-length mirror. She was wearing a flowered peasant top over what were once burgundy jeans that appeared to have had a tie-dye accident, with a pair of well-worn Keds high-tops that had once been red, but were now a rusty color.

Kaiser handed her a pair of white-framed sunglasses. She winced, put them on, and asked, "You got a cowboy bandanna I can tie over my hair?"

"Sure do," Mavis said. "Any color you want, long as it's black."

Mavis gave her a brown paper sack for her regular clothes.

Outside Mavis's door, Letty asked, "What do you think, Dad?"

"With that hankie on your head and those glasses, you look like you're from the Ukraine. In 1944. On your way to Mass after killing a Kraut."

"Thank you." She touched the hard lump in her jeans pocket. The pants were looser than her skinny jeans, and the 938 was right there, easy to get at.

"Let's get back to the motel and talk this out," Kaiser said. "Haven't heard any more gunfire."

They walked back to the highway, and at the corner saw a parked pickup partially blocking the highway, with two men in the truck bed, both with rifles. The men looked at them but didn't do or say anything. They turned downhill, stopped at Jeff's. The waitress in the pink dress recognized Kaiser, frowned at Letty as though she should recognize her but didn't. Kaiser asked, "Anything more happen?"

"Another one of them came in here, showing his gun off," the waitress said. "There's gonna be a town meeting at noon outside the border station. Everybody's supposed to come. No guns."

As they backed out the door, the waitress added, in a hushed voice, "They arrested the mayor and the city council. They said there's gonna be a trial."

"Who the fuck are they to arrest anyone?" Kaiser asked.

The waitress shook her head and let the door swing closed. Kaiser said, quietly, "Over there," and tipped his head: Letty looked back up the street, where the pickup they'd seen, partially blocking the highway, had stopped a truck coming into town. "Checkpoint," Kaiser said.

On the way farther down the hill, to the motel, Letty called Greet: "A woman at the local diner says they've arrested, detained, the mayor and the whole city council, for what that's worth. We've seen one armed checkpoint coming into town."

"Keep the information coming, you're the only good on-the-ground resource we've got there. I'm not giving your number to anyone, I'm routing all the traffic through our command center at FEMA. If somebody needs to hook up directly with you, we'll patch them through. We haven't seen any media coming . . ."

At that moment a Black Hawk helicopter swooped in over the town, moving fast, crossing into Mexico, and then banked and came back over, moving slower, and then, *bapbapbap BOOM bapbapbap.* The gunfire came from scattered places around the town, and the helicopter swooped back out, climbed, swung over the town again, much higher up, and Greet was shouting into the phone, and *bapbapbap BOOM bapbapbap . . .*"

Letty put a finger in her off ear and yelled, "What? What?"

"Was that gunfire?"

Kaiser reached out and took the phone and shouted into it: "A Black Hawk came over, way too low, took small-arms fire, almost all AR-15s, although I heard a bigger gun, could be an AR-10, and then another for sure was a .50-caliber that let off two rounds. You better tell your troops to get up higher and faster if they come back . . ."

Letty took the phone back. "Where's that caravan that's coming here?"

"They're still coming. I can't tell you how far out they are right now."

"Find out," Letty said.

Kaiser held out his hand and took the

phone again: "They need to bring in Delta or the SEALs if there's gonna be a fight. This is not something you want to try to do with the National Guard. These guys are all mixed in with local civilians."

Letty: "We're gonna do some recon . . ."

"I'll get all that going," Greet said. "Call me! Call me!"

At the motel, Kaiser said, "About the recon thing. We oughta split up again. If they were watching us at all, up in Midland or in El Paso, they know it's a skinny chick with a big guy. We can cover twice as much ground if we split up."

"Every time people split up in a movie, somebody dies."

"Try not to do that."

Letty nodded and said, "Most of them are down by the border station. I'll wander down there. Why don't you get in the truck, like you're trying to get out of town, see what the reaction is at that checkpoint. If we're lucky, you could make it up to the roadblock, make an assessment. Count the guns. The Feds are gonna want a live count."

"What if they wave me through?"

"Doesn't sound like they can. If they do, turn around, say you wanted to see what was allowed, you have to go back and get your wife and kid."

Kaiser nodded. "Good. You take care. You get killed, I won't get a gold star in my notebook."

Letty's phone rang. Senator Colles. He said, "I know you're life-and-death busy, but give me a one-minute recap."

"I will, but don't let on that you've got a source on the ground. They're willing to use their guns — they tried to shoot down an Army helicopter."

"What! Nobody told me that. But tell me, tell me . . ."

Letty gave him all the information she had, and said, "If you've got to talk about this, attribute it to a brave member of the Customs people. I'm sure they weren't all in the station when they were surrounded. Some must still have phones."

"I will. Call me! Call me!"

"That's what everybody says," Letty said. "Talk to you later."

Kaiser had clipped his carry gun to his jeans, handed Letty the extra magazines he'd been carrying for her, gave her a heavy but unexpected around-the-shoulders hug, and said, "Easy does it, Letty. See you back here in an hour." He grinned at her, added,

"Laissez les bons temps rouler," in what Letty suspected was a terrible French accent, and went out the door, dropping his blades over his eyes as he left.

Or maybe it was a good Cajun accent. She had no idea which. In any case, she thought, as she put the nine-millimeter magazines in her new/old socks, outside the motel door the good times were definitely rolling.

TWENTY-ONE

Earlier that morning:

Low looked back over his shoulder and said, "I've only seen one truck turning right. Chickenshit."

"One is good, one is good," Hawkes said. "There'll be more."

The sky was getting light in the east, the sun would be up before they made the turn at Van Horn. "I'm getting cranked," Low said, after a while.

"Everybody's cranked," Hawkes said. They had moved left and slowed, and were now thirty trucks behind the convoy leader, with more trucks strung out behind them for a mile or more, all rolling along at eighty-five miles an hour, just above the eighty-mile-per-hour speed limit. A blond woman in a red Porsche Panamera ignored them as she passed at a hundred and ten or so, focused on the application of her lipstick. Hawkes got on the phone and called the lead truck.

"Rick: did you lose anyone in your crew back at the turn?"

"Nope. They all knew what we were in for. They're all right with us."

"See you there." She called the chain saw crew, the last group in the convoy. "Lannie — you see anyone turning right?"

"I was about to call — I think we lost three trucks altogether. I thought it would be more. We didn't lose anybody from our crew."

"Excellent. See you at the trees."

"Couldn't do this first part without cell phones," Hawkes said to Low, when she'd hung up. "When we go to the walkie-talkies, we're gonna have some confusion."

"Can't avoid it," he said.

"I know." After a minute: "What do you have dialed in for music?"

They got on down the interstate listening to Joe Walsh and "Life's Been Good," part of what Low called his righteous prison mix.

The overnight meeting had taken place twenty miles northwest of Van Horn. The leading trucks made the turn and the rest followed like a loose-boned snake down the narrow highway to Pershing. Thirty miles in, they did catch an eighteen-wheeler, but it was moving briskly, a bit above the speed limit, so they let it go, and followed it toward the river as the mountain closed in beside them.

Low was silent, but Hawkes talked to the leaders of every one of the action teams. They'd all been thoroughly briefed, and everything was moving as expected, so there wasn't much to talk about, but she wanted them to hear her confidence. "We're absolutely on plan, it's all nominal . . ."

"Nominal," she thought, was a leadership-type word.

Five miles short of Pershing, they got to the grove of palm trees and Low pulled off and waved the rest of the convoy on. At the end of it, five trucks pulled off on the shoulder with them. The roadblock action team.

Low and Hawkes got out of their truck and Low said, "Let's get it on, guys. Get the pulley up on the other side."

"We got it," somebody called back.

Twenty tall palms stood on one side of the road, three even bigger trees on the opposite side. Two men hooked a block and tackle to one of the three big palms, and somebody else fired up a chain saw. The first palm fell a minute later. One of the men working the block and tackle hooked an end of the pulley line to the top of the downed palm, and the other end to the receiver on the back of an F-250. The truck surged ahead and pulled the downed palm all the way across the highway.

The rest of the palms came down one at a time and were dragged across the road, piled atop one another, to make a barrier of heavy entwined palms six feet high. The men were working fast and efficiently. When they'd finished, they retrieved the block and tackle, and then the chain saw crew dropped the three palms on the other side of the road, on top of those already down.

"That's a fine mess," Low said, pleased.

A tractor-trailer was coming down the highway from I-10, slowed and stopped. The driver watched them putting the tools away, then got out and shouted, "How long to clear it?"

"Couple days, anyway," somebody called back.

"Couple days? What am I supposed to do?"

"If I was you, I'd back it up and go to El Paso," he was told.

One of the chain saw crew clambered atop the pile of palm logs with an AR-15 in one hand. "Nobody coming through," he shouted at the driver.

Hawkes was watching. She clutched Low's biceps and said, "I'm fuckin' high on life here, Rand. We're doing it."

Low looked at her and said, "You know, this isn't the real big test. The big test is tonight."

Five trucks and six men and a woman were left at the roadblock as guards. Hawkes gave them a pep talk — "We're absolutely counting on you. If you let anybody through, we're screwed. We've all rehearsed what you've got to do, what you've got to say. Keep your faces covered and we'll be coming for you tonight. If you get more than you can handle, either call me or get on your walkie talkie. If things go right, won't be any phones after noon."

"Got it," the woman said.

"And you got your bullhorns and your food and drinks."

"We're good," the woman said. "You get on down there, Jael, we got your back door."

In the truck again, Hawkes took a phone call, listened, and said to Low, "We got the Customs people penned up. They've still got their weapons, but we're working on it."

"How about the ones who were off-duty?" Low asked.

Hawkes relayed his question to the militia

man in Pershing, who said, "I know we got people at their front doors, but I don't know what happened. Frank told me we got the mayor and the city council locked up."

"We'll be there in five minutes. Keep the lid on," Hawkes said.

"We got it. We're running smooth," the man said. "Oh: Rodriguez and the TV truck made it. They got here a while ago."

The town of Pershing started with a series of truck parking lots on both sides of the road, then two trailer courts, then the houses, most manufactured, some concrete-block, some wood-frame. They went by Jeff's Diner, where they'd eaten when they were scouting the town, and the motel, where they'd gone swimming, and down the long slope to the Rio Grande, which was nothing more than a thread of water sitting in a narrow gorge thirty or forty feet below the level of the towns on either side. The bridge over the river was empty.

The border station sat on a slab with an extensive parking lot behind it, a brown building with an American flag hanging limply from a pole near the front door. The militia's pickups were jammed around the buildings on three sides, men standing behind the trucks with rifles. A yellow concrete WELCOME TO TEXAS sign punctuated the cluster of trucks.

A long-haired man named Dick ran up to them as they stopped, a harried look on this face, and said, "We got the town, if we can keep it."

Hawkes and Low got out of the truck, and Low asked, "Where's the mayor and all them?"

"Jail. No problem."

"Somebody watching them?"

"Two guys, on the door," Dick said.

"Good. The Mexicans done anything?"

"Watching us with binoculars . . ."

"Get the first shift of bridge guys out there. Nobody goes across, either direction . . ."

"I know, we got that," Dick said. "We got the Customs guys nailed down, inside, but I kept the fast-reaction team here in case there's trouble. I could send them to their positions if you think it's time."

Hawkes shook her head. "Keep them here until the bridge guys are set up . . ."

The Customs and Border Protection employees were holed up inside the building, and some were armed. One of the El Paso militia members, wearing camo and armor, was negotiating with them, standing by the front door, shouting through it.

The negotiations went on for fifteen minutes, and the camo-clad man eventually walked away from the door and down to where Hawkes had met with Low, Duran, and Crain.

"They're being stubborn, but they're arguing among themselves," the camo guy said. "I think we'll need the demo."

"Okay with me," Low said. "Me 'n Vic will tell everybody."

"Like we talked about," Hawkes said. She was wearing a gunbelt with a Beretta nine-millimeter in a holster. She took the gun out, and when Low and Crain finished circling the trucks, Low waved at her, and she pointed the gun in the air, over her head, and fired a single shot.

At her signal, all the men around the trucks began firing in the air, downriver, where there wasn't much but desert. One full thirty-round magazine, they'd said. Hawkes put her fingers in her ears as eighteen hundred rounds went downriver.

The border station employees quit. Three militiamen went inside the station and collected sidearms, got keys for a secure file cabinet from the man in charge, and locked the weapons in the cabinet.

"I knew that would happen," Hawkes told Low. "As long as everyone thinks they can give up and nobody gets hurt, they'll do it."

"But they're pissed," Low said. He looked up the hill to the houses of the town. "And there are guys up there in town with guns as good as anything we have."

"We gotta stay on top of them. Pass the word to keep patrolling."

A while later, as Hawkes and Low were checking with their various militia squads, making sure their missions were on track, they heard the paddling sound of a helicopter, coming in fast.

Hawkes said, "Here we go," and Low said, "Holy shit," and the Black Hawk screamed down at them and the men in the trucks began shooting at it, and Hawkes dropped behind the pickup and *boom,* the .50-cal got in the fight and the chopper turned and climbed out, and as it went by a second time, Hawkes could see a man watching them from the door gunner's window, and a silent machine gun pointing down at them.

And from the ground, *bapbapbapbapbapbapbapbapBOOM . . .*"

The chopper disappeared over the mountain and Hawkes said, "Okay, we need to get the news to them that we're all mixed up with civilians. We need to get these trucks spread out, right close to the houses, like we planned. We don't want them to be able to blow us all up in a big cluster like this . . . That M240 would take us apart."

"I'll take care of that," Low said. "Dick's gotta get the bridge guys out there, why don't you find the TV guy and send them a message?"

"I'll do that," Hawkes said. And, "Hey, nobody's said anything about the cops."

"They won't be any trouble," Dick said. "We disarmed all four of them, made sure they didn't have any guns hidden in their houses. They're all part-timers, and Patty said she talked to all of them and they promised not to give us any trouble. They basically take drunks to jail. If they had a real problem, they sorta counted on the Border Patrol guys to help out."

The TV truck was parked on the shoulder of the highway, the right side pressing into the brush that lined the shoulder, fifty yards up the hill from the border station. Three militiamen, all with rifles, were standing beside it. Oliver Rodriguez was standing next to the truck with a camerawoman, named, Hawkes thought, Cherry something. They'd met once before, on a patrol along I-10; neither one of them had actually seen Hawkes's face.

She tightened her mask as she walked up, made sure her sunglasses were firmly on her nose; nothing to do about her hair, but her hair wasn't distinctive yet. In a week, it would be red, and her eyebrows were blond enough for red hair to look natural.

Rodriguez saw her coming and nodded, recognizing the green triangle on her hat and her general shape. "Jael," he said. He waved at the town. "Is this you?"

"I'm one of more than a hundred, all equal," Hawkes said. "We now have this town and we will not let the caravan pass."

"Say that again, in one minute," Rodriguez said. He turned to the camerawoman and asked, "Sound?"

The camerawoman nodded. "I got it while you were talking. You can go ahead."

Rodriguez nodded, turned to the camera, and said, "The town of Pershing was invaded this morning by the Land Division, a local militia intent on stopping the caravan now approaching the border crossing at Pershing, Texas. They have arrested the mayor and the city council, and are holding them in the city jail. The local policemen and the Customs and Border Protection employees have been disarmed. At the latest report, the caravan of migrants, most of them from Honduras and Guatemala, is nine miles out and moving steadily toward us . . ."

He turned to Hawkes and said, "I only know you as Jael, the leader of the Land Division. I don't suppose you'd remove your mask for this interview?"

"Might get COVID," she said. The COVID pandemic lingered on, though few people still wore masks. "I'll keep it on."

"You have conquered this town," Rodriguez said. "What are you going to do with it?"

"We're going to keep it American," she said.

As she spoke, the cluster of locals edged closer to listen to her. One of them, who appeared to be a young woman dressed badly, she nodded at. "We're going to try to protect American workers from immigrants, however pitiful their stories may be, from undercutting the wages of Americans. This is not a race thing, this is a wage movement: we have all races in our movement, black, white, red, Hispanic . . . The big corporations, and I'm looking at you, McDonald's, are desperate to keep us from succeeding in our efforts . . ."

The young woman had her hand in her jeans pocket, held there unnaturally, Hawkes thought, and she wondered if the hand were disfigured in some way. Maybe they could talk after the interview . . .

Rodriguez was saying, "There could be as many as a thousand refugees coming down the highway at you. You have guns. Are you willing to kill some of them to keep them from crossing the river? Because they seem pretty determined to cross . . ."

Hawkes spoke directly to the camera: "We will block the bridge. We will stop them." And, a little self-consciously, "They shall not pass!"

Rodriguez had more questions, and when he was done, and the camera turned away, Hawkes looked back to the locals, noticed that the young woman was no longer there.

Low called Hawkes on her cell phone: "We got a problem. A couple of Border Patrol guys have barricaded themselves inside a house up the hill from the border station. They sent a guy down to tell us if we didn't back off, they'll start picking us off. The guy they sent says they have rifles."

"Got it. How are we doing with the rest of the town?"

"We're all over it. We're being friendly and cool. Telling people we'll be leaving no later than day after tomorrow. But these Border Patrol guys . . ."

"I'll go talk with them," Hawkes said.

Hawkes trudged back down the hill, where Low was waiting with a tall Hispanic man who said he was with the volunteer fire department. "I know the two guys and they're tough guys," the firefighter said. "I was walking down the hill to see what was going on, and they waved me down and told me that if you don't clear out of the station and give the other border guys their guns, they'll start shooting you."

"Which house are they in?"

The man pointed up the hill, to the right, and said, "That one that looks like brick. It's really tarpaper, but . . ."

"I see it," Hawkes said. To Low: "Get the fast-reaction team up there above that house, out of sight, behind cover, tell them channel sixteen on the walkie-talkies. I may need to talk to them all at once."

"You sure you want to go up there?"

"Should be okay," she said. She grinned at him from behind her mask. "I'm a girl."

Low got on his phone to talk with the leader of the fast-reaction team as Hawkes climbed the hill toward the house of fake bricks. As she got closer, she saw that one side of the house had slumped to the right, and the tarpaper siding was warped and beginning to peel off. She looked back at the border station, and saw that the men inside the house must have chosen it because of their command of the station. On the other hand, they must not have thought clearly about the positions above the house, and behind them . . .

As she came up to it, a man inside the house shouted, "Who are you?"

She couldn't see anyone behind the windows. "I'm with the Land Division," she called back. "We need to talk."

"We sent a message down there. If you don't —"

"We're not going to do any of that. You need to listen to me, as I explain this situation." There was no immediate reply, and Hawkes turned her head up the hill where her fast-reaction team was concealing itself. The badly dressed young woman she'd seen at the TV truck was leaning against the side of a house, watching her, hand still in her pocket. Then a man inside shouted, "We're listening."

"We've got two hundred people here," Hawkes shouted back. She was lying; they had a hundred and seven. "We're all armed. I'm sure you heard the shooting when we were challenged by the Army helicopter. We've got AR-15s, AR-10s, AKs, we've got .50-cals, we got ten thousand rounds of ammunition. You guys are inside a house that couldn't stop a .22. If you shoot anyone, if you shoot *at* anyone, we'll put so many rounds through that house that it'll fall down on your dead bodies. On the other hand, if you don't shoot, we won't shoot at you. We won't even ask you to come out of there, or surrender, or give up your guns. We'll be leaving town tomorrow afternoon, or the next day, and you'll still be alive. We'll even send you a pizza for dinner tonight, if you don't have food. A couple beers, if you want them. Pancakes, tomorrow morning."

The man shouted, "Hang on a minute." Then, a minute later, "Okay, we won't shoot at you."

"Good. You guys chill out," Hawkes called. "I'm going to shout out my phone number, if you have any more concerns. Have you got a pencil?"

"Yeah."

Hawkes called out the number of her burner phone and a man inside said he'd written it down.

"If you need anything, call me," Hawkes shouted. "Take it easy, and day after tomorrow you can have a couple drinks with your friends and talk this all over. The TV people will probably want to interview you."

Back down the hill, Hawkes told Low, "We're okay. They won't be shooting at us. You got your speech?"

"I'm cool."

"Then you hold things here, I'll walk around town. I want to make sure that everybody's gotten a leaflet. Rodriguez should be transmitting my interview out to El Paso by now . . . Did you talk to Bernie about the caravan?"

Bernie was a one-legged alcoholic Iraq veteran largely confined to his house in El Paso, since the VA never quite got him walking right. He was a valued member of the militia, who spent his working days monitoring police radios, mining for tips he'd call to the local television stations and, a few years before, to Crain's and Low's car-theft ring.

Low said, "Yeah, I talked to him while you were yelling at those Border Patrol guys. He says all the cops are talking about it, on both sides of the border. The caravan will be here by six o'clock or so, unless the Mexicans decide to stop them. He says that won't happen, because the Mexicans want the caravan to confront us."

Hawkes nodded: "Okay. That's what we wanted, too."

She spent the next hour walking the town, constantly on her phone. Every house already had a leaflet stapled to the front door, laying out simple rules — go about your business, no guns, the road out is blocked, we don't want anyone to get hurt.

The border patrolmen barricaded in the house had given her phone number to the Border Patrol headquarters in El Paso, and a man who identified himself as a major from the Texas Highway Patrol called and told her that she and her militia had committed dozens of major felonies and that if they didn't surrender immediately, people could die, herself included.

She said, "Nobody will die unless you start shooting. Then people will die, and some of them will be you."

"Listen to me, lady . . ."

"No. You listen to me. We're going to stop this caravan from crossing the river and then we'll get out of your hair by tomorrow or the day after. Whenever the caravan gets turned around. You really don't want to come in here with tanks and helicopters and all that, because a lot of people will die. Most of our members are actual combat veterans, so we know what we're doing. You'll get us, but there'll be a lot of dead cops, too. Any possibility that you'll ever have a career in the Highway Patrol, that any of you will, you high-ranking officers, you can forget about it. It'll be another Waco massacre. We'll be dead and a lot of you'll be dead and you brass hats will get blamed. So shut up and sit down."

She smiled at her phone as she hung up.

Ah. The jail. She hadn't stopped there. She walked over to it, three blocks, and saw her two militiamen, faces obscured by bandannas, sitting on folding chairs.

"Y'all okay? Need anything?"

"We're okay. Got relief coming in forty minutes."

"I need to stick my head inside . . ."

The jail consisted of three cells, each just big enough for a cot, an outer space that was bare of any furnishings at all, and a windowless bathroom. The mayor and council members were locked in two cells, three men in one, two women in the other.

"Everybody okay?" she asked. "Anybody have to pee? Anybody need water or food?"

"What are you going to do with us?" one of the women asked.

"Well, we're gonna have a trial, a little later today."

One of the men stood up, gripped the cell bars. "For what?"

"Treason," she said. "If anyone needs to use the bathroom or needs food, water, or medicine, just call out."

"You can't put us on trial . . ."

The sound of his voice trailed off as she closed the door and walked down the hill toward the border station. Low had another big speech coming up. Rodriguez and his camerawoman — *Not Cherry,* Hawkes thought now, *but maybe Cameron?* — were working remotely, linked back to the truck electronically. Some of the locals were beginning to gather around them, where they might get on camera.

Hawkes flashed back to her job at Fleet & Ranch. Lifting batteries, for Christ's sakes. Not a woman that anyone would think about for one solitary minute; another human robot lifting seventy-pound deep-cycle batteries for nine dollars an hour.

No more, by God. Before the hour was out, maybe a hundred million people in the United States and Mexico would have seen her masked face, flashing across the screens at Fox, CNN, MSNBC, CNBC, Telemundo, Univision, and all the others.

Gonna work, she thought. And then, less certainly, *Has to work.*

TWENTY-TWO

Letty walked around the whole town, up and down every street. For a while, she watched a militia team that was stapling leaflets to the front doors of every house. The town had been heavily scouted before the invasion, she realized, because the team made no mistakes, knew how many people needed to go down each street, to get every house, with nobody standing around waiting, nobody returning for more leaflets.

Whenever she could, she joined townspeople who were mixing with militiamen, listening.

The leaflet crew was called the information team. Another, much larger, well-armed group was called the fast-reaction team. Because the town was built on a slope, virtually all the houses and businesses had a downhill side with a concrete foundation wall two or three feet tall. The fast-reaction team had begun taking positions behind those walls, with weapons facing uphill. Other teams blocked the bridge and the highway.

She lingered in the crowd that gathered to watch Hawkes's television press conference, checked the number of men and women blocking the bridge as she did that — there were twenty of them and they all wore armored vests and helmets and sunglasses and bandannas, with tactical pants and boots. They all carried AR-15s, and, to Letty, seemed disciplined. There were thirty-five more on the fast-reaction team. She could see two other, smaller teams working around the bridge, maybe fifteen people total. Another team set up checkpoints on the highways, and the main intersecting streets; they stopped all cars to check them, but let people walk through.

They were threatening, she thought, by their very heavily armed presence, without issuing any specific threats. She heard a woman on the bridge team call out to the Mexicans on the other side, in fluent Spanish, and the Mexicans called back, and then both sides laughed.

She wasn't close enough to hear what they actually said, but she thought, *Very organized and well thought out.*

Senator Colles called her twice, Greet

456

twice more, and she ignored the calls, her phone on vibrate, with the ring silenced. When she'd walked the full town, she called Kaiser: "Where are you?"

"On the way back," Kaiser said. "I talked to the militia at the roadblock, and I'm kinda impressed. They know what they're doing."

"Same here. I'll be at the motel. It's after eleven o'clock now and we need to talk. I want to go down to the town meeting at noon."

"See you back there."

When Letty returned to the motel, she found that two rooms had been taken over by the militia's medics, all but one female, all dressed in medical whites, all wearing white N95 masks. The militia had a thing about uniforms, she thought. She asked the medics if they thought people would get shot, and a woman told her, no, they didn't expect that.

"We've got a lot of people running around in the hot sun. We're thinking heat stroke, dehydration, that sort of thing. But we're all nurses here, so we can handle everything except major trauma. If somebody gets shot, we'll do what we can here and call in a medevac chopper from El Paso."

"Sounds like you got it under control," Letty said.

"We do," the woman said. "You from around here?"

"I'm from Midland, my boyfriend and I were headed across the river," Letty said. "We decided we better stay put, after . . . you know . . . you guys got here. Americans might not be too popular down there for a while."

As they were talking, Kaiser pulled into the parking lot and Letty said good-bye to the nurses and went to meet him. "I'm your girlfriend, we're going to the same room," she said, as she walked up. "The people I was talking to are militia, their medical team. Nurses."

Kaiser looked over at them: "Man, they've got it together. A medical team."

In Kaiser's room, he pulled his carry gun out from under his shirt and dropped it on the tiny desk, went over and sat on the bed. "No way anybody's going to get across that highway barricade in a hurry," he said.

He told her how the palm tree trunks had been woven together into an immovable mass. "A bulldozer could push it out of the way, but you'd have to get one down there and that'll take a while. The guys manning the barricade are flashing their guns. There are cop cars on the other side and people have been yelling back and forth."

"No way to get around it?"

Kaiser shook his head. "The mountain comes right down to the road on the west side, the east side is a steep downhill, and it's all stone rubble down there. You'd have trouble getting anything bigger than a trail bike through, even if you didn't have people shooting at you. A Delta team or SEALs could hike in overland. They could take out the guys on the barricade, no problem, but that'd mean killing a lot of people. I don't think we're there yet."

"What about that checkpoint? I saw it stopping cars."

"They waved me through when I was going out, stopped me when I was coming in. I guess they don't care if you go out, there's nothing out there, you're not a threat. Actually, there's a back way around the checkpoint, on the west side of the highway, that they haven't blocked off. Not yet, anyway."

"We need to brief Greet on what we've seen," Letty said. "I walked all over town, I've got numbers they need to know. The biggest thing right now is, they're talking about having a trial for the mayor and the city council. For treason. The way they're talking, they could hold the trial this afternoon or tonight. I don't think the council's gonna get found 'not guilty.' "

"That . . . doesn't sound good," Kaiser said. "The nutso militia guys usually talk about the penalty for treason being *death.*"

Letty nodded. "That's what I'm afraid of. So far, they're saying they don't want anyone hurt. But a trial . . . they might be backing themselves into a corner with their own people."

"You know where they're holding the council?"

"The jail. There's a jail here," Letty said. "I talked to this old lady who pointed it out to me. It's a little brick building with two guys sitting outside the door with ARs."

Kaiser dropped flat on the bed, crossed his ankles, wrenched a pillow around under his head, and said, "Okay. Here's something. On the way back down here, about, mmm, a mile this side of the barricade, there's this turnoff with a sign that says MESCALERO CAVE TRAIL. I went in to take a look. I thought if it was a trail out of here, maybe the cops or the Army could come in around the barricade. But it's just a campground, a couple of picnic tables, with a trail going out the back side. I walked up the trail and it dead-ends at a bluff. There's a cave there, more like a rock shelter. It's maybe fifty feet deep and probably that wide, with a lot of rubble in front of it, rocks that fell off the bluff. Boulders, big ones. If we got the mayor and council out of the jail, we could hole up in that cave and there's no way anyone could get at us. If I'm back there with my shotgun . . . if we took the ARs away from the guards . . . it's a perfect defensive site. We'd need about a five-minute lead getting out of town."

"We gotta talk about that," Letty said. "Let's see what Greet and Colles have to say. They've been calling me, but I've been too busy."

Letty called Greet and put the phone on speaker, so Kaiser could hear and chip in. Greet, sounding stressed, demanded, "Where in the hell have you been, goddamn it? We needed to talk to you. We've got a conference call set up here. Give me a minute to get everybody plugged in. It'll be Senator Colles and some DHS people here in Washington and an emergency task force at FBI headquarters in El Paso."

"El Paso? Who's down here? Who's on the road into Pershing?" Letty asked.

"They've got FBI and Texas cops down there, they're working out jurisdiction issues right now, but what they don't have, and they need, is intelligence. I mean like . . . military intelligence."

"How about the other kind of intelligence . . . you know, like IQ? They got any of that?" Letty asked.

"I'm not recording this yet, but I will be," Greet said. "I don't know about IQ, but watch your mouth."

"Got it."

After some clicking and static, Greet came up again and said, "Letty, John, I've got Senator Colles and a dozen of our DHS executives here, plus task force members in El Paso, all on the line."

Colles jumped in: "Letty! Are you and John okay?"

"We're in a motel room in the middle of town," Letty said. "John drove out to the highway barricade. He has some things to say about that. I've walked all over town, I watched the press conference that Jael, Hawkes, had here, I expect you've seen that. I talked to some of the militia people, I've got some numbers for you . . ."

A man's voice: "This is Tim Jackson, I'm a lieutenant colonel with the Texas National Guard. We appreciate any intel you can give us, but I have one question first: Why haven't they taken out the cell phones? We're getting calls from people down there."

"I looked at the cell phone tower," Letty said. "They've got three men guarding it, and one guy was working around the base. I can't promise you this, but I suspect he was putting some of that C-4 on it."

"Then they could cut us off at any minute."

"Yes. I expect they're planning to do that. If everybody will shut up, John and I will tell you what we know and what we've seen that you might not have gotten from the helicopter run or from other people. And hope we don't get cut off."

Jackson again. "Okay. Go. We're recording."

Letty began, "There are a hundred and five, to a hundred and ten, militia here, both men and women, counting the seven at the highway barricade . . ."

"Seven? We've been told there are twenty to thirty at the roadblock," a man said.

Kaiser: "There are seven. I not only counted them, I talked to them. Six men and a woman."

"Okay. If you say so."

A slight skepticism in the voice. Kaiser rolled his eyes and then snapped: "Seven! Exactly!"

Letty: "There are twenty of them — that's *another* exact number, by the way — blocking the bridge. They are on the Mexican side of the bridge. The bridge has six spans and they are about halfway across the last span. The Mexicans have taken positions on the other side, but there has been no shooting. They are shouting back and forth in Spanish, so that's well thought out."

She gave them numbers of militia she'd counted in town, as well as armament and personal protective gear: rifles, sidearms, bulletproof vests. She told them that the border station personnel had been disarmed and most of the employees were being held in the station, and that two others had barricaded themselves in a house above the station.

"We've talked to those guys," somebody said.

Kaiser chipped in, "Most of the guns are AR-15s, with a mix of AR-10s and AKs and at least one Barrett .50-caliber that I've seen. I haven't seen anything bigger. No grenades, no M320s. Everyone has a sidearm."

Letty: "They are very well organized into teams: the bridge team, the blockade team; there's a fast-reaction team, there are thirty-five members in it, equipped like full-on military with all the gear. There's a medical squad, five nurses. The leaders are this Jael woman, who I believe to be Jane Hawkes, and a man called Rand Low. Billy Greet has files on both of them . . ."

Jackson: "Are they digging in?"

Kaiser: "Yes. In a way. Not in the sense of emplacements of any kind, but the houses here are built on a slope, and the downhill sides of the concrete foundations are two or three feet high. They are setting up behind those foundations, which, in my judgment, is pretty substantial protection. If there was a real fight, it'd get ugly, overlapping fields of fire all the way down the hill to the river. And they've got that Barrett, if you thought you might send some choppers over . . ."

Greet jumped in: "For anyone who wasn't told yet, John is a former Delta master sergeant."

Jackson: "Good to know."

Letty: "They've detained the mayor and city council and are saying that they plan to put them on trial for treason because they let that other caravan across the bridge."

Colles: "We heard they were arrested. Are they talking about executing them?"

"Haven't heard anything about that," Letty said. "But . . . treason."

Kaiser: "The council's being held in the

city jail, guarded by two guys with ARs. Letty and I could take them out of there and make a run for the mountain. There's a tourist cave and a campground up there, a beautiful defensive site. If we could get the mayor and those guys to the cave, with some food and water, no way they could take us out."

Letty: "Right now, they're talking about being here until the day after tomorrow."

They could hear a cacophony of voices then, arguments breaking out among the listeners, and Jackson said, "Hold there, for a minute . . ."

Then Colles: "You don't know when this trial is going to be?"

"We expect we'll find out at the noon meeting," Letty said. "They've asked everybody in town to come to the meeting . . ."

Jackson: "Sergeant Kaiser . . . you believe there are only two guards at the jail?"

"Yes, sir. Letty has seen them."

Another buzz of voices, then a new one: "Kaiser, you're a stud. Could you take out both of the jail guards? Not kill them, but jack them up and push them into the jail? Lock them up? Take the hostages out of there?"

Kaiser: "I could. Depends on whether they decide to resist. If I had to shoot them, that'd attract a lot of attention. I don't think I'd get much resistance: they'd be looking down the barrel of a twelve-gauge from ten feet. The fact is, I've got enough gear here that I can look like one of them, put on a bandanna. I can get close, I'm sure of that."

Letty: "I don't think . . ."

The new voice said, "Miz Davenport, we really need you at that noon meeting. Your information is critical and we need to keep it coming. If everybody is focused on that meeting, Kaiser could push those guards into the jail, lock them up, and then make the run for this cave. If he makes it, we'd be in a hell of a lot better position for retaking the town, with no hostages to worry about."

Colles: "Have they taken any other hostages?"

"Not exactly," Letty said, "though they have all those border employees in the station . . ."

More talk, then the new voice again: "That noon meeting starts in fifteen minutes. We'll let you two decide whether to take the mayor and city council out of the jail. We don't have the on-the-scene knowledge that you do, so you're going to have to make the call."

Letty: "We can do that."

The new voice: "Any other critical stuff

that you can give us now?"

"One thing," Letty said. "All the trucks here have duct tape over their license plates."

A second new voice, but much younger, and again, with a skeptical note. "Why is that critical?"

Letty shook her head at Kaiser, then said, "Because it means that they don't want to be identified by their license plate numbers. That means they think they're going to get out of here somehow."

More garbled talk, then the first new voice. "Thank you for that. That *is* critical. You better get going now. We'll think about it. Good luck."

Colles: "Letty, don't take any chances, goddamn it. If you get killed down there, your old man will be all over me."

Letty smiled and said, "Yeah, I think you're probably right about that."

When they got off the phone, Kaiser said, "That guy who didn't identify himself, the first one — he's the weight up there, the one who says what they're gonna do. Could be military or intelligence."

"I picked that up," Letty said. "But — what are *we* going to do? Are we taking those people out of the jail?"

468

"I have to go look at it," Kaiser said. "If there are only two guards and nobody else watching, I can take them."

"If nobody notices that the guards are missing."

"There's that," Kaiser said. "If I get a five-minute lead, I'll be at the cave before anybody can react. Or really, probably, a two-minute lead would be enough."

They sat and stared at each other for a moment, then Letty said, "If you can pull it off, do it. Right now, sit here for a minute and try to visualize exactly what you'll be doing . . ."

They sat there, Letty staring at the ceiling, Kaiser at the floor between his feet, then Letty said, "If the guards don't have a key to the cells?"

"They must — in case there was an emergency or something."

"So you lock them in the cells?"

"Have to. I gotta be fast with this. If they have *two* keys, and I don't find the second one, they could be out of the cells ten seconds after I leave, before I even got the council in the truck. So I go in, I put them on the floor. I let the council out of the cells, we shake the guys down. Maybe yank them out of their uniforms, right down to their underwear. If I can get them locked up without being interrupted, we're good."

"Take their weapons," Letty said. "Should be two pistols, two rifles, ammo . . . Maybe pull off their vests, give them to members of the council. Everybody around here shoots, and if that cave is as good as you say it is, you should be fine."

"Need to run over to the convenience store, get some groceries," Kaiser said. "PowerBars and water and all that. If we're up there for two days, we'll need it."

"Might be closed before this meeting . . ."

"I should go right now," Kaiser said.

"Gets cool at night," Letty said. "We should pull the blankets off these beds, the pillows, stick them in the back of the truck."

"Yes. That's good," Kaiser said.

Letty said, "John: You're sure?"

"Yes. We gotta do something. They might be planning to shoot those folks," Kaiser said.

"Maybe I should go along."

Kaiser shook his head. "You intimidate *me,* but you're not intimidating to look at. If I can't herd the guards inside by myself, I don't think you'd be much help. All you could do is shoot somebody, which we don't want to do. Like I said, a gunshot's gonna draw a lot of attention. Like the big-shot guy said, they need you at that meeting."

■ ■ ■ ■

Letty went outside, didn't see the nurses, then walked down to her room, stripped the two beds, wadded up everything as best she could, carried it out to the Explorer, and threw it in the back.

Kaiser was out ten seconds later, threw his bedding on top of hers. "Okay, listen," he said. "When I get to the cave and we're good up there, I'll call you, if they haven't blown up the cell phone tower. Don't answer, put your phone on vibrate, if it isn't already."

"It is."

"Okay. If you get vibrated twice, in fast sequence, I'm good. Three vibes, find a place where you can talk, because I've got a problem."

"Twenty vibrations and I won't be thinking about problems at all," Letty said.

Kaiser got it, guffawed, and said, "A sex joke. The first sex joke I've ever heard you make. I am fuckin' *shocked.*"

"Not a very good joke, though," Letty said. She looked at him, a big, tough man, worried, then she said, "Hey. We got this, John." She lifted a hand in front of her shoulder, and he slapped it. She added, "Let the good times roll."

"Watch yourself," he said. "You go on down to the meeting, I'll head up to the store and get those groceries."

The townspeople were beginning to gather around the pickups outside the border station. Letty hooked up with a group of five women who were walking down together, to make herself less conspicuous, like a known member of the town. One of the women said, to the group. "They haven't killed anyone. Yet. Not that I've heard."

The other women agreed that they hadn't heard of any killing. One said, "We haven't gotten to the showdown yet. I can't believe they're all going to give up and go to prison, all three hundred of them."

A pickup cruised by, a masked man in the back with a rifle. He looked at them but didn't wave.

Somebody else, nervously: "Three hundred? That many?"

"That's what I heard, I don't know. There's a lot of them."

A hundred and five to a hundred and ten, Letty thought. *Enough.*

By noon, there was a sprawling crowd around the border station. The Wiki said

Pershing had eighteen hundred residents; Letty tried to count the crowd, but there were too many of them. She decided that there weren't two thousand people, though — perhaps half that. Almost no children.

Noon came and went and militiamen were running in and out of the border station, which they'd apparently turned into a headquarters. A man jogged up the hill, past the crowd, got in a pickup, and drove farther up the hill and out of sight. He was in a hurry, but not a huge hurry, Letty decided, more like a man with a mission than a man on an emergency run.

And she thought, *The cell tower is up on that hill.*

She walked away from the crowd, got behind a pickup, squatted, and called Kaiser.

"I got the groceries, I'm checking out the jail," he said. "Still two guards. Something happening?"

"Guy just took off up the hill in his truck. He could be going to the cell tower."

"Okay."

"That's all I got," Letty said. She clicked off, and was about to stand up when she noticed the truck's taped-over New Mexico license plate — and the renewal sticker in the lower-left corner. The renewal sticker had the tag number on it.

She'd vaguely known that about renewal stickers. She'd had to buy three of them for her car in California, and she'd asked about what looked like a random number on it. The DMV counter person told her that the sticker number went to the car's registration, and that the police could check to see that the right sticker was on the correct car. The California number wasn't the tag number, but it would identify a specific car or truck.

She pulled out her phone and took a photo of the New Mexico renewal sticker.

Did all the states do that? The next truck was from Texas — and had no renewal sticker. Neither did the next few Texas trucks. Since most of the trucks driven by the militia were from Texas, she thought, she was out of luck.

As she was walking down the line of trucks, looking for non-Texas renewal stickers, Hawkes and a man in a mask, who Letty thought was Rand Low, climbed into the back of a pickup, dropped the tailgate, and hit the switch on an amplifier. Hawkes lifted a walkie-talkie to her face and said something into it. She listened for a reply, then nodded to Low, looked at her watch, said something else to him, and picked up the microphone.

"You all know what this is about," she said. "We're planning to stop the caravan that's coming our way. We will not let them cross the bridge. The last we heard, they should be coming down the hill on the Mexican side around six o'clock, if nothing slows them down. We could have quite the confrontation here. We could be attacked from the east, by our own people, and from the west, by the people in the caravan. We don't want anyone to get hurt, so we're asking you, when you see the caravan arrive on the other side of the river, to stay in your homes. Between now and then, you're free to go about your business. We mean none of you any harm."

She looked out over the crowd, as if surveying them for signs of acquiescence; there was a shuffling of feet, glances exchanged, but nobody said anything, neither protest nor acceptance. The TV crew was standing directly in front of her, recording the speech.

Hawkes looked down toward the bridge. Letty caught it, and edged out to the side of the crowd and looked where Hawkes had. She saw the shoulders and heads of four men wearing camo shirts and hats sliding under the bridge; they'd apparently been concealed behind a house that stood closest to the riverbank.

Letty worked back through the crowd, where she could see the bridge at an angle. There were six sections spanning the river.

She did the numbers: blowing I-beams would take four chunks of C-4 for each section; six sections, twenty-four bricks of explosive, twenty-four timers, twenty-four detonators. Five support pillars would take more explosive to bring down, but only five timers and detonators. If they were planning to use one on the cell phone tower . . . twenty-nine detonators and timers. If the Army lieutenant had told the truth, they had more than enough.

Holy shit: they're going to take out the bridge. And they're waiting for the caravan to arrive before they do it.

Hawkes was still talking:

"You should know, or if you don't, I'll tell you . . . a lot of you people have been talking to the authorities in El Paso, and, as far as we know, Washington, D.C. We are hoping to convince these people to let us go peacefully, after we stop the caravan. We'll remove the highway barricade and drive in a convoy to El Paso. We're hoping that the authorities accept that. But: we're willing to die if we have to. We won't go alone. Most of us are, or have been, soldiers. We'll be a tough nut to crack. We've thought this through. We know what we're doing. We have more armaments than they realize — and if they don't let us go peacefully, we'll take them on, and a lot of Americans will die."

She looked at her watch again, lips moving as she did some math. "Some of you are talking to the authorities. Maybe right now. Maybe you have your phones on. We knew this would happen. But from now on, we're going to need additional security. So . . ."

She looked up the hill. Nothing happened. She continued to stare over the heads of the crowd, and people began to look in the same direction, and then, *CRUMP.* From the bottom of the hill, where they were standing, the crowd could see only the top of the cell phone tower, which seemed to hop sideways and then fall out of sight.

"I think AT&T can afford another one," Hawkes said. "For now, that's the end of the cell phone service. We're also taking out the Internet fiber-optic. We're trying not to damage it too badly. I know it's inconvenient, but it'll be back up in a couple of days."

A groan rippled through the crowd and

almost everyone held up a cell phone to check the screen. Letty did the same: there were no bars for reception. The phone was dead.

On the truck, Hawkes said, "Now, another one of the Land Division leaders would like to explain why we're doing this, better than I can . . ."

Letty checked around, peering at the members of the militia who stood at the edges of the crowd. They were, she realized, taking walkie-talkies from their pockets. The militia had communications, but nobody else did. Across the river, the Mexicans were all looking at their cell phones, talking with one another — they apparently only had phone access through the Pershing cell phone tower, which was now gone.

On the pickup, standing next to Hawkes, Rand Low began explaining the reasoning for the attack on Pershing, but the TV crew was backing out of the crowd, heading to their truck. Going to the cell phone tower for a shot of the damage, Letty thought: *If it bleeds, it leads.* She eased out of the crowd with several other people, started walking up the hill. One of the militiamen asked Letty, "Where you going, girlie?"

"I'm supposed to be looking after the

baby. He was sleeping good, but I got a feeling he ain't anymore. After that blast."

He nodded, said, "You're gonna miss the speech," and she went on, past the first four streets, then down a side street near the top of the rise, then through a scattering of trailer homes, and past a truck parking lot. At the crest of the slope, she saw the TV truck set up to record the downed tower, the camerawoman messing with her equipment while Rodriguez got back into a sport coat. There were still three militiamen at the site, examining the wreckage.

Letty watched for a minute or two, then walked back down the hill to the motel, went into her room, checked the Wi-Fi. The Net was down. She thought about it some more, then got her pack with the Staccato and extra mags, along with two bottles of water and some PowerBars, and went over to the motel office. The old man was there, with a somewhat younger woman, and Letty asked, "Are there any hardwired phones in town?"

The old man shook his head. "Haven't had those for years. Not even the Mexicans have them anymore, after AT&T put up the tower."

"Anybody in town got a ham radio?"

Again, he shook his head. "Not that I

know about. A few guys got CB radios, but they're short-range. A couple miles down here. Who do you want to talk to?"

"My mom. I want to tell her that I'm okay."

The woman said, "You're gonna have to be patient, honey, like the rest of us. Hope for the best."

Letty left the motel, crossed the highway, walked back a street, then carefully looked around the corner of a house. From there, she could see the front of the jail and a half-dozen pickups parked in front of it, several men standing outside with guns, people coming and going.

Kaiser had gotten away with it, she thought, or he was in desperate trouble.

Either way, there was nothing that she could do about it.

She turned back, recrossed the highway, walked to a street a block over, and started up the hill again, toward the downed cell phone tower. On the way, she passed a grocery store and a line of cars in the parking lot, people stocking up for a siege. As she walked by them, she noticed that each car had a sticker in the windshield, about half the size of a dollar bill — and all the cars were from Texas.

She swerved over for a closer look. Sure enough, Texas put its renewal stickers on the inside of the windshields, above and to the left of the driver. And each sticker, she found, had a tag number on it.

She continued up the hill. Two pickups peeled out of the cell tower lot as she approached it; the lot was surrounded by an eight-foot chain-link fence. The trucks headed east toward the roadblock — and also toward the cave where Kaiser would be holing up, if he'd gotten away with the mayor and city council.

The TV truck was still there at the cell phone tower, packing up. More pickup trucks went by on the highway, headed away from town, moving fast.

Letty checked one last time, then walked across the cell tower lot, slipping her DHS identification case out of her back pocket. Rodriguez looked up as she approached and asked, "Can we do something for you?"

"Yes. You can put me in touch with the government task force in El Paso. I'm with the Department of Homeland Security . . ." She held up her ID case so they could see the cards. "I know you can do that with this setup. One way or another, you've got to be talking to people. I've worked with these trucks before."

Rodriguez: "Wait, wait, wait, there's no way —"

"I'm not giving you a choice. You'll find a way unless you want to go to federal prison for the rest of your life," Letty said. She took the 938 out of her pocket, held it in her hand, pointing at the ground. "To make a point of how urgent this is, I'll shoot you in the kneecaps if you say 'no,' so you'll go to federal prison as cripples. Am I getting through to you now?"

Rodriguez and the camerawoman looked at each other, and then the woman said, 'You don't look like —"

"Because I'm trying to stay out of that jail they've got going down there," Letty said. "Now: how does this work? There must be somebody from the task force looking at your signal as soon as it goes into a TV station . . ."

"You could get us killed," Rodriguez said. "These people aren't fuckin' around. They could turn on us, if they thought . . ."

"That's your problem: killed later or shot now," Letty said. "Your choice. Besides, I don't hardly think they'd kill their PR team. Especially if the PR team keeps their mouths shut until this is all over."

■ ■ ■ ■

Rodriguez got in the truck and called the station; there was some back and forth and then he crooked an index finger to call Letty over. He handed her a pair of earphones and the microphone that had been clipped to the camera.

"You're on," he said.

Letty said, "Don't go away. I want to be able to see both of you. Neither one of you can outrun a nine-millimeter slug."

Without thinking about it, she'd been talking into the microphone, and a man asked, "Who is this?"

Letty said, "I'm a DHS investigator in Pershing. Who is this?"

"Oh my God. Wait, I gotta, I gotta make a phone call, we're gonna have to figure out how to . . . hang on . . ."

She could hear some fumbling around at the other end of the link and she kept her eye on Rodriguez and the camerawoman. Then a man's voice, not loud, but who she recognized as the first unidentified man from earlier in the day, asked, "Letty?"

"Yes. This is me. They blew the cell phone tower."

"We know that . . ."

"They're getting ready to blow the bridge. You've got to keep the caravan off the bridge. I think they're going to blow it up when they try to cross it."

"Okay, that's interesting. Tell me why you think that?"

She explained about the number of bridge sections, about the camoed men going under the bridge, the numbers of spans and support columns and the numbers of detonators and timers. "I can't be sure, but I believe that's what they're planning to do."

"We've had people call us and say that they were planning to come out peacefully, more or less . . ."

"You believed that?" Letty asked.

"No, I didn't. Some people think it has to be considered as an option. We've also had reports that they plan to crash the Mexican side and disappear into the backcountry there."

Letty said, "Right."

"Then what are they going to do?"

"I'm about ninety percent sure they're going to blow the fucking bridge," she snapped. "After that, I don't know."

"What else you got?"

"Militia trucks have been tearing out of here toward that cave John was talking about and I saw a swarm of people around the jail. I'm about seventy-five percent that he pulled it off. Seventy-five percent and climbing. I should know for sure, later this afternoon. I'm going to walk back into town and do my lost-fuckin'-waif act. See what I hear."

The unidentified man laughed: "Keep it up, babe. You're doing good. Is there anything we can do for you? *Can* do for you?"

"Yes. You can threaten this Rodriguez guy, the TV guy, about what will happen to him if he gives me up. And make arrangements for me to talk to you through this TV link."

"Have you checked other commo—"

"Yes, I've checked on everything. Even the Mexican side is shut down. They cut the fiber-optic cable, so no Net. They're using commercial walkie-talkies to communicate, so if you could monitor them somehow, that'd be good. There's only one other possibility that I can see, and that's CB. There are some tractor-trailer trucks stuck behind the roadblock, and if I could get to one, and use his CB, I might be able to communicate that way. Range is only two or three miles. But that's a long walk and I really need to get back to the bridge. You might tell the cops on the other side of the roadblock to monitor channel . . . what? Sixteen? For a call from Letty?"

"We'll do that, but we expect this TV truck to be in the thick of it, so why don't you focus on what you're doing right now? I'm exceptionally good at threatening people, so if you'd put Rodriguez on . . . And, hey, babe, easy does it. Okay?"

"Call me 'babe' again and I'll shoot you in the balls when I see you." She'd gotten that line from a Minnesota cop friend.

"Then thank God I haven't identified myself," he said, laughing. Letty suspected that she would like him. "Give me Rodriguez."

Letty waved Rodriguez over and he took the headphones and the mike. Letty walked over to the camerawoman and said, "I don't know your name."

"Candace. Not Candy. Not Cherry. Ochoa."

"Like the town across the bridge?" Letty asked.

"No relation. You got a pretty cool job. Could you give us ten minutes when it's over?"

"No. Anyway, I might want to use your link some more, so, if I come around . . ."

"We won't turn you in," Ochoa said. "Frankly, I think Rod-boy was an idiot to take this job. Though he'll make a shitload of money from it, of which I will get maybe

486

one-tenth of a shitload."

She talked like a camerawoman, Letty thought. "How long ago did you know this was going to happen?"

"This morning, about five o'clock. Rod was told to be ready, and they might have sweetened the pot for him." She rubbed her fingers together, meaning a cash payment. "We didn't know *what* was going to happen, but Jael called Rod at five o'clock and said there'd be a big deal in Pershing and we'd be stupid if we didn't get down here to cover it. There was nothing else going on, so . . . here we are."

"Don't give me up," Letty said.

"We won't. Listen, you got any chewing gum? My breath is like it's coming out of a dragon's asshole or something . . ."

Made Letty smile. *Just* like a camerawoman: world going to shit around her and she's looking for a stick of gum.

Rodriguez came back, in maybe a lighter shade of pale. "That guy," he said, "is somebody I *never* want to meet. Ever."

"Did he identify himself?" Letty asked.

"No, but I know who he is."

"Who is he?"

"You know those Romans who nailed Jesus to the cross and enjoyed it? One of them."

"Good. As long as he made himself clear about your position in all of this," Letty said. "Hey: catch you later, Rod-boy." She headed back down the hill.

TWENTY-THREE

Stepping back:

Gotta mosey. *Just fuckin'* mosey, *you can do that, for Christ's sake, John. Relax your shoulders. You're supposed to be here. You've taken over the town. Kick out those feet like some goofy fuckin' clodhopper.* Mosey!

Kaiser moseyed down the street, blades on his nose, blue cowboy bandanna over the bottom half of his face. Fifty yards out, he smelled barbecued hamburger, turned to look, saw a man cooking on a grill in his backyard, as if this were an ordinary summer afternoon. Smelled good.

Wearing jeans and a canvas shirt and bandanna mask, Kaiser looked more or less like the militiamen. He had the shotgun slung behind his shoulder, barrel down, so from the front, you really couldn't see exactly what kind of weapon it was.

The two guards were sitting on black

plastic chairs outside the single door into the jail. Kaiser had parked the Explorer a block away on a side street, out of sight of the guards. A pickup, with a gunman in the back, rolled past a block over, visible as a flash between houses. The guards turned to him as he moseyed up: they both had AR-15s sitting across their laps, hands on top of them, but not engaged with the triggers, and their eyes showed nothing but innocence. They had no idea.

Ten feet away, Kaiser reached back, caught the stock of the shotgun and swiveled it forward, the muzzle falling across their faces, and as they gawked, uncertain, he said, quietly, "I'm with the Department of Homeland Security. If you fight me, I'll kill you both. I can't miss from here. This thing is loaded with number-three buckshot."

One of the guards said, "Bro . . ."

Kaiser snarled, "Fuck that bro shit. I did eight tours in Iraq, Afghanistan, Syria, and Libya, and I'm more than ready to blow you guys up. I want you to take those rifles and prop them against the wall behind you."

One of the men said, "You're in a world of hurt."

Kaiser nodded: "Maybe. But you'll never know, because if I wind up in a world of hurt, you're gonna be in a world of *dead*.

Prop the rifles against the wall . . ."

They propped the rifles against the wall and Kaiser said, "Now go inside. Go inside. Line up, and go inside. If you think you can take me with those pistols, I can tell you, that's been tried, and I'm still here. Go inside now. Be good. No, no, don't put your hands over your heads, walk inside normal-like."

They did that, and one of them said, "We'll hunt you down like a rabid dog."

"Good luck with that," Kaiser said. He'd closed up behind him, the shotgun's muzzle three feet from the second man's shoulder blades. He said, "You, second guy. If your friend makes a play here, you'll have a hole in your back the size of a basketball. Then I'll kill *him.*"

Then they were inside. The interior was lit by a single window; the overhead lights were turned off. Kaiser said, "Stretch out on the floor. On your backs. On the floor."

The men obeyed, kneeling, then stretching out. Kaiser took in the jail's interior. There were three cells with yellow-painted bars, two side by side on the long back wall, another on a shorter side wall to the left. A bathroom with an open door and a window the size of a paperback book. There was nothing sophisticated about the cells, they were simply barred cages meant to hold drunks until they got sober, or other miscreants until they could be shuffled off to the jail in Van Horn.

"What's going on?" The cells held three men and two women, and Kaiser said, "I'm with the Department of Homeland Security."

One of the women blurted, "Thank God . . ."

"Not yet," Kaiser said. "I'm here all alone. Who's got the keys to the cells?"

Neither of the men on the floor spoke, and then one of the jailed men said, "The guy with the beard."

The guy with the beard turned his head to see who'd spoken and Kaiser prodded him with the shotgun muzzle and said, "Give them up."

"Fuck you, man —"

The guy got three words out and Kaiser kicked him in the ribs, hard, with an impact like a punt in pro football, and one of the council members said, "Oh my God," and the man on the floor bounced sideways and groaned and Kaiser said, "If I have to kick you to death to get the keys, I will. So now you've got some broken ribs. Next thing I kick will be your hip and I'll break your fuckin' hip bone off. Gimme the keys."

The bearded man groaned again, hurting when he tried to roll up on his side, but he dug in his jeans pocket and produced three keys.

One of the prisoners, a woman, asked, "What are you doing?"

Kaiser: "They're about to put you on trial for treason. The penalty for treason is death."

"What!"

"Ask the guys on the floor." He handed the keys through the cell bars to one of the women and said, "Try the locks."

One of the councilmen asked the bearded man, "Were you going to shoot us?"

The bearded man, now curled into a fetal position, said, "Fuckin' traitor."

Kaiser looked at the city council prisoners and nodded. "Tell me your names so I can talk to you."

They were all wearing jeans, including the women, and all had dark hair and eyes. A tall man in a white dress shirt said, "I'm Harry Lopez, I'm the mayor." He pointed at the two women: "Janice Moreno in the pink blouse, Veronica Ruiz in the white, the bald guy is Doug Hall, the other guy is Antonio Alonso."

Moreno had gotten her cell open, and Ruiz

493

stepped out behind her. Ruiz pointed to the beardless guard and said, "This one put his hands on me. Can I kick him in the head?"

The guard said, "Don't do that . . ."

Kaiser smiled at her and said, "No, that's not a good idea. You could break a toe, and you've got to walk to my car."

Moreno freed the three men and Kaiser pressed the muzzle of his shotgun into the stomach of the uninjured man and said to a councilman, "Get his pistol."

When they had both pistols, the councilmen took four .223 magazines and four nine-millimeter magazines from the men's belt pouches.

Kaiser said, "We need to get their walkie-talkies."

"Cell phones," one of the women said.

"Cell phones don't work anymore. They blew up the cell phone tower."

Lopez, the mayor, prodded the beardless guard's leg with his boot and said, "Goddamn it, did you have to go and do that? Took us two years to get that thing built."

"That's just the start," the man said.

Kaiser said to Alonso, a short, stocky guy with a tough face, "I'm gonna point this pistol" — he pulled his carry gun — "at this asshole's head, and I want you to go through his pockets. We want everything in them, wallet, knife if he has one, hidden gun, check his socks, his ankle . . . If he shows any sign of resistance, shout it out and jump back and I'll kill him."

The odor of urine suddenly suffused the jail, and Alonso said, "He peed himself."

"He has good reason to," Kaiser said, prodding the beardless man with his boot. "My trigger is delicate as a butterfly wing."

When both men had been searched — they were both carrying walkie-talkies and knives, but no additional guns — Kaiser kicked the uninjured man and said, "Crawl over to that cell. Go on."

The man crawled to the cell, and then Kaiser kicked the injured man again and ordered him to crawl to the adjacent cell. He looked around at the council members and asked, "You think they've got more keys? Like, you know, hidden somewhere on them?"

One of the men said, "I don't believe so. Somebody might have keys, but I don't think these guys do."

Kaiser told Moreno to lock the cells and to test them to make sure they were locked. When they were, he went to the door. He could see three women walking down the hill on the main street, one block over, apparently on the way to the noon meeting.

"I will tell you everything I know in a minute," Kaiser told the council people. "Right now, I want you to walk uphill, one at a time, to the first street. There's a Ford Explorer parked there, the doors are unlocked. We're gonna have to get six people in it, but that's the only transportation we got . . . You women are going to have to sit on somebody's lap . . ."

"Where are we going?"

"Tell you when we're on the way," Kaiser said. He tipped his head toward the cells. "I don't want these guys to know."

The bearded man said, "You guys are dead."

The five council members walked out, one at a time, the men picking up the AR-15s as they went. Up the hill, they piled into the Explorer. Kaiser went last, carrying the two pistols taken from the guards. He climbed into the Explorer and put it in gear.

"We think they won't be here more than a day or maybe two," Kaiser said. "I'm not sure, but it's possible that they'll be trying to get out of here tonight, after the caravan gets here. I don't know what they're planning to do about that. Anyway, I'm taking you up to the Mescalero Cave. I've got food and water and blankets for the night, we've

496

got guns. That cave is a fort."

"We could hide out in a house in town," Moreno suggested. "They can't search them all."

"Lot of reasons not to do that," Kaiser said. "We can talk about it up at the cave. The fact is, they *could* search all of them. There are a lot of militia people here and I think they'd enjoy doing that."

The path leading to the cave was three and a half miles up the highway. Kaiser got on the gas pedal and, a mile out, burned past two pickups coming from the other direction.

"They turn around? They coming after us?" he asked. He couldn't see anything in the rearview mirror except the women sitting on the councilmen's laps.

The councilwomen looked out the back window. "No."

The cave was a five-minute walk uphill from the campground, a cup-shaped hole in the soft red rock of the mountain, fifty feet across and fifty feet deep. Boulders and ragged chunks of rock from the mountain, some as big as buses, littered the ground in front of the cave, providing cover.

Kaiser loaded the council people with the food, water, and bedding he'd collected, and sent them up the hill. Running down the path to the road, he checked both ways and saw nothing. When he'd given the council people enough time to make it to the cave, he followed them up the hill, pausing to lock the doors on the Explorer.

"Now," he said, when they were gathered in a circle of boulders, "Who here hunts? Who knows how to shoot a rifle or a pistol?"

The five council people looked at one another, then all five raised their hands.

"Outstanding," Kaiser said.

The first militia truck pulled into the campground a half-hour later. A man got out, ran to the Explorer, peered inside, then ran back to the truck. Five minutes after that, there were eleven trucks in the campground area.

Kaiser looked down at them, then turned to the five council people and said, "You know what I said. I'll do the talking. I want you all in your holes, behind your rocks. I'll yell if I need you to open up. Main thing is, stay under cover. Nothing can get at you where you are."

"Will you shoot somebody?"

"If I have to. I'd rather not," Kaiser said. "If I do, stay in your spots."

The trucks could be negotiating chips,

Kaiser thought. Pickup owners often loved their vehicles like pets, and trucks with a couple of dozen bullet holes are not only expensive to fix, they tend to attract the eye.

He watched as the men below got themselves organized, split into three groups, and began climbing toward the cave, one well to the left, one to the right, one up the center. Kaiser put his two riflemen on the wings and said, "Everybody take it easy."

Veronica Ruiz, in the white blouse, had brought the two walkie-talkies from the Explorer, and now said, "They are talking on channel twenty-two."

"Great. Listen in. The minute you hear anything interesting, let me know. Keep your fingers away from the transmit button. We don't want them to know we might be listening."

Down below, the men were scrambling from one rock to the next; not very good technique, Kaiser thought. He could shoot one of them in the open, and if anyone tried to help him, he'd get another. A thought to be put on reserve.

"We could pick off a few of them right now," the stocky councilman said.

"Let's wait," Kaiser said. "But I like the way you think."

The approaching squads stopped behind cover forty or fifty yards down the hill, and a man in the center squad shouted, "Come out of there."

Kaiser shouted back, "No. We got food, water, lots of ammo, and a hell of a lot better cover than you've got. We could kill all of you before you got to us."

"We don't want anyone to get hurt," the man shouted.

"Come on up here and talk. We won't shoot you. You can see how we're set up here, what you're up against."

The man, who'd stuck his head up for the shouted exchange, ducked back down, and Ruiz said, "They are talking on the radio."

They listened as somebody talked to a woman: probably Hawkes, Kaiser thought. The woman asked, "What can they do to us?"

Man's voice: "There are only six or seven of them, I think, but they're higher than we are, and they got real good cover. They'd shoot the shit out of us. No way to get at them from above, they're set back in that cave. If we had grenades, maybe."

"Don't have grenades . . . You think the

guy was telling the truth when he said he wouldn't shoot you if you went up to talk?"

"Who knows?" the man said. "Probably . . . If he shot me, there'd still be nineteen more of us, pissed off. I think he wants to show me how dug in they are. Intimidate us."

"Okay. Listen, go talk to him. See what you can see. Tell him if he shoots anyone, we'll crawl up that mountain and drop grenades on them."

A moment of ratiocination, then the man said. "I'll try it."

The radio talk stopped, then the man who'd been doing the talking shouted, "I'm coming up. Don't shoot me."

"Come up."

A man stood up, raised his hands over his head, and shouted, "I'm not armed."

"Come on," Kaiser shouted. He turned to the others and said, "Veronica and Janice, get behind those rocks over there . . . Lean in to them, so this guy can only see your backs, and he might think you have rifles. Veronica, turn the radios off — we don't want them to know we can hear them talking. Antonio and Doug, I want you out where he can see you. Point your rifles at him when he comes up. Harold, stand

501

halfway behind that rock, hold that pistol on him, let him see it . . ."

The man down below said something to somebody out of sight, then began climbing the hill until he was standing fifteen feet from Kaiser, who stepped out with his shotgun.

"You made a bad mistake," the man said. "Don't make it worse. Give up, and I'll guarantee your safety."

"What about the trial for treason?" Kaiser asked. "That's usually considered a capital crime."

The man shook his head. "We weren't gonna kill them, though they deserve it. We were going to find them guilty and then cut them loose."

"That's nice of you, but we're safe right here," Kaiser said. "Let me tell you something. There are only eight of us, but we've got six ARs and two combat shotguns full of number-three buckshot. Three of us are with the Department of Homeland Security and we spent years with Delta fighting in Iraq and Afghanistan. We'd have no problem killing all of you and we're very good at killing people."

"You oughta be with us," the man said.

Kaiser: "You're all . . . deluded. Talk of treason, you're the traitors. Anyway I'm not going to argue. We're not coming down. If you look around, you'll see that you can't come up. The best thing for all of us would be if you walk back down the hill, get your men, and go on your way."

The man stared at Kaiser, more thinking, then said, "Here's what we're gonna do. I'm going to leave a bunch of guys down there — won't tell you how many. Then the rest of us are going back into town. If you don't fuck with us, we won't fuck with you."

"Deal," Kaiser said. "You go on now."

The man turned, walked back down the hill and out of sight.

Veronica stepped out from behind her rock and turned the radio up. They huddled around it and heard the man report back to the woman. The woman said, "Leave four men — the caravan is getting close and we may need the rest of you down here."

"Got it."

Then another man's voice: "Don, I got about a fifteen-, maybe twenty-foot run to that big rock, the one on the left. They won't expect it. If I can get to there, I can make it further up the hill. Maybe I can see down on them."

The woman: "Don't do that, Rick. We've got the problem contained, no point in taking a chance that you'll get shot up."

"Not much of a chance, if I could get up there . . ."

"Rick. I'm telling you . . ."

Then the man named Rick: "Those fuckers. He made me pee myself. I'm going up there."

Kaiser said, "Goddamn it, it's the jail guard." He jogged to his right. "He's going to try to . . ."

The beardless jail guard broke up the hill in a stoop, his AR in one hand, his other hand almost touching the hillside as he ran, running like he might have seen on a TV show.

Kaiser, tracking him with the shotgun, shot him in the legs and the man went down, screaming.

From down below, the negotiator shouted, "Stop. Stop. He wasn't supposed to do that. He wasn't supposed to do that."

"Then come up and get him," Kaiser shouted. "He's hurt bad, he's gonna need a medevac."

"I'm coming up . . ."

The negotiator and another man hustled up the hill and the man on the ground sobbed, "I'm hit bad, man, I'm hit bad."

Kaiser shouted, "Leave the gun. Take him and leave the gun. We're going to pick it up.

If anyone shoots at us, we'll kill all three of these men."

Janice Moreno said, "I'll go. They're less likely to shoot a woman. If you see anyone poke a head up, shoot him."

Kaiser nodded: "Good. Go. Hurry."

Moreno scrambled out from behind her rock, ran to the AR, picked it up, looked down the hill where the two militiamen were still only halfway down, then ran back to cover.

"Got it," she said.

The wounded guard was put in a pickup and the pickup turned down the hill and disappeared.

"You think you killed him?" asked Lopez.

"I messed him up, but I was basically shooting at his ankles," Kaiser said. "He's gonna need a hospital, but I don't think he'll die. Does that . . . bother you? Me shooting him?"

Lopez: "Nope. I was more curious than anything. A good thing — they know we're serious."

The negotiator shouted up the hill: "We're pulling out some of our men, but we're leaving most of them. You stick a head up, we'll kill you."

"Likewise," Kaiser shouted back.

"Fuck you, man!"

"Likewise!"

On the radio, they heard the negotiator talking to the woman. "We're leaving four guys. They can't get out and we can't get in. I don't think the Delta guy was lying, I think they've got food, water, cover, and guns."

"Not to worry . . . Listen, did Rick and Bob still have their walkie-talkies on them?"

"I don't know. I can check."

"Wouldn't be good if they were listening to us," the woman said.

"She was right about that," Kaiser said.

When the chatter ended, Veronica Ruiz said, "Okay. So we're camping out for a couple of days. If only we had some weenies and marshmallows . . ."

"As a matter of fact," Kaiser said, "If you check those grocery bags . . ."

TWENTY-FOUR

Letty walked down toward the border station, headed for the crowd still hanging there. An elderly man was pushing a weather-worn bicycle up the hill, and as they met, Letty asked, "Is there a sporting goods store in town?"

"Ham's Guns 'n' Gifts 'n' More got some stuff," he said. "It's over there, around the corner."

He pointed up the hill and she went back that way. As she turned the corner, she heard a single gunshot in the distance, a *boom* rather than a *crack,* that she thought might be Kaiser's shotgun.

She whispered, *"Shit,"* and hurried along to a house with a sign stuck in the dirt by the front porch, with the store's name on it. She climbed the porch and knocked on the closed door; a woman peered out past a safety chain. She asked, "Wut?"

"You got walkie-talkies?"

"You buyin'?"

"Yes."

"Got a package of two for one-oh-nine-ninety-nine," the woman said. "Work on nine-volts."

"I'll take them," Letty said. "And the batteries."

"Stay there." The woman closed the door, came back a minute later with a plastic clamshell package that still had the $79.99 price tag on it.

Letty opened her mouth to complain, then shrugged and took two fifties and a ten out of her purse and gave it to the woman, who said, "The batteries are another ten." The battery package said $5.99.

"You're doing all right for yourself," Letty said, passing over another ten dollars. "You wouldn't have a pair of binoculars in there?" Kaiser's binoculars were in the Explorer.

"Got a monocular. It's pretty good. Sixty bucks."

The Celestron Nature monocular still carried the $39.99 price tag.

Letty passed over three twenties. To the woman she said, "You ought to be proud of yourself."

"Gotta make hay while the sun shines, and right now, it's shining. It's either pay me or walk to Van Horn," the woman said. "And for the money, I don't tell no one that you were here, or what you bought."

"That's a really, really good idea," Letty said. She put some gravel in her voice, and the woman took it in, then closed the door and locked it.

Letty walked along the side street until it ended, then found a spot behind a sick-looking shrub and broke the walkie-talkie handsets out of the clamshell and put the batteries in. The packaging said that the handsets had thirty-six channels. She clicked through them one at a time, listening, and eventually found spurts of conversation on channel twenty-two.

Listening, she eventually worked out that somebody had been shot, and, shortly after, learned that the gunshot victim was a member of the militia and that the city council and Delta troopers were holed up in a cave. Kaiser had made it. A voice she recognized as Hawkes's said that they could use the TV van to request a medevac from El Paso and a man replied that they should do that, and that they'd be at the station in one minute. "Tell the chopper to land on the bridge."

The handset went silent.

If Kaiser had taken out the jail guards, Letty thought, he wouldn't have left the walkie-talkies behind, and he might well be monitoring the only channel on which they seemed to be talking: twenty-two.

She thought, then clicked transmit and blurted, "Kaiser, date we flew."

She clicked down to channel fourteen, listened, and Kaiser said, "We good."

Letty: *"Cada media horas."* Kaiser didn't speak Spanish, but all but one of the city council had Spanish surnames. If there was a militia listener on channel fourteen, maybe he/she didn't.

Kaiser: "Got it."

"Later."

With any luck, they'd talk at every half-hour interval on the clock. Letty realized she was only a block from the used-clothing store, and she went that way, knocked on the door. The woman inside recognized her. "You're back."

"I'm back. I want to buy a dress. And some different shoes. Maybe a hat."

"We got that. What are you up to, girl?"

"You don't want to know," Letty said.

Letty bought a loose neck-to-ankles gingham shift, a pair of worn Levi's jeans, sandals, and a slightly battered straw hat, for twenty-three dollars. She borrowed a pair of scissors from the store owner and cut the legs off the jeans. The woman said, "You might be showing a little more than you want there . . ."

"They're underwear," Letty said.

She went into a tiny dressing room, checked the time on her cell phone, pulled on the shorts, transferred the Sig 938 in its Sticky Holster to one pocket, DHS ID to a back pocket, then checked the time again, took out the walkie-talkie, and called Kaiser: "Nothing here."

She got back, "Nothing here."

She turned off the walkie-talkie and pulled the shift over her head. She looked in the mirror — she was hippier because of the jeans — and groped for a one-word description of her new self. She came up with "helpless."

Perfect.

One walkie-talkie went in a back pocket, the cell phone and the other walkie-talkie in her purse, which was becoming a problem: too bulky and too expensive. The clothes she had been wearing and the white-rimmed sunglasses went in a brown paper grocery sack.

She said good-bye to the store owner — "I could be back" — and walked out and down the hill to the motel. There were militia trucks at almost every corner: security had been kicked up, apparently because of the shooting. The nurses were no longer in their two rooms and she thought they might have gone to help the man Kaiser had shot.

In her room, she traded the purse for her backpack. The Staccato was there, and she was tempted, but if anyone should check the pack . . . She hid it under the bare mattress, with one of the walkie-talkies, put on her straw hat, and went out again and down the hill.

The TV truck was again parked up the hill from the border station, and she saw Hawkes and Low standing next to it. A crowd was still hanging around the station, where the meeting had been held. She eased into it and asked a woman there, "Anything going on?"

"One of their men got shot by some crazy up at the cave. I heard they're calling for a helicopter, but . . . that's just what I heard. I don't really know."

"Anything about that caravan?"

"It's not too far away. Some guys on bicycles came down the road on the other side, and looked over at us, and went back. I think they were with the caravan and came to see what was happening."

As Letty watched, Hawkes broke away from the TV truck and ran down toward the bridge. Low stayed talking to Rodriguez for a minute, then jogged after her. The nurses Letty had seen at the motel were gathered on the bridge, and Letty realized they'd almost certainly called for a helicopter evacuation, as the woman said. Hawkes and Low joined the nurses, and they all began talking at once.

Letty walked back up the hill for a short distance, crossed the highway, and got the TV truck between herself and the people on the bridge. She hurried down to the TV truck, eased up to the right side, which was pushed against the brush on the shoulder of the road, and rapped on the closed door.

The camerawoman, Ochoa, pulled the door open a couple inches and looked out. "You can't be here," she said.

"Did they call for a chopper?"

"Yes. It'll be here fairly soon." She started to push the door closed, but Letty blocked it with her hand.

"When you get a chance, send a message from Letty. Tell them, 'Letty says council is safe with Kaiser.' Get that out right away."

Ochoa nodded and said, " 'Safe with Kaiser.' I don't know what that means, but you gotta go."

Letty walked away, up the hill again, and when she felt she was far enough up, recrossed the street and then walked back down again, rejoining the crowd. One of the women, in her early thirties and pregnant, said to another woman, "I can't take this much longer."

"You gotta be patient," the second woman said. "They're okay, they said they wouldn't hurt anyone."

"Then why won't they let us see them?"

"Because . . . I don't know. Maybe they're just jerks."

"I'm gonna ask again."

"Don't make them angry. There's that one guy, I think he wants to shoot somebody. Anybody."

Letty asked, "Your husbands are in there? Customs people?"

Both women nodded.

"Okay, over there . . . the lady in the blue mask . . . If you talk to her, she might let you visit. She's the boss, I think."

Hawkes and Low were talking to the nurses, then Hawkes turned away, got on her walkie-talkie, spoke to someone, said something more to Low, and started up the hill toward the TV truck.

The pregnant woman called out, "Ma'am? Ma'am?"

Hawkes looked across the street at her, still walking, and the woman hurried toward her, skipping once.

Letty trailed, with a couple of other woman who'd heard their conversation. "Us girls would really like to see our men inside there, couldn't you just let us go in for a couple words? Couldn't hurt nobody."

Hawkes kept walking toward the TV truck, but she turned and shouted down the hill. "Hey! Hey! Rand!"

When she got Low's attention, she pointed to the pregnant woman and shouted, "Talk to this lady."

Letty and the others walked down the hill as Low walked up. The nurses were huddled around a man on a blanket. Letty used Low's body to block their line of sight to her, should one of them turn around to look. The pregnant woman said to Low, "That lady said it would be okay if we went inside to talk to our husbands . . . We wouldn't do anything, we just want to see them."

"Ah, crap . . ."

He shouted at a militiaman on the edge of the crowd. "Hank! Hank! Talk to these girls."

The women walked over to Hank and

Letty said to the militiaman, "The lady and that gentleman said it would be okay if you let some of us girls in to talk to our men . . ."

"Sure. Thought they should have already done that. Don't be pulling anything funny in there."

Letty went over to the crowd and said, "If you've got a man inside, they said we can go in."

Three more women joined the group going in. The pregnant woman stepped up to Letty and asked, "Who the heck are you? You're not from town."

Letty smiled at her: "Why don't we talk about that later. When we talk to your man, let me talk to him, too. Let me be his sister, Joan. I need to get a head count and . . . pass the word along."

The woman gave her a long look and nodded.

Fifteen Customs and Border Protection employees were sitting on chairs or on the floor on one side of an open room, facing three militiamen with guns. Letty went with the pregnant woman, whose name was Alice, and whose husband's name was Parker. Parker stood up and kissed Alice and as they stepped apart, Alice said, in a whisper, "This is your sister, Joan. She's . . .

with somebody."

With all the women talking to their husbands at once, the conversational noise level had gotten high. Parker looked around and then said, quietly, to Letty, "You're too young to be with somebody."

"But I am — I'm an investigator with DHS, out of Washington. I can talk to some outside people every once in a while, police, military."

Parker nodded and said, "We're all okay in here. Something awful might happen, though. They've got all those guns on the bridge and we've heard them talking about the caravan. It isn't stopping, it's still coming on."

"They're not doing anything out in town," Alice said. "The kids are with Gabriela, they're fine. You don't be doing anything brave that gets you shot."

One of the militiamen had stepped toward them, overheard that, smiled and said, "He's doing fine. Couple more hours and we'll be all done."

Another militiaman overheard that comment and said, irritated, "Hey . . . Reg . . ."

"Oops. Sorry," Reg said.

Letty thought, *Really? A couple of hours?*

In the continued gabbling of talk around them, Letty asked Parker, "Any hint they're

517

going to hurt any of you guys?"

He shook his head: "No. They seem to think we're more or less on their side."

"Are you?"

"Fuck no. But we're being nice," Parker said.

"Do you have any access to weapons? Any hidden weapons?"

"They took them all," Parker said. "They were all over us, they body-searched us."

"Would you want one?"

He stared at her for a moment, then said, "Not right now . . ."

Letty nodded toward the windows at the far end of the room. "If things get . . . desperate . . . in here, if you think they're going to start killing you guys, get three guys and all of you line up and lean against those windows. Put your shoulders right against the glass. We'll try to help."

"Who's 'we'?"

Before Letty could answer, a militiaman near the door shouted, "Okay, that's all. Let's get you ladies out of here."

Alice and Letty both gave Parker a hug, and they went back outside and rejoined the crowd. Hawkes was walking away from the TV truck and called to Low and the nurses, "They're saying ten or twelve minutes."

Alice asked, quietly, "Are you DHS? Really?"

Letty smiled and patted her on the arm. "There's a bumper sticker I saw in El Paso; it said, HEAVILY ARMED AND EASILY PISSED. That's more or less me."

Letty lingered with the crowd. Ten minutes later, she heard the helicopter coming in, and the nearby militia pressed down to the bridge. Rodriguez and Ochoa went down with them, working remotely from the truck, recording the evacuation scene. As people shuffled around to watch the helicopter come in, Letty joined the group near the bridge, edging closer to Ochoa.

When they touched elbows, Letty said to Ochoa, in a near-whisper, "Another message, when you can. Say, 'Message from Letty. They will break out tonight.' "

The camerawoman: "You're sure?"

"Send it." And she moved away, watching the helicopter circling the potential landing zone on the bridge.

The militia's pickup trucks were lined up around the parking lot, all facing the entrance, as if prepared to make a break for it. Letty walked down the line with her cell phone held to her face, as if listening to music, snapping photos of the trucks' windshields. With everybody's attention on the helicopter, she got more than twenty shots, she thought, though she wasn't counting.

At the end of the line of trucks, she walked off a short distance and looked at the photos. They'd been taken from six or seven feet from the windshields; the stickers were shown clearly enough, and when she used her fingers to spread the photo size, she could clearly read the tag numbers on all but four trucks. Those trucks had a hot spot from a sun reflection; she could go back later, she thought, and try again.

As she was doing that — and the whole photo walk took no more than two minutes — the helicopter came in, hovered, turned, landed on the bridge. Two paramedics got out and checked the wounded man, unfolded a gurney, loaded him in the helicopter, and two minutes later, the chopper was gone over the mountain. Rodriguez and Ochoa hurried up the hill to their truck and Ochoa caught Letty's eye and nodded.

Two militiamen had been watching the chopper go, and Letty eased up to them and asked, "When's the caravan get here?"

"Maybe three hours, I guess," one of them said. "Maybe . . . six o'clock or a little after?"

The other one asked, "So . . . what're you up to? You live here?"

"Up the hill," Letty said.

"You ever make it to El Paso?"

"It's kind of a long trip with the baby, the bottle warmers and diapers and all . . ."

"Okaaay . . ." The interest vanished and Letty ambled away.

The afternoon dragged: even the militia seemed bored, waiting for the caravan to come in. Letty continued taking renewal tag photos whenever she could do it inconspicuously. When she'd gotten most of the trucks around the lower part of the town, she went back to Jeff's diner, ate a very late lunch, checking in with Kaiser on the half-hour. Neither of them had anything to report except that they were still alive and operating.

Letty went back to the motel and lay on the stripped bed. She'd been down for five minutes when somebody knocked on the door with a key, like housekeepers do. Letty rolled onto her feet, put her hand in her gun pocket, looked out through the peephole she'd forgotten to plug, and saw the old man who managed the place. He was unhappy, but alone.

She opened the door and he said, "I saw

521

you come in. The housekeeper checked your room and your friend's room and she said you've stolen the blankets and sheets and pillows."

Letty said, "Step inside for a minute."

She stood back and the old man followed her inside. She shut the door, took out her ID, held it in front of his face, and said, "My friend and I are agents with the Department of Homeland Security. We took the city council out of the jail and up to the Mescalero Cave campground, where my friend is holding the militia off."

He had to think about that for a minute, then asked, "What about the blankets and pillows?"

"We thought we might have to stay up there for a couple of days . . . couple of nights . . . and it gets cold at night. We needed something for people to wrap up in."

"Are we going to get them back?"

"Yes. Or, if they get damaged, we'll buy them from you. Do not let on to anyone that I'm with DHS. These people here, the militia, have kidnapped people, they're committing treason. You *don't* want to be on their side."

The old man's Adam's apple bobbed and he said, "I'm going back to the office. I won't tell nobody."

"Keep your mouth shut and you'll be fine," Letty said.

He backed away from her, groped for the doorknob, let himself out, and very quietly shut the door.

Letty said, aloud, "Ah, God. Pillows and blankets?" and lay on the bed again. She'd been up a long hard day, most of a night, another high-stress day, and she might have to make it through another night. Young as she was, she was feeling it. There didn't appear much new she could learn by wandering up and down the hill, at least not until the caravan got close. If she could get a couple hours of sleep before the caravan came in . . .

On the half-hour, as she was nearly asleep, Kaiser buzzed her and she picked up the walkie-talkie and said, "Going down for two."

"Good. Same here."

She couldn't make calls on her phone, but its clock still worked. She set an alarm for two hours, and was gone.

When the alarm went off, she bolted upright, shut down the alarm. She had time for a quick rinse before Kaiser would check with her, and she staggered to the shower, dazed, fought an absurd fight with the plastic shower curtain, peeled open a bar of motel soap, and scrubbed up.

Steaming hot water, followed by cooler water and finally by thirty seconds of a torrent of cold, shook the sleep from her brain. She dried off, dressed in her first set of thrift-store clothing, transferred the 938 to the pocket of the red jeans, but this time, took the Staccato XC from its carry pouch, checked it, jacked a shell into the chamber and clicked the safety on, and put it, locked and loaded, into the pack.

She now had to be very careful, she thought. She had the tag numbers of at least forty-five trucks from Texas and five other states; she couldn't risk losing her phone to the militia. And, in fact, taking a chance with that was stupid. She spent ten minutes writing down a list of tag numbers on a motel envelope, and hid the envelope under the mattress.

Just before six o'clock, she walked out the motel door, crossed the parking lot, and looked down the hill. A dozen or so people were milling around on the Mexican side and she could see bicycles. The crowd on the American side had grown, both of townspeople and militia.

At six, she stepped behind an ivy-covered trellis outside the motel, buzzed Kaiser, and said, "Caravan close."

"Got it."

What he would do with the information, she didn't know — probably, if he was stuck under guard, nothing. She put the walkie-talkie in her pack and headed down the hill.

The TV truck was parked where it'd been since Rodriguez and Ochoa got back from the cell tower explosion, but the street-side door they used was shut and locked. As she got farther down the hill, she could see Ochoa floating above the crowd, and as she got closer, realized that she was sitting on the shoulders of a husky dark-haired man that Letty hadn't seen before, a mobile video platform.

She joined the crowd, watched and listened for a couple of minutes — they were expecting the caravan at any time — and saw Hawkes, Low, Duran, and Crain standing by the end of the bridge, with a dozen militiamen with rifles braced on their hips, all looking across the river. The original crew of twenty militia were standing on the far side of the bridge, no more than twenty yards from the Mexican side.

Letty threaded her way through the crowd until she was beside Rodriguez. He didn't see her coming up, didn't turn until she asked, quietly, "Where did Candace get the ride?"

He glanced down at her and said, "It's like Uber. Twenty bucks and you get a ride. Go away."

"I'll wait with you," Letty said.

He sighed and said "Goddamn it" and turned away. A man with a cowboy hat moved in front of Letty and she couldn't see past him. She poked him in the side. "I can't see."

Without looking at her, he said, "Tough."

She said, "If you don't move, I'll take out my knife and cut your belt and your pants will fall down."

Now he looked at her and Rodriguez said, "She'll do it," and the man moved sideways. Letty said, "Thank you."

Across the bridge, a dozen people appeared on the highway behind the group already gathered by the Mexican border post, and then an old yellow school bus that resembled all the old yellow school buses in the world edged around a turn behind them.

Rodriguez said, "Here we go."

TWENTY-FIVE

Standing in the crowd, Letty was gripped by the idea that she was stuck, that she was letting events run over her. As the school bus edged forward, a group of Mexican border patrolmen lined up at the edge of the bridge to block the bus and the people behind it. Then nothing happened.

But something *was* going to happen.

The highway down to the bridge was flanked on the left side by the substantial American border station, which included the main building plus two smaller buildings surrounded by a large parking lot meant to hold eighteen-wheelers while they were being inspected. On the right side of the highway, the mountains sloped down to the Rio Grande flood plain, which was several hundred yards across. Probably once used for agriculture, it was now half-covered by scrubby brush, while a portion of the plain closest to the river was plowed and mown bare, right down to the dirt, with hardly a weed poking up.

Letty walked back up the hill, far enough that she wouldn't be noticed as she crossed the highway and pushed into the brush and began to make her way through it, back down the hill again. The going was rough: scrubby, tangled pinions and woody bushes plucking at her blouse, her hat, the backpack, and her hair. She made her way to the sandy flood plain, crossed a dirt track, and then moved carefully on through the jungle of brush and weeds on the plain to the point where the plowed ground started. Sitting just inside the brush line, she slipped off the pack, took out the monocular, and looked at the bridge, where she'd seen the men disappear earlier in the day.

She didn't see them immediately, because they weren't moving, but after a fast scan, she did a slower inspection, and one of the men raised an arm, and she picked him up. There were two of them, tucked in the shadows under the Mexican end of the bridge, dressed from head to toe in camo.

Scanning the underside of the structure, she began picking up what she thought might be the explosives; she wasn't sure of that, but she could see changes of color at the ends of the red-painted support beams.

The beams, she thought, were the same size as the one that had been cut in half by the C-4 experiment they'd seen with Hawkes and the others at the mountain off I-10.

Then the men stood up, as if on a command, did something under the bridge that she couldn't see, then moved down the slope toward the river, still concealed beneath the structure from eyes at either end.

One of the men was carrying something metallic. As she watched, the two men paused near the end of the first slab on the Mexican side and began working with the metallic object . . . a lightweight aluminum extendable ladder. They put it up against the bridge support structure, one of the men climbed it, did something under the bridge, came down, carried it over to the other side of the two-lane bridge, climbed again, and did something again.

Setting the timers on the explosive, Letty thought. The C-4 was already in place. They were going to take down the bridge.

The river, which might not even have been called that in Minnesota — more like a big creek — was shallow beneath the bridge, and the men waded halfway across to a support structure that stood in the middle. The ladder was extended, and one of the men climbed it while the other supported the ladder.

Letty watched: they'd have to do this six more times. That would take a while.

She backed into the brush, and, careful not to disturb the foliage any more than she had to, she worked her way back across the flood plain, across the dirt track to the mountainside, then up a hundred feet or so, and cut back toward the highway. At seven-fifteen, as she was approaching the highway, the handset vibrated, and she sat down on the hillside and called back: "You there?"

"Here," Kaiser said.

"Gonna blow the bridge," Letty said.

"How soon?"

"Don't know. I'll find out. Monitor this channel."

Before she emerged from the brush, Letty plucked the twigs and burrs from her clothing, then checked across the street. There were townspeople moving around, some walking uphill, some down toward the bridge. Two pickups went by fast, heading down the hill, then another one.

She stepped out of the brush, and walking down the hill, no one paid her any attention. The militia was buzzing, people moving fast, loading up trucks. Two more pickups went by, and near the bottom of the hill, they turned off on a dirt road that she'd crossed on her way to spy on the bridge.

Letty rejoined the crowd at the bottom and edged as close as she could to the front, where a line of militiamen was blocking the American crowd from the bridge.

Hawkes, Low, Duran, and Crain were standing at the near end of the bridge, looking across at the militiamen who still stood in a line nearly at the Mexican side. Rodriguez and his camerawoman were standing next to Hawkes. Ochoa had taken the camera off her shoulder and was resting it on her foot, talking to the husky man who'd been her mobile platform. They apparently didn't think anything was imminent.

The sun had dropped below the hills on the Mexican side, puffy clouds going orange and then lavender overhead. Letty checked her phone: 7:40.

She felt the handset vibrate. She walked back out of the crowd, up the hill to the locked-up TV truck, stepped behind it, then around to the far side where she couldn't be seen.

She called Kaiser: "What?"

"Something's happening here. The guys watching us pulled out. They're gone."

"Are they playing you?"

"Don't think so . . . wait one . . ."

She waited, then Kaiser came back.

"A bunch of pickups just went past, moving fast, heading your way. They must be coming down from the roadblock. What do you want me to do?"

Letty hesitated. They had no plan for this. She pushed the transmit button and said, "Do what we planned, you know, *ven aqui.*"

Pause: "Got it."

With any luck, Kaiser would leave the council at the cave, with guns, and would join her near the bridge.

More pickups went by as she walked from behind the TV truck. They didn't pause as they went by, the passengers didn't look at her. As she walked back down the highway, toward the bridge, they turned right at the dirt road and out of sight.

The sky was going dark, and lights were coming on around the town. Six more pickups, running together, went past, took the right, and disappeared. Letty rejoined the crowd, saw the pregnant woman, Alice, who'd been worried about her husband, and stepped close to her.

Letty asked, "Where are the pickups going? Is there a road out down there?"

Alice shook her head. "There's a gun range a ways down there. Then the old ag plain runs along for four or five miles, then the mountain comes right down to the river. There's no way out. There's a deep arroyo, Arroyo Grande, but there's no way in or out of it that I know of. Maybe you could hide in it . . . Look."

Letty looked.

Low was walking up the hill with a megaphone. "Let me have your attention, folks. We've gotten word from our people at the roadblock that the Army is clearing out the roadblock and is coming down the hill with troops. There's gonna be a hell of a fight down here, all over town. You gotta get out. Get in your cars and get out . . . we're turning the Customs loose right now, follow them out of here. This is gonna be a goddamn nightmare, this is gonna be a free-fire zone. We understand they're coming in with Black Hawk gunships to take us out, and we ain't going, we're gonna fight back . . ."

Most of the crowd began to move, headed up the hill, slowly at first, then more quickly; some people began to run. The front door of the border station opened, and the captured Customs and Border Protection employees surged out and began jogging up the hill and into the town, headed for their homes and families.

Low was chanting into the megaphone, "You gotta hurry, you gotta run . . ."

Bapbapbapbapbapbap.

There was a burst of gunfire, picked up by other guns, to the side, and far up the highway.

Another man, up the hill, began shouting into a megaphone, repeating the message. *Army's coming in . . .*

Letty ran with the crowd, but when she got to the TV truck, she stepped behind it, and then around into the brush beside it. Dark back there. Stars were popping out overhead, with a bare orange line defining the tops of the hills on the Mexican side of the river.

Her handset buzzed and Kaiser asked, "Where are you?"

Had to risk it: the militiamen seemed too busy to be monitoring the unused radio channels and she blurted, "Behind the TV truck."

"Two minutes."

The orange line that defined the Mexican hills was fading when Kaiser appeared. He had come down the hill inside the brush line, and had the shotgun slung behind his shoulder along with an AR.

534

"I'm clean," he muttered. "I didn't see anyone watching me."

He unslung the rifle and handed it to her. "One mag, thirty rounds."

She took it. "The council's okay?"

"Still up at the cave, but I don't think the militia cares anymore. They're evacuating." He reached out and touched her shoulder. "You okay?"

"So far. But they've set charges on the bridge." She told him about talking to the woman who said there was no way out along the river, but that it appeared all the trucks were going there.

"Then they've got a backdoor, somehow. Maybe there's a ford up there, somewhere. They head into Mexico, come back across one at a time, maybe at another ford."

"I don't know . . . Let's take a peek."

They edged around to the front of the truck and looked down the hill. A couple of townspeople were lingering there, along with a crowd of militia. Everybody was looking across the bridge.

As they watched, in the lights from the Mexican border station, the line of militia at the far end of the bridge, the Mexican side, suddenly and all at once, broke and began trotting toward the American side. The militiamen on the near side of the bridge jogged into the border station's parking lot and began loading into the pickups parked there.

Across the river, the school bus edged onto the bridge.

Rodriguez, Ochoa, and her husky helper hurried up the hill, and as they got close to the truck, turned back, and then Ochoa, with a boost from Rodriguez, got on the shoulders of the big guy. She began recording the militia running off the bridge.

"They can't, what's going on?" Letty asked. "I told the people in El Paso to warn the caravan to stay off the bridge, but they're coming . . ."

"Somebody didn't get the message," Kaiser said. "Or they didn't believe it. Or us. Or something."

Hawkes and Low were with Rodriguez, Duran, and Crain farther down the hill, all watching the bridge. They heard Hawkes call to Rodriguez and Ochoa, "One minute. One minute . . ." and then ". . . Thirty seconds . . ." and then ". . . Ten seconds."

Ten seconds passed, nothing happened.

Hawkes shouted at Low, "What happened? Are we —"

Low interrupted her, shouting back, "I told them to add on five minutes."

"What? What are you talking about?"

Hawkes looked back toward the bridge. "You'll kill them."

"Gotta draw the line," Low shouted. "We're drawing the line. You wanted the Alamo, you got it."

"What! What!"

Letty: "Did you hear that?"

Kaiser: "He delayed . . ."

The school bus, with one good headlight, rolled farther onto the bridge; the Mexican border patrol let it go.

And Kaiser said, "Oh, *shit!*"

Letty leaned the AR against the TV truck and turned into the brush, and began pushing through it, away from the highway and then down the hill. *Five minutes,* she thought. *Now four-forty. Now four-thirty. Now four-fifteen . . . Now four.*

There was a thrashing behind her and she realized that Kaiser was following, not delicately, but bulling his way through the brush. She let him come. They broke out of the thicket near the end of the bridge. On the other side, a crowd was walking parallel to the school bus, on both sides of it. Letty and Kaiser ran onto the bridge and started across it, Letty screaming, *"Detente! Detente! Stop! Stop!"*

Kaiser was looking at his Rolex and

shouted, "Three-thirty."

Letty continued to scream, but the bus and the crowd kept coming, and Kaiser unslung the shotgun and aimed it up in the air and pulled the trigger.

Boom! Boom! Boom!

Letty began screaming, *"Hay bombas abajo del puente! Detente! Regresa!"*

Kaiser shouted, "Three!" and "Go back! Go back!"

The bridge was three hundred yards long, the school bus already fifty yards out from the Mexican side when they reached it. The bus was driven by a heavyset woman who looked out the driver's-side window, which was missing, and Letty shouted at her, *"Hay bombas! Hay bombas abajo el puente!"*

The woman seemed confused. *"Que? Hay bombas?"*

Behind and beside the bus, the crowd had slowed its march, and some, not many, had turned back. Letty kept screaming *"Hay bom-bas!"* and Kaiser shouted "Two!" and Letty screamed out the countdown: *"Hay bombas* in *dos minutos."*

There were a hundred and fifty people on the bridge, maybe more. The front of the crowd had turned and was beginning to step backward, uncertain about what was happening, as Letty continued to shout at them. The school bus was now backing up, a foot at a time, slow, too slow, with people stacked up behind it, some of them banging with their fists on the fenders to stop it. The crowd on the far side of the bus had continued to move forward or had stopped, confused.

Boom! Boom!

Kaiser fired two more shots and the crowd began to move back, a few tried to run, stumbling along the edges of the bridge. Some of the caravan members, who hadn't heard what was happening, continued to press forward from the Mexican side, blocking the escape of people trying to get off the bridge, but then, like a turning tide, people began to get off, picking up Letty's voice, shouting at the people behind them: *"Hay bombas abajo del puente!"*

The school bus was missing its front door and a woman jumped out of the bus, followed by another, both carrying and dragging kids, and Letty realized that the bus was full of women with small children who couldn't keep up with the caravan on foot.

Kaiser screamed, "One minute," and Letty ran to the rear door of the bus and began banging on it, but a woman's face appeared in the window and she made a windshield-wiper motion with one finger, telling her that the door didn't work. Two more women, each with a child, jumped off the bus at the front door as the bus continued to slowly back up.

Kaiser shouted "Thirty seconds."

They were twenty yards from the end of the bridge and some of the crowd was still standing on the last slab, and Letty yelled at Kaiser, "We gotta get the kids off," and Kaiser shouted back, "Can't," and he shouted, *Ten seconds,*" and Letty started back to the bus's forward door and Kaiser picked her up as though she were a heavy coil of water hose, holding her under one arm, ignoring her as she beat on his legs with her fists, and ran for the Mexican end of the bridge, smashing through the crowd like a linebacker.

Dropped her on her feet when they got off the bridge and he said, "Should have blown . . ."

WHOMP!

The first bomb went and a handful of people who were still on the bridge managed to leap off, as the slab nearest them tilted crazily to one side, and then, *WHOMP! WHOMP! WHOMP!*

The charges began going off, not quite simultaneously, and spans began to drop into the river and onto the riverbanks on both sides, and Letty put her hands over her ears and *WHOMP! WHOMP! WHOMP!*

The explosions stopped; Letty took her hands away from her ears, to the screams of injured and dying people who'd gone down with the bridge.

The nearest slab had fallen fifteen or twenty feet onto the riverbank and the bus and thirty or forty walkers had gone with it. The bus was nose-down, the slab canted sideways, and the bus began to tilt to the side, as though in slow motion, and then toppled over as the slab beneath it wrenched free of its moorings and fell another five feet.

Letty looked at Kaiser and shouted, "We gotta get the kids out of there . . ."

Kaiser shouted back, "This way," and they went to the side of the bridge, where a railing still stuck up, and they went around the railing, and now Mexican border patrolmen and members of the crowd began to follow them down where the slab was lying on the ground under the bridge.

The people who'd been on the slab when the bombs went off were all hurt; some of them badly, broken bones, broken backs, skull fractures, people screaming for help and crying. Mexican border patrolmen were swarming down the slab, trying to give aid, one man with a tiny kit of small bandages, Band-Aids, and disinfectant ointment.

The bus door was underneath the chassis and they couldn't get to it, but the back door had popped open a few inches and one of the Mexican border patrolman unloaded his rifle and used the barrel as a crowbar, and with somebody inside kicking at it, they managed to wedge the door open eight or ten inches, but the patrolman was too thick to squeeze through.

Letty said, "Let me! Let me!" and with Kaiser and two border patrolmen prying at the door with their hands, she managed to squeeze through.

Looking down, the seats of the bus were like a sloping ladder to a stygian hell, dark, stinking of blood and sweat and desperation. Lights began to flicker inside, as people outside began shining flashlights through the windows on what was now the top of the wrecked bus. A woman was climbing the seats toward Letty, holding a small child with blood all over the kid's head; the mother was shouting at her and Letty took the kid and pushed her upward to the back door, and a man on the other side of the door took her through the narrow opening, still screaming, and then the mother climbed past, trying to get out.

Letty went the other way, down and sideways. Forty people were piled up at the bottom of the bus, half of them children, all of them hurt, some trying to push out of the pile and pull others up. Letty shouted in Spanish, "Take the children up . . . Take them up."

Women began climbing the seats, carrying children. Some were getting out, but in the pile at the bottom, many more were hurt too badly to move, and others had to be dead, Letty thought, twisted into impossible shapes; and some of them were small bundles of flesh and clothing.

She began to cry; cry and carry and climb, her body shaking, tears pouring down her face, handing injured children upward. Cry and carry and climb. A woman below her handed her a baby, and Letty began climbing toward the top again, and when she got to the door, three women were there. Two went through and the other started back down to bring more people up, and Letty handed the baby up to one of the Mexican border patrolmen, and as she did that, she realized something was terribly wrong with the baby's neck and head; the baby was dead.

That nearly broke her. She slumped

against a crazily tilted seat and pressed her hands to the sides of her head, weeping, and dimly heard Kaiser, "Bring the pole, bring the pole."

The sound of his voice brought her back and she wiped the tears off her face and went back down. More women were climbing the seats, the backs of the seats functioning as narrow platforms. Children were being handed up, placed on the seats, then passed upward, and uninjured women kept trying to lift children and injured women out of the nose of the bus and pull them up to platforms . . .

As Letty was climbing upward with a little girl, a thick, rusty steel pole that might have held a stop sign pushed through the narrow opening of the back door and people outside began yelling, and the pole pried the door open to a point, and then with a sudden crack it was wrenched fully open and women began to climb out. Letty passed the little girl upward, and a woman below handed her a bloody toddler and she climbed up the seats and passed the child up and then border patrolmen began climbing down past her.

The bus was becoming jammed with rescuers and Letty crawled out, wet with blood and saliva and snot and urine, one sleeve nearly ripped off her blouse. She climbed out and found Kaiser there, who took her by the arm and pulled her up.

"They got it; we can't help much more," Letty said. She began to cry again, looking at a line of bloody, injured women, children, and a few dead bodies, now laid out on a tarp on the road, the Mexican border patrolmen working over them with towels, sheets, anything they could find to help.

Kaiser was still holding her arm, supporting her. "We *gotta* help," he said.

"Then *you* help," Letty snapped. "I'm gonna cross the fuckin' river and kill some people."

TWENTY-SIX

Some of the slabs hadn't been blown free and were hanging by one end or the other from the vertical supports. The supports themselves had big chunks blown from their sides, but none had actually fallen. The two slabs over the river *had* gone down, so there was a bridge of sorts back to the American side. Hopping from one slab to the next, Letty and Kaiser crossed the water, Kaiser leading, then dropped onto the American riverbank, and Kaiser said, "There'll still be some people up there with guns."

"Can't see us in the dark."

"Not here, but there are lights up on top."

They scrambled up the riverbank, Kaiser leading with his shotgun. Behind them, they could still hear the screams of the injured and dying, and the shouts of the rescuers. Dozens of flashlights and cell phone lights now illuminated the bus, and from Letty's point of view, the rescuers were reduced to black shadows as they worked around the outside of the bus.

On the American side now, the streetlights lining the highway down to the bridge were still on, as were lights at the border station and in town. They could see militiamen moving around, trucks pulling out, two men directing traffic, trucks disappearing down the gun range track.

"Don't see anyone we know," Letty whispered, as she looked over the top of the riverbank. "We need to get up there."

"C'mon," Kaiser muttered. He led the way, in a crouch, sideways along the riverbank and a few feet down from the crest, so they couldn't be seen from the highway. After poking their heads up a time or two, they climbed back to the top of the riverbank and crossed the border station's back parking lot. They stopped behind an emergency power generator, from where they could see across the highway.

"There they are," Kaiser said.

Low, Duran, and Crain were standing in a semicircle in the light outside the open door of the TV truck, as Rodriguez and Ochoa worked inside.

"That's them. Getting the propaganda out," Letty said.

"Can't get at them without hitting the TV

guys," Kaiser said. "We need to get closer."

Letty could see cars leaving, heading up the hill toward the roadblock, townspeople fleeing what they thought might be a fire-fight. There was nothing coming down the hill and only five pickups waited by the end of the flood plain track. Two of the militia-men standing by those trucks pointed their weapons in the air and began firing them, *bapbapbapbapbap . . .*

Two full magazines went out, and Kaiser said, "Still trying to panic the town — if they get enough cars trying to get out, the cops can't come down, even if they clear the palm trees."

"We're on the wrong side of the highway," Letty said. "If we go up the hill a couple hundred feet, like we're running away, we can cross over between the cars that are leaving and come down behind the TV truck, in the brush."

They did that. They ran through the dark, Kaiser tripping, going down, cursing, then back on his feet. They crossed between two outgoing cars, the driver and his passenger gawking at them. They walked back down the hill, inside the brush line, to the right side of the highway, in the dark, and then, again:

Bapbapbapbapbapbap . . .

They both flinched, the shots very close, some sounding as though they were hitting the TV truck, then Kaiser said, "They're close, but they weren't shooting at us . . ."

They heard Rodriguez shouting something and then another man's voice, different, that Letty thought might have been Low, but quieter, and they couldn't make out what he was saying.

Letty stood back up, Kaiser beside her, and said, "I think we lost the last of our communications . . . I think they shot up the satellite feed."

They moved slowly, deliberately, along the back of the TV truck and peeked around it. Rodriguez was standing there, thirty feet away, Ochoa beside him, watching Low, Duran, and Crain walking away toward the last two pickup trucks still on the highway.

"Where's Hawkes?" Kaiser whispered.

Letty said, "Don't know. C'mon." They went back to the off-side of the TV truck, where Letty recovered the pack she'd dropped and the AR that was still leaning against the truck.

"What are we doing?" Kaiser asked.

Letty: "Like I said: I'm gonna kill some people."

They pushed into the brush, the branches

and tree limbs catching them, scratching; Letty walked into the end of a broken limb and felt it jab into her forehead. She touched the wound with her fingertips and came back with blood that trickled into her eyes.

"Watch your eyes," she told Kaiser. "Watch your eyes."

As they approached the track going onto the flood plain, Letty said, "We'll ambush them when they come by."

They heard truck doors slamming and Kaiser said, "Here." He caught Letty by the arm, said, "There's a ditch here, or a hole. Cover, if they shoot back."

In the hole, Letty put her pack down, lifted the AR, and asked, "You jack a round into the chamber?"

"Probably is one . . ."

Letty pulled back the charging handle on the AR, let it slam forward, felt, or heard, a shell flip into the brush as she did it. "Twenty-nine now," she said, of the AR's thirty-round magazine. She thumbed the safety into the firing position. "You're the ambush expert. Tell me what to do."

"Two trucks left, with the leadership. Aim at the door of the lead truck and put fifteen or twenty rounds through it, keep ten or so in case you need them. Visualize how they'll be sitting inside. I'll take the second truck.

If it gets past me, dump the rest of your rounds into it."

"Wonder where they are?"

"Coming . . . I can hear them . . ."

Hear them but not see them. The trucks were rolling down the hill without lights, both black, hard to see.

Kaiser said, "Here . . ."

Letty saw the lead truck creeping toward them in the dark, fifteen feet away. She half-stood, to clear the weeds around their hole, and, when the truck was directly across from her, began firing the AR, the gun leaping in her hands, *bangbangbangbangbang,* half a mag going out in three or four seconds.

The truck rolled to the left, rudderless, Kaiser's shotgun banging along a few feet farther up the hill, louder but much slower than the AR, and then, her ears ringing and Kaiser shouting, "I don't know, he may have bailed when you opened up . . . I'm going around the back of the truck, watch this side, watch this side."

Letty shouted "Yeah" and pointed the AR at the front left headlight of the second truck, looking for motion. Five seconds later, *BOOM,* then Kaiser's voice, "Never mind" and "Stay right where you are. I got a guy down here, I'm checking him . . .

Okay, I'm moving up to the first truck . . ."

A moment later: "We got three down, no sign of Hawkes."

Letty shouted, "Take care, take care, she was in the military . . ."

They moved around the truck, covering each other, and eventually heard Rodriguez shouting down the hill, "Who is that? Who is that down there?"

"We're looking for Jael," Letty shouted back.

"She's gone. She's gone. She ran down there . . ."

Letty took her phone from her pocket, turned on the flashlight app, shined it into the first truck. Duran and Crain were there, exceptionally dead. She'd put seventeen rounds through the pickup door and had shredded the two men.

Low lay in the dirt beside his truck. He'd been hit in the leg with a solid slug, but had managed to get out of the truck, gripping his pistol, when Kaiser came around the end of the truck with buckshot shells loaded and shot him in the stomach. He was dying as Letty came up, but wasn't quite gone.

His now paper-white face, untouched by the violence, turned up at her and he groaned and said, ". . . Can't make it here."

And he died.

Letty and Kaiser spent the next ten minutes moving around the bottom of the hill, one covering the other, until they decided that they were clear. Hawkes, Ochoa told them, had a violent argument with the three men about the bridge explosions, and left them to run down the hill to the gun range track, where they saw her catch up with one of the last departing pickups.

Letty said, "What about your satellite feed?"

Rodriguez said, "We can't transmit, the fuckers shot out our cables to the dish. We can still record, though . . ."

Ochoa lifted her camera to her shoulder and turned on her light, and Letty said "No," unconsciously gesturing with the Staccato. Ochoa put the camera down but turned away, smiling.

Kaiser said, "If the cops have pulled out that roadblock . . ."

"Then where are they?" Letty said.

They both looked up the road and saw no headlights coming toward them, only the taillights of people fleeing the town, well toward the top of the long hill.

Rodriguez: "Did you kill those guys?"

Letty didn't answer, but asked Kaiser, "Where you'd leave the car?"

"Up by the motel."

"C'mon. Run," Letty said. She began running up the hill toward the motel.

Kaiser caught her at the motel parking lot and said, "I'll drive, but I'm not sure that following those pickups down the river . . ."

"That'd just get us killed," Letty said. "We need to get to the cops, get some communications."

"Attagirl," Kaiser said. When they opened the car's door, he looked across at her and said, "Your face is covered with blood."

"Fuckin' tree branch," Letty said. "Stabbed myself."

As Kaiser pulled into the street, Letty looked out the back window. Down the hill, Rodriguez and Ochoa were standing by Low's truck, shooting video of the dead men.

The roadblock was five miles out, but they'd gone less than a half-mile up the highway when they caught the cars and trucks of the fleeing townspeople jamming up both lanes and the narrow shoulders.

"Now what?"

"We *gotta* talk to somebody in El Paso," Letty said. "If the cops have cleared the roadblock . . . I can run."

"So can I." Kaiser pulled the Explorer on to the shoulder, parked it, and said, "Let's go."

They ran.

They ran, jogged, and walked four and a half miles. Back in Washington, on her regular run, which was flat, Letty could do four and a half miles in a little over thirty minutes if she pushed hard. She and Kaiser took more than an hour and a half to run, jog, and walk the four and a half miles, mostly uphill, through the jammed-up cars, with the crowds trying to move on foot between them. At places, they were simply stopped, unable to push through. From time to time, they could hear gunfire behind them, the militia, they thought, still encouraging the panic. The sound of the ARs and AKs was punctuated by the *BOOM* of the .50-cal.

There was a crowd at the roadblock. As they came up to it, they were told that the police on the far side weren't letting people through, apparently worried that some of the militia would try to get out that way.

At the roadblock itself, they found that the cops on the far side had made almost no progress in moving the palm trees off the highway. Letty and Kaiser walked around to the side, jostling through the crowd waiting there, into the headlights of a half-dozen Highway Patrol cars and a man shouting, "Hold it, hold it . . ."

Letty held up her ID case and shouted "DHS . . . DHS."

A man, invisible behind the headlights, called in a Texas accent, "DHS? That you, Letty?"

They had radios, and the radio linked to the task force in El Paso. Letty told the task force about the trucks going out along the river, to the gun range.

"They must have a way out. You need to get somebody up in the air to look for them. I talked to a woman who said the track runs four or five miles along the river and then stops. There's an arroyo out there that apparently blocks the road. She said you can't get up the arroyo, but I'm not sure she knew what she was talking about. You need to put some helicopters out there with searchlights. You need to put medevacs over on the Mexican side, lot of medevacs, everything you got . . ."

"That's under way. We saw the TV crew's video of the bridge going down, the school bus, and you and Kaiser running across there . . ."

"Lot of hurt kids," Letty said. "Some of them . . . they're gone."

"Ah, no."

A second cop: "They're all out of Pershing? The militia?"

"All of them," Letty said. "Well. Except the dead ones."

Twenty-Seven

Hawkes made it out.

When she saw the bridge blow up and the school bus go down, she abandoned Low, Crain, and Duran and ran down the hill to the dirt road, caught up with the last slow-moving pickup, banged on the door until the truck stopped, then climbed inside.

"Need to ride with you," she said to the driver.

"Happy to have you." He was from Michigan, his name was Carl Waltz, and he had a rough red beard. "Hope we can get out. I dunno . . ."

"We'll be fine," Hawkes said.

"The bridge went down . . ."

"Yes."

"Think anybody got hurt?" Waltz asked.

"I hope not. That wasn't the intention," she said. That wasn't her intention; she had no doubt that Low and some of the others had fully intended to blow the bridge with people on it, and no doubt that some had been killed. Low hadn't told her in advance because he'd known she'd refuse to go along.

She'd gone along too many times, she thought now, nodding when she shouldn't have, beginning with the killing of the two illegals in the desert. Nodding when the men had proposed the killings of the Blackburns and Winks. Sending Max Sawyer off to die . . .

For a good cause? She still thought so, but might there have been another way? One in which the Blackburns had been allowed to live? Winks . . . she didn't care about Winks, she admitted to herself. Max Sawyer she cared about.

The pickups in front of them were running dark, barely visible in the thin moonlight, a loose caravan kicking up dust as they passed the gun range. They could see the truck in front of them bouncing over rough spots, so they could slow for them. Everything seemed to be working except . . . there were no trucks trailing them. They were the last in the long line and Hawkes kept looking back, wondering: Low in one truck, Crain and Duran in the other. They should be coming up from behind, but they weren't.

They took twenty minutes to drive the five miles to the hole, the Arroyo Grande, where there was another ten-minute wait, the pickups slowly going over the edge, men getting out to look at the situation. When it came their turn to go over, Waltz said, "I dunno."

One of the El Paso militiamen was standing on the edge of the arroyo, knocked on the driver's-side window, and when Waltz lowered it, said, "You'll be fine. No problems so far with trucks less good than yours. Don't hit the gas hard going up the other side. Just drive up, you don't want your wheels spinning."

"Like I was on ice."

"I dunno, I never been on ice. But glad you could make it, buddy," the militiaman said. "Say hello to your folks back home. And take it easy, you got a valuable passenger there."

Waltz took it easy, and they went down, over, and up. On the far side, they caught up with the end of the caravan and Hawkes said, "We should be good now. It smooths out."

"I looked at the maps. I'd like to get on the interstate, but what do you think?" Waltz asked. "You're the brains of this operation."

"When we get up to that loop . . . the farm

loop . . . we should keep going north instead of cutting over to I-10. If there are any cops hunting for us, that's where they'll be. The farm roads are fast enough and we get ten more miles in, there's a whole network of roads, branches all over. Might not be the fastest, but it'd be the safest."

"Safe is good for me," Waltz said. "Think we made it on national TV?"

"Oh, yeah. Before we took the cell tower down, I talked to our intel guy in El Paso," Hawkes said. "He told me we were on every network, all the time."

"Hell of a thing," Waltz said. "Hell of a thing. The Alamo."

"You got our publication on what to do when you get home?" Hawkes asked.

"Yup. Makes sense to me."

"Keep your mouth shut, and when people ask if you were here . . ."

"Smile." He laughed, his head bobbing in delight at the thought. "So they'll know, but they won't know."

"Use cash in the gas stations, stay off your credit card . . ."

"I got it," Waltz said.

They drove on, and then Waltz, looking in his rearview mirror, said, "Look back there. A helicopter."

Hawkes looked back, and she could see a

brilliant light shining down on what had to be Pershing, a police helicopter with a searchlight. "Too late," she said. "Too late."

"Might not be looking for us," Waltz said. "Might be looking at that bus."

"Might be," Hawkes said. She didn't want to think about the bus.

An hour after they left Pershing, they hit the farm service roads. Most of the trucks turned to the right at the first state highway, heading toward an on-ramp at I-10. Hawkes pointed Waltz to the left, and, two hours after they drove out of Pershing, directed him onto a highway that went northwest into the backside of El Paso.

They made it into the city shortly before midnight and Waltz dropped her at the twenty-four-hour Walmart where she'd left her Subaru. They spent a minute pulling duct tape off his license plates, then she gave Waltz a hug and said, "Stay under the speed limit, take care, Carl. I don't know your plans, but if I were you, I'd head on up to Albuquerque tonight . . ."

"I got it," he said. "I'm going through Albuquerque all the way up to Santa Fe and then cut cross-country back home."

"Maybe I'll see you up there someday,"

Hawkes said.

"Always got a place for you."

When Waltz had gone, Hawkes got out her burner phone and tried to call Low, then Crain, then Duran, and got no answer from any of them. Something bad had happened, she thought. And maybe something bad *should* have happened, since Low had delayed the blowing of the bridge.

She got on I-10 a few minutes after midnight, pointed the car at Tucson, four and a half hours away. She'd find a motel there, with her new ID, get some sleep, change her hair color, and head north into the Rockies.

She had a hundred and fifty thousand dollars in cash, an AR and a Beretta, and a bottle of L'Oréal Paris Excellence Crème Hair Color in the Red Penny shade.

A new life coming up, a life underground.

Red hair and guns.

Made her heart beat harder.

By the time Letty and Kaiser got to the roadblock, the first militia trucks were turning onto I-10, streaming up toward El Paso, although some turned back toward Van Horn, planning to catch I-20 north toward Midland, or to simply stay on I-10 east.

The few available police and military helicopters didn't make it to the Pershing area for more than an hour after Letty requested them and they found nothing. Police on the highway north of the road-block managed to drag the palm trees out of the way, but it was more than three hours after the bridge explosion before the first police cars nosed into Pershing.

With directions from people who had stayed in town, the first cars carefully followed the dirt track to the gun range, and then on to the Arroyo Grande, where the cops saw the newly carved-out escape route. The police cars were too low-slung to follow past the arroyo, and it was the next morning before the first official truck covered the entire route out.

At the roadblock, a highway patrolman told Letty that they'd been told to get her and Kaiser to the El Paso command post.

"We got stuff in Pershing, at the motel . . ."

"When we get through the roadblock, we'll collect it for you," the cop said. "For now, I'm running you up to Van Horn, where a helicopter will pick you up. They don't want to land here on the highway — too iffy."

"I'm a mess," Letty said. She plucked at

her torn blouse, a hole big enough to expose her entire shoulder.

"That's true," the highway patrolman said. "But you might be the only person who cares. You two are sort of a big deal, whatever you look like."

As they got in the backseat of his patrol car, he grinned and said, "Buckle up."

Her father had warned Letty against going for rides with highway patrolmen. "When it comes to driving, they're a little . . . out there, I guess you'd say. 'Fast' isn't good enough for them."

Driving to Pershing from Van Horn had taken Kaiser an hour. The trip back to Van Horn took a little more than forty-five minutes. Letty suspected her fingers had made permanent grip holes in the seat in front of her. A version of the Black Hawk military helicopter was waiting at the Hampton Inn parking lot off I-10 in Van Horn, and a half-hour later it dropped Letty and Kaiser into the parking lot at the FBI headquarters in El Paso.

Two FBI agents, one male, one female, walked out to meet them and take them inside. "Got a pretty large contingent of brass hats in here . . . Got some questions," the female agent said. She'd introduced herself as Lauren Fix.

The male agent said, "Saw you guys on TV running across the bridge . . ." His name was Rudy Fischer. "That was pretty heavy. We could see everybody crawling around the bus, then we lost the satellite feed . . ."

"You've got medevac people on the way, right?" Kaiser asked. "Lotta hurt people there."

"We do," Fix said. "We're using everything we got to lift people out. Last count from the Mexican side is we have seventeen confirmed dead. At least thirty injured, some might not make it."

"Ah, my God," Kaiser said.

Letty, stone-faced, said, "We knew that, didn't we? We got their blood all over us."

The Pershing task force was scattered around four conference rooms, but the main center was in what looked like a classroom into which somebody had carried all the cafeteria tables and chairs, if there was a cafeteria. Before they went in, Fix asked Letty, "You want to . . . freshen up?"

"I'm okay," Letty said.

"You're covered with blood," Fix said. "Your forehead is still bleeding."

Kaiser: "She can wash her face later. We need to find out what's going on. How many militia have you nailed down?"

"That might not be the best question to ask," Fischer said. "Because I think the answer is not many."

"Or even damn few," Fix added.

When they walked into the task force center, the dozen people inside stopped talking and turned to look at them. A tall, square, forty-ish man with a graying mustache said, "Well, you guys look like shit."

Letty recognized his voice: "Didn't have time to put on a dress."

He smiled and said, in a dry Texas accent, "We've secured your rooms at the motel. We got the first cars down there a half-hour ago. There seems to be some issue about sheets and pillows."

"Yeah. We stole them," Kaiser said. He scraped two chairs around, and he and Letty sat down.

Letty: "How many have you rounded up? The militia?"

"Five, at this point," the man said. "We are troubled by that. By the way, I'm Carter Walsh, I'm a major with the Texas Rangers. I was elected to run this show . . . Have you got anything new for us?"

Letty looked at Kaiser, who said, "We believe the militia was run by four or five people. One of them we killed up near Seminole, Max Sawyer. Of the other four, Jane Hawkes, who called herself Jael, got away, as far as we know . . . unless you guys got her?"

Walsh shook his head. "No. Not a sniff of her."

Kaiser said, "The other three, Rand Low, Victor Crain, and Terrill Duran, are dead. Letty and I killed them as they were trying to escape after the bridge explosion."

Walsh nodded. "We heard there were dead militiamen . . . apparently that TV crew has shots of the bodies. This is critical: Do you have *anything* more we can work with? Our well is running dry . . ."

Letty dug in her pocket and held up her phone. "Did you know that license renewal stickers have the tag numbers on them? We couldn't risk pulling the tape off the plates, but I've got photos of the renewal stickers from sixty-two trucks. Not great pictures, but you can read the tag numbers."

In the sudden hubbub, Walsh laughed and then said, "Ah, babe: you make my heart sing. And . . . please don't shoot me in the balls. Please. And give me that fuckin' phone."

Letty poked a finger at him: "One more thing that I didn't notice until after they took out the cell phone tower — all these guys were taking selfies. You know, themselves at the invasion, like with that mob that attacked the Capitol. When you locate these guys through the tag numbers, you gotta grab their phones. Immediately. They'll hang themselves with their selfies. A lot of them took their masks down while they were taking them."

Walsh: "You're . . . You guys . . . I had no idea what you could do. Senator Colles told me, but I wasn't sure I believed it. Selfies. Jesus H. Christ!"

In the next hour, highway patrol officials began compiling names and addresses linked to Letty's renewal sticker photos. The process was all computerized and didn't take long. Many of the suspects lived in El Paso or within a few miles of El Paso; many of those who didn't would still be on Texas highways. The patrol would coordinate early-morning raids by a task force of state and local cops to grab all the suspects simultaneously, and to seize their phones.

Letty and Kaiser were hit with a barrage of questions from Walsh and the others — agents from the FBI, the ATF, even an officer with the Army's CID. The Army officer told them that the young captain they'd spoken to, Colin, used Letty's iPhone photo to identify a soldier who Colin believed had stolen the C-4. "That's not certain. We're working on it. He's a guy we've suspected was involved in black-market activities, selling stolen government equipment. But he's good, so we haven't been able to catch him at it."

At eleven o'clock, Letty and Kaiser were faltering in their responses: they'd been asked too many repetitive questions. The news from Pershing wasn't getting better: there were now eighteen confirmed deaths, and there were still seriously injured people awaiting transport to El Paso hospitals.

Letty got to an empty restroom, locked the door, stripped down, and took a sponge bath with paper towels. Her clothing was in shreds, but Fix, the FBI agent, was close to her size, and went to her apartment and brought back a pair of jeans and a blouse that fit well enough.

"Nothing we can do about the rust-colored gym shoes," Fix said, shaking her head. "If I was wearing those shoes, I'd cut off my feet."

Letty smiled for the first time that night.

At midnight, as Hawkes was getting in her Subaru at the Walmart, a few miles away,

Senator Colles walked through the task force door, dressed as though he was on his way to a dinner in his honor. He shook hands with Kaiser, slapped him on the back, then gathered up Letty for a major squeeze.

"Okay, guys . . ." He put her down and looked around. "Who's Walsh?"

Walsh lifted a finger and Colles said, "Let's send these two off to a motel to get some sleep. We gotta lot of stuff to do tomorrow. Every network in the country wants them for the morning shows. We need them looking good . . ."

Letty said, "Aw . . ." and Kaiser said, "I need a haircut."

"We want you just like you are," Colles said, rubbing his hands together. "We can do a lot of good tomorrow. Good for our border policy, good for our relationship with Mexico . . ." He turned to Walsh: "Hey: did you guys catch this Jael person? Hawkes? Last I heard, you hadn't . . ."

Colles got them out of bed the next morning at five o'clock, already seven o'clock on the East Coast; the highway patrol had delivered their suitcases from Pershing, so Letty and Kaiser looked reasonably like themselves. Welp, who'd traveled with Colles, arranged for them to use a studio at

KTSM in El Paso for a series of remote interviews with the morning shows on all the major networks — seven interviews altogether, which took a bit more than an hour.

Colles sat between Kaiser and Letty, introduced them at each interview, took some credit for sending them to Texas, and let them talk. Kaiser stumbled through the first two interviews before smoothing out. Letty, who'd worked at a Twin Cities station as a teenager, knew how it all worked, and spoke succinctly and seriously, never a smile. The Telemundo interviewer spoke Spanish with Letty, while Kaiser and Colles sat like dummies. The Fox interviewer asked Colles if he was planning a run for president, and Colles said it was the wrong time to talk about such possibilities, given the horrific disaster in Pershing. He didn't say he wasn't thinking about the presidency.

The live interviews were cut with video of Rodriguez's interviews with Hawkes and Low. There were after-action shots of Low's, Duran's, and Crain's dead bodies. More video showed Letty and Kaiser dashing across the border bridge, of the explosions that took the bridge down. Of Letty and Kaiser, talking with Rodriguez after they had recrossed the Rio Grande, Letty's face awash in blood, the images taken surreptitiously by Ochoa.

Letty told of crawling up and down inside the school bus, of passing children up through the jammed back door . . . of passing the dead baby's body out of the bus.

Hawkes had checked into a Tucson highway motel at five o'clock in the morning. She got three hours of sleep, and watched the interviews, repeated in endless loops all day. She was also genuinely horrified. Her friends dead, eighteen members of the caravan now . . . dead. More hurt.

And just as bad, she saw video from the El Paso television stations of raids on the homes of El Paso militia members. She didn't know how the police had found them so quickly — and she was stunned to hear that the police were seizing telephones for the selfies they might hold. She remembered that militia members had been taking them . . . and it had never occurred to her to stop them. It should have, because she'd seen it during the Capitol riot, and how the images had been used against the rioters in court.

Hawkes stayed in the motel all day and the following night, eating food she'd packed in her Subaru. By noon, she was a convincing redhead. She watched the president make a statement at midafternoon, and she saw the Republican Speaker of the House challenge the president's statement, referring to the members of the Central American caravan as criminals and carriers of coronavirus variants. The usual bullshit storm ensued.

Eighteen dead, not counting the three militiamen, her friends. She muttered to herself, over and over, "Eighteen."

She left the hotel twenty-four hours after she arrived, in the dark, headed north for the Rockies.

Letty and Kaiser remained in Texas for a week, being debriefed, making statements. They would later be required to return for trials, and were told they'd probably be there for several months. In a trip back to Pershing with prosecutors from the Texas attorney general's office, they retraced their movements during the invasion day. That evening, Kaiser was taken to dinner at the pizza place by the city council and the council members' spouses.

Letty's father called her every day, and sometimes twice. He wanted all the details; and not just details, he wanted all of her thoughts, both at the time of the invasion and afterward.

When they had exhausted the what-ifs and how-to's, he said, "You did well. I can't think of anything anyone could have done better. You have a gift."

Letty and Kaiser were minor stars around their respective departments for a week or two after they got back to Washington, but that went away quickly enough.

Colles was making a lot of television appearances without Letty or Kaiser, and regular life began to assert itself. Kaiser was sent to Chattanooga for a conference on TVA security. Letty found a rifle range in Virginia.

The brown-eyed political aide was no longer coming around to visit with her, though he left a note, hoping to see her on his trips back to the capital. He'd gone to Ohio to prepare for a congressional run, still two years away, but he said he needed to be there, on the ground. He would miss their chats.

One rainy day in October, Letty took a phone call in her closet/office. She said hello, and after a moment of silence, a woman asked, "Letty Davenport?"

"Yes, this is she."

"This is Jane Hawkes . . . Jael."

Letty fumbled for something to say, and came up with "Where are you?"

"I'm in Washington State. Leaving Washington State, I should say. When I finish talking to you, I'm going to take the batteries out and throw this phone out the car window."

"What do you want?"

"I've read about you. You should have been with us — you're another version of me. White trash. You got lucky and got adopted by rich people, but you won't escape it. Not in the long run. I had to try to make it on my own, and you know what? I never did. I kept getting pushed down. Kept getting dragged down. Tried to do something about it and you wrecked my Land Division."

"You murdered nineteen people altogether, the last one died only a week ago," Letty said. "Six of them were babies and small children."

"That was Rand . . ."

"Bullshit. That was you," Letty said. "You killed those people, Jane, you and your fucked-up militia."

"I didn't want to kill anyone — but I've been thinking about it, and I guess I'll take it. My share of the responsibility. We're mobilizing people in this country and they're coming my way. Pershing will be a monument."

"You're deranged," Letty said. "You're nuts."

"No, I'm not. I'm right. As for you . . . we're coming for you," Hawkes said.

Hawkes couldn't see it, but Letty stood up and nodded, touched her pocket with the 938 nestled inside. "Do that, Jane," she said. "Bring it on. Bring everything you fucking got."

ABOUT THE AUTHOR

John Sandford is the pseudonym for the Pulitzer Prize–winning journalist John Camp. He is the author of twenty-nine Prey novels; four Kidd novels; twelve Virgil Flowers novels; three YA novels coauthored with his wife, Michele Cook; and three other books.

The employees of Thorndike Press hope you have enjoyed this Large Print book. All our Thorndike, Wheeler, and Kennebec Large Print titles are designed for easy reading, and all our books are made to last. Other Thorndike Press Large Print books are available at your library, through selected bookstores, or directly from us.

For information about titles, please call:
    (800) 223-1244

or visit our website at:
    gale.com/thorndike

To share your comments, please write:
    Publisher
    Thorndike Press
    10 Water St., Suite 310
    Waterville, ME 04901